SPIRIT MISSION

SPIRIT MISSION

A NOVEL

TED RUSS

HENRY HOLT AND COMPANY
NEW YORK

Henry Holt and Company
Publishers since 1866
175 Fifth Avenue
New York, New York 10010
www.henryholt.com

Henry Holt® and 🏛® are registered trademarks of Macmillan Publishing Group, LLC.

Library of Congress Cataloging-in-Publication Data

Names: Russ, Ted.
Title: Spirit mission : a novel / Ted Russ.   **33614057737495**
Description: First edition. | New York : Henry Holt and Company, 2016.
Identifiers: LCCN 2016001250| ISBN 9781627799669 (hardback) | ISBN
    9781627799652 (electronic book)
Subjects: LCSH: Air pilots, Military—Fiction. | Special operations (Military
    science)—Fiction. | Military helicopters—Fiction. | Suspense fiction. |
    War stories. | BISAC: FICTION / War & Military. | FICTION / Thrillers.
Classification: LCC PS3618.U746 S65 2016 | DDC 813/.6—dc23
LC record available at http://lccn.loc.gov/2016001250

Our books may be purchased in bulk for promotional, educational, or business use. Please
contact your local bookseller or the Macmillan Corporate and Premium Sales Department at
(800) 221-7945, extension 5442, or by e-mail at MacmillanSpecialMarkets@macmillan.com.

First Edition 2016

Designed by Meryl Sussman Levavi

Printed in the United States of America

1 3 5 7 9 10 8 6 4 2

For the Corps

ONE

I BANKED THE HELICOPTER SLIGHTLY TO THE RIGHT TO adjust for the crosswind. It was stiffer than forecast, and our ground track was skewing south. As we skimmed above the desert at 120 knots, I checked the navigation display. Forty-three minutes to the landing zone. The terrain-following radar showed nothing significant for as far as it could see. The vacant expanse of northwestern Iraq rose gently in front of us for almost 160 kilometers. The forward-looking infrared imagery was the same, showing only occasional terrified sheepherders in an otherwise empty desert sandscape. There is nothing like a war machine the size of an MH-47G sneaking up and flying over you at less than a hundred feet.

I looked at the clock: 0035 hours. I hoped we would get there in time.

"Pete, can you take her for a while?" I asked.

"Roger that," Pete said from the left seat. "I have the controls. Heading three one zero, one hundred and twenty knots, one hundred feet."

"You have the controls."

I leaned back in my seat and tried to relax my lower back. More than twenty years of flying, marching, sleeping on cots, and a couple of hard landings had wrecked it. But it was a different pain that clouded my brain tonight.

This would be my last flight in a Chinook, my last flight as an army aviator. There was no doubt about that. We were going to be shot down or court-martialed. I flipped my night-vision goggles up and rubbed my eyes.

I felt the tweak of impending loss worse than before my divorce. The feeling of being past the point of no return, headed directly and irrevocably toward the permanent absence of something good.

I loved flying Chinooks, but not in the one-dimensional way of a pilot. I loved it in the sick, over-the-top way that special operations army aviators do. Army pilots are not like air force pilots, flying missions and then tossing the keys to the crew chief and taking a golf cart to the O Club. Army pilots live on their airframes, positioned as far forward as possible with the units they support in the desert, jungle, mountains, or wherever they need to be. That has meant a lot of nasty places over the past fourteen years of war.

Chinooks steal your heart in a way that other army airframes can't. I had thousands of hours flying them, mostly at night, but I probably had ten times that living in them, eating in them, sleeping in them, shitting in them, planning and briefing missions in them. I knew the inside of a Chinook better than any house I'd lived in. I knew her contours, shapes, hard and soft spots more intimately than I knew my ex-wife's. I knew the Chinook's systems in detail and understood how they collaborate to keep two engines turning five transmissions driving two rotor hubs spinning six rotor blades that intermesh like an egg beater. It is a complex and elegant design from the 1950s that somehow yields the best stick-and-rudder flying I have ever experienced. I have told people that their great-great-great-grandchildren will ride to battle in a Zulu model Chinook. And I believe it.

The special operations variant we flew westward was highly modified. It could penetrate the weather and follow the terrain with its onboard radar. It could see in the dark with its FLIR pod. It could refuel in the air behind a C-130. It carried two 7.62 miniguns and two 7.62 M240s. The digital mission-management system and max gross weight of fifty-four thousand pounds made it Special Operations Command's long-range insertion/extraction platform of choice. In Afghanistan it was just about the only machine that could carry enough guys and supplies high enough into the mountains to take the fight to the Taliban.

But as cool as the Golf model Chinook is on its own, its best qualities are the customers it serves: Rangers, SEALs, Delta, and the others, the best warriors the country has to send.

And this was the last time I would be on board one. I would miss the hell out of it, but I was okay with that, because after fourteen years of war without victory, this was the best mission I'd ever go on, the purest I'd ever fly, and the most illegal. That night my Chinook truly was a divine wind, a platform of salvation with a dozen trained killers in back speeding at over 135 miles an hour across the desert, weapons at the ready, seeking our friend. I wished every mission could have been like this one, like I had imagined they would be when I was a cadet.

The radio interrupted my thoughts.

"Bulldog 71, this is Thunder 06. If you're hearing this transmission, I'm ordering you to return to base immediately."

"He sounds pissed," said Zack, leaning into the cockpit.

"Yep. He is." I leaned forward and turned off the UHF radio. We had needed it during the earlier mission, but now I didn't want to deal with the enraged voice of the task force commander, Rear Admiral Brick. He was a good guy, and I was not looking forward to the next time I'd see him. I would do so gladly if we were able to return successfully, though at this point I didn't want the distraction.

We flew in silence for a few minutes. Silence is a relative term in a Chinook, of course. Sitting under the forward transmission and rotor hub puts you in a cone of noise that sounds like a fight between a freight train and a hurricane. Gears rotate madly only a couple feet from your head, and thousands of pounds of hydraulic pressure articulate the entire flight-control system a couple feet behind you. Without a flight helmet and noise-canceling earplugs, your ears would probably dissolve.

The satcom radio crackled. "Bulldog, this is Elvis."

"Go ahead, Elvis."

"Sitrep follows. Single individual left the target house. He walked a couple of blocks south, got in a vehicle, and departed north. We kept eyes on as long as possible. He just left our field of view."

"Roger, Elvis."

"I hope he's not going to get any friends," I said to Zack.

"Me, too. How far out are we?"

"About forty minutes."

"Relax, Sam," said Zack, putting his hand on my shoulder. "This is going to be a piece of cake." As always, his cavalier attitude drove me crazy. I shrugged his hand off.

"You've got a strange definition of 'cake.'"

"You are still such a pussy."

Zack shook his head and looked at Pete, saying, "Chief, I can't believe you guys let him call himself a Night Stalker." He unhooked his headset and went aft.

"I thought you said you guys were friends," Pete commented.

"We are."

"You guys are weird."

"You have no idea."

The word "friends" didn't cover it; we had endured West Point together. We were Beast roommates together, were tested for four years together, and, though we were not the best cadets to ever wear dress gray, we graduated together. And then we went to serve. We followed different paths as officers. He, infantry. Me, aviation. But the arcs of our service intersected again that night, long after graduation and far away from where it started. Giving us the opportunity for a common end point: to complete our final spirit mission together. And, like our last spirit mission as cadets, we knew that if we somehow succeeded, people were going to talk about this one for a long time.

TWO

WEST POINT IS FASTENED TO A MOUNTAIN THAT HAS nudged the Hudson River from her desired course for millions of years. Because of its location on the west bank of the Hudson almost sixty miles north of New York City, it played a critical role during the Revolutionary War. It has since become the longest continuously occupied military post in the United States and the home of the United States Military Academy.

America never wanted a military academy. So recently unfettered from England, she was afraid of a military elite. But finding herself in possession of a foreboding and vast natural wealth, America needed sons who could build railroads, dam rivers, oversee the construction of her cities, and win her occasional wars. There was so much resistance to the idea of a standing military academy that even George Washington could not get it done. Washington's first secretary of state, Thomas Jefferson, opposed the idea. Yet it was he, as the third U.S. president, who, in 1802, finally signed the law that created West Point. It was the reluctant act of a nation that felt it needed engineers so badly it would tolerate professional warriors.

On the last day of June 1987, our train punched its way out of Manhattan and rolled up the east bank of the Hudson toward fortress West Point. It might as well have been carrying me to the moon. Every railroad tie that fell behind us was a small measure of the extent to which I was leaving what little I knew.

As is the case for the vast majority of my generation of Americans, the last person in my family to serve in the military was my grandfather, in World War II. He never talked about it. Growing up in the suburbs of Charlotte, North Carolina, afforded me zero interaction with the military. I didn't know a single person in uniform as I came of age in the shiny, happy eighties.

The truth was, I was bored. Uninspired. The prospect of college dismayed me; it all looked the same: insipid paths to a bland life in the merchant class. Of no service. Without consequence. I thought of myself as tough, honest, and good. In short, I deemed myself worthy of a quest; I thought I deserved it. When I learned about West Point during the rising martial tide and national spirit of Reagan's tenure, my imagination was captured. My fate was sealed. It was the only college I applied to.

So the train carried me north toward one of the nodes of American history, a place that had forged men who had cast long shadows. I was going to offer myself up to that forge. I would do whatever they told me to do; I wanted only to measure up, to be accepted, and to make it.

The next day, my parents and I and thousands of other people gathered at the sports complex. Once we were all seated inside the immense basketball arena, a senior cadet stepped up to the microphone in the center of the court.

"Good morning, parents and candidates," he began. "In a few moments we will begin the in-processing for the candidates and orientation for the parents. The day will conclude with the swearing-in ceremony on the Plain. At this time, please take a moment to say your good-byes." He stepped away from the microphone. Everyone in the stands looked around for a minute before we realized that he was serious.

Soon hundreds of weeping mothers and fathers clung to their embarrassed sons and daughters. I stood up, grabbed my duffel bag, and turned to give my mom a hug. She was crying but managing not to sob. I shook my dad's hand and walked away.

We filed out of the stands and toward a door on the other side of the gym. Our parents remained behind. Standing next to the door, waving us through, was another senior cadet. I was struck by his magnificent appearance. His form-fitting uniform was set off by numerous silver and brass insignias. A straight silver saber hung at his side. I could not take my eyes off it as I walked by. Noticing my gaze, he stepped forward to cut me off. He leaned down next to my ear and said softly, "Take your beady eyes off my saber and keep them fixed to your front. You don't want me to smoke you in front of Mommy and Daddy, do you?" I must have looked ridiculous as I stammered and continued out through the doorway.

"Head and eyes to the front! Welcome to Cadet Basic Training, cadet candidates!" shouted a first classman who had been waiting on the other side. "Pick a spot on the back of the head in front of you and bore a hole in it with your eyes!" We filed out of the huge sports complex into a large parking lot, where streams of confused candidates were directed by shouting first classmen into small groups and herded onto buses.

After a short, angst-ridden trip down the mountain, the bus stopped and we poured out like a litter of scared puppies, into a large rectangular area bounded by sinister, gray stone buildings on all sides. They looked like old castles. A drum team pounded out a marching cadence from the center of the area.

"Move out!"

They marched us quickly into a tunnel and then down a dark hallway into what looked like a big locker room. "Males this way. Females that way!" directed a cadre member. Soon there were about fifty of us in a room with several tables against the wall. On the tables were neatly folded stacks of dark socks, shorts, and athletic shirts. "At this time you will file through the clothing station and receive a gym alpha uniform. You will also be given a duffel bag. You will change into the gym alpha uniform and place your civilian clothes in the duffel bag."

There was a flurry of activity. The uniform was a ridiculous combination of black shorts, white T-shirt, and knee-high dress socks with black leather shoes. We each had a large tag hanging from our waistband. The uniforms heightened my feeling of threatened self-consciousness. I felt silly next to the regal-looking cadre members.

"Move, move, move!" boomed the cadre. We snaked quickly through a few short hallways and rejoined the main tunnel. The drums grew louder as the tunnel got lighter. We flew up a short flight of steps and burst into the daylight.

The drums were loud and had an eerie potency. The concussions rebounded off the towering gray stone walls that surrounded us.

Suddenly we stood shoulder to shoulder as the cadre divided our long column into rows of ten stacked one in front of another. We faced the center of the large area, our backs to the barracks.

A giant cadet stood in front of us. Unlike the other upperclassmen, he wore a large red sash around his waist. Next to him on a tripod stand stood a status board.

"Don't move a muscle!" yelled an upperclassman stalking back and forth behind us. "Backs straight, head and eyes to the front, hands cupped and held behind the seam of your pants! This is called the position of attention. For the next year, if you are not in your barracks room or some other place in which you are authorized to fall out, you will be at the position of attention . . . unless, of course, you are pinging, which is to move at a minimum of one hundred and twenty steps per minute, arms locked, head and eyes always to the front. Do you understand?"

"Yes, sir!"

Another cadet walked up to our formation. "At this time you will report to the cadet in the red sash and will be given instructions on what to do next. You will follow his instructions precisely." The cadet looked us over as he walked down our file.

I was the right-most cadet candidate in my row and first up. "Cadet candidate, step up to my line," the cadet in the red sash growled.

He was a massive, intimidating figure. The black brim of his white hat covered his eyes. His block nose and square jaw angled down at me from atop broad and muscular shoulders.

When I moved toward the line he shouted, "Eyes off the ground! You will keep your head and eyes to the front. You will not gaze around at the ground, or the sky, or anywhere else. Try again!"

I tried again. This time I kept my eyes focused straight ahead in the direction of the cadet in the red sash. I walked up to him and saluted. "Sir, Cadet Candidate—"

"Stop!" he yelled. "Look down at your feet, cadet candidate."

I looked at my feet. One of them rested on the tape line.

"I said step up to my line, not step on my line or short of my line or next to my line. Do you understand, cadet candidate?"

"Yes, sir."

"Try it again."

After a few more iterations of this process, the summer sun and my own panic had drenched me in sweat, but I was standing in front of the cadet in the red sash, having finally placed my feet in an acceptable spot. He was tall, and my eyes were on about the same level as his chin. I was able to read his name tag: Wilcox.

He leaned slightly over and grabbed my tag. He looked at it, then straightened and said, "Cadet Candidate Avery, you will join the group of candidates over there and report with them to Issue Point Number Three. Do you understand?"

"Yes, sir."

"Then move out, Cadet Candidate Avery."

I began to spin and leave.

"Stop!"

Startled, I spun awkwardly back around to face the cadet in the red sash.

"Cadet Candidate Avery, when dismissed by a superior officer you must render a salute."

"Yes, sir." I gave him my best salute.

"Straighten your fingers."

I did.

"Align your thumb with the plane of your hand."

I did.

"Angle your hand slightly down."

I did.

"Okay. Now move out!"

We spent hours like that, reporting to the cadet in the red sash, being assigned to small squads of companions and sent off through alternating periods of walking at a near sprint and standing still in the sun. We were sent from issue point to issue point. At some points we were given equipment, at others uniforms, at others training manuals. At one station we were told to strip. As we were led along, they gave us inoculations, took blood samples, examined our genitals, and recorded our heights and weights. In between these stations were short and intense blocks of training on how to salute, march, assemble into a close interval squad, and perform other basics of drill and ceremony.

The tags that dangled from our waists contained our statuses and shipping instructions. They told which stations we had been to. As we stepped up to the cadet in the red sash's line, he would examine the tag, then send us off to wherever it said we needed to go next.

It was hot. The high granite buildings that ringed the asphalt area formed an effective oven. Despite the ridiculousness of the outfit, I was thankful we were in shorts and T-shirts.

After a few hours, my arms screamed as I tried to stand at attention while holding two large duffel bags full of gear. A cadre member walked up and pointed in my direction.

"You three follow me." He escorted us to a barracks room, waved us in, and departed immediately.

The three of us stood mute in the middle of the room, too dazed to even introduce ourselves to one another. The sudden peace of the room with only us, and no cadre, was disconcerting. It was short-lived.

The door burst open. A cadre member strode into the middle of the room and looked us over as we stood at attention. "I am Cadet Lewis." He didn't raise his voice, but it was full of authority. "I'm your squad leader. I will be back in one hour. At that time you will be in the proper uniform and have this room squared away. Do you understand?"

"Yes, sir."

"Good. From now on you will salute when you greet upperclassmen outside and when we enter or leave your room, do you understand?"

"Yes, sir!" we said in unison.

There was an awkward second; then he spoke slowly: "Good afternoon, candidates."

Our hands snapped up. "Good afternoon, sir!"

He saluted and walked out, closing the door behind himself.

We exhaled as a single set of lungs and regarded one another for a moment. Panting and dripping in sweat, I wondered if my new roommates were also having serious second thoughts about the next four years.

"My name is Zack Dempsey," said the tall one. He had a few inches on me, but his build was substantial, not skinny. He had a classic Irish complexion, pale with light freckles. His cheeks were red from exertion.

"I'm Sam Avery," I said.

"Bill Cooper." Bill was an inch or so shorter than me, though more stocky. His powerful build favored his legs, which were not fast or quick. But, I would soon learn, they were steady like a diesel engine. Once he got warmed up, Bill could walk forever with a heavy load. He was the strongest road marcher in our class.

Knowing one another's names woke us up.

"Dump your bags and get organized," said Bill calmly. Zack and I followed his lead, throwing our gear into piles in the middle of the room. Then we excavated for the uniforms needed for the swearing-in ceremony. This version was called "white over gray" and consisted of gray trousers and a short-sleeved white shirt. The shirt was worn with epaulets that bore the cadet's class and rank. Our epaulets were plain gray. They were humorously blank, compared to the cadre's epaulets, which bore gold stripes and black and silver brass.

"That's not how you do it."

Bill took the white shirt from me and swapped the epaulets around while Zack and I watched. "See here? Wider end goes toward your shoulder and the narrow end to the inside."

"Thanks."

Zack changed his.

"Find your belt buckle. It looks like this," said Bill, holding up a brass buckle still in a plastic bag. Zack and I dug through our piles.

"How do you know all this stuff?" Zack asked.

"I'm prior service. Was artillery and then a year at the prep school."

"You were in the army before this?" I asked.

"Yes. You guys obviously were not."

"Naw. Just graduated high school. From Chicago. I played lacrosse," said Zack.

"Me either," I said. "I'm from Charlotte, North Carolina."

"Were you a wrestler?" Zack asked me.

"Yes."

"I figured. My best friend in high school was a wrestler. You've got his build: big shoulders. I hope you're smarter than him, though. He's a rock."

We learned quickly that Zack had no verbal filter. He said what he thought as he thought it. This made for a humorous running narrative as we slogged our way through West Point, because he was always bugged about something. He was quick to irritation with the world but slow to anger with his friends.

"Don't worry about it," Bill reassured us. "In a few weeks, no one will be able to tell us apart. Just follow my lead. It's just a bunch of reindeer games." Bill was intelligent, street-smart, and experienced. This was a boon to Zack and me but often left Bill frustrated.

Cadet Lewis returned and took us, along with the seven other candidates who made up our squad, to parade practice with the rest of the platoon. We spent an hour doing as a full platoon the things we had been doing earlier in the day as just a squad. We learned how to march in column, execute right and left wheel turns, stand at parade rest and attention, and present arms in unison as a platoon. After that we were marched out onto the Plain for the swearing-in ceremony.

We stepped off at six p.m. Cadet candidates marched in white over gray. We wore white gloves on our left hands. Our right hands were bare, in preparation for the oath. The first classmen wore their India whites with red sashes and sabers.

The ceremony took place on the Plain, the large flat expanse in front of the cadet barracks that had served as a bivouac site and training ground for American soldiers during the Revolutionary War. The Plain was green under a blue sky, and the gray stone barracks rose behind us as if they were part of the mountain.

The West Point Band played as we marched out, the drum beating loudly as every left foot in the regiment hit the ground. Nine Cadet Basic Training companies emerged from the barracks sally ports. There were more than a thousand of us. Every gloved hand swung at once. Every foot fell in unison. Thousands of people watched from the stands and all around the far edges of the Plain. In the distance behind the crowd and below the Plain, the Hudson River flowed south.

Once the regiment had assembled, companies on line, facing the superintendent's reviewing stand, the music ceased, and we stood at attention. Someone began to speak into a microphone, welcoming dignitaries, congressmen, and generals to the ceremony, as well as all of the proud parents. Mom and Dad were somewhere in the crowd. Our good-byes in the arena felt like years ago; I missed them already. Before I knew what was happening, the voice on the microphone began to lead us in the oath.

"I, Samuel Avery, do solemnly swear that I will support the Constitution of the United States, and bear true allegiance to the National Government, that I will maintain and defend the sovereignty of the United States, paramount to any and all allegiance, sovereignty, or fealty I may owe to any State or Country whatsoever, and that I will at all times obey the legal orders of my superior officer and the Uniform Code of Military Justice. So help me God."

What had I just done?

THREE

"**G**OOD MORNING, SIR."
"Good morning, Sergeant Weber."

I walked into the tactical operations center and headed directly for the coffeepot. Just halfway through this rotation to Iraq, it already seemed like I'd been there a year. It was probably because all the previous times I had been here blended into one fuzzy, endless event in my mind. This was a strange one, though. No one knew we were here—or, more accurately, no one wanted to admit we were here.

President Obama had pulled the last of the U.S. combat troops out of Iraq with great fanfare in 2011. Of course, we still had a lot of people in-country working for the embassy, the various consulates, and as military trainers. But all of our muscle was gone. We had ceased being a land power in the Middle East. This made us all nervous. We crossed our fingers and tried not to think about the cost of getting to that point.

After a long and nasty fight, we'd finally achieved a little peace and stability. The sheer weight of "the surge" and our radically improved covert tactics had put all of the insurgent groups under excruciating pressure.

We'd killed a lot of them. It had looked like we might actually pull this off. In 2010, the situation had been tenuous but offered a foundation the Iraqis and we could build on. And then we'd taken the pressure off. Meanwhile, guys like Abu al-Baghdadi had been laying their preparations. By 2012, he had pulled together a critical mass of insurgent groups and nursed them back to fighting strength.

Then Syria went to hell. Baghdadi expanded his operations into that fertile chaos, obtaining access to more zealous, anti-Western insurgent volunteers. With breathing room from us and new recruiting sources in Syria, ISIS caught fire quickly.

In June 2014, major Iraqi cities began to fall to ISIS. In early August, ISIS even defeated the Kurds in the field and captured the Mosul Dam. It was clear that the situation was not going to get better on its own. The president publicly ordered air strikes and gave a secret order for the military to be prepared to evacuate the embassy and other personnel . . . none of which we could do without having assets in-country.

So, over a year ago, in the middle of the night a couple of C-5s cycled into an airfield outside of Kirkuk and disgorged a small Joint Special Operations Command task force under the command of a navy one-star, Rear Admiral Brick. We're still here, with no status of forces agreement, no acknowledgment from our government or the Iraqis, and not much backup.

We picked Kirkuk for two reasons. First, it was far enough north that we could be responsive to any needs in Mosul or Irbil, which were both less than an hour's flight away. Second, it was safe. We knew the Kurds wished they had taken Kirkuk during the First Gulf War. They had moved in during the ISIS-induced chaos, and we figured they wouldn't let anyone wrest it from them now that they finally had it.

I was responsible for the aviation operations of the task force and reported to the task force commander. Brick was a SEAL and could be gruff and arrogant, but we worked well together. He gave me full authority for crew selections and all other aspects of our flight operations. I was good at this. It was the kind of job I had done a lot of recently while I waited to see if I would get promoted. I'd been a lieutenant colonel for a while. If I didn't get picked up for full-bird colonel this year, they were going to make me retire. Despite my weariness, I didn't want that. I loved my unit and wasn't ready to leave it. I loved Chinooks, and though I didn't fly them as much as I used to, I liked being around them. And I had no idea what else to do with my life. I was not ready to leave.

Our immediate job was to provide insertion platforms for special ops teams that conducted targeting for the air strikes as well as any required downed-pilot search and rescue. We also had to be ready for an evacuation of the embassy and other civilians and assets. Beyond that, we served as a general-purpose, highly capable quick-reaction force made up of two Chinooks, four Black Hawks, and a contingent of Green Berets, Pararescue, and SEALs.

In the beginning, we couldn't decide if this had the feeling of a last hurrah or the start of something bigger. We still couldn't tell. Despite the "air strikes only" approach, we'd managed to stop the ISIS advance for a time. We were occasionally able to launch successful raids against the ISIS chain of command, killing them even in Syria. Still, over the last few months they had mounted a comeback, and in May, they had taken control of Ramadi. This victory put them only about 120 kilometers from Baghdad.

At least we have coffee, I thought as I looked at the map.

"Colonel Avery, you have some visitors," Sergeant Weber said behind me.

"Visitors?"

"Yes, sir. Two gentlemen out at the airfield gate. They say they really need to talk to you."

This was strange. How would anyone know I was here? I looked at Sergeant Weber skeptically. "I'm going to need more than that before I shag my ass out to the perimeter gate. They didn't give their names?"

"No, sir. Just said to tell you to 'Go naked,' whatever that means."

I smiled. "Major Obrien, I'll be back in a bit. Radio me if you need anything."

"Roger that, sir."

"I'll tag along if you don't mind, sir," Weber said as he grabbed his M4 and followed me out.

"Sure, Weber. I'm touched."

We hopped into the van, Weber in the driver's seat, and headed toward the airfield gate. We weren't even halfway there when I spotted the silhouettes of two armed men on the other side of the guard shack and vehicle barrier. One tall and lanky standing motionless, watching our vehicle approach. The other stout and muscular, shifting his weight back and forth between each foot. I chuckled, comforted by the duo's unchanging nature, and shook my head.

"Sir?"

"I know those guys."

Weber pulled up next to the vehicle barrier, and I hopped out. Waving the guard away, I walked up to Zack and Turtle. They were grinning, but something was off. They'd each grown scruffy beards—not uncommon for guys like them in this theater—and were wearing full combat kit. Modified M4s hung from their shoulders, and they each had at least one sidearm that I could see. Though their eyes were covered by sunglasses, I could tell that they were narrowed in calculation of something. My friends were on edge, as if a clock was ticking.

I extended my hand to Zack. "Come here, you son of a bitch," he said, wrapping me in a bear hug. Turtle laughed and slapped me on the back.

"How the hell are you?" Turtle asked. His tan face was framed by jet-black hair and wore a wide and friendly smile.

"I'm good. What's it been? Ten years?"

"More than that, I think."

"I can't believe it."

"Not since Walter Reed, my friend," Turtle said. "I appreciated that, by the way."

"I was disappointed I couldn't visit more."

"You were deployed most of the time. That makes it hard."

"And you," I said, looking at Zack. "A full bird, and I heard you were on the short list for squadron commander."

Zack shrugged. "What can I say? Clean living."

Zack had been promoted below the zone to colonel and pinned on full bird a full year before the rest of us were even considered. It was a surprise to all of us, since his career had been built on pure competence. He was terrible at politics. There was no way he would ever pin on general, but I was certain he would get picked to command Delta. I had seen him more recently than Turtle, since we worked in the same community.

"Did you hear about his daughter?" Turtle asked me, gesturing at Zack.

"I did. I think everyone did. She started West Point this summer, right?"

"Yep. I can't believe it." Zack shook his head.

"I know. We are getting old, aren't we?"

"That part I believe. It's how good a kid Susan turned out to be. Better than I deserve."

"What are you guys doing in-country, anyway?"

"I'm over here on a temporary tasker at the embassy. A joint liaison gig. They've been giving me bullshit busywork like this while the command board is sorted out."

"Uh-huh. Since when did an embassy liaison duty require all that kit?" I gestured at Zack's weapon with a smile. He shifted on his feet.

"Thankfully, it's a short rotation. I'll hear the board's decision on squadron commander in about thirty days and should wrap up here about the same time. How about you? You should hear about your colonel's board soon, right?"

"Yes. Any day now," I said, noting the diversion. "It's my last shot. You guys working together?"

"Hell no," said Turtle. "Zack wouldn't sully his professional reputation by working with a sellout private contractor." He punched Zack in the shoulder. "He just sneaks out after taps to drink with me, like the old days."

Zack rubbed his shoulder. "I ran into Turtle in the embassy dining facility."

"We picked up a couple nice security contracts in Baghdad after Blackwater got kicked out," Turtle added.

I looked past Zack and Turtle to the beat-up van they had driven up to the gate in. Baghdad was almost three hundred kilometers to the south.

"Did you guys drive here in that?"

Turtle chuckled. "No. I had one of my Little Birds give us a ride up."

"One of your Little Birds?"

Turtle shrugged. "It's a big contract."

"Where did you get the van?"

"Sam, can we talk?" asked Zack, gesturing at the vehicle.

"Sure." I looked at Weber. "I'm going to talk to these guys for a few minutes." He nodded unenthusiastically.

Zack, Turtle, and I walked over to the van, twenty meters and just out of earshot from Weber and the gate guard.

"What is it?" I asked.

"We need your help," said Zack. "The bastards got the Guru."

"Who got the Guru?"

"ISIS."

"What? I'm confused."

"Do you even know what the Guru has been up to for the past few years?"

"Vaguely. Charity work, right?"

"Sort of. He's got a group that works with the Iraqis to help them rebuild their country, schools and infrastructure kind of stuff. Not a big organization officially, but in addition to a dozen employees, he's got about a hundred Iraqis pitching in, Sunni, Shia, Kurd. All of them just following him around the country helping with projects."

"Sounds like the Guru."

"They've been working in the north and in the Kurdish-controlled zone."

"So?"

"ISIS captured him about twenty-four hours ago."

"Shit." I stared at the ground, thinking about the last time I'd seen the Guru. We'd run into each other about five years ago in a mess hall in Mosul. He had looked tired. I remembered thinking it was odd that he wasn't excited at all for his colonel's board. Everyone had said he was a shoo-in for the command list, and that he would definitely get a brigade. This was all the more impressive because the Guru had become well known for his searing, iconoclastic assessments of U.S. strategy and foreign policy in multiple professional journals. He had been published in *Foreign Affairs* twice.

But he was fried. He'd had seven tours in Iraq and Afghanistan at that point. I hadn't heard the details on his charity outfit, but it sounded true to form.

"Ordinarily," Zack said, "it would be a death sentence. But he got lucky. The guys that got him seem to be more bandit types than ISIS devotees, and they're in a chaotic region. We're not sure if Baghdadi even knows they have him yet. We've got a window, Sam. But it's a small one."

"A window to what?"

"To go get him," said Turtle.

I looked at Zack. He looked back at me, motionless, and then nodded.

"You guys are crazy."

"We're dead serious, Sam," Turtle said.

"Don't you think they're planning an op to get him back as we speak?"

"Who would 'they' be, Sam?" asked Zack.

"Well, you know. SOCOM. CIA. Somebody."

"Aren't you SOCOM? You getting ready for a rescue mission tonight?"

He had a point. I hadn't even heard about a recently captured American. Much less been involved in any planning to get him back. "Maybe there are other assets in-theater?"

"I've got pretty decent access, Sam. Trust me, nothing is being cued up."

"Yeah. Think about it," said Turtle, noticing my confused look.

"How the hell do you guys know all this?"

Zack smiled. "I'll tell you later."

"You'll tell me now."

"Not until you're on the team."

"Come on, Sam!" Turtle said. "You've got to help. It's the Guru, for Christ's sake. You of all people—"

"Will you shut up for a second, Turtle? Let me think."

"We don't have time for this!" Turtle yelled. His muscular body tensed, and he took a step forward.

"Is everything okay, sir?" Sergeant Weber stepped forward, his M4 hanging in front.

"Yes, Weber. Thanks. Everything is fine."

Sergeant Weber stood motionless, looking at Turtle. When soldiers have lived in an insurgent war zone as long as the group of us had, they develop a sense for threat ID. Turn the corner and see six men approaching, an instant evaluation occurs. It's not conscious, but in half a step the brain has prioritized each individual from friendly to threat, closest to farthest, easy to deadly, and it calls forward three or four sequential techniques to deal with them. Weber's brain was doing that now. The funny thing was that he had it wrong. He was focused on Turtle. Zack was deadlier.

Zack smiled and waved at Weber. "We're a lot nicer than we look, Sergeant. Besides, we've known Lieutenant Colonel Avery here for, what, Sam? Twenty-seven years?"

"Twenty-eight, I think."

"Ouch."

I gave Weber a subtle okay sign, and he moved back reluctantly.

"They're not going to try to get him back, Sam. They are trying to keep everything quiet and make it seem like things are not so shitty. If they acknowledge that another American was captured at all, it will cast everything in a new and shittier light, especially after we lost Ramadi."

"I can't believe they would just leave him."

"Ever heard of Benghazi?" said Turtle sadly.

My head was spinning. I turned and looked back through the gate, across the airfield, at the helicopters on the far ramp. The two Chinooks pointed eastward, their massive rotor blades drooping low at rest.

"Let's say for the moment I'm in. What are you proposing we do, anyway?"

"Simple. We know where he's being held. I need you to fly me and Turtle, with his guys, up there with a vehicle, so we can grab him. Then we need a ride back. That's all."

"Oh. Is that all?"

"Long as we hit them tonight."

"So you want me to steal a Chinook and fly you on an unauthorized mission tonight to try to get the Guru back?"

"Borrow a Chinook, not steal," said Turtle, smiling.

I shook my head, trying to clear it.

"Don't you have a contract bird and crew?"

"No. All I've got access to is two Little Birds, and one of them is down for maintenance. And you know they don't have the range or payload. Sorry, Sam, but you're the best heavy-assault asset in-country. Besides, we thought you would care the most."

"Zack, if you do this, you're giving up squadron commander. You know that, right? You'll probably go to jail."

"I'm aware of that," Zack said slowly. "Look at us, Sam. For the past fourteen years we've lost friends, limbs, wives, our way . . . all of it for what? Afghanistan is still a shit show. Iraq is coming apart again after we just about had it fixed. For nothing! We're going to be stuck here for another fifty years, net oil exporter or not. We'll keep sending unit after unit after soldier after soldier forever, and I'm not saying that we shouldn't. I'm saying all that matters to the three of us right now is that our friend is out there. They've got him. He's dead in twenty-four hours. And not just shot dead. And for whatever reason, in all of this chaos, a couple of his best friends are in a position to do something about it."

It was classic Zack. He had boiled a complex, decades-old geopolitical quagmire and a personal moral dilemma down to a simple overriding question of duty to a friend.

"I don't know. I haven't flown a hell of a lot in the past few years. I'm a staff weenie now, Zack. I might kill us all."

"I doubt that, Sam. I remember you being a pretty good stick. Besides, I don't really have any other choices over here."

"You know I can't fly a Chinook alone, right? I'm going to have to convince some other dumbasses to go with us."

"I have confidence in your powers of persuasion. And, again, you're all I've got."

Turtle made a show of looking at his watch. Zack fixed him with a stare and pointed at their vehicle. Turtle objected silently, but Zack waved him off.

"It's good to see you, Sam, sincerely," Turtle said. He stepped over and shook my hand.

"You too, Turtle." His face was roiling, but he did not speak. He pulled me in for a quick hug, patting me twice on the back. He was as strong as ever. Turtle then walked around to the driver's side of the van, hopped in, and cranked the engine.

Zack watched Turtle until he had closed the van door. Then he stepped closer and put his hand on my shoulder. "Sam, I've always respected how you deal with things. Strategic. Thoughtful. But I don't have time to run down all the scenarios with you right now. If you're not in, I need to know by noon."

"Why then?"

"Because that's the cutoff for us to infil over land."

"Drive up there?"

"Roger that. Turtle's Little Bird flew us up here, so we could talk to you. His team got their kit and vehicle together and has been driving this way. Should be here in about an hour and a half. We're headed northwest of here and will have to move slow."

"That's ISIS-held territory. You'll never make it."

"Probably not."

"That's just stupid. Why the hell would you do that?"

"You once told me, a long time ago, that you wished you had handled things differently . . . with Bill, I mean. That you regretted it. That made a big impression on me. I'm not going to have any regrets. I don't think you want them, either."

The reference to Bill caught me off guard. For an instant I was back at West Point.

"Sam, don't let that happen with the Guru. Help us stop it. Don't regret anything this time."

He turned and walked away. Turtle put the van in gear. Zack opened the door and got in.

Decide who you will be and then be him.

I stepped over as Zack closed his door and rolled down the window.

"I'll need lat/longs for the PZ and LZ and whatever timeline you've planned so far. My main concern is fuel."

Turtle pumped his fist. "Hell yeah!"

"Roger that. Can you meet us at this address in about two hours?" Zack handed me a folded piece of paper.

"Yes, but first I need to talk some other crazy bastards into helping."

FOUR

IFIRST MET THE GURU AFTER THE MARCH BACK TO WEST Point from Lake Frederick. It was a long march at the end of a long summer.

I'd been assigned to room 5324 in Scott Barracks with Cisco Guerrero, and we were trying to get moved in.

Cisco was a second-generation Cuban American and army brat. His father had gained citizenship after enlisting in the army and serving in Vietnam and had then gone on to become a command sergeant major. He had dragged his family all over the world. Growing up never spending more than two years in any one spot had imbued Cisco with an adaptability and resilience I came to envy. He was also a troublemaker. His father had sent him to a military boarding high school to try to straighten him out. It must have worked, because he'd made it to West Point. Barely.

Cisco also possessed an army brat's indifference to rank. He'd grown up around it, so the system lacked any mystery or menace in his eyes. His father had been the highest-ranking U.S. Army enlisted man in Europe when they were stationed there, responsible for the welfare and readiness of over a hundred thousand soldiers under arms. To Cisco, though, this accomplished and powerful soldier was just his father. He was fallible and imperfect.

And yet reporting to our academic barracks terrified Cisco as much as me.

These barracks were different from the ones we had lived in that summer. Referred to as "the Divisions," they were old, having been built in the thirties. Rather than forty-plus rooms on the same hallway, they had four rooms per floor, stacked one on top of another. A stairway ran up the middle of each division, serving as a vertical hallway that connected the five floors. Each division was numbered. The Corps of Cadets called the divisions that housed E4 "the Lost Fifties" because of their location on the extreme western edge of the cadet area, next to the gym.

After the march back, Cisco and I dropped our rucksacks on our beds before heading out the door again to get the rest of our gear. Pinging out into the hallway, we ran into a cadet's trunk that had not been there moments earlier. I nearly fell over it and into the lap of the cadet seated in a chair on the other side.

"Whoa there, stud," said the upperclassman. I righted myself and stood at rigid attention. "Hey, smack," he said, gesturing to Cisco, "stand next to your classmate. I can't see you behind him."

"Yes, sir." Cisco moved to my left side. We stood facing the upperclassman. There was a silver mess hall pitcher of water and a mess hall glass on the trunk.

"You're slow, Guerrero. You ping like a damn turtle."

"No excuse, sir." Cisco was shorter than the average cadet, but more muscular. He moved his stout frame deliberately and often did not convey the sense of urgency that upperclassmen expected.

"Your name is Turtle from now on."

"Yes, sir."

I couldn't tell if he was a yearling, cow, or firstie, because he wore only his cadet-issue robe and shower flip-flops. I hoped he was a yearling, since the newly risen sophomores of West Point tended to take it easier on plebes.

I was most scared of cows, the third-year cadets. Corps legend said they got their name over 150 years ago, when cadets were not allowed to take their first leave until after the completion of their second year. This inspired the adage "When a man goes to West Point, he doesn't come home until the cows come home." Though the academy's leave policies had since changed, the nickname had not; nor had the fact that cows were generally the meanest of the classes.

His cadet robe was covered in old military unit patches, which gave it an impressive bathroom flight-jacket appearance. There were two cigars in its pocket.

"Do not gaze at my robe, Cadet Avery." His voice was stern.

"Yes, sir." I swiveled my eyes off his robe and looked him in the face. His hair was curly, sandy blond, and so long that it was only barely within regulations.

A grin spread across his face, exposing his teeth and dimpling his cheeks. His eyes crinkled at the corners. I would learn that his classmates referred to this as his "Loki grin" because it meant mischief.

"Long road march, huh?" he said in a conversational tone.

"Yes, sir."

"Have you guys been drinking enough water?"

"Yes, sir."

"Good. Why don't you drink some more?" He motioned to Cisco. "Pour yourself a glass of water, Turtle. It's very important to stay hydrated. Don't you think, New Cadet Avery?"

The cadre had harped on hydration the entire march back. They would have been held responsible for any of us who fell out as "heat casualties," so, with classic military overreaction, we were told to drink water every fifteen minutes. Our bladders had suffered. My stomach was already taut and uncomfortable. I didn't like where this was going.

"Yes, sir."

"Good. Recite 'The Corps' for me, please."

"The Corps" is a hymn that was written in the early 1900s and has since become foundational to the academy. Sung by the cadet Glee Club at most important events, its verses are embedded in every cadet's mind by the time they graduate. It was primary among our plebe knowledge during the summer and was hammered into us daily. "Sir, 'The Corps'!" I said, and I launched into it while Turtle drank water.

"The Corps! The Corps! The Corps!
The Corps, bareheaded, salute it,
With eyes up, thanking our God."

"Now pour New Cadet Avery a glass of water," the upperclassman told Turtle. "When he begins to drink, you will pick up 'The Corps' where he leaves off." He turned his attention to me. "More feeling, Avery. It's a goddamn important poem, not a grocery list." I tried to liven up my enunciation. He arched his eyebrows and rolled his eyes in mock appreciation.

Suddenly Turtle was holding the glass of water in front of me. I grabbed it and started to drink. Turtle stuttered a bit and then continued:

"We sons of today, we salute you.
You sons of an earlier day;
We follow, close order, behind you,
Where you have pointed the way;
The long gray line of us stretches,
Thro' the years of a century told."

"Not a smooth transition, Turtle. I think your performance is being hindered by your dehydrated state." He reached down behind the trunk and produced a canteen. "Drink this, please." He handed it to Turtle. "When you have finished that canteen, continue where New Cadet Avery leaves off."

This went on for a long time. It was terrible. I was bloated. Turtle and I started to spill as much water as possible down our chins as we drank. Our uniforms became soaked in front. He seemed to quiz us on the entire contents of *Bugle Notes*, a book we had been issued our first day that contained all of the plebe knowledge we were responsible for. It was small, so it could fit in a cargo pocket, but over a hundred pages long. We had to memorize everything in it during Beast Barracks.

Finally, the cadet held up his hand. I stopped reciting Schofield's Definition of Discipline and Turtle stopped drinking.

"I am Cadet Stillmont. Most cadets call me Guru. You will not call me Guru until I authorize it. I am a cow and your squad leader, and you will be sharing this floor with me until Christmas leave. As your squad leader, I will be assigning numerous duties to you, but we will start with the basics. Make sure I get my newspaper every day, my mail and laundry when they're due, and that you've mastered all your required knowledge. Do not ever embarrass me. You are my plebes now. You are a reflection on me. Are my standards clear to you, new cadets?"

"Yes, sir," we said.

He looked at both of us for a long moment. "Do you know how to properly greet your company mates?"

"Sir, the company motto is 'Go Elephants.'"

"The Corps has," he said, sadly shaking his head. Short for "The Corps has gone to hell," it is an old saying that has been declared by upperclassmen and old grads for centuries. By the end of that summer, my classmates and I had heard it a thousand times.

"I hate that Beast Barracks bullshit," the Guru continued. "Gentlemen, the proper greeting to other members of E4 is 'Go naked.'"

Turtle and I looked at the Guru, trying to determine if he was setting us up.

"I'm serious about this," he said as he stood up from behind the trunk. "They have been trying to stamp out our company motto for decades now. In my squad we uphold company traditions. It's important. Do you understand?"

"Yes, sir."

"Never use the company greeting when there is an officer nearby. And you should take care when using it if cadets from other companies are around, particularly those duty-dick Frogs from F4. But in these halls and among your company mates, both contemporaries and superiors, the greeting is 'Go naked.' The only other acceptable greeting is 'Go Elvis.' Do you understand?"

"Yes, sir."

"Good. 'Go Elephants' is a stupid motto. Don't ever let me hear you say it."

"Yes, sir."

"Where were you two new cadets going when you so rudely bumped into my trunk and me?"

"Sir, we were going to retrieve our trunks in order to continue setting up our room."

"Good. I will inspect your room at eighteen hundred hours this evening. Be ready. You are dismissed."

"Go naked, sir," we said as we moved down the stairs. The water sloshed painfully in my stomach.

Later that night, Turtle and I lay in our beds, trying to calibrate to yet another jarring transition.

Cadet Basic Training, or Beast Barracks as it was referred to by cadets, had been an endless progression of regimented drudgery: physical training, classes, issue points, instruction in the honor code, parade practice, room inspections, and plebe duties. Zack, Bill, and I had quickly gelled into an effective roommate team, and we did better than most. But it still sucked.

Mealtimes most of all. For plebes during Beast Barracks, meals are torture. Sitting at attention without your back against the chair, not being allowed to chew unless your hands are in your lap, restricted to tiny bites so that you can swallow instantly in order to respond to an upperclassman, and performing plebe table duties. The worst of which is cutting the dessert.

At the start of the meal, the gunner at each table is responsible for asking who wants dessert and cutting the appropriate number of pieces. The firsties always conspire so that an odd number of pieces must be cut. Cutting a cake into seven even pieces is difficult. Once cut, the cake is always inspected by the first classmen. If the pieces are not even, the gunner gets hazed for most of the meal. Not only does this mean he can't eat, his tablemates also can't eat, because no plebe is allowed to eat while a cadre member is talking. So everyone depends on everyone else's ability to perform their duties. This makes cake cutting a high-stakes activity.

We learned quickly to use a template, a small cardboard circle marked with all of the possible piece counts from halves to tenths. It was like an Old World compass folded in half and stuffed in our hats. It was critical. And at dinner three days into Beast Barracks, I had forgotten mine.

I sat down at the table and froze in fear. I knew immediately where it was: sitting on my desk in my room. I had been double-checking the markings just before dinner. One of the cadre declined dessert, of course. I had to cut that night's Martha Washington cake into nine even pieces. I was fucked. Worse, I had fucked the whole table.

Someone nudged my left knee. I had been a cadet for less than seventy-two hours, but I had already killed the instinct to gaze around when startled; even so, I knew it was Bill. I subtly yet quickly extended my arm under the table. Bill thrust something into my hand. It was his template. He saved me. He saved the table.

That night after taps, I thanked him.

"Don't mention it."

"How did you even know I needed it?" I asked.

Bill shrugged. "I just did. I could tell something was wrong."

"So sweet. You guys are gonna make me cry," said Zack from his bed.

That was the first instance of what quickly became a strong bond. I was good friends with Zack, of course, and several of the guys. But Bill and I had a connection. Several times over the summer, one of us instinctively saved the other. It just worked.

Still, Beast Barracks was a stressful grind punctuated by frequent moments of fear. Wilcox was a terror. Nothing we did was ever good enough for him. He and the rest of the cadre circled us like angry sharks all summer, constantly reminding us how weak we were as individuals and as a class. They let us know, whenever they could, how much worse they'd had it when they were plebes, and how bad they would have made things for us were it not for the commissioned officers staying their hand. "The Corps has," they would lament.

Lake Frederick, the capstone training event, was a one-week bivouac. The contrast between the field and the garrison was dramatic and welcome. The garrison had been briefings, classes, and drill periods followed by late nights of polishing, shining, cleaning, memorizing, and reciting. The field was tactical training: rifles, machine guns, hand grenades, land navigation, and first aid. Best of all, since we were out in the field, there was no *New York Times* to memorize daily, and the incessant knowledge quizzes abated slightly. When we were tested on our plebe knowledge, the questions focused more on military stuff than, say, how many gallons of water were in Lusk Reservoir.

But the march back to West Point had been tough, and not just physically. The sense of dread got heavier the closer we got to post. The entire Corps had converged back on West Point from summer training assignments around the world and was waiting for us.

Most of the march back was tactical, but when we entered main post at the back gate off Storm King Highway, we formed up into companies.

There were people waiting for us: families, friends, faculty, and tourists. All cheering as we marched toward the barracks to join the Corps.

The band intercepted us at Keller Army Community Hospital and marched in front of our column as the crowd thickened. The cheering became louder and more raucous, the flag and sign waving more vigorous. The closer we got to the barracks, the more upperclassmen I saw in the crowd. By the time we passed by the superintendent's house and the Plain, the clusters of yearlings, cows, and firsties were thick. The math had turned against us. Upperclassmen now outnumbered us three to one. Academics didn't start in earnest for a week. They had nothing better to do than haze us, their new plebes.

Billeting on the same floor as the Guru and having him as our squad leader was terrifying, but Turtle and I quickly realized that it also granted us status, even with upperclassmen. No one hazed us too much because they knew the Guru was constantly riding us, and it seemed like they didn't want to irritate him by doing so. This also applied to the firsties, even though the Guru was only a cow.

The other plebes were terrified of him and wanted to know more.

"So what's the Guru like?" asked Zack.

"What did you hear about him?"

"I heard he's a third-generation legacy," said Creighton Patterson, Zack's new roommate. "His father and grandfather were grads. His father was killed in Vietnam."

Creighton was the first son of a renowned black armored cavalry officer. His father named him after General Creighton Abrams, a West Pointer who fought under Patton in World War II and was regarded as the best armor commander the country had ever produced. Creighton's father had worked for General Abrams in Vietnam after achieving his own fame as a smart and aggressive armor officer.

If family and professional expectations weighed on Creighton, it did not show. We learned quickly that he was a lifer. There was no other school for him than West Point, no other place for him than the U.S. Army, and no other branch for him than his father's. Armor.

Creighton was black and of average build, but in the super-fit environment of West Point, he seemed smaller than average. Wearing glasses did not increase his stature, but he had an advantage over all of us. He was a natural cadet. He wore the uniform and moved through the cadet area with ease. He was a master of military history, which enhanced his sense of self and place. He knew why he was here, what to expect, and how to optimize himself within the system.

"The yearlings on my floor were talking about him," said Bill. "He sounds pretty cool."

"I don't know about all that, but cool is definitely not how I would describe him," I said. "My stomach still hasn't recovered."

"Where did he get the balls to go by 'the Guru'?" asked Zack.

"I heard he had a habit of correcting firsties and being right," said Bill.

"Okay. So that is ballsy," acknowledged Zack.

"No kidding."

"Supposedly," Bill continued, "a firstie freaked when Stillmont corrected him on how Edgar Allan Poe got kicked out. The firstie was in his face: 'What? You think you're some kind of damn guru?' But Stillmont wouldn't cave. The firstie put him through a couple hours of uniform drills, trying to get him to back down."

Zack groaned. Uniform drills were painful. The cadre would say simply, "Report back to me in three minutes wearing your full dress uniform," and you were off on a doomed quest to meet their timeline. Each time you reported back, the cadre would shake his head and give you a new assignment. "Not fast enough. Report back to me in three minutes wearing your class uniform under raincoat." A couple rounds of this and not only were you exhausted but your room was destroyed from your spastic efforts to get in and out of different uniforms quickly. Firsties could dial up the cruelty easily by adding small requirements. "Report back to me in three minutes wearing your battle dress uniform under field jacket and holding your mattress cover." Bed destroyed.

"They say each time Stillmont reported in new uniform the firstie would ask him if he wanted to admit that he was not a guru. That he was wrong and correct himself. Stillmont never did. Finally other upperclassmen told the firstie that Stillmont was actually right. So the name stuck."

"I heard a different story," Creighton said. "A crazy one. I heard he got the name in the House of Tears."

We all shuddered, remembering one of the worst segments of Beast Barracks: NBC, or Nuclear, Biological, and Chemical, training. The goal was to teach us how to use, and have confidence in, the army's protective gear. The method was to file us, by squad, into a small, one-room cinder-block building known as the House of Tears. The structure was full of CS gas, a powerful riot-control agent. We were sent in wearing full protective gear, including our gas masks. After a few minutes of demonstrating that the protective gear worked, we were told to take off our masks and recite "The Corps."

The effect was instantaneous. Sandpaper scraped our eyeballs, and breathing felt like inhaling molten glass and thumbtacks. Our lungs rebelled and tried to stop the inflow of poison, but our bodies demanded oxygen. Long ribbons of snot poured from our noses, and our eyes burned. They held us in there for a long time. The room filled with grunting noises and strange shrieks as our respiratory systems tried to reject the CS gas while we choked our way through the sacred verse.

Finally we completed our recitation of "The Corps." By the time we were released, we had been reduced to a retching, heaving gaggle of blind people. My eyes felt like they were dragging across the cement floor as I stumbled toward the light. The cadre ushered us out and made sure no one fell over. It took hours for the effects to wear off.

"They said Stillmont didn't miss a beat. Said he belted out 'The Corps' like he was reciting it back in the barracks. Everyone else was reduced to choking tears, and he was fine. One of the cadre members, in his gas mask, looked at Stillmont and said, 'Look at this stubborn plebe, the fucking guru of the House of Tears.' And the name stuck."

Both stories had the ring of truth to me. That's how nicknames happened in the Corps. They sprang forth from moments of embarrassment, rage, or hazing. The universe assigned them through upper-class revelation, and they stuck when their essence was true. Stillmont's had not only stuck, it had spread. He was known Corps-wide as the Guru.

"They also told me why he is on the area," Bill said. Being forced to walk the Central Area for hours in full dress uniform was a common form of punishment. "This summer at Air Assault School, he organized a group of cadets one night and they painted a giant cadet insignia on the big rappel wall!"

"How did they get caught?" asked Zack.

"A pair of Apache gunships were in the area and spotted them on their FLIRs."

"That's actually a really cool way to get busted."

"They said the Air Assault instructors were super pissed! They wanted to kick the Guru out immediately, but the school commandant wouldn't let them. He was a grad. They put the Guru on restrictions instead."

"What did they write him up for when he got back here?"

"Conduct unbecoming of a cadet."

"Conduct unbecoming? Really?" mumbled Zack. "Seems like you would want cadets to be just like that: proud, ballsy."

"Don't kid yourself," answered Bill.

Like the rest of us, Zack was still coming to terms with the reality of West Point and its emphasis on professionalism. Plebe summer had been bewildering. It was difficult to connect most of what we were put through to our quest to become warriors. It was hard, but in a tedious, pedantic way. We accomplished something by surviving it. But we weren't sure what.

This dissonance stayed with us long after the summer ended. We were still grappling to understand it, Zack most vocally.

✦ ✦ ✦

The start of the academic year did not alleviate any of the pressure of our plebe duties. Our first week back, I was assigned "paper carrier" responsibility with Emily Simons, a female plebe from Ohio. In high school, she had been class president and captain of the basketball team. Here, like the rest of us, she was a scared and sweaty human with closely cropped hair.

Paper carriers retrieve the *New York Times* each morning from the Fourth Regiment drop-off point in North Area and deliver them to each cadet barracks room before morning formation. Of all the cadet duties, paper carrier is the most visible and stressful. Everyone wants their paper in the morning: plebes because they have to memorize it before formation, and upperclassmen because they want to quiz and stump plebes on it.

Emily and I failed miserably our first morning. The paper drop-off was on the opposite corner of North Area from the Lost Fifties. At 0605 hours, when we arrived to grab our allotment, there was only enough for about half of E4's rooms. We panicked and had no system for prioritizing our deliveries. Plebes we missed were pissed because they got slaughtered at morning formation. Upperclassmen we missed were incensed: "You gave a paper to a damn yearling before you gave one to me?"

Emily and I took heat all day, from upperclassmen and fellow plebes alike. The worst for me, though, was the Guru's rebuke at lunch formation: "You've really let me down, Avery. What happened?"

"No excuse, sir."

"I don't want to hear that bullshit. What happened?"

"Sir, we left our rooms as soon as we could, right at oh-six-hundred, but most of the papers had already been taken by the other companies." Cadets were not supposed to leave their rooms before 0600 hours. It was the academy's effort to try to offer some protection from too much hazing and too many extracurricular challenges during the academic year. In situations like this, however, it was an obstacle to getting things done.

"Do you really think I don't understand the rules here, Avery?" he said, glaring at me.

"No, sir. We will be sure to be there in time tomorrow morning."

He leaned forward.

"Does that solve your problem?"

I looked back at him, my mind flailing. I had no idea what he wanted me to say or do.

"My plebes are problem solvers, Avery," he said before walking away in disgust. He ignored me the rest of the day.

Emily and I held a war council after classes.

"We've got to get to the drop-off point earlier," she said. "I know it's a risk, but I think we should leave our rooms at oh-five-forty-five to get the jump on the rest of the regiment."

"That won't solve our problem."

"What are you talking about?"

"We'll just have to do that every day from now on. And once the other companies get wise, they'll just do the same thing and we'll just have to get up earlier and earlier."

Emily frowned. "Okay, smart guy. Do you have a better idea?"

"I think so."

The next morning at 0400 hours when the *New York Times* delivery contractor pulled into North Area, Emily and I were waiting for him. As he came to a stop and hopped out, we stepped out of the shadows and Emily made our offer.

"Good morning, sir."

"Mornin', cadet. What do you want?"

"We'd like to request a daily delivery of fifty papers each morning to the Lost Fifties." Emily pointed at our barracks.

"No way. That's not the deal. I drop 'em here and in Central Area."

He tried to push past Emily, but she blocked him.

"How about for fifty bucks a month?"

He straightened up at that, surprised.

"For real?"

"Yes, sir. Fifty bucks now and then fifty at the completion of each month, based on performance." She raised her hand, holding the money we had collected from each plebe in E4 after dinner the previous night.

He took the money and counted it slowly. Then he smiled. "Show me where you want 'em, cadet." For the rest of the year, plebes happily coughed up the small fee, and E4 had its papers every day.

A few days later, the Guru asked what we had done. After I debriefed him, he smiled and nodded. "I would have started at twenty-five dollars a month, but you solved the problem. Good work."

✦ ✦ ✦

As the semester ground on, the Guru regularly pulled us aside to teach us arcane aspects of cadet lore. His lessons were always a little skewed from the party line and much more interesting. He was connecting us to the ancient heretical spirit of the Corps. We loved it.

On the Friday of Ring Weekend, the Guru strode up to breakfast formation. I watched him approach out of the corner of my eye. He was of average build but stronger than he looked. His gait was always slightly off tempo from the disciplined and purposeful movements of the Corps in general. Even in parade formation, it looked to me as if he was struggling to restrain himself.

"Avery, you ready for Ring Weekend?"

"Yes, sir."

"Let me hear the ring poop."

"Oh my God, sir. What a beautiful ring! What a crass mass of brass and glass! What a bold mold of rolled gold! What a cool jewel you got from your school! See how it sparkles and shines? It must have cost you a fortune! Please, sir, may I touch it?"

The yearlings had been teaching us the ring poop since we had returned from Frederick. We were supposed to wait outside the mess hall while the firsties were given their rings at the secret ceremony. As they emerged to meet their dates for the weekend, we were to ambush them and recite the ring poop until they allowed us to touch their rings.

"Good. But do you know the true meaning behind the ring?"

"No, sir." I had learned to recognize when he had a lesson to teach.

"Ever heard of Prometheus?"

"The Greek god, sir?"

"He was one of the oldest. One day he looked down on man and took pity on his nasty, brutish, and short existence. He stole a little bit of fire and ran it down to earth. Zeus found out and was pissed. He had Prometheus chained to a rock in the Caucasus for the rest of eternity. Every day a gigantic eagle would come and dig at Prometheus's side and eat his liver. Since Prometheus was an immortal, his liver grew back every night. Every day the eagle would return. This went on for hundreds of years, until Zeus relented and released him. Zeus decreed that until the end of time, Prometheus would wear a link of the chain that had held him to that mountain, to remind him and the other immortals of exactly what had happened and what he had been subjected to." The Guru looked at me for a moment.

"Do you understand?"

"Yes, sir."

"Good. Pass it on." He suddenly glanced past us, to the rear of the formation. "Ugh. Without fail. The bicycling bastard arrives."

I heard what had become the familiar clicking of Captain Eifer's ten-speed bike. He made it a practice most mornings to ride up behind the company to observe our formations. The upperclassmen hated it. More often than not, a handful of them would get written up for uniform violations. The chain-on-gears noise alone was now sufficient to put the whole company on edge.

Captain Eifer was E4's tactical officer, responsible for the discipline and development of all the cadets in the company. Every company at West Point had a tac, but ours was a tyrant. He was rumored to have written up more cadets than any tactical officer in history. There was no way to validate that, of course, but everyone believed it, including Captain Eifer. He was aware of his reputation and wore it like airborne wings on his chest, but he didn't swagger. He was always the most precise and professional thing moving in the cadet area. His movements were efficient and unexpressive. He could scan cadets effortlessly and from great distances; his head would swivel smoothly on motionless shoulders as he wrote the quill in his head. The Guru told us of a time when Captain Eifer wrote him up for inappropriate uniform from the other side of North Area. Eifer had spotted the one button on the Guru's shirt that was unfastened from over one hundred meters away. "No shit. I was guilty, and he got me." The Guru shook his head with grudging respect.

Captain Eifer was such a force that the other tacs in Fourth Regiment let him walk all over their cadet companies. Whether it just wasn't as important to them or they didn't have the stomach for the conflict, they allowed Eifer to rule the regiment. Adding special insult to Eifer's terror was the fact that he was not a grad. It was one thing in the eyes of the Corps to be a hard-ass if you had done it yourself. But Eifer was Ivy League ROTC: Yale. He had not been through what we were going through. Not only that: he was proud he hadn't been through it. He was not impressed by West Point. "Anachronistic," he called it when he lectured us. "A terrible way to create officers, cloistered as you are here on the river, alienated from the society you are tasked with leading." His antipathy for us was so great, we'd wondered what he was doing here.

Creighton had set us straight: "After more than a decade of peace, and no real conflicts in sight, assignment to West Point is an excellent career move."

Bill had nodded ruefully in agreement.

"I'm going to fucking barf" had been Zack's response.

E4 was not only Eifer's assignment; we were the main focus of his disdain. It was so bad, most cadets in Fourth Regiment believed that Eifer was on a special mission from the commandant to "fix E4." The administration had viewed our company as slack troublemakers for years. Maybe decades.

E4's long, slow divergence from the academy ideal was surprising to some, but cadet companies at West Point have always been potent alchemies of legacy, legend, and the now. You would never know, just watching the Corps in formation on the Plain; every cadet company that marches by looks identical to the next, but the personalities and culture of each one are disparate and stretch back into fuzzy and exaggerated prehistories. Captain Eifer was pushing against the full weight of this tribal identity in E4. We pushed back.

✦ ✦ ✦

Turtle and I learned early on that spirit missions were a special emphasis for the Guru. One Thursday evening early in the semester he pulled us into his room for a lesson.

Clad in his distinctive robe and blowing the smoke from his cigar out the window, he held forth: "A spirit mission, gentlemen, is an activity undertaken by cadets that is typically somewhat against regulations yet demonstrates qualities that the academy supposedly seeks to develop: audacity, teamwork, creativity, and mission focus. The successful accomplishment of a good spirit mission enhances the spirit not only of the cadets involved but also that of the whole Corps and the greater West Point community in general."

We smiled, completely under his spell.

"You have to be careful, though. Do not expect to be thanked for your service on a spirit mission. In the view of the tactical department and academy leadership, spirit missions are dangerous. Not to be tolerated. The higher-ups don't appreciate the cadet perspective on motivation or justice. They will try to prevent spirit missions from taking place, and if they cannot prevent them, they will punish the cadets they can catch."

He smiled his Loki grin and blew a large smoke ring out the window. "This persecution, of course, lends spirit missions a greater share of honor."

He released another smoke ring for emphasis.

"We must aim high. The best spirit missions are too bold, too foolhardy, and too outlandish. They make a statement; they right a wrong; and they demonstrate that the impossible can be achieved. Remember, it was MacArthur himself who, as a cadet in 1901, snuck out of the barracks after taps and moved the heavy reveille cannon all the way across the Plain to the top of the clock tower of Pershing Barracks." The Guru smiled widely, out of respect. He was inspired just talking about it. "That tower is sixty feet tall! It took the engineering corps over a week to figure out how to get the cannon down. Can you imagine? It's a legend now." He nodded to himself.

"Of course, if he did that kind of thing today, he would be slammed for destruction of government property and conduct unbecoming. He'd get at least a hundred punishment tours on the area." He shook his head and looked at us earnestly. "In our time, spirit missions are risky and thankless. Nevertheless, gentlemen, they serve the greater good."

FIVE

I SAT IN SILENCE AS WEBER DROVE US BACK. "SO, WHAT DID those guys want?" He pulled up to the TOC building and looked at me.

"Oh. Nothing. Just saying hi."

Weber was a smart guy. An air force combat controller, he was Ranger-qualified and had served with me for the past three years. We knew each other well.

I returned his gaze with my best poker face. He rolled his eyes and smiled. "That's nice." He hopped out of the van and preceded me into the TOC.

This is crazy echoed in my head as I walked through the TOC to the coffeepot. I was amped on adrenaline and didn't need the coffee at all, but the ritual was calming. I stood in front of the pot for a few moments and slowly went through my process: half a packet of sugar, then add half a cup of coffee and swirl, visually inspect to make sure most of the sugar had dissolved, then add the rest of the coffee. *What the hell am I doing?*

I looked at my watch. Fortunately, there was not a lot of time to sit around and worry about what was next. It was time to talk to Pete.

A Chinook takes a crew of three to fly on a milk run: two pilots and a crew chief. In combat it takes five, adding two more crewmen. The crew is critical. They make sure the pilots do not put the ass end of the helicopter, extending about seventy-five feet behind them, into a building. They monitor external loads, manage myriad aircraft systems, and man the miniguns and other weapon systems. It's easy to say that they are an extension of the pilots' eyes, ears, arms, and legs, but it's not true. That is too simple an explanation. Often it is the other way around; the pilots are an extension of the crew's mind. In reality, no one is an extension of anyone on board a Chinook in battle. It's more like a seamless quintet.

But right now, I was a wannabe crew of one that would probably not even remember how to start the engines correctly. Though I was still qualified on the Chinook, as a lieutenant colonel, my role obligated me to focus more on leadership and administration. I was rusty.

I stepped quietly into the pilots' quarters and found Pete's bunk. They were all sleeping, trying to stay "reversed out" so they would be fresh for the inevitable night missions. I gave Pete a nudge.

"Huh? What's up, sir?"

"Can we talk?"

"Sure—what's up?"

"Outside?"

"Shit, sir, everyone else is asleep. They won't hear anything. What's up?"

"I'll wait outside."

I left him grumbling in his bunk, went outside, and sat on a bench under a lean-to about twenty meters from their trailer. Pete Shephard was one of the most senior warrant officers in the regiment. As a warrant officer, he had flown thousands more hours than I, the commissioned officer, but at this point we were like brothers.

We'd met in Germany at what was the first unit for both of us. I was a second lieutenant, and he was a WO1. From that first day, our careers were commissioned/warrant mirrors of each other's. We each worked our way through our respective career tracks while posting, repeatedly, to the same units. We cycled through Germany, then back to Fort Rucker, and then Fort Campbell together before being selected by the 160th Special Operations Aviation Regiment the same year.

The 160th had been a goal for each of us since we'd graduated from flight school. The "Night Stalkers," as they are called, were formed in 1980 after the debacle at Desert One. When President Carter asked for a military option for the Iranian hostage situation, Delta Force, composed of the best special operators in the world, was the clear choice. They would go in and rescue the Americans. The problem was how to get them there. The military had no dedicated special operations aviation capability, so they cobbled together an ad hoc unit of scrounged-up navy helicopters flown by marine pilots.

After the deadly failure in the desert, helicopter crew selection and performance was criticized and studied intensely. President Carter ordered the military to get ready for another attempt and to get it right. This time the National Command Authority turned to the army for the helicopter piece. The release of the hostages put an end to the specific preparations, but the Joint Chiefs regarded the aviation capability the army had built at Fort Campbell as too valuable to let it disperse again.

So they formed the 160th, the Night Stalkers, to continue to preserve and perfect the anytime, anywhere, any weather capability. The Night Stalkers were dedicated to supporting Delta, the SEALs, and other similar assets. From then on, U.S. special operators knew that, no matter how bad things got, the 160th would put them in exactly the right spot and would always come back to get them out of whatever pinch they got into.

By the mid-1990s, when Pete and I were trying to get in, the unit was legendary.

Pete stepped out of the converted trailer that served as the pilots' quarters and walked toward me. I smiled despite my anxiety. Pete was not only a great pilot; he was a great-looking pilot. His lean six-foot-two frame, symmetrical face, and dark, wavy hair won him a lot of attention from the ladies wherever we were deployed. It also earned him constant abuse from the rest of us.

Pete sat next to me while I pitched him straight up and in simple terms. He listened quietly as he smoked one of his trademark Backwoods cigars. He always had a pouch of the cheap, rough-looking cigars in one of his flight suit pockets. His Ray-Ban sunglasses and those damn Backwoods cigars were the two things I never saw Pete without.

"Is this a joke, sir?" he said when I was done.

"I wish it was."

Pete turned his head and stared out at the helicopters. He looked sad. I knew what he was thinking about. I did not want to make this about that night.

"This really how you want to go out, Sam?"

Pete was a pro. As close as we were, he never called me Sam unless we were away from the military and out of uniform. He never dropped his "sir"s.

"I think so."

"You better be sure."

"I am, Pete. I won't be able to live with myself if I don't try."

"Really? Seems like we've lived with it for a while."

"That was different."

Pete just stared back at me.

"Doesn't seem like it."

"I know," I said sadly. "I almost asked someone else because I was afraid you would get weird about this."

He shook his head. "There is no one else you could ask to do this, and you know it," he said, giving me a weak smile.

"I know."

"What if I say no? What if it's not how I want to go out?"

"You and I will still be square. One hundred percent. And I hope you'll understand that I had to ask."

He nodded, looked away, and took a big tug on his cigar.

"I mean, what will you do if I say no?"

"I'll join my buddies on a ground infil north to try to get him out."

"You'll never make it."

"I don't know. These guys have grown up to be pretty tough. They're good at what they do."

"ISIS is cutting people's heads off."

"And they have my friend."

Pete nodded and stomped out the stub of his cigar. "You know I'm also pretty good at what I do." He stood up. "Sir, this actually sounds like a pretty damn meaningful mission. Count me in."

"You sure?"

"Now you're going to try to talk me out of it?"

"No. I just want you to be sure. Don't do this to balance any scales, Pete. It doesn't work like that."

"We'll see. Besides, I'm a fucking CW5. What are they going to do to me?"

That made me laugh. There was no saltier dog in the U.S. Army than a CW5. "Beware the general with no ambition, right?"

"Whatever. You're the deep thinker. Let's go get your friend."

" 'Thank you' doesn't seem to cover it."

"You're damn right it doesn't. When we get back I don't expect to buy a drink ever again."

"Deal."

"You said this was a single-vehicle-team insertion and then an exfil?"

"Yep."

"I'd like to meet your guys, Zack and Turtle, as soon as I can to talk particulars."

"Roger that. I'm going to meet up with them around fourteen-thirty a couple miles from the airfield."

"I'll grab a quick shower and join you."

"What about a crew?"

"Let me worry about that," Pete said, smiling. "Couple of those guys owe me big-time."

"I don't want to know."

"They don't want you to, either."

I looked at my watch. It was 1335 hours. We were burning daylight quickly.

✦ ✦ ✦

I walked back toward the operations center trying not to think about that night. I tried to push it aside and focus on my next task, but it was futile. I was pulled back to just before midnight on January 7, 2002.

Our aircraft had throbbed like a locomotive as we climbed up the mountain two hundred feet above its surface. The engine temperature indications had been in the red for eighteen minutes. We were high and we were heavy as we flew toward our destination. There was no avoiding the engine abuse.

LZ Troy was 11,347 feet above sea level. Our payload was Boxer 25, a fully equipped Special Forces A Team. They were packing heavy with no idea when they would be pulled off the mountain.

By that time we were used to the challenges of high-altitude flying. We had learned how long the aircraft's systems could take such brutal punishment. The engines could be operated at those temperatures before causing damage for another twelve minutes.

We would be at the LZ in nine.

"Hammer 22, this is Raven 21, approaching LZ Troy. Requesting status," Pete transmitted over the VHF radio.

Hammer 22 was an AC-130 gunship orbiting five thousand feet above us. They had been on station for several hours observing the LZs and supporting the two Special Forces teams already in the area. We had been monitoring the transmissions between the gunship and the SF teams. Both ground units had been in contact with the enemy since sunset, particularly Dragon 45, which had been in sporadic enemy contact all day. Hammer 22 was having a busy night.

Hammer's imaging and targeting equipment enabled it to peer through the night down onto the LZs and other areas of interest with decent accuracy. We did not want to unwittingly insert our team directly into a firefight.

"Raven 21, Hammer 22. Be advised that we have not had eyes directly on Troy for two zero mikes. But it was ice at that time," responded the gunship. "Ice" was the code word signifying that the LZ was clear—or, at least, it had been twenty minutes ago.

"Let the team leader know. Landing in six minutes," Pete said to the crew chief in the rear.

"Roger that, sir. Six minutes."

I was sitting in the companionway jump seat, centered and behind Pete and Kevin, the copilot. Pete was the pilot in command of our aircraft and I was the air mission commander of our flight of two. We had both been with the unit only a few years at that point, and this was our first combat tour.

Raven 31, our sister ship, had broken off from us twenty-five minutes earlier and was inserting its A Team into a mountainside LZ on the opposite side of the valley. Once in place, these two teams would perform a deadly overwatch of the mountains and the valley below, conducting direct actions against the enemy as well as providing targeting and guidance for air force sorties. After Tora Bora, the previous month, we were getting more aggressive in our fight against the Taliban in the mountains.

LZ Troy wasn't bad, as high-altitude Afghanistan landing zones went. It was large and level enough for us to set down rather than have to execute a two-wheel pinnacle landing.

"I'll take the controls," Pete said.

"You've got the controls," Kevin responded.

As we approached the LZ, I could feel the tension radiate off Pete. High-altitude landings like this were tricky, and it was very easy to bake an engine. Doing so would be a disaster, since at that altitude it takes both engines to fly. We wouldn't have single-engine flight capability until we got back down into the valley.

I trusted Pete, though. Rather than stress myself out by staring at the instrument panel as the engine indications spiked, I turned to watch the team exit.

Knee-high snow covered the LZ. Our rotors kicked up a cloud of it that engulfed us before the aircraft crunched down onto its surface. The flight engineer lowered the ramp, and ten soldiers ran out into the cold night.

"Ramses 03, Raven 21 is Durham," I transmitted on the satcom radio. Ramses 03 was the task force operations officer monitoring our progress from our base at the airfield at Bagram, about 160 kilometers away. "Durham" meant we were on the LZ.

"Team is off. Rear is ready," announced the crew chief.

"Roger that. Moving," Pete said as he increased power. Raven 21 jostled as she skidded forward through the snow before laboring back into the air. Pete turned the aircraft downslope and nosed her over slightly to accelerate.

The mountain fell away sharply, and Pete dropped us over the edge like a cliff diver, trading altitude for lift-giving airspeed. I passed the code word "Birmingham" to the operations center, signifying we were airborne again. Once back at cruising speed, Pete eased the aircraft into a gentle climb, and soon we were orbiting five miles away, above the valley.

After an insertion like that, we typically loitered at a safe distance while the ground team got their bearings and ensured that there were no enemy in their vicinity. Once we started down the mountain, it would be at least an hour before we could climb back up to get them. We didn't want to leave them in a firefight if we didn't have to.

Raven 31 was supposed to join back up with us as we orbited; we would then proceed back to base as a flight of two. But their insertion did not go smoothly.

"Raven 21, this is 31. Primary LZ was Killjoy. Moving to alternate."

"Roger that, 31." Killjoy meant that the LZ was not suitable for landing. Sometimes, no matter how thorough the planning, the flat patch on the side of a mountain that looked so nice on a map and satellite imagery turned out to be a sucker hole, and there was simply no way to land a heavy helicopter on it. That's why we always had an alternate landing zone or two on missions like these. The problem was, switching to another site required more fuel and meant the helicopter's noise signature persisted longer, giving the enemy more time to figure out our intentions.

As we orbited, Pete reported what we were all observing: "The weather is deteriorating." Small clouds were forming near the mountains, and the cloud ceiling above us was coming down.

We monitored the radios, waiting for the team to give us the all clear. On the VHF and satcom radios it was apparent that Dragon 45's long day was not over yet. They were still exchanging fire with the enemy on another mountaintop, approximately ten miles to our north. The methodical back-and-forth on the radio between them and Hammer 22 belied the violence taking place. Soon a familiar voice reached out on the FM radio.

"Raven 21, this is Outlaw 01, over?"

I smiled. Outlaw 01 was a friend of mine, Major David West. Though he had graduated just one year ahead of me at West Point, we weren't close until we served in the 101st together in the mid-1990s. One year my senior in rank, he preceded me in nearly every assignment and became a mentor and coach as much as a friend. He transitioned to special operations two years before I did, and his encouragement and recommendation had been helpful there also. He had been promoted to major shortly before 9/11. It had been a hell of a party, and afterward he had enjoyed referring to me as "just a damn captain." He was a good pilot and officer.

That night he was serving as an embedded liaison to the Special Forces teams. He lived and fought with them while providing aviation planning and communications expertise. Sometimes it works better to have pilots talking to pilots on the radio. David had been on the mountain with one team or another for two months.

Pete turned his head, smiled, and nodded at me when he heard David's transmission. Everybody liked David.

"Go ahead, Outlaw 01."

"Raven 21, we've got three wounded that are surgical urgent. Requesting medevac."

"Outlaw 01, standby."

Pete was a few steps ahead of me. He checked our fuel and other systems. He gave me the thumbs-up over his right shoulder without looking back.

"Outlaw 01, say LZ."

"Raven 21, we are moving the wounded to LZ Argos."

"Roger that, Outlaw. Stand by."

Pete and Kevin called up LZ Argos on the navigation display and calculated a route while I made the call to the operations center. "Ramses 03, Raven 21, requesting permission to respond to Outlaw medevac request in support of Dragon 45. We are green on fuel."

"Raven 21, Ramses 03. As soon as Boxer 25 releases you, you're cleared to LZ Argos."

"Roger that, Ramses."

Pete pointed at the information on his navigation display. I read it quickly. "Outlaw 01, we can be there in twelve minutes as soon as we are released here."

"Roger that, Raven. We'll be ready."

"Will be good to see you, Outlaw."

"Likewise."

A few minutes later we were traversing a valley en route to Argos. As we neared the other mountain, I shook my head at the Afghan night. I was still not used to how dark it was, especially up in the mountains. There was absolutely no ambient light. Nothing. Having flown missions extensively in the United States, Europe, and Asia, I was used to dark nights. But in almost every other part of the world, there was always some kind of light source. A streetlight, a remote farmhouse, an industrial facility, something. In northeast Afghanistan there was nothing. Our night-vision goggles worked fine, and we had the forward-looking infrared imagery as well, so we were far from blind. Still, it was unnerving to stare out the cockpit unaided and see nothing but black, as if we were flying deep underwater rather than next to looming mountains.

"Raven 21, this is 31. Be advised our alternate LZ was hot. Unable to infil ground team. Took multiple hits. No wounded but aircraft damaged. Number two engine questionable. Need to return to base immediately."

"Raven 31, roger. Will advise when we are off Argos," I responded.

This was not good. I'd been worried when they had shifted to their alternate LZ. Hammer 22 was tied up supporting Dragon 45's fight and was unable to properly clear the LZ from above. Now my flight of two was permanently split. At least there were no casualties.

"Raven 21, Outlaw 01. Make your approach from the west. We've pushed the enemy off to the east. LZ should be clear. But no guarantees."

"Wouldn't expect any," I responded.

"Hammer 22, what can you see on Argos?" Pete transmitted to the gunship.

"Raven 21, Hammer 22. No enemy activity on Argos that we can see. Good little firefight approximately one kilometer to the east, though."

"Roger that."

We flew in silence for a few more minutes before Argos came into sight.

"Outlaw 01, we've got a visual on Argos. Will be on the ground in two minutes."

"Roger that, Raven."

Beyond the landing zone we saw the green of old, Soviet-manufactured tracer rounds occasionally pierce the darkness. When they did, a burst of red tracers would answer in force. It looked more like harassing fire than an assault, but Dragon 45 was probably in for a sleepless night.

Pete put the aircraft into a gentle descent. We passed through a couple of low-hanging scud clouds short of the LZ. They were getting thicker and more frequent.

Pete approached from the west and pointed the aircraft downslope before putting us firmly on the ground. He took the power back to idle, and the aircraft settled heavily onto its landing gear. There was less snow here. I judged it to be ankle-deep.

"Ramp coming down. Personnel approaching the rear of the aircraft," the crew chief announced.

"Make this quick," said Pete.

I got out of the jump seat and headed back to the rear of the aircraft with my M4, to assist if needed. The stretchers were loaded one by one. It was an awkward process. As I stood on the ramp, a soldier bounded on board and grabbed me.

It was David. His weapon was slung over his shoulder, and he was carrying two radios in his backpack. One headset was attached to his shoulder strap; he held the other. He was filthy but smiling. He put his hand on my shoulder and shouted something, but under the aft transmission there was no way for me to hear what it was. I shook my head at him. He shrugged and smiled. I nodded and winked at him, a ridiculous thing to do in the darkness.

At that moment the western side of the LZ erupted with gunfire. Green tracer rounds flew toward the aircraft. The ramp gunner next to me was struck in the shoulder. His uniform caught fire as the tracer burned in his body. He fell backward, screaming. A medic dove on the writhing crew member, putting out the fire and applying direct pressure to his wound. I lunged into the fallen gunner's station and returned fire with the M60, pointing the weapon at the enemy muzzle flashes. The right mini-gun also responded. Still firing, I looked toward David. He was running back to Dragon 45's position, shouting into his radio headset and firing his weapon.

SIX

"**G**O NAKED, YOU NASTY-ASS PLEBES!"

The Guru and the rest of E4's upperclassmen stood joyfully on the stoops of the barracks as our platoon of naked plebes spilled out of the Lost Fifties and streaked toward North Area. We wore nothing but shoes and our black cadet-issue ski masks, for plausible deniability. But everyone in the regiment, leaning out of their windows screaming encouragement, knew who it was. "Go naked" was not just the company motto; it was what we did. Often.

This was the traditional first "running of the plebes" for E4, held annually just before taps on the night before the first football game of the season. Initially it was awkward, but after a few strides, it felt terrific. As the year went on there were many such runs: for the first snow, the first exam, the first Army football win, or simply whenever the Guru decided to whip up a reason. But on those runs many upperclassmen joined in, the Guru usually in front. Many times other companies did as well.

Though E4 did it more often, the entire Corps was prone to these juvenile bursts of nakedness. Like other spontaneous mischief, they were brief escapes from the grayness of cadet life. Lame in comparison to what went on at any "real college," the ridiculousness reminded us that we were still alive. We had to be careful, though. A cadet caught naked like that by a tactical officer was in for a big slug. We were taught early how to scan the area and to never, ever stop running. Turtle, Zack, Bill, and I learned a lot of things that first semester.

✦ ✦ ✦

"What the hell, Turtle?"

"Get up, Sam. Cadet Stillmont is here."

"Huh?"

I sat up quickly. The Guru was standing in the middle of our room, wearing his camouflage battle dress uniform and his Loki grin.

"Good morning, Cadet Avery."

"Good morning, sir."

"Be in the basement. BDUs. Five minutes."

"Yes, sir."

In the basement we met up with the Guru as well as Cadet Wilcox and a couple of other upperclassmen I didn't know. Zack and Bill were also there.

"Follow me," said the Guru.

We crept out of the Lost Fifties. The Guru peered around the corner. "It's clear. Let's go!"

He ran to a manhole cover in the corner of North Area. "This is it. Get it open." Several of the upperclassmen used a metal tool to quickly jerk the cover off the manhole. The Guru vanished into it.

We climbed down the rusted ladder one at a time, into the darkness. The dank tunnel was too short to stand up in and was crowded by large metal pipes that ran its length. There was a loud clang as someone dragged the cover back into place. The Guru, at the head of our column, had a flashlight. I focused on that light and wondered where we were going as we shuffled though the grimy tunnel.

After scuttling along for about fifteen minutes, we bumped to a stop. There was a discussion at the front of the group, and then I heard a squeaking noise.

A loud crash startled me, and I sensed Turtle jerking in surprise behind me as well. Then a dim light illuminated the end of the tunnel, and the group shuffled forward.

One by one, each man dropped out of the tunnel; when I got to the end, I realized why. It was about a ten-foot fall to the floor.

I shuffled forward, swung my legs out, and hung from the opening.

"That's it, Avery. Now go ahead and drop," said Wilcox.

I hit the ground and moved to the side. I looked around while we waited for the rest of the group to exit the tunnel. All I could tell was that we were in a dark hallway.

When the last person dropped, Wilcox and the rest of the upperclassmen started taking off their clothes. I looked at Zack. He shrugged and started to strip.

Once we were all naked, Wilcox led the way through a pair of double doors. When we stepped into the large, dark space, I realized where we were. It was the cadet swimming pool.

The huge natatorium was dark. No one spoke as we followed the flashlights around the pool to the ten-meter high dive. Wilcox stood on the end of the diving board, waiting for all of us to get to the top of the platform. One of the upperclassmen spotlighted him with a flashlight. His large, pale, naked body bounced slightly on the board, suspended in the darkness. I looked down but could not see the water.

"Plebes, I recommend you enter the water like this." He grabbed his balls with both hands and stepped off the board. There was a long delay and then a splash.

We spent about an hour jumping off the high dive and swimming in the pool. It was ridiculous. As a spirit mission, it was a joke next to Mac-Arthur's bold and ingenious effort. I did not have the guts to ask the Guru if this was what he'd meant earlier when he'd said, "We must aim high," but it was fun, and I was proud that they'd included me. The steam tunnels were legendary in the Corps; this network of utility tunnels had been constructed almost two hundred years ago and ran beneath the cadet area. Every cadet had heard about them, but no one really knew how to access or navigate them except for E4. Wilcox and the Guru were rumored to have a map of the steam tunnels that enabled them to enter any building in the cadet area.

When we finally got back to the barracks, Turtle and I followed Cadet Stillmont as we snuck back up the 53rd Division, to our room. When we reached our floor, he stopped at his door and turned around, saying, "Good job tonight, gentlemen. You may refer to me as the Guru from now on."

"Go naked, sir."

I had a hard time falling asleep that night. For the first time since I'd gotten to West Point, I felt that I had been accepted as a cadet. I felt that I belonged and that I had joined something special. It felt good.

✦ ✦ ✦

We slogged through our first semester as plebes, caught between the triple pincers of Captain Eifer, constant hazing from upperclassmen, and academics. The course load was stiff, and we spent our Friday nights cramming for Saturday's classes. It was depressing. We coped by studying together and complaining.

"What the hell was I thinking?"

"I'm sure I don't know, Zack," said Creighton.

"I thought the academic year would take a little heat off us."

"A math study party at eight o'clock on Friday night is not what you had in mind?"

"No, Creighton. I'm not a military legacy freak like you. You're in heaven, aren't you?"

"No. I hate math. We should be studying military history."

"You guys are killing me," I said. "I'm hitting the latrine." Zack and Creighton bickered constantly. It got old sometimes.

The only positive effect of the academic freight train was its ability to compress the weeks and months, even as the days seemed to last forever. We were all counting the minutes until Thanksgiving leave, the first time we would get to go home. On Friday nights like this, I was acutely aware of Amanda, my high school girlfriend, having a totally different college experience than I. Immersive as well, I was sure, but a lot different. I thought about how excited I had been after graduation last summer. I'd been ready to leave boring civilian life behind and join the military. Amanda and I broke up, and I left without looking back. Now I missed her, and I was sure she wasn't missing me.

In fact, none of us were having much relationship success in our first semester of college. The E4 "Dear John" board was nearly full. This Corpswide tradition had evolved over decades to deal with the predictable trajectory of cadet relationships. For plebes who show up with girlfriends, it doesn't take long for the letter to come: "You're a special guy" and "I really respect what you are doing" followed by the windup: "but my life is changing so much . . ."

There are never letters from guys breaking up with female cadets on the board. The average civilian guy doesn't have the confidence to be in a relationship with a female cadet. They break up before the new female cadet departs. Plebes who post their letters on the bulletin board get a week of big bites at meals and are relieved of all duties like mail carrier or minute caller. Upperclassmen then take a red pen to the letter to correct the English, point out common phrases and clichés, and question the chastity of the writer. In less than a day, each letter has been savagely edited and is nearly illegible for all of the comments scrawled over it. The dumped plebe always feels better.

"Avery. Come here!"

I snapped out of my self-pitying trance. It was the Guru. He was typically the only upperclassman around on Friday nights, because being on the area curtailed his privileges.

"Yes, sir."

"Do you have any shoe polish?"

"Yes, sir."

"Go get it," he ordered as he stepped back into his room.

I retrieved the shoe polish, crossed the hall, and knocked three times on the Guru's door.

"Enter!"

I stepped into his room. Music played softly from his stereo. His dress uniform was arranged neatly on his bed, and his hat brass lay on top of a polishing rag on his desk. He sat by the open windows with his dress shoes at his feet. He was in blue jeans and his robe. I got a good look at it as I approached with the shoe polish.

High on his right shoulder was an Eighth Army Air Force patch, which I had heard was his grandfather's unit in the Second World War. The First Cavalry Division patch underneath it must have been his father's unit in Vietnam. Over the breast pocket, which bore the standard academy crest, a large armor insignia had been embroidered in gold thread. Beneath the academy crest he had sewn a yin-yang patch. There were a dozen other patches that I did not recognize and a cigar poking out of his breast pocket. A half-smoked cigar smoldered on the windowsill. A thin finger of smoke threaded its way out the window and up the mountain behind the barracks.

Smoking in the barracks was against regulations, of course. If an officer caught the Guru, he'd get another twenty hours piled on the punishment tours he was walking off for his spirit mission.

"Thanks, Avery. Put it over there on my bed. I'll return it in the morning."

"Yes, sir." I hesitated.

"What do you want?"

"Nothing, sir. It's just that I heard what you did at Air Assault School. That was ballsy, sir."

"Do you know why I did it?"

"No, sir."

"The NCO cadre at that course were simply talking too much shit about West Point."

I chuckled. The Guru looked at me harshly. I froze.

"I'm serious, Avery. You're going to find that West Point is an easy target out there." He gestured out the window at the world. "Don't stand for it."

"Yes, sir. I mean, no, sir. I won't."

"You should have seen their faces. They were so pissed. It was totally worth it. I probably would have gotten off much lighter if I hadn't argued with them so effectively when I was caught." He smiled. "To hell with 'em. I still qualified and got my wings."

"Must be weird to walk hours for defending West Point, sir. Are you angry?"

"Nope. Before any spirit mission, you must ask yourself if you are man enough for the punishment. I had just heard enough shit about West Point 'kaydets.' It had to be done."

He leaned back in his chair and looked at me for a moment, sizing me up.

"'Waste no more time arguing about what a good man should be. Be one.'"

"Sir?"

"Marcus Aurelius."

"Sir, I do not understand."

"Decide who you will be. Then be him."

I just stood there.

"Listen, Avery, right now for you it's all about survival, but soon, sooner than you think, you're going to have to decide what kind of cadet you're going to be." He looked at me patiently.

"Sir . . . I want to be a good cadet."

"Everybody wants to be a good cadet."

I just blinked.

He shook his head.

"What does being a good cadet mean to you?"

I had no idea what he was talking about.

"Let me give you an example. You are pinging to class. You're going to make it just in time, but then you remember that your roommate is probably asleep. He told you he was going to sneak a nap after lunch, before class. Tough luck for him, I guess. A good cadet always gets to class on time, right?"

"Um . . ."

He shook his head and waved his hand at me so that I would not answer wrong. "Bullshit. I go back every time. A good cadet goes back for his roommate and makes sure he gets to class. Always. You save him from a major slug. You're both late and get minor quill, but you go back for your buddy. Fuck being on time." He realized his voice was rising and stopped talking.

"It sucks, Avery. But it will happen. And be glad when it does. You'll know you are being prepared for something."

"Yes, sir."

He got up and walked to his stereo. As he did, I saw that on the back of his robe he had sewn a large Grateful Dead symbol. About six inches in diameter and sitting high on his back, the skull seemed to be his rear guard. "Say, Avery, do you like the Grateful Dead?"

"Not really that familiar with their music, sir."

He looked out the window. "Thanks for the shoe polish. Leave the door to your room open."

"Yes, sir. Go naked, sir."

"Go naked, Avery."

"What are you doing now?" asked Turtle when I returned and propped the door open.

"He said leave our door open."

The guys looked at me with "what the hell is coming next" faces. I shrugged.

Just then the Guru turned up his stereo. Jerry Garcia was singing "Eyes of the World."

> *Sometimes we live no particular way but our own,*
> *And sometimes we visit your country and live in your home,*
> *Sometimes we ride on your horses, sometimes we walk alone,*
> *Sometimes the songs that we hear are just songs of our own.*

We were transfixed. No one spoke. Plebes were not allowed to listen to music in their rooms until after Christmas, when we were authorized to have stereos. Those caught with a Walkman or similar contraband in their possession got an automatic twenty hours on the area. Though we had been only a few months without it, music now had a special power over us. It was exotic and beautiful.

We studied for another two hours, listening to the music from across the hall. Creighton and Zack left at about 2230 hours. The moment they were gone, the music quit.

SEVEN

EVERY WEAPON ON RAVEN 21 OPENED FIRE: MINI-guns, M60s, grenade launchers, AR-15s, and even sidearms. Sitting on the ground broadsided by the enemy, Raven 21 became a lead-spitting porcupine.

Another crew chief grabbed my shoulder, and I gave him the M60 position.

Bullets struck the aircraft like thrown hammers as I ran forward to the cockpit.

"What's the status back there?" yelled Pete.

"Almost done, sir!"

Hammer 22 opened up from above with its 40mm cannon. At David's direction, the gunship pounded the enemy with well-placed high-explosive rounds. The detonations came systematically, about five seconds apart. Each detonation killed enemy. Finally, the inbound gunfire began to wane.

"That's it, sir! Passengers secure. Rear is ready! Go! Go! Go!"

"Roger that. We're out of here," Pete said as he rapidly increased power.

The engines screamed as they tried to suck in the thin air. The aircraft got light on its gear and began to slide forward in the snow. Raven 21 rose a couple of feet as she gained momentum. The aircraft ran off the small plateau, and Pete nosed her over aggressively. We dove down the mountain into dark. The green enemy tracer rounds flew farther and farther above us as we descended beneath the crest of the mountain.

Red warning lights flashed in the cockpit.

"We've lost the number one flight hydraulics!" Kevin announced.

"Roger that, sir. Levels and pressures are zero on the number one back here," responded the crew chief. "Number two is normal and holding, though."

Flying a Chinook without flight hydraulics is impossible. The aircraft becomes uncontrollable. That is why there are two independent and redundant systems. Flying on one flight hydraulic system is considered an emergency situation, and the crew is supposed to land the helicopter as soon as they can. For us, that night, that meant more than an hour getting back down to Bagram.

We flew in and out of small clouds as we descended. They were definitely thicker now.

"What's our status?" I asked over the intercom.

"We got five wounded, sir. Including the three critical we picked up. We need to hurry."

I keyed my mike to transmit. "Ramses 03, this is Raven 21, we are off Argos. Five wounded on board. Three critical. ETA is approximately sixty minutes."

"Raven 21, Ramses, roger. We'll be ready."

I exhaled deeply. Pete had us descending rapidly down the mountain. It had been hairy. But we were headed for home.

We still had one of the FM radios tuned to the ground commander's frequency and our VHF monitoring Hammer 22. Though it had receded into the background, we monitored the battle with one ear. Hammer 22 had continued to tear up the enemy. That made us smile as we dropped into the valley and steered toward base.

We were twenty minutes into the flight down the mountain to Bagram when we overheard the call on the satcom radio.

"Ramses 03, this is Dragon 45, we've got another wounded. Surgical urgent. Request immediate medevac." Satcom was the only way to communicate with stations that were not line of sight. It was the ground elements', and often our own, only reliable link to headquarters.

I saw Pete sit up straight. He looked over his shoulder at me, then at Kevin. I listened intently.

"Ramses 03, this is Dragon 45, Outlaw 01 is down. It's bad. Rounds to the lower abdomen. Need to get him off the mountain ASAP." The firefight raged in the background of Dragon 45's transmission.

I sagged in my chair as my blood ran cold.

"I've got the controls." Pete reached forward and took the aircraft's controls.

Kevin lifted his hands in the air. "You've got the controls."

"What are you doing, Pete?" I asked.

"I'm turning us around."

"Hold on. Let me get some more information."

"Outlaw is down. What else do you need to know?"

"We've got three surgical urgent on board, shitty weather, one hydraulic flight-control system, and a contested LZ, from which we are halfway down the damn mountain. How about you give me a few fucking minutes to do my job?"

From my vantage point, the back of Pete's helmet was expressionless. But his shoulders were stiff with rage.

At times like this, the dynamic between the pilot in command and air mission commander could get sticky. Pete commanded the aircraft and everyone in it, but I commanded the flight of the two helicopters. Truthfully, I did not give a shit whose call it was. I pictured David lying in the snow almost ten thousand feet above us, blood seeping out of him. A creeping dread welled up within me. To say that "Leave no man behind" is a code we lived by doesn't say it well enough. It was an ethic, edict, aspiration, and minimum.

But it did not have the power to change the laws of physics, weather, aerodynamics, or mathematics. And it had to be balanced with the principle "Don't make a shitty situation worse through a bad decision."

"Dragon 45, this is Ramses 03, what is the weather at your position?"

"It's getting worse, Ramses. Visibility less than two hundred feet."

"Roger that, Dragon. Stand by. We are working on something here for you."

Pete shook his head. I knew what was coming.

"Sir, we need to go back," he said.

I didn't respond. I was not able to say it yet. I stared at the clock. I estimated that David had had bullets in his gut for over ten minutes now.

"Sir, we are the closest asset. We can be there in about thirty minutes. I am going to turn us around and we are going to extract Outlaw."

I wanted to vomit.

Pete increased power slowly, arresting our descent. The helicopter mushed through the thin air as the rotor blades clawed harder for lift. We leveled off, flying away from the mountain. He was setting the aircraft up to climb back to Argos.

I could not say it yet. So I said other words to the flight engineer. "What is the medical status back there?"

While I waited for the update, I watched Pete as he leaned forward and called up Argos's coordinates on his navigation display. He was plotting a course back.

"Two of these guys are fine. No factor," reported the flight engineer. "One is still critical but stable. But two of the surgical urgents have worsened. One is a femoral artery job. Altogether, they've gone through at least four IV bags since they've been on board. We're probably going to have to let them use ours before we get there. Other one is a head trauma. Medic says they are going to have to crack him open as soon as possible to relieve the pressure on his brain."

Pete banked the aircraft slowly to the left to pick up the course back to Argos.

I still didn't want to say it yet.

"What's our maintenance status?" I asked instead.

"Zero pressure on the number one flight hydraulics," said the flight engineer from the rear. "Levels on the number two are within limits but are decreasing slowly. I've got one of the crew chiefs back here looking for a leak. Numerous holes in the aircraft and one of the guys back here said he thought he smelled something burning. But I don't smell shit."

Halfway through the turn, Pete increased power to get the aircraft into a climb.

"Dragon 45, this is Raven 21, request weather status," I transmitted.

Pete rolled the aircraft out of the turn. We were now heading back up the mountain.

"Raven 21, this is Dragon 45. Weather deteriorating. Visibility now between a hundred and a hundred and fifty feet." An explosion rang out in the background as Dragon spoke. Hammer 22 was still giving them hell.

"Roger that, Dragon," I said.

The dread was lodged in my throat. I pictured David.

The aircraft was churning up the mountain again as the blood ran out of one soldier's leg and the brain of another pressed against his skull as it swelled. At the same time blood seeped out of David's gut. I couldn't swallow.

I waited thirty more seconds, hoping Pete would make the decision himself. But then I had to say it. "Pete, turn us around. We're going back to base."

"Negative, sir. We are going back to Argos."

"Pete. You know I'm right. We've got three critical on board that need to be in surgery ASAP, our aircraft is shot up and is down to one flight hydraulics system, the weather is shit, and I haven't asked you to confirm our fuel status but I'm sure we don't have enough for this. I hate it, too, but we need to return to base."

"It's Major West, sir. One of us." Still climbing the mountain.

"I'm aware."

"Doesn't seem like it." That made me mad.

"Okay, Pete. Should I go back there and throw the three criticals out of the aircraft? We might as well. It will lighten the load and decrease our fuel burn. You're killing them anyway."

His head fell slightly forward at that. He knew I was right.

A few rotor beats later, Pete turned the aircraft back down the mountain. I almost cried out at him to stop, to head back up. "I'm sorry, David," I muttered to myself.

I still hoped they would get to him. That they would find a nearby asset or just pull off a fucking miracle. But they didn't.

The enemy harassed Dragon 45 all night. They made a few more radio calls requesting extraction for David. But the weather on top of the mountain quickly worsened; there was zero visibility by the time we landed. Ramses was out of tricks.

Our wounded were downloaded as soon as we landed and went

directly into surgery. The head wound never recovered consciousness. The leg wound made a full recovery.

David died on the mountain before we even landed.

Pete and I did not talk about that night much afterward. When we did, he never said I made the right call. He never said I made the wrong one, though.

EIGHT

THE NEXT MORNING'S MATH CLASS WAS A GRIND. OUR instructor, Major Winslow, gave the command "Take boards!" within the first ten minutes of class. We spent the next eighty minutes at the chalkboards doing problems as he circled the room looking for mistakes and making sure that we were not peeking at our neighbor's work. After the bell rang, he held us there to emphasize his expectations for neatness and honor code compliance.

"What am I going to become here?" said Zack dejectedly as he, Bill, and I walked through the bowels of Thayer Hall toward the barracks.

"What do you mean?"

"I mean, what do all this trivia and bullshit reindeer games do to a guy after four years?"

"It's a game, Zack. Suck it up."

There was bad news when we returned to the company area. In his Saturday morning inspection sweep of E4, Captain Eifer had written up 99 of 121 cadets and had dispensed 498 demerits. This became the norm for our Saturdays.

✦ ✦ ✦

The weeks passed slowly. Long days of grinding academics and inspections heightened the nerves in the company. Soon it was mid-October and parade season was in full swing.

Parades are tradition, training, and torture for the Corps of Cadets. By the time a cadet graduates, he has been in hundreds of parades. "Drill and ceremony," as the army calls it, is a symbolic and stylized direct descendent of the movement techniques used during the Revolutionary War. In those days, and long before, a unit's ability to maintain a formation while marching under arms actually influenced and sometimes decided the outcomes of battles. Commanders who maneuvered units more efficiently than the enemy were able to flank or envelop them with devastating results.

Now it had no bearing on actual battle. Technology and tactics have evolved beyond those Baron Friedrich von Steuben taught the Continental Army. What does drill and ceremony have to do with leading a flight of assault helicopters, or erecting a river-crossing bridge, or managing a communications satellite? Nothing, most cadets thought. Nothing, perhaps, other than that it requires alertness, discipline, and teamwork, the proponents of D&C would argue. Debate aside, it is during this useless endeavor that cadets first begin to perfect a skill that actually is critical to military success: the ability to check out and to put their minds somewhere else.

On the Plain of West Point, cadets learn to unplug their brains from their bodies. They put their minds into the gap and ignore the sweat pooling in their shoes and the heavy rifle in their hands during an extended presentation of arms. They can stand for hours in a cold wind and their minds are away, considering a homework assignment, planning a road trip, or undressing a girlfriend. A cadet can drive his body around in perfect sync with his unit and execute a flawless "eyes right" with only a fraction of his mind at the wheel and the majority of it away. To the viewers in the stands, the Corps of Cadets on parade is a splendid display of coordination and unity of thought: thousands of identically dressed soldiers thinking and moving as one single, military hive mind. In reality it is some four thousand bodies left vacant by minds wandering in separate, individual respites.

We drilled twice a week. Every weekend there was at least a double regimental review. Football Saturdays saw a full brigade review. Each parade was graded, and E4 came in dead last in all of them. The Guru was quick to quote the timeless maxim: "No combat-ready unit ever passes inspection; no inspection-ready unit ever survives combat." But we knew the truth: E4 just didn't like to drill.

✦ ✦ ✦

Early one Saturday morning in mid-October, Turtle shook me by the shoulders.

"Sam, wake up!"

I sprang out of bed. Turtle was already standing at attention. I wondered what time it was but did not dare to look at my watch. The Guru stood at the door, smiling.

"Meet me in the basement in five minutes. BDUs. Each of you, bring your entrenching tool."

"Yes, sir."

"What time is it?" I asked Turtle.

"Oh-three-thirty."

A couple of minutes later, we were in the basement. Zack and Bill were there. The four of us stood groggily looking at the Guru with our E-tools.

"Avery, give your E-tool to Turtle and carry these." The Guru handed me three large pieces of cardboard.

"If anything happens while we're out there, we're going to split up. Everybody run toward a different sally port, but absolutely no one come back to E4 until you are sure you are not being followed. Is that clear?"

"Yes, sir."

"Good. Let's go." The Guru turned and walked quickly out of the barracks. We followed closely behind. When he hit North Area, he started jogging briskly.

We ran out onto the dark Plain. Soon after we got onto the grass, the Guru halted. "You guys wait here for a minute." We knelt down as he continued out into the darkness. He stopped about fifty meters from us and started pacing around, periodically looking back at the barracks.

"What the hell are we doing?" grumbled Bill.

"Shut up," said Zack. "This is cool."

"Kneeling outside in the cold instead of sleeping is cool to you?"

"At ease, guys. He's waving us over," I said.

We trotted over to the Guru.

"Dempsey, give me your E-tool," the Guru said as he knelt down. "Look, gentlemen. This sod is really high quality, and if you make a cut in it like this, you can peel it back like carpet." The Guru made a couple of quick slices into the Plain with the edge of the E-tool's spade. He then pulled back on the grass and a large piece of turf came up in his hands.

"I want all of the sod lifted from here where I have marked the corners. Stack the sod to the side. Hurry!"

We started slicing the sod and pulling back long swaths of it. Within minutes we had cleared a large area.

"Good." The Guru stepped into the large bald spot and marked off four corners of a rectangle within it. "Now I want a one-foot-deep hole dug out of this rectangle. Put the dirt into these trash bags." He pulled several large black plastic bags out of his BDU pockets. "Hurry!"

With the four of us working together, the digging went quickly. Soon we were looking at a large rectangular hole. Four large trash bags of dirt sat off to the side.

"Avery. Hand me the cardboard." The Guru knelt down and placed cardboard supports in the middle of the hole, then laid the larger pieces over them. The hole was about two meters wide.

The Guru stood up and examined his work. He nodded to himself. "Okay, gentlemen. Hand me pieces of the sod."

One by one, we passed the Guru pieces of sod, and he painstakingly arranged them to cover the cardboard and, ultimately, the entire area. It took some time, but when he was done, it was difficult to see where our excavation had taken place. It started to dawn on us what we had done. Zack laughed.

"At ease, Dempsey." The Guru looked at his watch and continued: "Grab the bags of dirt and let's go."

We followed the Guru to First Regiment's area, where we deposited the heavy bags of dirt in a dumpster. Then we headed back to E4. It was almost 0500 when we got back in bed. Turtle and I both laughed in anticipation.

The bad blood between F4 and E4 was long-lived. We hated each other. But recently, the feud between Cadet Mathison, the F4 cadet company commander, and Wilcox had become more intense. Mathison had assigned two of his firsties to observe E4 during formations and report on which cadets were talking. Talking during formation was not allowed, and E4 regularly ignored the prohibition. Often the talk was ridicule of F4 and their cadet chain of command. When demerits began to come down from Eifer for talking in formation even when he and his damn bicycle were not around, it didn't take Wilcox long to put it together. He fumed. The Guru, however, had acted with no coordination or knowledge on Wilcox's part.

That day at 1100 hours, the Corps of Cadets marched out for a full brigade review. General Vuono, chief of staff of the army, stood in front of the reviewing party, which included another two dozen general officers, one senator, and three congressmen. It was a football Saturday at West Point. There is nothing quite like it. The air was crisp, the sky was clear, and the leaves were changing.

The first part of a brigade review is the most impressive. Four thousand cadets in full dress uniform bearing arms emerge suddenly from the barracks. Initially, it looks disorderly. Thirty-six cadet companies seem to weave and intermesh as they step out of the six sally ports and onto the Plain. For those in the crowd who have never seen a brigade review, there is a moment of anxiety. Is it supposed to look like this? Is this the vaunted United States Corps of Cadets? Then, after just a moment, the timeless pattern takes hold. Order becomes apparent.

As the cadet companies get clear of the sally ports, they head for their positions on the Plain. One by one, each company comes to attention in a massive formation. E4 always precedes F4 to its assigned spot by about thirty seconds. That was all we needed to have the perfect vantage point that day.

Those of us who knew what was coming maintained the position of attention with our heads pointed to the front but strained our eyes to stare to our left. Seconds later, the entire F4 chain of command tripped and fell spectacularly. Hats, sabers, and guidon all scattered to the ground as the company commander and his staff stepped into the hole we had dug and camouflaged the night before. Cadet Mathison cursed loudly as he lost his grip on his saber while breaking his fall. There was an audible gasp from the viewing public. The entire Fourth Regiment laughed quietly under arms as Mathison and his staff awkwardly picked themselves up. The Frogs were humiliated. It was perfect.

The mysterious quills for talking in formation abruptly stopped.

✦ ✦ ✦

The next week a rumor swept through the Corps. E4 held its breath, hoping it would prove true, the Guru most of all. He had more reason than any of us to be excited about the possibility of a visit by President Reagan.

When the commander in chief visits West Point, he has the authority to grant the Corps amnesty. That means all demerits and area tours are expunged.

If true, it would be huge for E4. The entire company was sagging under the weight of the demerits we had been racking up under Eifer's sustained assault. Several of us were serving punishment tours on the area, as we had exceeded the monthly demerit limits. *What a sweet karmic victory this will be,* we thought. It was October, with only about six weeks left in the semester. Getting reset this late would give us all a good buffer to weather Eifer's crusade until we got out for Christmas. The disciplinary tally would reset for second semester.

Less than a week later, on October 28, 1987, after a full brigade review, the president stood before the Corps of Cadets in the mess hall.

"Brigade, attention!" came over the loudspeaker.

The Corps was motionless. I could see the Guru standing at attention at another of E4's tables. Most cadets were looking at one another, making hopeful, excited faces. The Guru stared down at the center of his table.

Suddenly, we heard that signature voice that sounded like your grandfather and the prom king all at once: "I know I'm going to be speaking to you after lunch, but I just wanted to tell you how great it is to be back at West Point. And I have never seen a more impressive and spirited Corps of Cadets; you make me proud." He hesitated for a few seconds. "But I know the real reason why all of you are so warm in your greetings, so glad to see me. It has to do with this directive I have written." A peal of excited laughter ignited simultaneously from all points within the Corps. We struggled to hold ourselves back.

"Consistent with past practices that have been established, as commander in chief, I have directed the superintendent to grant amnesty to the Corps of Cadets."

We exploded. The noise bounced around the stone of the mess hall and gained force as we continued to add energy to the roar. The Guru stood on his chair, saluting toward the poop deck.

It felt sweet. It felt like a victory. For once, we'd landed a blow. The superintendent let us go on for about a minute, and then the command to take our seats was given.

We were giddy as we ate lunch. The president addressed the Corps about his administration's efforts toward nuclear arms reductions between the United States and the Soviet Union, a relationship that he described as "likely to shape the whole course of your careers as professional soldiers." But he was really talking to the press. We were a colorful backdrop, and we knew it. And we didn't care.

+ + +

The end of the semester finally arrived and, with it, the Army-Navy game. Always the last game of the regular season, the game typically falls just two weeks before exams and Christmas leave. The match means everything to the Corps, who had to make peace long ago with the reality that, by modern standards, West Point will never have a great football team. The academic and disciplinary demands and the five-year military obligation following graduation make recruiting a challenge. So, Army has a tough time against even the most unremarkable football programs.

In Navy, however, we had a true peer for an opponent. One that we had respected and hated since the first game, nearly a hundred years ago. Twelve years older than the Rose Bowl, the Army-Navy game was an intense rivalry from the very first snap. So intense, in fact, that a near duel between a rear admiral and a brigadier general in 1893 resulted in a five-year cooling-off period. The game was not played from 1894 to 1898.

Every year since then, with only a few exceptions, the teams have met. And to this day, for the Corps, if the Army team loses every game but this one, it's a winning season.

Like a long-anticipated signpost, when the game swings into view, the mood of every cadet lifts. It's not just the game itself; it's also the fact that the Corps is about to put another semester behind it. Plebes, yearlings, cows, and firsties alike look at their calendars during Army-Navy Week and say to themselves, "I'm a semester closer."

By that time, plebes possess finely tuned antennae, able to detect the slightest shift in the mood of the Corps. They must. Everything flows down onto them. When the Corps is happy, plebes can breathe easy. When the Corps is not, plebes know to be cautious. Just stepping into the hallway at the wrong time can earn a plebe half an hour of hazing by a grumpy upperclassman.

Army-Navy Week is signal overload for the plebe survival instinct. The atmosphere in the cadet area is electric in anticipation of a frenzied collective release for the long game weekend. Thursday night, the last night the Corps is in garrison before the game, is always crazy. That Thursday night of our plebe year, however, was historic. It was the infamous food fight of 1987.

We could sense the energy in the air as we pinged into the mess hall. We were nervous, suspecting that the vibration indicated a night of stepped-up hazing, but when we took our seats, we could tell there was something different animating the Corps: mischief.

Dinner was listed as "BBQ goat." We all knew it was really roast beef, but we loved pretending. Then, as soon as the mid-meal announcements from the poop deck were complete, it started.

Later I heard that it kicked off in multiple places at once. All I know is that, for our table, it began when a single potato wedge landed in our midst.

"Did someone just throw food at us, Avery?" asked the Guru.

"I think so, sir."

"I think so, too."

We looked around to see where the potato had originated. All of the adjacent tables were also scanning their areas. The mess hall crackled with potential energy. The key was not to be spotted initiating a food fight. That offense was an automatic twenty-five hours on the area, but defending one's table in kind? That was a matter of honor.

As we craned our necks, another lone potato wedge struck the middle of the table.

"Arm yourselves, men," said the Guru quickly. "If it happens, it's going to happen fast."

He barely got the words out before an entire "Beat Navy" sheet cake slammed into the table next to us. It hit a water pitcher at the plebe end of the table and exploded. Sticky cake fragments covered Emily and Creighton. Emily grabbed a handful of barbecued goat and let it fly as Creighton heaved the stainless-steel water pitcher in outrage.

The Guru leapt to his feet, beaming. "It was the Frogs!" he yelled.

A dark cloud rose above and around the Guru, but it wasn't smoke or mist. It was a dense mass of airborne food. In an instant, everything edible was in the air, sailing toward a target.

Our target was the Frogs, of course, and we were theirs. I slung my entire plate of food just as their first salvo hit us. It was devastating. Turtle yelped under the impact of a shower of hot broccoli. I started to laugh but was cut short by an open carton of milk striking me in the chest. I ducked just in time as a silver water pitcher flew through the air where my head had been. It clanged loudly on our table and ricocheted into the wall.

We windmilled our arms onto the table and toward the Frogs. We threw everything. The same drama played out across the mess hall. All of the petty cadet company rivalries were celebrated as the Corps let off steam. For an instant, the air was so thick with projectiles I couldn't even see the mess hall ceiling. It was joyous. It was cathartic. It was over in less than a minute.

There was a lull in the fighting as every table in the hall ran out of ammunition at the same time. Our table was empty. A few cadets threw food that they picked up from the ground or off their own heads, but almost everyone stared at their tables and reached the same conclusion at once.

"Run!" yelled the Guru.

Turtle and I lunged for the doors at the same time as the rest of the Corps. No one wanted to be caught in the mess hall when the tac officers showed up. They couldn't be far away.

The Guru grabbed our arms from behind. "No. Not back to the company area," he ordered, pointing toward the poop deck, a large spirelike stone structure in the middle of the mess hall. Thus we did the opposite of the rest of the Corps, who surged toward their company exits. The Guru gave us instructions as we ran through the poop deck exits and down the stairs into the basement. "Don't go back to the company area until taps. The tacs and company commanders will be pressing everyone they see into cleanup duty tonight. You want to avoid that."

We followed his instructions that night and escaped the mighty task. I couldn't get the image of the dark cloud of food that had obscured the ceiling out of my mind for weeks. I knew that I was right to be impressed when I overheard the Guru telling some yearlings that he had never seen a food fight like that before.

Even though thousands of cadets were pressed into immediate service, the mess hall did not recover for almost a week. The administration had to bring in a professional cleaning crew two nights in a row. The commandant was enraged. Remarkably, no one was written up. It was impossible to determine how the fight had started. The tactical department made it clear that food fights were a thing of the past, though. The punishment for throwing food was doubled to an automatic fifty hours on the area. Officer patrols were doubled on nights the Corps was keyed up. I didn't see another food fight for the rest of my time at West Point.

✦ ✦ ✦

The weekend of the Army-Navy game is one of the few times plebes are given privileges. Turtle and I tagged along with Zack and Bill on a plan the two of them had put together. We stayed at a dive hotel near UPenn. Zack knew a bunch of girls at the university. It was a rowdy weekend, and it was just what we needed. We went bonkers. Turtle got so attached to one of the girls that he snuck her into the Corps during the game. Tacs hate that kind of thing, of course, and it took Eifer no time to spot her. Turtle got slammed with twenty hours on the area. "Totally fucking worth it!" was his response.

Army-Navy Weekend was also the first time the four of us had seen one another in civilian clothes. When we got to the hotel, we quickly ditched our cadet uniforms in preparation for meeting up with the girls. We changed in a frenzy of anticipation and then stood still for a full minute, knocked into silence by one another's appearance. Turtle wore a black studded leather jacket, ripped jeans, and a red bandanna tied on his head do-rag style. Bill looked like an imitation 1950s motorcycle racer, with a brown leather jacket and dirty black jeans. He wore an old, dark brown hat with a small black brim that had obviously spent a lot of time in the wind. Zack was a tall vision in denim: blue jeans with a blue denim jacket and a gray Chicago Blackhawks hoodie underneath. I'm sure I looked as funny to them: the straight-laced goober right out of the J. Crew catalog. Having been thrown together six months ago in West Point's cauldron of sameness, we found it jarring to see one another in our chosen social uniforms. In the "real world," we would never have been friends. Our appearances would have been too foreign, the assumptions about one another too negative. But at West Point, all of the visual cues had been taken away. Our friendships had formed based on proximity, mutual hardship, and a common code. Forged in that way, our bonds now made our clothes seem silly, an afterthought. We made fun of one another for a few minutes and then left to meet our dates.

The weekend followed what I came to learn was the standard Army-Navy Weekend program. Friday was a frenzied and drunken exploration of Philly, followed by a painfully hungover Saturday morning. We struggled to sober up and get into uniform for the Corps' march into the stadium a ridiculous three hours before the game. Eifer stood by to make sure we made it. The several that did not were quilled hard. By the time the game ended—with a big win over Navy—we were ready for more action and headed back out to South Street and another long night.

On Sunday, we returned to West Point for final exams. The Corps' high Army-Navy Week spirits were replaced by a collective siege mentality. Since we'd beaten Navy, our class had been given the privilege of falling out. We did not have to ping or be at attention when we were out of our rooms; we just couldn't talk. We played it safe, though, and didn't wander around casually, but it was nice not to be at attention all the time. It felt strange. I noticed things I had not observed in six months of living in the cadet area: gargoyles, insignias, carvings of cadets' faces, cannons, and officers' sabers were everywhere. Then, suddenly, the semester was over, and I flew home for Christmas leave.

NINE

BACK IN THE TOC, I GOT ANOTHER CUP OF COFFEE, then wandered over to an empty corner of the planning area and tried to clear my head. I didn't notice Weber until he was standing almost right in front of me. He did not look happy.

"Who were those guys, sir?" he asked.

"West Point classmates of mine."

"They didn't seem like West Pointers."

"They were actually two of my best friends in the world."

"'Were'?"

"Still are, I guess. We just haven't seen much of each other lately."

"The shorter one just seemed like trouble to me."

"Oh, he definitely is," I chuckled. "Could you tell he was an amputee?"

"No, sir. Not at all. Where did he lose it?"

"Day three of the initial invasion of Iraq in 2003. He was with Third ID. High-caliber gunshot wound below the left knee. When he got back to Walter Reed, he worked out like a fiend for about a year. He found an experimental artificial-limb start-up out of San Francisco to work with him on a specifically designed prosthetic. I heard he bugged the hell out of them. You can't tell now, but he majored in aerospace engineering at West Point. After a couple of iterations, he had a kick-ass leg and could move better than most full-limbed soldiers."

I did not tell Weber how ugly it had gotten with Turtle. The reason he worked so hard was to regain his combat status with the army. He was facing his personal abyss: life out of the military or, worse, life as a REMF in the military. So, in Turtle fashion, he told the system to fuck off and fought back. Hard.

He became a minor celebrity at Walter Reed. Generals and congressmen would visit to shake the hand of the "inspiring army major" who had such a great attitude. I got to Walter Reed twice to visit him during that time. He was an animal.

But the army ultimately denied his appeal one year to the day of his wounding in Iraq. Not only was his combat status denied, the army then insulted him deeply. They offered him a staff job at the Pentagon.

Turtle walked out of Walter Reed Army Medical Center that day and moved to a trailer park in Virginia Beach. He lived off of his disability pay, spending his time either in the gym or drunk. I was overseas then but heard that he was circling the drain when Zack found him. Zack spent three weeks by Turtle's side, getting him sober. Rumor was that Zack missed a deployment with Delta to stay with him. I didn't know if that's true, because ordinarily that kind of thing is called being AWOL and ends careers. But Zack's reputation in JSOC at that point was such that he could probably have gotten away with it.

Zack told Turtle about the contracting bonanza going on in Iraq and put him in touch with Creighton. Creighton pulled some strings and got him a small contract working with the CIA. Turtle's abilities and attitude did the rest.

"You ever heard of Thayer Tactical?"

"No, sir."

"Most people haven't. It's a small contract shop that Turtle started. They're not as well known as Blackwater or some of the others. Turtle has kept them small and focused."

"Turtle?"

"Long story."

"What do they do?"

"Mostly direct-action jobs for the CIA. They've got a one hundred percent success rate and have done well. It doesn't hurt that Turtle still has friends at the CIA who are influential."

Thayer Tactical had been an immediate success. Turtle was a million-aire by the end of the first year. He kept trying to recruit me. "You'd be perfect. I need a SOAR operator." I kept rebuffing him, giving him grief about the name Thayer Tactical, instead. I thought it was hilarious that a double-century man who had nearly been kicked out for discipline issues no less than half a dozen times had named his company after such a prom-inent and revered figure in academy history. "It's good branding, Sam" was his only response.

He must have been right. By the end of its second year, Thayer Tacti-cal's revenue exceeded thirty million. From time to time, I'd hear about Turtle's success and would feel happy and relieved for him but also a little jealous. Looking back now, I wondered if what I'd been experiencing was regret.

"What about the other guy? The tall one."

"That's probably the toughest guy you've ever seen. Infantry, then Fifth Group for a few years before being selected for Delta. He's been there forever and is now up for squadron commander. I think he would have gotten it."

"What do you mean 'would have'?"

I ignored the question and looked at the map of Iraq on the wall behind him.

Sergeant Weber glanced over his shoulder to see what I was studying. He then looked back at me with a face that was equal parts puzzled and angry.

I couldn't worry about his feelings at that moment. I needed to figure out a way to ditch him and sneak away from the TOC with Pete to plan tonight's bootleg mission.

"Look, Weber, I'm sorry, but can you excuse me? I've got to get some things together for a briefing with the admiral here in a little bit."

He hesitated.

"Sure, sir. Roger that. Don't let me get in your way." Weber stalked off.

TEN

FEBRUARY 1987

"I SWEAR TO GOD I HAVE NEVER SEEN A PLACE AS depressing as this," I said to Creighton as we trudged through the snow on the way back from class.

"What is so depressing about it?"

"Look around, Creighton!"

I gestured at the bleak landscape. No place on earth can match the gloom of West Point from January to March. The sky is gray. The stone buildings are gray. The snow is gray. The uniforms are gray, and even the pallor of the Corps is gray. The cumulative effect of weeks without sun and the crushing amount of time until spring weigh down the Corps' spirit. It becomes mole-like and depressed. Even firsties, weathering their final cadet winter, become skeptical that it will ever end. This span of time is called the "gloom period." And by February, it has fully descended. The river's complexion is dark beneath a dirty crust of ice as it moves, unperturbed, southward.

"What did you expect?" Creighton asked.

I just shook my head at him. Creighton and I were roommates for second semester plebe year. For the most part, it was a good match. He was a much better student than I was, and he helped me raise my academic game. I tended to be more social, apt to go to the gym or goof off. When my influence prevailed in our room, it helped integrate him further into the company.

I quickly learned to respect Creighton's strategic mind. He worked at sharpening it constantly and, after a while, forced me to do the same. We often ended our day with a quiet game of Risk before taps. It was the simplest of the several strategy games he played regularly. Most of his games were more complex, involving ten- and twenty-sided die and voluminous rules. For those, he had to travel the cadet area to visit his fellow strategy geeks. I was not up to the task.

We were one of those odd pairings that West Point often throws together, improving each of the individuals. He was a "gray hog," though, and it really chafed when I wanted someone to share in my misery. Gray hogs love being cadets: the uniforms, the regimented lifestyle, the traditions, everything. They love it all and cannot understand those who don't. Creighton, like all gray hogs, was totally at home living in the cadet area.

Carefully delineated by the *Regulations for the United States Corps of Cadets,* the cadet area is a physical boundary in which all of the rules and restrictions apply; plebes have to ping. Cadets have to be in the full, designated uniform. No civvies. Only firsties are allowed to drink alcohol. No cadet is permitted to eat or drink while walking in uniform. No carrying books in backpacks.

The regulations were endless, consisting of all of the things Bill scornfully referred to as the "reindeer games." The specific area was a strange geographic concoction of just about everything "at the level of the Plain," mean sea level for cadets. Beyond this border, a cow could drink a beer; inside it, he could not. On one side of this street, my classmates and I were at attention and at the mercy of upperclassman; on the other side we were not.

But, actually, we were always within the cadet area. That's the potent, inescapable reality. The cadet area is mental. Once a cadet, you're never able to leave it. The cadet area is burned into your head, and you carry it with you. I've heard general officers say, "Sometimes I have to remind myself I'm not a cadet anymore."

I first felt this stamp on my psyche while home on my first Christmas leave. I had reveled in the freedom to take big bites, decide what to wear, and plan my own day, but I found myself looking around every corner for upperclassman. I was sure they would jump into the dining room as I ate with my family. "Goddamnit, Avery! That was a big bite! You're done eating. Take your plate to the sink, and when you get back, you better have your neck and back straight! You're a disgrace!"

+ + +

Captain Eifer wasted no time digging into the company. He had quilled me twice before the end of January: once for improperly aligned uniforms in my closet and once for insufficiently shined shoes at dinner formation.

It took no time for Turtle to land hard on the area. He had become the go-to plebe for spirit missions. Firsties and cows were constantly grabbing him in late-night conscriptions for their purposes. He often pulled me into the mix, until I begged him to stop. I needed sleep.

He got busted a few times for minor infractions and then finally got caught rappelling down the face of Washington Hall in an attempt to hang a "Beat Navy" flag over the commandant's office windows for the Navy basketball game at the request of one of E4's cows.

He got twenty hours on the area for that one, and Wilcox went nuts. He forbade any further enlistments of Turtle in spirit missions. "The kid needs to graduate!" Wilcox was no longer the company commander, but no one dared cross him.

Classes were hard. Creighton helped us all study for military history. He was better than our professor and held weekly study sessions in our room for all the guys. We felt under siege but united.

I'd been a fool to want to get back after Christmas, though. Camaraderie and companions were no match for the place and season. By February, I was chest-deep in gloom.

Fortunately, Colonel Krieger refused to let me wallow. I got back from class one Wednesday to find a note from him on my desk.

"Be at Mac's statue at fifteen-hundred hours this Saturday. Bring a friend. We are grilling steaks. No excuses. Col. Krieger."

Every cadet is assigned a sponsor after Beast, an officer to provide informal mentoring and a window into what life as an army officer is like. Many of these matchups fade quickly or are replaced by other informal relationships. My assignment to Colonel Stan Krieger had lasted. Visits to his quarters were relaxing, and he was fascinating. He didn't talk much about the things he had done, but I knew they included Vietnam and Grenada and probably some other things I had never heard of.

He wore his hair close-cropped, in the style of an old Roman general. The cool gray hair on the sides blended to black on top, framing a face that was weathered and tired but happy; the crow's-feet were deep. He walked with a slight limp, but I could never tell which leg it was. It changed each time I saw him, and I never asked to clarify. He was slow to get out of a chair but could run ten miles easily. His arms were toned, and his belly was flat. He looked exactly how I thought an American warrior would look, and I wanted to be like him.

Best of all, I liked to eat, and he and his wife liked to feed cadets.

I invited Bill along, so Saturday afternoon he and I stood beneath the statue of General MacArthur and waited for Colonel Krieger.

"It's cold out here," I said.

"You don't get winters like this in Charlotte, do you?"

"You might get a cold snap, but that's it. It's a snap. You don't get this sustained death march of a winter."

"We get it in Pennsylvania. Stomp your feet."

"Oh, please."

"I'm serious. I never did it growing up. Sure as hell did it when I was stationed in Korea."

I looked at Bill dubiously and stomped my feet.

"See!"

"Yeah. Balmy."

"You know it worked."

"Here he is."

Headlights reflected off the supe's road; it was the colonel's old Blazer. The ice crunched as he pulled to a stop, and we hopped in quickly.

"Evening, boys," he said. "Happy gloom period to you."

"Thank you, sir," I said in mock appreciation. "This is Bill Cooper."

"Good to meet you, sir. Thanks very much for having us over."

"It's our pleasure, Bill. Sincerely."

The colonel was not a department head, so he didn't live on Colonels' Row, though some considered his location more desirable. His was the last house on Lee Road just before the gate, sitting on a wooded plateau a couple hundred feet above the Hudson. There was no million-dollar view of the river, due to a thick patch of old-growth trees, but it was a quiet corner that seemed far away from West Point. The large brick Tudor-style quarters were old but comfortable.

His wife greeted us warmly, giving each of us a strong hug. She took our dress gray tops and hung them in the hallway closet as we continued to the living room. Along the way, we passed the colonel's study. The door was open, and Bill and I slowed to peer inside. The walls were covered in keepsakes and gifts from friends and former units. Framed old battle streamers, guidons, and photos of tough-looking men and dirty, beat-up helicopters. On the wall, centered behind his desk, hung half of a tail rotor blade on a simple wooden plaque. It was bent and scarred and hinted at something rough.

"Whoa," said Bill softly.

"Keep moving, cadets," said the colonel in a friendly but forceful voice. He shut the door to his study and nudged us along. "Let's eat, fellas!"

After gorging ourselves, we lay on the sofa, watched TV, and chatted with the colonel and his wife. For plebes, it was about as good a Saturday night as we could hope for: no upperclassmen around, food just an arm's length away, and a TV that responded to a remote control.

"So, how does it feel?"

"How does what feel, sir?"

"To be this close to having it in the bag?"

"Are you kidding, sir? It's not even March yet. We've got over three months to go."

"Trust me, guys. It's going to start accelerating. You've got it licked," he said, though he could tell we were skeptical. I smiled politely.

The colonel grinned. "You'll see. There's something about rounding the corner at the end of February. Gloom period starts to weaken, not right away, but by the end of March, you'll be sticking a knife in its belly, and then, boom! You're yearlings."

Bill and I looked at him and nodded, unconvinced.

"Just promise me you bastards will tell me when you realize I was right."

"You got it, sir."

✦ ✦ ✦

With the spring came the return of E4's shame: drill. We marched at least twice during the week to get ready for the brigade reviews, which took place nearly every Saturday now that the weather was nice again. We were terrible. We were still last in the regiment, and it drove Captain Eifer crazy, which made us happy, of course.

It was a strange feeling to be happy about poor performance, but after a year in E4 that is exactly what I felt. Drill was a senseless waste of time. I had come to West Point because I wanted to be a warrior. Marching around with an antique rifle in my hands and a feathered hat on my head accomplished nothing toward that goal; therefore, doing poorly in it didn't matter. In fact, doing poorly seemed to make me more of a warrior because I endured the heat of disapproval from Eifer and the rest of the machine. It was twisted E4 logic, but most of us felt that way—in fact, everyone but Creighton.

"I don't understand you guys," he would protest. "Drill is an important part of being a cadet. It is historic. It is required. You guys don't get to pick what's important. You can't change what is tradition. It's disrespectful."

"Whatever, Creighton. Pass me a piece of that pizza."

Creighton handed Bill a slice of Schade's pizza and looked at me for support. I shrugged.

"I don't know what to tell you, Creighton," said Zack. "But when I first got here, I thought like you. I wanted to excel at being a cadet, you know?"

Zack reached for another piece of pizza as he continued: "Then I got to know how fucked up this place is. I got written up this week for dust on the bottom of my shoe. On the bottom of my shoe!" He took a huge bite of cheese and pepperoni.

"I was quilled this week for improper book alignment on my bookshelf," Turtle interjected.

"'Xactly what I am talkin' about!" yelled Zack with a mouth full of pizza. I held up my hand to shield myself from flying food particles.

"Big bite, Dempsey?"

Zack swallowed hard, burped loudly, and went on: "How can I take anything they say seriously when they try to tell me that lining up books from tallest to shortest, left to right, is important? Or when every Saturday morning until noon I have to leave all of my drawers open so that officers and upperclassmen can come peer into them and make sure my tighty-whities are folded just so into neat fucking squares in the proper place next to my rolled-up socks?" Zack ran out of breath and inhaled deeply to continue, but Creighton cut him off.

"It's a simple requirement," said Creighton.

"Doesn't matter," Zack said. "It's stupid. Makes them all seem stupid when they make such a big deal out of bullshit."

"They don't make a big deal out of it. How many demerits did you get for books out of alignment, Turtle?"

"Four," said Turtle.

"Not a big slug. Insignificant, in fact. Rather proportionate, if you think about it. Seems like you're the one making a big deal out of it, Zack."

"Fuck you, Creighton. You're missing my point."

"No, you are missing *the* point."

"What does proper book alignment have to do with winning wars?"

"You hear that, gentlemen?" Creighton looked around at us theatrically. "After less than a year in uniform as a plebe, Cadet Dempsey is qualified to tell us what regulations we should follow and which ones we do not have to follow."

"Why's that so ridiculous?"

"Because you have no sense of history. No sense of context."

"Well, you have no sense of common fucking sense."

Zack stood up abruptly, glaring at Creighton. Zack was a big guy. Even though Creighton was genuinely angry, he was too good a tactician to ever confront Zack physically. Creighton sat motionless, staring coolly back at him.

The rest of us ignored them, used to their standoffs. Turtle winked at me as he chewed his pizza.

"Yeah. Well, for the record, I thank God I am in E4." Zack dramatically crossed himself and then took another huge bite of greasy pizza.

"I agree with Zack," said Turtle. "I tell ya, if I hadn't landed in E4, I doubt I'd graduate. I'm grateful, too."

"The irony is, Turtle, you would have been better served in another company."

I put my hand on Creighton's shoulder and smiled at him. Zack and Turtle shook their heads and kept eating. Creighton looked at me, conflicted, at once disgusted by us and drawn in. We were his brothers. We'd survived plebe year together. That never goes away.

✦ ✦ ✦

On May 27, 1988, Recognition Day, plebe year ended. The Corps marched onto the Plain together as a brigade, and then the first class marched away from us to the reviewing area. The full regiment of the class of 1988 stood at attention as the lower three classes passed in review and marched back into North Area.

In North Area the companies were dismissed, and each executed its recognition ceremony. We plebes stood in two long ranks, and the upperclassmen, beginning with the firsties, who had marched back from the Plain after us, walked down each rank and introduced themselves to us, one by one. It was strange. It was a letdown and great at the same time. It was hard to process. The upperclassmen I had been so terrified of were now talking to me like a human being, using my first name and telling me theirs.

Like most of my classmates, I found it hard to drop the "sir" and "ma'am" when speaking with them. They would chuckle politely: "You don't have to say that anymore, Sam. You made it."

I had the hardest time with Wilcox. "Congratulations, Sam," he said, holding out his hand. "I'm Steve Wilcox."

"Sam Avery, sir. Thanks . . . I mean, Steve. I appreciate it."

He could tell I was flustered; he held the handshake and pulled me in slightly.

"I've got high hopes for you. Keep it up."

"Thanks. But I didn't really think that was what you thought about me."

He smiled and nodded knowingly. "You know it really doesn't matter what I think of you. How do you feel?"

"Proud. Confused. Excited and let down, I guess."

"Get used to it. Good luck to you, Cadet Avery. I hope to see you out in the army."

"Me too, Lieutenant."

"Not till tomorrow." He smiled. "But thanks."

The rest of the line was a blur except for the Guru, who said simply, "Sam, I'm Henry Stillmont, but you will continue to call me Guru."

"Sure, Guru. You got it."

"You did well, but the hardest part is still ahead. Remember, decide who you will be . . ."

"Then be him."

"Good." He smiled and nodded. "Go have fun this summer. See you in August, Sam."

He walked away before I had a chance to answer.

We signed out on summer leave the next day, after the graduation ceremony in Michie Stadium. Plebe year was over. Zack, Bill, and I shared a cab to Newark Airport. We walked into the terminal together and then hesitated in the grimy departure hall.

"How fucking anticlimactic is this?" asked Zack.

"What do you want," said Bill, "a tear-jerking good-bye?"

"Jerk this, asshole."

"You did it, Zack. We all did. Don't overthink it." Bill extended his hand to Zack.

Zack shook it slowly, "Thanks, Bill. You're right, as usual. Couldn't have done it without you. Now come here."

Zack yanked Bill into a bear hug. Zack was a hugger. I didn't fight it when he released Bill and turned to me.

Bill shrugged, saluted, and walked away. "Your summer leave is wasting away, Avery," he called over his shoulder. "Go naked!"

Zack winked and turned around. I watched them both go, confused by what I had accomplished but grateful for the friends I had made.

ELEVEN

"THIS IS THE HOUSE WHERE THE GURU IS BEING HELD. It's your standard two-story Iraqi house with a small garden area surrounded by a mud-brick wall."

Zack held his laser pointer's dot on a house on the southeastern edge of the town in the satellite image.

"Fucking Tal Afar," mumbled Pete as he and I grimaced. We sat in a dusty garage facility a couple of kilometers from the airfield. Turtle had paid off the owner for the day and placed four discreet guards around the building, so we were assured of having the space to ourselves. His guys were using it as their staging area for tonight's mission, and their gear was laid out in neat piles behind us as we sat on metal folding chairs for Zack's briefing. To one side he had taped a large map of Tal Afar; on the other side, a portable projector threw images against the dirty wall.

Zack looked at the map and nodded. Tal Afar sits mostly on the south side of Highway 47 about fifty kilometers west of Mosul and nearly sixty kilometers east of the Syrian border. This stretch of road and the border crossing into Syria had been a troubled, lawless area for hundreds, maybe thousands of years. The route was overrun by land pirates and mafia types all the way from Mosul to the border. When the town had been success-fully taken over and controlled, it had been so only under a heavy hand. Even then, extremists had maintained a hidden but brutal influence just below the surface. Pete and I had actually been on several operations into Tal Afar over the past decade. One had been with Zack's unit. Those mis-sions were never fun for our customers or us.

"Well. At least we got a little lucky on the specific target location," I said, trying to lighten the mood.

"It definitely could be worse," Zack agreed. The satellite image of Tal Afar showed the circular-shaped city snuggling up to a slight northward bulge in Highway 47. But the circle was only about four-fifths complete, with a dark green wedge of a partially cultivated, scrubby river valley jut-ting north, taking up the final fifth. The city looked like a south-facing Pac-Man.

"The target house is well south of the city center and sits only about one hundred and fifty meters to the east of this unpopulated area of vegetation"—Zack gestured at the green wedge—"and about eight hun-dred meters from the easternmost edge of the city. Much better than if he had been taken somewhere here." Zack put his dot in the middle of the ancient city, home to two hundred thousand people.

"So what are you thinking?"

"The concept of the operation is pretty simple: you guys drop us off with our vehicle about ten miles to the southeast of the target. There is suf-ficient terrain development so an insertion out here should be acousti-cally masked and far enough away that it won't be heard. We will infil along this route and assault the objective. Then, depending on how it goes, we will either exfil in the vehicle to a spot about ten clicks south of the city where you will pick us up or we will call you guys to come get us right from the objective."

"If you have to call us into the objective, it would be really good if you could get into that scrub area," said Pete.

"Roger that. We'll try."

"What intel do you have on the house so far?" I asked.

"Not much in terms of layout," said Turtle. "But we know that three men got to the house at twenty-three-thirty hours last night with the Guru. Other than stepping outside to smoke a cigarette or walk around the walled garden area, they have not left. The Guru is definitely still in the building."

"How do you know that?" Pete asked.

"Because we've had eyes on the house continuously since he entered."

"Continuously?"

"Roger that," said Zack.

"How are you doing that?"

Zack looked at me. I nodded.

"We've got a guy in the CIA."

"You've got a guy?" Pete shook his head slowly and looked at me. "Let me guess. Another fucking West Point classmate?"

I shrugged and smiled.

"We also know that ISIS does not know exactly where they are yet," said Zack. "Intel has been pretty clear on that. They seem to be looking for him primarily in Mosul, where he was captured."

"That's strange."

"Not really. I figure the guys who got him are your basic opportunistic pirate-thug types. This city has bred a lot of them. They probably didn't really know what they had and decided to run it back to their own neighborhood before figuring out their next move."

"Lucky for the Guru."

"So far, but it won't take them much longer. That's why we have to exfil him tonight. We won't get another window."

"What time frame were you thinking of doing this?" I asked.

"I want to take them before they leave the house. Turtle is right that we don't have a layout for the place, but we've been in a thousand of these houses. We should be able to clear it quickly enough. I'd much rather do that than try to hit them in a moving vehicle. It's only sixty kilometers to Syria and Baghdadi. I think they'll wait until later in the night to get rolling. So, I'd like to hit them about an hour after sunset, if possible."

"What if they leave before that?" asked Pete.

"If that happens, we'll get the word and will have to adjust the plan en route."

Pete leaned back in his chair and rubbed his eyes. "So basically what you're telling me is we're going to make all this shit up as we go along."

"Yes," said Zack.

"Okay, then."

"I've got a question for you guys," said Zack. "Are you sure you can get the helicopter?"

"Don't worry about that part," Pete said. "Who's going to stop a lieutenant colonel and a CW5 in flight suits?"

Turtle chuckled.

I agreed with Pete. Our operations tempo had been slow the last couple of days. The aircraft would be available, and we wouldn't have a problem getting access to it.

We stayed with Zack and Turtle for about two hours, talking through scenarios and agreeing on contingencies. We had all been at war for close to fifteen years. We were professionals with a common experience set and language. It was like putting four experienced musicians in a room together: the music flowed easily.

Turtle's six commandos were also pros and had done this kind of operation numerous times. They'd all been veterans of multiple deployments with SOCOM before signing on with Thayer Tactical and exuded the air of men who had been in-theater for a long time. Their bearded, grizzled faces and the bags under their eyes conveyed the aggressive pace Turtle's organization was laboring under. But they were also motivated. In addition to the righteous cause of rescuing an American citizen, Turtle was giving each of them a bonus for going on the mission, with promise of a larger bonus contingent on their success. They paid close attention during the planning session but spoke very little. I could feel the heat of their focus as the meeting went on. They were trying to assess Pete and me. Could we be counted on?

As it approached 1600 hours, I looked at Pete. "We need to get back. Admiral Brick is sure to be wondering where I am by now."

"Roger that, sir. I think we're ready anyway."

It was actually Sergeant Weber I was worried about. Sneaking out without him at my side was hard. He must have noticed that I was gone in less than five minutes.

"Can I walk you out, Sam?" Zack asked.

I made eye contact with Pete and looked toward the door. He nodded and headed out.

"See you gentlemen tonight."

Zack and I followed him out at a discreet distance.

"What do you think?" Zack asked.

"About what?"

"The plan."

He looked worried in a way he had not conveyed yet. "You've seen a lot of these ops. I need your honest opinion."

"I think it's as solid as it can be. We have a good shot."

"Good. Good." He kneaded his forehead as we walked, and I could see the pressure weighing him down. There is nothing as lonely as being responsible for a plan in which lives hang in the balance. No matter how many times you've done it, no matter how good at it you get, no matter how mechanical it becomes, you wonder, *Did I plan this one right?*

+ + +

On the drive back to the airfield, Pete pressed me on our CIA source. He'd seen me get the full download from Zack, across the room from him. I decided that since Pete was going to be putting his ass on the line with us, he deserved to know the whole story.

"So who is your guy at the CIA?" he asked. "Must be pretty high up."

"He is. His name is Creighton Patterson. We graduated together."

"I figured that much. What's his story?"

"He left the army in 1997, which was a huge surprise to all of us. He had been the hardest charger of any of us as cadets—not physically, more of a cerebral strategy type, and he was a little weird. It was almost like he was bred to be a cadet."

"Like you, right?"

"Right," I answered sarcastically.

"Creighton graduated as the top-ranking armor-branch officer in our class. Bound for glory. After a few years where he'd been off the radar, we learned that he'd entered the CIA. This confused the hell out us. We could not see him as a spy. Creighton was just too socially awkward. He was definitely not the kind of guy you could picture recruiting assets in a foreign country. After 9/11 and the war kicking off, though, it became obvious he had found his calling. We all knew he was a superior analyst and strategic thinker, but it turned out he was also a savant with drones. He was the architect of the CIA's drone program, and by 2009 he was overseeing global drone operations with the highest access and ridiculous influence. He sits on the president's 'kill list' council and probably a lot of other things I don't know about."

"Let me guess: now he is supporting you guys with one of his drones."

"Because of his command and oversight role for CIA drone operations, when the Guru got nabbed, Creighton knew soon after."

"That was lucky."

"I don't know. I think Creighton has been watching over a couple of us for a while without letting on about it. In any case, he was also involved in the discussions when it was decided there would not be a rescue mission."

"And he didn't like that."

"Nope. Somehow he got a small cell of trusted guys to cycle a drone over the site. Since he's CIA, the military has no idea what he is up to. Then he got in touch with Zack. The truth is, I don't know exactly what he's doing back there, but I know he'll do whatever he has to do to help us succeed."

Pete chuckled. "Bunch of fucking pied pipers."

"What do you mean?"

"Look at you three. The CIA guy talked a couple folks into helping. The Thayer Tactical guy talked a couple guys into helping, and you talked my dumb ass into helping."

"It's kind of what they trained us to do."

"I just hope you West Pointers don't all go bad at once. You could wreak some serious havoc."

"Don't worry. We've all sworn to use our powers only for good."

Pete laughed loudly.

"Your CIA friend, though, why is he doing this? All you guys are tight, but it seems like he's throwing away a big career over this. I guess we all are, but it sounds like he's got a lot further to go."

"Long story. West Point. We all go way back."

Pete nodded, and we drove in silence for a few minutes. I had to ask: "Why are you doing this?"

"Because you and I go way back."

TWELVE

THE M1 TANK LEAPT INTO VIEW, SAILING OVER A HILL A quarter of a mile away. Dirt flew from its sides like sawdust from a massive chain saw. It rocked back and forth on its chassis, absorbing blows from the uneven terrain in a violent gallop as it raced downslope. It screamed toward us and at the last minute executed an abrupt hockey stop, skidding sideways and throwing rocks our way. Poised at a forty-five-degree angle to the bleachers we were seated in, its turbine engine spun reluctantly down and settled into a high-pitched growl. The dust cloud it had kicked up along the way caught up to it and swept over us. We inhaled the acrid combination of burnt fuel and Kentucky mud as we waited to see what would happen next. It was the most powerful machine I had ever laid eyes on. A fast, angular, low-slung, and massive killing beast. It was Armor Week at Fort Knox.

Cadet Field Training at Camp Buckner is commonly referred to as "the best summer of your life." That's part truth and part rueful lie. Eight weeks of intense field training exposed the newly risen yearling class to all of the major combat branches. Plebe summer is narrowly designed to enable new cadets to fit into and survive the West Point system. The "real army" is a distant backdrop. Yearling summer has a more expansive charter. It is an orientation to the "real army" that enables third-class cadets to begin to think about where they belong and where they will spend their careers as officers. It includes driving tanks with armored units, building river crossings with combat engineers, and patrolling with infantrymen. Most of it takes place on the West Point military reserve at a site called Camp Buckner, which sounds idyllic but really isn't. The decrepit World War II–era facilities bake in the summer heat.

There is no saltier member of the Corps than a yearling. The emotional bounce of promotion from plebe status is shorter lived than anyone ever expects; rounding that corner is sweet. For most cadets, for the rest of their lives, there are days when they find themselves saying with genuine happiness and relief, "At least I'm not a plebe anymore." Once the foreshortened perspective of just-get-yourself-to-recognition-day is lifted, a young yearling is able to measure how far he has yet to go and how low on the ladder he remains. There is a reason most refer to it as "yuk" year.

The Fort Knox portion was the most memorable for me. But it wasn't because of the impressive armor demonstration and training; it was because Bill and I left Fort Knox with a big problem, a Captain Eifer problem.

After the armor training was complete, we got a day off before flying back to Buckner to continue the rest of our training. Bill arranged a diversion for himself and me. We snuck off post and spent a few hours drinking beer with a newly graduated lieutenant who had just posted to Knox. The lieutenant had invited a few girls over. We grilled and drank beer next to the pool in his backyard. It was a fun afternoon and evening; we almost felt like normal college kids. That night, though, Captain Eifer caught Bill vomiting outside the barracks; it was bad luck. Bill had gone outside to avoid waking people up.

Eifer confronted Bill, who immediately confessed. But Bill made things much worse for himself when he refused to answer Eifer's question "Did anyone else participate in this unauthorized activity?"

"Sir, that is an improper question," he responded.

The fact that cadets live under an honor code is not supposed to be used against them, but it is an inescapable fact that the concept of honor and regulations are intertwined in their daily lives. Some cadets would say that there is often a cynical exploitation of the honor system to enforce regulations. The tactical department, charged with maintaining the good order and discipline of the Corps, is most often the culprit in the eyes of cadets. The academy, recognizing the potential for this practice to corrode the concept of honor within the Corps, actively discourages this behavior. Tactical officers are not supposed to line up groups of cadets, for example, and ask them directly if they are guilty of violating one regulation or the other. They are supposed to operate within the bounds of reasonable probable cause, and cadets are encouraged to speak up when they perceive a question to be improper. This is part of the extensive honor training cadets receive.

The improper question is an important concept at West Point that underscores an unspoken hierarchy of cadet conduct; honor matters more than anything, and regulations are expected to be broken.

Cadets break regulations every day, and there is a mechanism for dealing with those shortfalls. Quill is written, boards are held, punishments are dispensed, and time is served. In fact, a century man, a cadet who has served more than a hundred hours on the area, holds a certain status in the Corps and even among the officers of the tactical department. A century man has screwed up a lot, but he has paid the price. He has served the time. In the eyes of the system, he has been honed and chiseled and improved; he didn't quit, and the academy did not quit on him.

Honor is different and always has been. In the early years of the academy, honor was taught and maintained through an informal, cadet-enforced system. In 1922, Superintendent Douglas MacArthur formalized the Cadet Honor Code and its enforcement, establishing much of the structure and administration that is still in place today. It's been tweaked a few times since, but the specifics and spirit of the system have not changed much from the original standard. The honor code has remained simple. Stark. Uncompromising. "A cadet will not lie, cheat, steal, or tolerate those who do."

Cadets hold honor above regs, just as the academy does. The same century man who willfully breaks regs again and again stops cold at the prospect of violating the honor code. Cadets have even been known to reject academy decisions of leniency in honor cases. A cadet found guilty of an honor violation who is not expelled faces the "silence." No cadet speaks to them. No cadet eats with them. No cadet will acknowledge their existence. They are dead in the eyes of the Corps. This devastating practice drove all those who faced it to resign until the 1970s, when the administration worked to end it. It has since lost much of its effectiveness but is still sometimes invoked by an angry Corps.

So the improper question is supposed to be a buffer between honor and regulations, but in practice, invoking the concept of the improper question is difficult. It requires the cadet to face down a superior commissioned officer who is typically already upset. This usually occurs when the cadet is alone with the officer and the difference in rank is most apparent. It takes a hardy constitution to tell the officer that they are wrong and need to back off. It takes balls. This was not a problem for Bill Cooper.

Eifer had him dead to rights on drinking—Bill's vomit was all the probable cause the captain needed. But when Eifer asked if anyone else had been involved, Bill drew the line. He was not going to let Eifer use his honor to compel him to give me up as well.

"Sir, that is an improper question."

Eifer was enraged.

But Bill did not crack. I felt a terrible combination of relief and guilt, which grew as the summer dragged on. Bill was put on restriction pending a disciplinary board that would be held after the summer training was complete. Still, Bill did not waver.

"Bill, it's not worth it," I often said to him.

"No. I've thought about it. I don't care what they do. I don't have to rat anyone out. They got me. Fine. But I'm not giving up anyone else. Fuck him."

Finally, Buckner came to a close, and we cycled back to our academic barracks.

+ + +

E4's company area was relocated for the new academic year. The old Divisions were closed for extensive and much-needed renovations, so we would spend the year in the long wing of MacArthur Barracks. As I walked up the stairs and rounded the corner, I ran into the Guru. He was returning from the shower in his distinctive cadet robe.

"Go naked, Cadet Avery. How are you?" He extended his hand.

"Go naked, Guru. I'm good. How was your summer?"

"Good. Airborne School and Cadet Troop Leader Training in Germany. Really enjoyed it."

"What kind of unit in Germany?"

"An armored unit, of course. What other kind is there?"

"I didn't realize you were an armor fanatic, like Patterson."

"Patterson is a strange fellow, but his branch preference is spot-on."

"Where in Germany were you?"

"Little town called Wiesbaden. I had tried to wrangle my way to Fulda, but the Eleventh ACR doesn't do cadet internships. They take their East German border mission seriously. It was very cool nonetheless. How was Buckner?"

"Oh, you know . . . best summer of my life."

"I heard about the unpleasantness with Cooper and Eifer."

"Not a good scene."

"Glad you weren't involved. That is going to be a hefty slug." He looked at me. I didn't know what to say. After an awkward moment, he let me off the hook: "Not watching the march back?"

"No. It's actually pretty boring when you're not a plebe."

"Agreed. Well, I'll leave you to it. I need to get into uniform to be properly prepared for the new beanheads' arrival." He turned and continued on to his room.

"What? No water torture in your robe?"

"Nope. That was my preferred technique in the Divisions, but these long hallways are much less conducive to that method. Too many people pinging by, and you never know when an officer is going to come up on you. That spoils the mood." He shook his head and continued on. It was still weird to speak in normal terms to some of the upperclassmen. There was a lingering edge to things. It was as if, at any moment, they would pounce and scream that it had all been a cruel joke, that plebe year had been extended.

I straightened our room for about half an hour before Steven came bounding in. Steven Thompson was a tall, good-natured Montanan with a knack for math and engineering. He and I were rooming together this semester.

"Here come the new cadets!"

I heard hundreds of feet climbing the stairs against a backdrop of shouting upperclassmen. E4's new batch of plebes was arriving; the feeding frenzy had begun.

I stepped out into the hallway to observe as they burst out of the staircase carrying trunks and rucksacks. They staggered down the hallway toward the orderly room to find out their room assignments. Upperclass-men circled and harassed them as they went. When weaklings identi-fied themselves through inaction or mistakes, they were culled from the herd. The weakened ones would be set to the side, where they would be devoured by two to three upperclassmen yelling, "The rest of you move out!"

The centuries-old dynamic was at work. Upperclassmen did not expect perfection. Having taken every step that these new cadets took now, they understood that this was hard, that it wore you down, that fatigue and stress doused everyone in a fog; yet an instant and unwritten algorithm was at work, churning through both the obvious and the non-verbal data points pouring out from every new cadet. This one is not really trying hard. That one is simply too weak. This one doesn't want to be here. That one thinks we can't get to him. It was involuntary. It was pervasive, and it felt infallible.

I scanned up and down the hallway, at once observing the scene and remembering it. Some of my classmates were tearing into new cadets. Turtle had selected a short, sweaty beanhead and was screaming in his ear. His words were straight out of last summer. I smiled as I headed down the hallway toward room 527.

I had been assigned two new cadets for the semester. I knocked twice on the door and heard, "Enter, sir!"

The two cadets stood at attention. "Sir, New Cadet Morris, Third Squad, Fourth Platoon, reports."

"Good afternoon." I returned their salute. "Stand at ease. My name is Cadet Avery. I'm your team leader. I know things are nuts right now. Just focus on getting yourselves and your rooms squared away ASAP, and remember, tomorrow you need to have memorized your daily knowl-edge before morning formation. That means the *New York Times,* the meals, the Officer of the Day, 'The Days,' all of it. We will meet ten min-utes prior to any formation in my room, so that I can be sure you're ready. If you have any questions between now and then, come find me. I'm two doors down to the left. Any questions for me right now?"

"No, sir," said Morris.

"Good. The heat will be bad until classes start. Just accept it. Focus on executing what you have been trained to do, and if you screw up, just take the heat and move through it without screwing up again. Multiple screw-ups in a row will kill you."

"Yes, sir!"

"One last thing: do you guys know the company greeting?"

"Sir, the company greeting is 'Go Elephants,'" said Morris.

I shook my head in disgust. "God, I hate that Beast bullshit." I looked at them and set them straight.

The next day, Saturday, was the first real barracks inspection of the year. This first SAMI inspection after Reorgy Week was always a bitch.

Every day of a cadet's life is divided up into different expectations for the state of their room. Despite the fact that a cadet's room is where they live, the closest thing they have in the cadet area to a private space, it is the first focal point of the tactical department's developmental attention. The two primary divisions are "AMI" and "PMI," which denote the a.m. and p.m. inspection periods. AMI is the worse of the two; the requirements are more stringent, forbidding any trash in the trash can and even naps. Cadets may not take a nap at West Point until after noon, at which time PMI begins. SAMI is a notch up from AMI and is in force on Saturday mornings until noon. It imposes all of the limitations of AMI with the added requirement that drawers, closets, sink vanities, and laundry hampers must be left open so that officers can assess the folded underwear, toiletry configurations, and other critical room specifications.

The first SAMI of the academic year is always the classic "tone setter," during which the tactical department declares itself. I looked in on my plebes' room prior to the inspection. "Not too bad, guys, not too bad," I said as I walked around. I ran my finger over the windowsill; it came back clean. I looked at Cadet Morris, asking, "How late were you guys up cleaning last night?"

"Sir, lights-out is at midnight."

"Morris, what did you read in the *New York Times* today?"

"Sir, today in the *New York Times* it was reported that after almost eight years of war and a million lives lost, a cease-fire between Iran and Iraq was reported to be holding. The truce was brokered by the United Nations and took effect today at seven a.m. local time. There—"

"Cease work. Good. But talk slower, so you have more runway. Remember, if you spit out too much detail, you'll have upperclassmen sharpshooting you on the small stuff. What did I tell you guys about reporting on the *New York Times*?"

"Sir, you said read the whole article, but in reporting, try to stick to just the first sentence of each paragraph."

"Right. Anderson, what is for lunch?"

"Sir, the menu for lunch is baked chicken patties, baby carrots, and fresh fruit."

I made a face. "What do you think about that, Anderson?"

"Sir, I think the chicken patties are gross."

"Me, too. Seem more boiled than baked." I turned and walked toward the door. I was pleased. They were good plebes.

"Keep this up for the first few weeks of class, and all the upperclassmen will decide you are squared away and won't bother you until after Christmas."

"Yes, sir."

"The room looks good. Just remember, SAMI is not over until twelve hundred hours. It's only oh-seven-thirty now. Don't do anything stupid. Stay in uniform, and for God's sake, don't take a nap."

"Yes, sir," they said in unison.

"Good luck. Report to my room immediately after SAMI to let me know how it goes."

"Go naked, sir."

"Go naked."

The inspection did not go well for E4. Steven and I got written up for "dust under bed" and "improper clothes hanger spacing." We earned eight demerits each; it was not a great way to start the year. The firsties really got hammered, though. Captain Eifer hit their area about ten minutes prior to the end of SAMI. He got nearly every one of them but slammed the Guru particularly hard. He was in the shower and had left his uniform on his bed when Captain Eifer inspected. Having a uniform out of place like that during SAMI is a huge hit.

After consoling Steven about our results for a few minutes, I checked on Morris and Anderson. They were unscathed. Plebes tended to do well on inspections since they had so many eyes on them all the time.

I went to Bill's room. Today was his disciplinary board. He was not back yet, so I sat at his desk. I didn't have a good feeling.

I read the newspaper while I waited. Karl, Bill's roommate this semester, futzed with his computer. After about twenty long minutes, Bill came back. He entered the room without acknowledging either of us and changed into his PT uniform. Karl and I looked at each other as Bill stood with his back to us, slowly hanging his class uniform back in his closet. I motioned to Karl to give us a moment, so he got up and left the room quickly, without saying anything.

Bill, now in regulation shorts and T-shirt, walked over, sat down on his bed, grabbed one of his running shoes, and began to put it on. He didn't look angry or sad. His face was blank.

"For violating the United States Corps of Cadets Regulations, I have been given three months of room restriction and seventy-five hours on the area," he announced while he grabbed the other running shoe, still staring straight ahead. "While on room restriction, I must be either in class, in my room, in the mess hall with the rest of the Corps, or engaging in one hour of authorized exercise."

"Bill—"

He shook his head to shut me up. "I've done the math. It's almost the whole semester. I'll be off restriction sometime around Thanksgiving and might get off the area in time for the Navy game."

"Bill—"

He cut me off again. "Colonel Vanson made it clear that a major factor in the severity of my punishment was my refusal to cooperate with the investigating officer, Captain Eifer. Had I been more cooperative, the punishment would have been half as severe, and, he said, in the future, I should spend some time reflecting on the importance of supporting my chain of command."

"Bill, I'm really sorry."

"Don't be. I did the crime. Both crimes. I got busted, and I didn't cooperate with the investigating officer." He turned his head and looked at me. "This is going to be a long semester, Sam. But I can manage through it. It helps now that I know what I have to get through, and it's not your fault. I'd handle it the exact same way if I had to do it over again." He turned back and stared toward the wall. I realized that it wasn't a blank look; it was one of resolve. He was steeling himself against the months-long task in front of him.

"Well, I'm going to say it one last time."

Bill held his hand up to stop me, but I ignored it.

"Thanks."

"Fuck you. Can we go to the gym now? I want to use my hour well."

THIRTEEN

MAJOR OBRIEN GREETED ME URGENTLY THE MOMENT I walked back into the TOC.

"Good. You're back, sir. We've got a mission tonight. Received it about half an hour ago."

"What's the mission?"

"High-value target near Haditha. The flight crews are in the planning cell looking at imagery with the ground element now. Package looks like three Black Hawks and two Chinooks. Air mission brief is at nineteen-thirty hours."

I cursed our luck. After a couple of days with almost no operations we get hit with this, a mission that would take both Chinooks.

"Who's the target?"

"Abdul-Ahad," Obrien said with a smile. Abdul-Ahad had been on our HVT list for a long time. He was one of Baghdadi's main lieutenants; snagging him would be a big win. I followed Major Obrien to the large map on the other side of the tactical operations center.

"Intel puts Abdul-Ahad in this house north of Haditha tonight. The landing zones are small, so it will be a Black Hawk mission with Chinooks in support. You can see that the distance to the LZs is almost two hundred and fifty kilometers. The ground commander wants to maximize his shooters on the objective so the Black Hawks will carry only just enough fuel to make the insertion and get back to the forward refueling point. The first Chinook will be configured as a fat cow, and the second will be an on-call casualty-evacuation bird."

A "fat cow" was a Chinook helicopter stuffed full of internal fuel tanks and used as a flying gas station. It could serve up thousands of gallons of jet fuel wherever it landed. A cas-evac bird was basically an empty Chinook with a medic that could stabilize any wounded as it sprinted with them to the hospital in Baghdad, should the need arise.

Other than the terrible timing, it was a straightforward mission. It was a mission profile we had executed thousands of times over the past few years. Ordinarily I would've have been fired up for this one, but now I was too concerned about the Guru. I was scared for him. The major could see the conflict on my face.

"You okay, sir?"

"Yeah. I'm fine. It will be good to get the bastard. I'm going to head over to the planning cell."

"Roger that, sir. You should. They need you to make the final crew assignments."

I grabbed my flight-planning bag and headed for the door.

"Colonel Avery."

"What is it, Obrien?"

"Just so you know. When the mission came down, the admiral got pretty irritated that you weren't here. I told him I was covering the desk for you, but . . . well, you know how he can get."

"Thanks." *Just what I need,* I thought.

My mind raced as I strode toward the planning cell. Zack had given me a burner phone for coordination; I called him as I walked.

"Go ahead," Zack said when he picked up.

"We've got a problem. A mission just came down. It's an HVT hit."

"Damnit. What does that mean for us?"

"Not sure yet. I'm walking to the planning cell now, but I think it will tie up both Chinooks."

Zack was silent. I could picture his eyes narrowing as he thought the situation through.

"Sam, it has to be tonight, or we'll lose him. The Guru will be dead."

"I hear you. I'll call you when I know more."

"It has to be tonight, Sam."

"I know. Give me time to solve the problem."

FOURTEEN

THE FIRST SEMESTER OF YEARLING YEAR PASSED slowly for E4, particularly for Bill.

As a punishment, the area is effective. Cadets dread it and work hard to ensure that they don't end up on it. Punishment tours on the area are awarded in multiples of hours and accompanied by the revocation of all privileges until the tours are walked off. Since punishment tours are served primarily on the weekends, and because of the way the process is structured, it's not possible to walk off more than eight hours a week. So a twenty-hour slug usually meant a monthlong sentence. It is a powerful behavior-modification tool.

As a way to spend one's time, it is a mind-numbing, Sisyphean torture. It begins with a thorough inspection, inspiring the cadet maxim that "area breeds area." Then cadets walk back and forth under arms from one end of the Central Area to the other. For hours. In the summer, the heat is oppressive. Cadets march in their gray, woolen, full dress uniforms on a black asphalt surface as sweat soaks through their clothes and white gloves and pools in their shoes. In the winter, it's cold. The wind hurtles down the ice-covered Hudson, scrapes over the frozen Plain, and then shrieks as it squeezes and accelerates through the sally ports of Eisenhower Barracks into Central Area. Strangely, uniforms that are ovens in the summer are frigid wind sieves in the winter.

The area is another of the powerful, unintended mental workshops in which cadets master the art of escape. Back and forth. Back and forth. Left, right, left, right, left, right, left. Stop. Order arms. About-face. Right shoulder arms. Left, right, left, right, left. The body suffers. The mind escapes. The hours pass. The punishment is served. Same as it ever was.

I had already logged thirty hours on the area at that point—not a lot relative to some, but enough for me. Turtle had racked up twice my tally and was well over halfway to becoming a century man.

I was not on the area with Bill, but the semester was tough. As a yearling, I had only a few more privileges than a plebe, amounting to just one forty-eight-hour pass for the entire semester. It was plebe year without pinging. Worse, it was plebe year without mail.

When a cadet first starts his journey at West Point, he is on everyone's mind back home. There is an open seat at the family dinner table, a vacancy on the buddies' road trip, an absent sweetheart, and everyone knows that plebe year is a trial. They write letters regularly and send care packages.

There is no better feeling than going to the cadet mailroom under the mess hall, turning the key in your assigned metal mailbox, and finding a handful of letters. This is not just for plebes. Even firsties cry for joy at the sight. But after plebe year, the novelty of one's absence wears off. The concern expires. The letters cease.

For yearlings, however, the taunting daily trip to the mailroom is not only a sign that the full weight of West Point's social isolation has descended; it also reminds them that romantic relationships are hopeless.

Zack and I fought hard against the dynamic but failed. When a girl I'd met over the summer break dumped me, I was despondent. I made the mistake of seeking comfort from Creighton.

"Tell me, Sam, what does her father do for a living?"

"He's some kind of banker something, I think."

"And his father?"

"Why does it matter?"

"I'm just trying to figure out why you expected her to understand you at all. From what you've told me, I'd say her family has not known a day of geopolitical fear in a couple of generations. I bet they don't personally know anyone in the military."

I was irritated and just stared back at him as he continued.

"Combine that pervasive ignorance of the military with the accelerating deterioration of civilian colleges into vacations from responsibility rather than a course of preparation for life, and it's ridiculous of you to expect to have a 'relationship' with any of them."

"Are you done yet?"

"You are like a brother to me, Sam, so I say this with love: get used to it. The public, for the most part, does not care. Why should any of your parade of pretty civilian girlfriends be any different? The public will never really care unless we go back to the draft. They think they do, but they don't really, and we will never, ever go back to the draft."

"Creighton, only you would try to comfort a friend through a breakup with a discussion of the draft," I said, shaking my head. "Besides, they'll care next time there is a war."

"You are not hearing me. They will care even less when we are at war. The next conflicts will last for decades, for generations, because there is no real immediate cost for the citizens of this country anymore. We have the population and resources to sustain limited conflicts indefinitely. We could fight forever, and the public won't care. That's the funny thing. The scales will never fall from their eyes. They are never going to suddenly stop funding or supporting us. They always will. They will be fine with us fighting and dying forever."

"You can't fight forever in the time of nukes."

"Don't be ridiculous. We won't get nuked by another country. A terrorist maybe, but not another country."

"You can't be sure of that."

"Nor do I care. That is what the air force trains for. Even if that did happen, they would just throw more resources at us."

"So what you are saying makes you happy."

"Yes. Other than the pain it causes you, my friend, it does. I understand where I fit in all this. You will continue to get hurt and feel depressed until you do the same. Just accept it. You are studying to be an army officer and are stuck here for another two years. The vast majority of your civilian contemporaries don't understand and don't care, and you should not expect them to. Once you graduate and go to flight school, you will be able to chase women to your heart's content. So, for now, you need to get over it."

"I can't decide if revulsion at you has simply displaced my loneliness and hurt feelings or if I actually feel better."

"Regardless, I'm glad to have been some help."

As the semester wore on, the isolation and reindeer games of the cadet area weighed on me. What made my persistent yearling gloom nearly intolerable, however, was the constant unfavorable comparison I made to Bill in my mind. He was a rock. After a week of sharp irritability, he snapped vigorously back into frame. He was on the area every weekend and could leave his room for only an hour each day to exercise, but I never saw him down. I was amazed and shamed all at once.

Everyone tried to keep him buoyant in the beginning. Zack, Turtle, Creighton, and I would be sure to all check on him at different times, stopping by to hang out or to study for a class. After a few weeks, however, it became apparent that he didn't need special help. That he had emerged. Bill was one of those blessed people who could say, "It is what it is" and really mean it. When his mind threw the mental switch of acceptance, it was done. He resisted only those things that he determined both could and needed to be resisted. He did not recycle decisions or second-guess beliefs. Ever. He was not crushed by the massive slug, plus room restriction. It was merely an obstacle. It was a task, like shining shoes, and it would pass.

One of the few things I derived pleasure from was working with my plebes. It felt good to find that I had a knack for individual leadership. Also, despite my mood and my yearling cynicism, I was glad to be engaged in something timeless. I felt a connection to the long gray line. I made sure to teach my plebes not only by the official book but also in the spirit of E4. I took them on numerous spirit missions, with Zack often tagging along. Several times I even asked the Guru to participate. He loved it, of course, and played the devious visiting professor well. I pushed them hard and burnished them under constant pressure. By the end of the semester, they were the best of their class—Mike Morris, in particular. He had become a better cadet than I would ever be.

✦ ✦ ✦

The week after the Army-Navy game passed quickly. It was the final week of class. The weather was cold and gray, and exams loomed over the Corps. On Thursday, Colonel Krieger invited me up for a pre-exams dinner, and I brought Bill along. Now that he was off room restriction, we were all trying to integrate him back into our activities.

It was nice to relax at the colonel's. Bill and I tried to sneak into his study to get a closer look at his photos and the mounted tail rotor blade, but he again busted us. "Halt!" he said when he spied us in the hallway. "No cadets allowed in there." We went back to eating.

The next day I was the midnight cowboy.

The CQ, or cadet in charge of quarters, is always a yearling. In addition to mail runs, weapons checks, and inspections, the CQ does the final taps accountability check at midnight and renders the report to the brigade's Central Guard Room. It is a twenty-four-hour duty, and the CQ has to man the desk and phone all night—thus the cadet nickname "midnight cowboy."

The daytime and evening duty hours were usually not so bad. There was a lot of interaction with company mates and other folks as one went about their duties. It was the graveyard shift that dragged. Despite housing more than four thousand young men and women in their late teens and early twenties, the cadet barracks were quiet and boring after taps. The Corps, forever exhausted, slept soundly. The fact that I was pulling duty on Friday meant that I'd have an easy recovery day on Saturday. It could be worse.

The day passed easily. With less than a week until exams, cadets were quiet and focused. Usually a Friday night CQ duty involved dealing with a couple of drunk firsties staggering back to the company area just before taps and not wanting to hear any shit from a "damn yuk." Tonight there was none of that. Even the first classmen were buckled in and studying.

Around 1145, I stood up to stretch my legs and prepared for the final taps accountability check. I grabbed the clipboard with the inspection checklists and hit the latrine. It was a little early, but it seemed like most everyone was already in their rooms, so I started my check. The first couple of rooms I hit were good, and then I got to Karl and Bill's room. Empty.

I glanced at my watch: 1155. Five minutes. I quickly looked up and down the hallway. No one. I remembered something about another Math

Team trip for Karl and checked his card. It was marked "Off post for authorized absence." Bill's card was unmarked, of course. A knot formed in my stomach.

"Son of a bitch," I muttered as I continued to check off the rest of the company rooms. I remembered that Bill had a girl visiting him from somewhere this weekend. Earlier in the week he'd told Zack and me how eager he was for the weekend to get here. I had an idea why. I hoped he wasn't doing anything stupid.

As I finished the rounds and approached Bill's room, I was certain he had come back while I had been gone. I was relieved. I opened the door to the room and stepped inside.

No one. *Shit.*

A wave of panic swept over me. I was going to have to hammer Bill. He wasn't going to make it. I would have to render a report that would earn him at least twenty-five hours on the area, maybe worse. It would be at least a second-class board following quickly on the heels of his big slug from the summer. He would be kicked out.

I didn't want to do it. I was torn. Why the hell did I have to be the guy who was on CQ for this? And what the hell was Bill thinking? How stupid can you be? I started to get angry. Realizing that I was pacing around his room, I left and headed for the company orderly room.

I looked at my watch again. It was 0008 hours. After taps, he still wasn't there. I suddenly remembered a brief conversation Bill and I had had on the way back from the colonel's.

"So, you got the midnight cowboy on Friday, huh?"

"Yeah. Sucks."

He had consoled me for a few minutes and then laughed about Karl being gone this weekend for the Math Team trip. The knot in my stomach grew larger. Had he planned this? If so, what had he thought I would do?

I got to the orderly room and sat down at the desk, then looked at the accountability report I had yet to fill it out. The clock on the wall said 0009. At that moment every company across the Corps was calling in their reports. I had a couple of minutes but not more than that. I stood up and walked back toward Bill's room, even though I knew he still wasn't there.

"Shit," I said to myself, standing in the middle of the room. Bill had taken a huge slug for not turning me in over the summer. Period. Now I had to decide if I was going to hit him with another one.

Or tell a lie and break the honor code.

I walked back to the orderly room. The phone was ringing. I was sure it was Central Guard Room calling to get our accountability report. I let it ring. They would call back. I started to think about how I would explain this to Bill. *I know you took a slug protecting me, but I'm sorry. I had to turn you in. The alternative was to lie and render a false report.* I was starting to get angry. "Fucking dumbass."

The phone started ringing again. I might as well get it over with. I picked up the receiver. "Echo Company, Fourth Regiment, Cadet Avery speaking. May I help you, sir or ma'am?"

"What the hell, Avery? We need your accountability report. All the other companies have reported in."

"Yeah. Sorry. I was pulled into something for a few minutes. . . . Uh, we're good. All accounted for here."

"All right. Good night."

"Yeah. Good night."

I hung up the phone but couldn't lift my hand off the receiver. I was paralyzed. I wanted to take it back. I had just lied—without hesitation. On an official report. I felt faint. Terrified. What the hell had I just done?

I paced around for a few minutes and then walked over to the window, opened it, and stared outside. It was freezing, and ice clung to the sill. The window looked out onto North Area; everything was still, other than a light flurry of snow. My mind raced. I was at once ashamed of myself and enraged at Bill. Wherever he was right now, he knew exactly the position he had put me in.

Sitting down at the orderly desk, I put my head in my hands. I couldn't believe what had just happened. I had been winding myself up for a difficult conversation with Bill, but when the phone rang, I'd told a lie rather than turn in my friend. I focused on the instant I had told the lie. There had been no decision process. It had simply happened. *What does that mean? Am I simply a liar?* I shook my head and stood up. It was hard to be still when my mind was bouncing around like this. I closed the window and stepped into the hallway. I begin to quietly walk laps, waiting for Bill to get back.

An hour later, the repetitious walking had settled my mind from a racing, emergency condition to a low-grade, functioning panic mode. I went back to the orderly room and grabbed the clipboard. I walked down six flights of stairs to inspect the company trunk room. I recorded it as secure and walked like a zombie back up the stairs toward the orderly room. My brain was sliding off two hours' worth of adrenaline. I felt a hard crash coming on.

Bill was sitting at the orderly desk when I got back. He looked at me and smiled. The clock behind him said 0235.

I hung the clipboard back in its spot and sat down in the chair across the desk from him. I had been obsessed with this moment for the past two hours. Now he was back. I was exhausted and sad.

"Look. I'm sure you're pissed at me, but I've been locked up for over three months. I needed this badly, and if I had told you what I was going to do, you would have tried to talk me out of it. You would have gone into your worried mode, and from what I can tell, we're cool, right? No one the wiser." He leaned forward and winked at me. "Got to love math camp, baby! Am I right?"

My vision narrowed with rage, and I stammered to get the words out. "What the hell? Are you out of your fucking mind? I can't believe you did that to me!" I tried to keep my voice down so as not to wake anyone. My words came out in an angry hiss. I was standing now, leaning over the orderly desk, jabbing my finger into Bill's chest.

"Whoa, whoa, whoa!" Bill leaned back in his chair to get away from my finger and my spit. He was startled. "Sam. Hey, Sam, spin down. Let's talk about this."

He stood up behind the desk and reached out to my shoulder. Tears were streaming down my face now, and that enraged me. I punched Bill in the nose as hard as I could. He fell backward over the chair and landed on the trash can. It skidded loudly across the room. I didn't care who woke up now. My fate was sealed. I would be back home in Charlotte in a few weeks. I would be branded a liar. I would be kicked out of West Point. I was going to punish Bill Cooper. I leapt around the desk and was on him. He tried to fight back, but he was on his back. I had my knee in his sternum. My blows landed hard on his face. I bawled like a baby.

Someone tackled me. I fought. I wanted to get back on top of Bill and continue hitting him in the face. Someone slapped me. I saw stars. Another hard slap. I realized I was in the orderly room. The Guru was standing in front of me, his hand gripping my shirt in the middle of my chest. He reached back to slap me again.

"Guru," I panted, "I'm good."

"You sure?"

"Yeah. I'm done."

Across the room, Zack knelt over Bill, whose nose was bleeding. Zack wore only his cadet robe. He looked scared.

"Cadet Dempsey, go change into your class uniform. I would like for you to relieve Cadet Avery."

"Roger that, Guru. I'll be right back." He helped Bill stand up.

"Thank you. It's only for an hour or so, to give Avery here time to clean up and get his wits back about him."

Bill was standing on his own strength now, holding a cleaning rag to his nose. Zack looked at me with obvious concern, then darted out.

"Cooper, I recommend you leave now."

"Okay, Guru. I just—"

"I didn't say speak. I said leave." There was an edge to the Guru's voice I had not heard even as a plebe.

I watched Bill as he left. He stared fiercely back at me until he was out of the room. When he disappeared around the corner, my head sagged, my chin falling to my chest. I was glad I wasn't crying anymore.

The Guru slowly loosened his grip on my shirt and cautiously let his hand return to his side. His knees were still slightly bent, in a ready stance.

"I mean it, Guru. I'm done. I'm not going to run after him."

"Okay. Good. Go shower, change your uniform, and return." His voice had that same edge he'd used with Bill. I didn't have the will to argue with him. "I'll wait here for Cadet Dempsey to return. When you're ready to resume your post, you will swing by my room first. Do you understand?"

"Yes."

The rest of the night took forever to pass. The shower helped to clear my head, but with the clarity, my mind just burned hotter. I swung by the Guru's room first, as instructed. He said simply, "Hold your mud, Avery. I don't know what happened, and I don't want to know, but hold your fucking mud."

"Sam, what the hell happened between you two?" Zack asked when I relieved him. "I thought you were going to kill him."

"Let it go, Zack."

He persisted. I shook my head. "If our friendship means anything, drop it."

I spent the rest of the night with my head in my hands. I'd lied. I'd falsified an official report. I expected that within a day or two, they would figure it out. Eifer would come walking down the hall to find me and escort me to the honor committee for a perfunctory hearing. I would be excoriated for the liar I was, summarily found guilty, and expelled that day.

I was baffled and enraged by Bill. I felt betrayed and manipulated, which made me feel stupid and sad, which made me hate myself for not possessing the strength to do what I should have done. I should have recorded him as absent from room check and let the process work itself out. It shouldn't have been my problem. It would not have been my fault if he'd gotten hammered and expelled. But he had taken a slug for me. He had weathered more heat than I probably could have and still stuck to his commitment to me as a friend, and he'd never gotten mad at me. Even when he was walking the area in the freezing rain in November for hours, he'd never uttered a single cross word. He'd sucked it up. He'd lived by his code, but was his code then to manipulate and take advantage of his good friends? What kind of a fucked-up code was that?

And so it went for hours.

Around 0530, the Corps began to wake. The first sign was flushing toilets. Singles at first, widely spaced and some far off, but soon they were firing off in groups of twos and threes, followed by the rush of showers. Since it was a Saturday and there was no morning accountability formation, this awakening was a more gradual and staccato process than it would be on a weekday, when the barracks toilets flushed about five thousand times in a twenty-minute window. Proof enough that West Point knows how to train engineers.

As 0630 approached, I sat and stared at my duty log. In the middle of the page read a simple entry: "0008: Company all accounted for." I picked up my pen to draw a line through it and correct the report.

"Hey, Sam, good morning," said Emily as she walked into the orderly room to relieve me. "How was midnight cowboy?"

I dropped the pen and grabbed my stuff. "Same old."

When I got back to my room, I quietly kicked off my shoes and lay down on my bunk. Steven was still sleeping. I was suddenly exhausted and fell asleep, too.

✦ ✦ ✦

I slept until noon and woke up disoriented. Steven was not in the room, and it took me minutes to figure out where I was. By the time I had reoriented myself, panic and anger were welling up inside me. My class uniform was damp from nap sweat. I quickly took my clothes off, put on my cadet robe, and went to shower. When I got back to the room, Bill was waiting for me. He sat on my bunk like it was a church pew.

"Don't hit me," he said with a wan smile. His nose was scratched and bruised, and he had cotton stuffed into one nostril. His eyes were puffy but didn't seem blackened.

I ignored him and started to get dressed, stepping slowly into my gray cadet trousers.

"Sam, I'm sorry. I probably should have told you what I was going to do. I see now you don't appreciate not having been in the loop, and I get that."

"You think I don't appreciate being left out of the loop?" I asked angrily. "Are you kidding me? You think that is what this is about?"

"Sam, I get it. I'm trying to apologize here. I'm sorry!"

"For what?"

"Like I said, I should have told you what I was planning."

"This is not about me feeling left out, you selfish idiot!" I shook my head in disbelief and jerked my white undershirt over my head.

"What are you talking about?"

"Bill, I lied to cover for you," I whispered viciously.

"I know. I'm grateful."

"Are you serious? Don't you know what that means?"

"Sam, it means you're a good friend—like I said, I'm grateful."

"I lied!" I repeated loudly.

"Keep your voice down, idiot."

I was breathing heavily now. He suddenly seemed alien to me. "Do you realize I am a West Point cadet?"

"That's why I'm telling you to keep your voice down!"

"I can't believe you put me in that position!" I was close to crying again. My body language must have communicated something else, because Bill stood up from my bunk and held his hands up, palms down.

"Sam, easy. Don't fucking go off on me again. I'm trying to talk this out with you. Should I come back later?"

I remembered the Guru's admonition to hold my mud. I kept it under control. Barely. "No. I don't ever need to see you again. There is nothing for us to talk about. I fucking hate you." I grabbed my black shoes and sat down at my desk to put them on.

"What is your problem?"

"I broke the honor code for you."

"I know you did, and I said thank you, and we got away with it. So what is the big deal?"

I regarded him blankly and then looked down to try to focus on my shoelaces rather than my rage. I tried to ignore his voice.

"Sam, I've told you a hundred times, this place is not the army, not even close. Ask your precious sponsor Colonel Krieger if I'm right!" He was indignant now. He closed the space between us in deliberate steps and continued: "I happily play all the fucking reindeer games here because that is the way it is. I don't complain. I certainly don't cry, and, as you well know, I don't rat out friends. Period!"

I stood up and faced him. "Well, I guess we all proved last night that I don't, either."

"That's right. You don't, but don't expect me to be grateful to you for giving me the minimum fucking respect I deserve after everything I've been through for you!"

"Finally, I'm glad you said it. You know I didn't ask you to do that."

"You didn't have to."

"And I certainly didn't ask you to lie for me."

"Well, I would have."

"What?"

"For you, Sam? Of course!"

"I would never ask you to do that."

"I don't even know what we're fighting about. We got away with it. Other than your tantrum, which we now have to explain away . . ." He pointed at his face. "It's over. Done."

"I'm not so sure." I stepped past him to my closet.

"What? Let me guess. You feel guilty. Is that what this is about?"

He calmed down incrementally, as if a piece of a puzzle had snapped into place. I took my dress gray top from its hanger.

"Sam, in the army you have to make choices between honor"—he made air quotes around the word—"and friends every day."

"I get it, Bill. I'm a big boy. I'll be fine with that, and I understand now that you don't give a shit about honor."

"Sam, that is not at all what I am saying. Why do you have to be such a drama queen?"

I raised my hand to shut him up. "You don't give a shit about *my* honor."

"Sam."

"You didn't ask. You chose." I spoke slowly as I donned my dress gray top. "You chose your pleasure over my honor. Despite our being friends, I didn't even rate a conversation."

We stood quietly for a few seconds as the air ran out of our friendship. "I can't blame you for my decision, but I can't forgive you for putting me in that situation."

His head tilted slightly as he regarded me, and then he looked at the floor and took a deep breath. "I'm sorry."

"Me, too."

"So, what happens now?"

"You're going to leave my room."

"You're not going to do anything stupid, are you?"

"I honestly don't know."

I heard him quietly shut the door as he left, and I put my head in my hands.

Exam week passed slowly. When I wasn't studying, I was rerunning the moral calculus in my head, over and over, trying to find a solution that made me a not terrible person.

Steven was a good roommate during that time. He could tell something bad had happened that night that was worse than a few thrown punches, but he never asked me about it. For the most part, the other guys gave Bill and me space as well.

The most useful advice came from the Guru halfway through exam week, half an hour before taps.

"I said, Cadet Avery!" he called loudly from a few feet behind me in the hallway.

"Sorry, I didn't hear you."

"That is apparent. I said your name three times." He was returning from the showers wearing his trademark robe, towel over his right shoulder and toothbrush sticking out of his breast pocket. "What's going on in there?" He tapped his finger on my head.

"Exam week."

"Bullshit." He crossed his arms.

"I'm working through some shit, Guru."

He grabbed my arm as I turned to leave. "I have no idea what's really going on, but my strong sense is that it has something to do with what happened last week while you were the midnight cowboy."

I stared at the ground.

"Sam, look at me. Hold your mud. Go home for Christmas. Try to relax. Come back in January and deal with what you need to deal with then. I don't know what you're trying to work through right now, but your process doesn't seem to be helping." He winked and walked back to his room.

Having no better course of action, I followed the Guru's advice. I figured I could turn myself in come January. I staggered through exams and onto an Eastern Air Lines flight out of Newark, back to Charlotte.

FIFTEEN

THE TASK FORCE WAS POINTING AT A TIME ON TARGET of 2200 hours. Moonrise was shortly after midnight and, as always, we wanted the illumination to be at a minimum when we struck. It was exactly the right tactic for the hit on the HVT, and it totally screwed our mission to get the Guru.

I assigned Pete as pilot in command of the cas-evac bird and slotted myself as his copilot. It was a crew assignment that no one would think twice about, putting the rusty old lieutenant colonel on the simplest piece of the mission. But I still was a little nervous as I posted the assignments. Pete and I spoke quietly as we left the planning cell after the air mission briefing.

"Any thoughts?" Pete asked me.

"Only one."

"What's that?"

"Get the Guru after the Abdul-Ahad hit."

Pete thought about it. "It could work, as long as we hit the fat cow to top off our fuel first."

"That's what I was thinking. Top off, fly back and get Turtle and the team, then hit Tal Afar."

"That could do it, especially since you assigned us to the cas evac. We'd never be able to pull it off if we were in the fat cow. Even so, if there are casualties, we're screwed. We'd be flying to Baghdad with wounded and have no way to know when we'd be done."

I just nodded. "I need to grab the rest of my gear from the TOC. I'll see you at the aircraft."

Pete was right. If the hit on the HVT went bad, we were done. I didn't see another way, though. Zack agreed.

"I don't like it, but I think it will work," he said when I called him.

"It's the best I can do."

"Okay. Let's go with it. Same LZ. We'll just plan on seeing you a lot later. If you get activated as cas evac, we'll improvise a ground op."

I didn't say anything back to that, because if it happened, it would be a disaster.

"Okay, Sam, good luck. See you on the PZ."

I stepped into the TOC to grab the rest of my gear and walked right into Rear Admiral Brick.

"Avery. You're back."

"Yes, sir, just grabbing my gear for tonight."

"May I speak with you for a minute in my office?"

"Can it wait, sir? I'm in a bit of a rush."

"No. It can't."

He walked to his office. I followed and shut the door behind myself.

He gestured at a folding table covered with maps and target diagrams and sat at one end. I sat at the other.

"Where were you today?"

"Reconnecting with a couple classmates."

"West Point guys?"

"Yes, sir."

"How did they know you were here?"

"One of them is with Delta on a temporary assignment at the embassy. He seems to know everything."

Brick looked at me, not smiling.

"That so?"

"Yes, sir." I smiled back at him nonchalantly.

"And the other guy?"

"Sir?"

"You said you linked up with 'a couple' of classmates. Who was the other guy?"

"He's a PMC now. Actually, he owns the company. He's working a contract down at the embassy. They linked up, thought of me, and decided to come say hi."

"Decided to drive a couple hundred miles through ISIS-infested territory to say 'Hi'?"

"They actually flew up on a Little Bird."

"That's an expensive reunion."

"Like I said, he owns the company. They'll be fine." I was getting irritated. "Is there a problem here, sir?"

"I guess I'm old-fashioned, Avery. When my battle captain leaves the TOC for a couple hours without telling me, my feelings get hurt. When my feelings get hurt, I can be a real dick."

"There was nothing going on, and Major Obrien took over for me. We had coms with each other the whole time, but I'll keep that in mind going forward, sir."

Brick leaned back in his chair. "Look, Avery, I don't mind you leaving to link up with old classmates. I would do the same if any of my Annapolis buddies were in reach. But I like being in the loop."

I nodded. I didn't have time for this.

The admiral looked back at me in silence. Brick and I had been at MacDill together for a few years. We were not friends but were familiar. He seemed like a good officer to me but a little uptight. This mission, in particular, had him wound up and on edge; that was understandable. We were the only JSOC quick reaction force in-theater, which meant his role as our commander was extremely high-visibility. He was on the secure video conference back to MacDill and Washington, D.C., several times a day, updating them on our aircraft maintenance status and aircrew readiness. When we flew off with one of his Chinooks, it was going to be a very high-level embarrassment that he wasn't going to take well at all. I didn't want to think about that right now.

"We done here, sir?"

"Actually, no. There is one more thing. Your promotion board results came in. You got picked up for colonel." He actually smiled. "Congratula-tions."

"Thank you, sir." I couldn't believe it. Today of all days.

"You don't look happy."

"No, sir. I mean, yes, sir. I am happy, just surprised. I wasn't expect-ing to hear today."

The admiral stood up and extended his hand. "Well, congratulations anyway, Avery."

I stood up and shook his hand. I couldn't believe the timing.

"Sir, you heard anything about a kidnapped American?"

"Which one? You know we're tracking about half a dozen now."

"A new one. A recent one in the Mosul area."

"No. Why?"

"My buddies heard a rumor down at the embassy."

"It doesn't surprise me, but if there were any Americans in that area recently, they were idiots. They've probably had their heads chopped off already. I'm sure we'll see the video in a week or so."

SIXTEEN

BY MARCH, IT WAS CLEAR THAT CAPTAIN EIFER HAD SET his sights on the Guru. The captain's campaign against E4 seemed to have evolved into one directed at him in particular. He was getting dinged on a regular basis. Insufficiently shined hat brass at breakfast formation. Shoes improperly spaced beneath the bed during class. Improperly cleaned mirror and sink. The minor offenses mounted as the scrutiny increased. Captain Eifer was taking advantage of the fact that no one was perfect, and if you inspected any cadet often enough, you would find the imperfections. The Guru took it in stride.

"Cadet Morris, tell me about the elections in Russia!" the Guru said cheerfully as he approached breakfast formation.

"Sir, today in the *New York Times* it was reported that Soviet voters relished their freest elections in more than seventy years, choosing a new national Congress of Deputies. Boris N. Yeltsin, the deposed Moscow Communist Party leader, campaigned against party privileges and for greater political pluralism. Mr. Yeltsin appears to have beaten the candidate backed by the Moscow party machine."

"Interesting, eh, Cadet Morris?"

"Yes, sir."

"The first nationwide election since 1917. You see, cadets, there is hope!" People within earshot of the Guru's comments smiled and gave each other the "that crazy Guru" roll of their eyes. But as I watched him walk to his spot in formation, I noted that his hair was shorter than usual, his shoes were highly shined, and his gait was measured, not jaunty. I saw in these cues Eifer's quarry, not the most cavalier cadet in the Corps. The Guru was under much more strain than he was letting on.

That morning, I joined him for coffee. I found the post-breakfast time in the mess hall one of the most peaceful respites in my cadet day. It was strange, considering the scope and frenzy of the activity that kicks off instantly at the official close of the meal. The mess hall orderlies begin to reset the vast feeding machine for the lunch meal, only about five hours away. Four thousand dirty place settings and hundreds of serving dishes must get off the tables and into the massive dishwashing operation while fresh replacements are deployed. Giant mixing bowls, basters, dough scrapers, cooking sheets, and other oversized utensils are put to work as the ovens and grills are lit.

Still, as a cadet sits with coffee after a meal, the furiously clanking dishes, scraping chairs, and hustling orderlies somehow recede. The massive space is full of noise and activity, but sitting at the table is quiet and peaceful. The window of calm lasts only about fifteen minutes, though, because the orderlies start slamming clean plates and silverware down on the table, signaling that any remaining cadets have worn out their welcome. It's nice while it lasts.

After breakfast, I walked over to the Guru's table and sat down next to him. He looked straight ahead, not acknowledging my presence.

"What do you want, Avery?"

"Nothing. Just checking in."

He smiled. "Are you actually checking to see if I'm doing all right?"

"I guess."

He nodded.

"I'm fine. It does seem I have become Eifer's special project, but no matter. It is the middle of March, and I graduate in about two and a half months. I could stand on my head for the rest of my time here if I had to."

"I know that, Guru. I just think it would suck to have that kind of constant heat."

"It's not much fun, but, to be honest, I'm more worried about E4."

"What do you mean?"

"I've heard rumors of a scramble."

My heart sank. "Scrambling" was an old academy practice of blowing up a cadet class after yearling year and reassigning each cadet randomly to a new company. It hadn't happened in a long time, decades probably. It was constantly rumored to be under serious consideration, particularly as company personalities had so drastically diverged. Like E4, some companies were on trajectories the tactical department disproved of. To me, A1 seemed like it belonged to a foreign military organization. I know those cadets felt the same about E4.

"What do you mean, rumors?"

"I have my sources," he said without irony or mirth. "Eifer is making a big argument for it to the commandant. He thinks it's the only way to bring all of the cadet companies to a uniform level of excellence."

Scrambling would mean that I'd lose Zack, Creighton, Turtle, and everyone else. We would be scattered to the four corners of the Corps. I shook my head; I couldn't think about this right now.

The Guru could see my concern. "It's not a done deal yet, Avery. We just need a quiet end of the year, and we should be fine." He seemed unconvinced himself.

"I'm sorry I mentioned it," he said. "By the way, I can't help but notice that you and Bill Cooper don't seem to be on great terms."

"You're just a laugh a minute these days, Guru."

I didn't know what else to say. Christmas leave had actually ratcheted up my anger at Bill and my guilt at what I had done. Bill and I had still not spoken since our fight.

"Now, that is a sad face. You should see yourself."

"Well, I'm sure we'll patch it up after a while."

"Real convincing. I hope you guys do patch it up. Good friends are hard to find, Avery. Especially here."

Good friends wouldn't have done to me what he did, I thought. I looked at the Guru and began to explain what had really happened that night but stopped myself as soon as my mouth opened.

"My Lord, Avery, you had better make peace with whatever is bothering you. Pass me the coffee, will you?"

He warmed up his cup and resumed staring straight ahead. I did the same.

A bowl of silverware clanged as it landed at the other end of the table. The mess hall orderly glared at us as she moved to her next station.

"Well, Avery . . . onward." The Guru stood up, put on his gray overcoat, and moved on.

✦ ✦ ✦

"What is your friend Bill up to?" asked Colonel Krieger late the next week as he handed me a bratwurst. It was Saturday afternoon, and he had invited me up for a grill. When we'd spoken briefly on the phone, he'd made a point of telling me that Bill was welcome to join us. I had not mentioned it to Bill.

"Same old." We left the grill and I followed the colonel back inside. We sat in their living room and devoured our bratwurst.

"He seemed like a good kid to me."

"Yeah," I said as I played up the fact that I had just taken a big bite. I had zero desire to talk about Bill.

Colonel Krieger shook his head. "I thought they taught you knuckleheads not to take big bites. The Corps has." He winked.

"You have no idea, sir."

"Oh, come on, Sam—you've got about six weeks left in yearling year and then a big chunk of leave coming your way, and it's all downhill from there."

"Yes, sir. All downhill. For two more years."

"Did you get your final assignment for the summer?"

"Yes, sir. Airborne School after graduation, then leave, and then Drill Cadet Leadership Training."

"Excellent. Where are you doing DCLT?"

"Fort Benning."

"A Fort Benning summer!" He chuckled. "If I didn't know better, I'd think you were an aspiring infantryman."

I rolled my eyes and replied, "No, sir. I put the bid in for Benning DCLT because it's close to home."

"Good thinking. What are you doing for leave?" He was genuinely excited.

"Europe, sir."

"Now we're talking!" He just about came out of his chair in excitement. "Where?"

"Germany and Austria. I've always wanted to see the Berlin Wall. I'm going to explore Berlin for a couple of days and then do some hiking in Austria. Clear my head for a while."

"Outstanding. You know, a classmate of mine is with the Berlin Brigade right now. JAG Corps. If you want, I can give you his contact info. Great guy!"

Involuntarily, I shook my head. The colonel leaned back in his chair.

"Only if you want."

"Honestly, sir, a commissioned officer is the last person I'd want to hang out with over there. I really want to get off the grid."

He took a swig. "Sure. I get it, son. When I was a cadet, I felt the same way."

We sat in silence. I didn't know how to talk about it; I felt like a jerk. The colonel quietly watched the TV, giving me space.

"I'm sorry, sir. It's been a long year. I don't have a problem with officers. To be honest, it's my own classmates that have worn on me lately."

"It's okay, Sam, really." He held his hand up to stop my babbling and continued: "I don't take it personally. It's the never-ending cycle. Plebes are scared. Yearlings are depressed. Cows are mad, and firsties are just excited to graduate.

"You're an end-of-year yearling. Everything is rubbing you the wrong way. You need to get the hell out of here for a while." He chuckled. "It's such a funny thing."

"What's that, sir?"

"You guys start to drive each other crazy after a while. The stakes get so high. The differences between each of you seem so stark. The truth is, by the time you graduate, you guys are nearly identical."

"I don't like the sound of that."

"I'm sure you don't right now, but, trust me, it's like your DNA has been spliced with all of your classmates'. At this point, there is only about a two percent difference between any of you, even between the best and worst cadets. Right now, that two percent makes all the difference. It causes friction; it's all you guys focus on while you swim around chafing each other in the fishbowl. After graduation, it's that ninety-eight percent commonality that you will seek out. For the rest of your life, long after you take your uniform off, you will feel more at ease, more understood by other old grads than anyone else in your life. All of that rubbing will be distant memories."

I didn't know what to say.

"I swear. I don't know why I bother," he added, winking to let me know he understood.

After dinner, I said good night to the colonel and his wife and declined their offer of a ride back to the barracks. It was a crisp spring evening, and it felt good to walk. As I passed the cadet cemetery, I realized how desperate I was for the summer to start. The feeling had come into focus at Colonel Krieger's house and was now heavy upon me. The secret shame I had been swallowing for half the year was still heavy. So, too, was the feeling of loss and anger between Bill and me. Ladle on top of that the standard comic opera and pedantic idiocy of cadet life, and I felt like I was suffocating.

It was getting close to 1800 hours when I took a right on Jefferson Road, the last stretch to the barracks. I walked by the supe's quarters and was soon passing MacArthur's statue. I paused and looked to the northeast, back over the Plain toward the Hudson River. It was a perfect evening, and, reluctantly, I admitted to myself that West Point would be a lovely place to visit. Zack greeted me breathlessly when I got back to the company.

"Captain Eifer and the Guru just got into it. Holy shit, Sam! It was incredible. I think the Guru is fucked!"

✦ ✦ ✦

For the next few days, E4 tried to digest the earthshaking news. The Guru had been suspended.

His disciplinary cycle had been one of the quickest anyone had ever seen. Monday morning at 0800 hours, the Guru was in Eifer's office. The regimental board was held Tuesday morning. On Wednesday, his suspension was finalized.

The demerits and area tours the Guru had racked up under Captain Eifer's grinding second-semester campaign had combined with

Saturday's incident of "gross disrespect" to create a narrative that doomed him.

"You can't get slugged that close to graduation," I said to Zack later as we studied for exams. "The Guru knows that." A cadet could not graduate with outstanding area tours. His ledger had to be clean. As a result, there was a practical limit to the size slug you could take as a second-semester firstie and still graduate. This ceiling ratcheted down as the academic year expired. During grad week, there was always a platoon or more of firsties madly walking off their final hours. There was a maximum to how much a cadet was allowed to walk off, though, and one had to get authorization to walk off more than that. This approval hurdle was an effective way to decide who could graduate. I was sure the Guru had requested to serve his tours prior to graduation, and I was just as sure Eifer had denied the request with pleasure.

"You should have heard him go after Eifer," Zack said. "I thought the captain was going to punch him."

"I bet the Guru wishes he did. I would slit my wrists if they pushed me back to a December grad."

"Knowing Eifer and how much he hates the Guru, I bet he pushed to have him kicked out completely."

"I'm sure you're right."

"They are not going to do that to someone with the Guru's pedigree: a third-generation legacy whose grandfather fought in World War II and father fought in Vietnam."

"I thought the Guru had this place totally figured out. I can't believe he let himself get out of control like that."

"Sam, this place gets to everybody. Period."

SEVENTEEN

AFTER PREFLIGHT, PETE SMOKED A BACKWOODS CIGAR and we briefed the three crew members on the follow-on mission we would attempt if we had the chance. Pete had done a good job of crew selection; they were all in. Pete's charisma and his relationship with them combined with the righteousness of our cause to make our bootleg mission irresistible. When we were done, Staff Sergeant Crawford, 458's flight engineer, smiled and said, "Sounds like a big fucking hip shoot to me."

Crawford was a muscular twenty-nine-year-old from Ohio. Having joined the army straight out of high school, he was a veteran of over a decade of war and had been crewing Golf model Chinooks for eight of those years. As a longtime crew member in the 160th, Crawford was used to missions that were planned down to the gnat's ass, much like the one we were about to undertake to get Abdul-Ahad. These tightly orchestrated operations involved multiple agencies internal and external to SOCOM and timelines that were planned and executed to the standard of plus or minus thirty seconds.

"That's right, Crawford."

"Cool. I love a good hip shoot," he said genuinely.

As the flight engineer on 458, Crawford was personally responsible for her readiness at all times and was in command of the crew chiefs, Sergeant Thomas and Sergeant Wilson. It takes years to become a Chinook flight engineer. The path typically involves working one's way up from ground-based aircraft mechanic duties to crew chief to, finally, full flight engineer. When an FE is assigned to an aircraft, it is like adopting a child. All aspects of the care and feeding of that bird fall to him. The rhythm of his life is dictated by the health and status of his Chinook. The FE is at the aircraft hours before the pilots show up and leaves hours after the pilots have left. It causes him physical pain when his bird is unable to fly. FEs get nervous when the less proficient pilots are at the controls of their Chinooks. Pete, being the pilot in command, had to make Crawford feel good. I'm sure having me on the controls as well did not.

I stepped past Pete into 458 and walked up to the cockpit alone as he and the rest of the crew sat on the ramp. I prepped my helmet, snapping the night-vision goggles into place and then resting it on the cyclic. I placed my M4 next to the seat on the outside of the armor panel and laid my kneeboard and checklists on the instrument console.

Looking at the cockpit, I tried not to think about how long it had been since I had actually been on the controls for a mission like this.

I turned and surveyed the dark aircraft. The left and right front mini-guns had been swung to their stowed position on their mounting arms. They rested with their barrels pointing down and full ammo cans strapped to the floor around them. Looking aft through the dark aircraft toward the open ramp, I could see Pete and the crew silhouetted against the desert airfield. Pete stood on the tarmac facing the guys, who sat on the ramp. His cigar cast a soft red glow over his face every time he pulled on it. As he took the next pull, I realized that he was looking at me and shaking his head. He knew what I was doing and thought it was ridiculous. He always had.

I didn't care. Standing just outside of the cockpit facing aft, I closed my eyes.

Every pilot will tell you that aircraft have personalities. No two are alike even among identical models. Somehow the sum of all of the microvariations in each of the hundreds of thousands of component pieces that make up the aircraft stack up to a unique performance signature. You learn early on in a unit how each tail number performs. Which one is a dog. Which one is spry. Which one handles better than all the rest.

When it comes to Chinooks, my belief goes further. Chinooks have more than personalities; they have old warrior souls. They've carried scared men into battle and carried dead men out. They've seen pilots and crewmen be brave, skillful, bold, stupid, incompetent, and cowardly. They've been shot, burned, pranged, bounced, and crashed. Chinook 458 had seen a lot of this herself, and I'm not talking about the last fourteen years. I am talking about the last fifty.

In 1962, the army began taking delivery of what would eventually number 349 A model Chinooks. The fledglings did not get much time to acclimate to their role. By 1965, they were fighting in Vietnam. Before the war was over, 314 of the original A model aircraft had served in Vietnam. Every one had been damaged in combat. Seventy-nine were lost, and they'd taken more than one hundred crew members with them. Many more crew members and soldiers were killed and wounded on the aircraft that survived the war.

After Vietnam, the tired A model Chinooks returned to the States and to bases in Europe with their units. They continued to fly until the early 1980s, when, after twenty years of service, they were sent to the Boeing plant in Philadelphia to be given new life. Stripped down to their metal ribs and studs, the aircraft were overhauled. Every major system was upgraded in a process that yielded aircraft that were brand-new in the eyes of the army. The factory even zeroed out the flight hours and gave the helicopters new tail numbers.

But they weren't new. Their bones and souls were old.

The reincarnated D model Chinooks were then sent out to army units around the world, where they worked for two decades. They saw combat again in the Second Gulf War and duty in places like Haiti and Bosnia.

Then, shortly after 9/11, they were reincarnated once more. This time the extensive process yielded G models with glass cockpits, aerial refuel probes, terrain-following radar, and global communication and navigation capabilities. Flight times were again zeroed out. New tail numbers assigned.

But they had the same old bones. The same old souls.

Boeing started to deliver the reincarnated Golf model Chinooks to us in 2004. Each time they did, I would call a friend at Boeing and get the history of the tail number. I was fascinated. I just liked to know.

Chinook 458 had served eight years in Vietnam as an A model, and from what I could determine from the accounts of battles and missions, she had seen the death of about half a dozen men on her airframe, both aircrew and soldiers. Then she'd returned to combat in the First Gulf War as a D model and had taken part in the largest air assault operation in history. She'd been reborn as a G model in 2005 and had been fighting with us ever since. She'd been serving for over five decades.

Years ago, I had developed the habit before each mission of closing my eyes and quietly acknowledging to the aircraft that she had been flying and fighting longer than I had been alive. That she had seen and done a lot more than me. Then I'd let my Chinook know I was going to do my best to get her, the aircrew, and the soldiers on the flight back unharmed, or if not unharmed, then at least alive, and that I didn't have a right to ask, but if she could pitch in where she needed to, apply what she had learned, help me be a good pilot, I'd be grateful.

I wrapped up this pre-mission session with a little extra. I let her know that we wouldn't have any help on this one. No wingmen. No medevac. No close air support. So we both needed to be as good as possible. Finally, I told her that this would be my last run, no matter what. And that I would miss her.

Lucky ritual complete, I joined the others on the ramp. It was almost time to strap in.

EIGHTEEN

I WENT BY THE GURU'S ROOM THE EVENING BEFORE HE left. The door was open, and I walked slowly in, knocking a couple times as I did. He wasn't there. The room was spotless and oddly spacious. All of the Guru's uniforms, books, and gear had been removed. There was a small stack of books on what had been the Guru's desk. At the top was a class of 1964 *Bugle Notes;* it was dingy and beat-up but otherwise looked a lot like our class of 1991 edition. I picked it up and flipped through the pages. They were stiff and dirty.

"That was my father's."

"You startled me," I said, putting the *Bugle Notes* back down on the small pile.

"Stay alert, stay alive, Avery," he replied as he walked over, picked up the books, and put them into his backpack, except for the *Bugle Notes.* "We also still have my grandfather's *Bugle Notes.* Class of nineteen forty."

"He still alive?"

"Yep. Retired in Florida. My dad is not. He died in Vietnam." I knew his father had died in Vietnam. Everyone did.

I looked at him, not knowing what to say, but he wasn't looking at me. He was staring at his dad's *Bugle Notes*. He held the little book in his left hand and ran the fingers of his right hand along the pages like he was loosening up a deck of cards. As he did, I noticed that the stone was missing from his class ring. Instead of glistening faceted aquamarine, a gaping woundlike cavity yawned in the middle. I could see his finger through the hole. It was bruised. In fact, all of the fingers on his right hand were bruised and scratched.

"What happened, Guru?"

"I fucked up. I played right into his hands."

"I mean your ring. Your hand."

"Oh, when I found out my punishment, I had a moment. I punched the wall a few times." He smiled sadly. "The stone popped out."

"Did you find it?"

"Yes. Luckily. Aquamarine is not cheap."

"That's good. I bet any jeweler can snap it back in."

"I suppose so," he replied while holding his hand out at arm's length to look at his ring. "To tell you the truth, I'm starting to kind of like it."

I nodded.

"Let me be a lesson to you, Avery. I was right, of course. A mock turtleneck is a type of collared shirt, but it doesn't matter. I know better than to let a careerist prick like that get the best of me. I'm supposed to be smarter than that—the 'Guru,' right?"

I chuckled. I'd been surprised when Zack had told me what had happened. The Guru was leaving post on first-class privileges that Friday night and was stopped by Captain Eifer for being in improper civilian clothes. Cadets were supposed to always be in collared shirts. The Guru was wearing a mock turtleneck, and Captain Eifer did not accept it as proper. He wrote the Guru up for the infraction and told him to go change. The Guru refused. I thought it was a ridiculous hill for him to die for.

As I digested the events, I realized that Eifer had transgressed the Guru's sense of fairness. In the Guru's worldview, fairness was more important than right and wrong. For him, it was okay to be hammered for breaking the rules. That was fair. He never complained when he got slugged. He took it and walked it off. What's more, he didn't tolerate whining from cadets who got slugged for violating rules or standards. In that way, he and Creighton were in perfect sync. Unlike Creighton, however, in the Guru's universe it was okay to break the rules. It was fair—honorable, even, when done for the right reasons by a cadet willing to do his time. For Creighton, this kind of thinking was heresy. That night, in the Guru's mind, a mock fucking turtleneck was a collared fucking shirt. End of story. It didn't matter if it was Captain Eifer or the president. He was not going to accept unfair treatment. He was actually honor-bound not to accept it, especially not from Eifer.

As for Eifer, he saw an obvious violation by a cadet who had been on his list for some time and was now refusing a direct order. It was an outrage. It would be written up, and justice would be dispensed. Zack said that at the end of the episode, the Guru had lost it and started yelling at the captain. Eifer had smiled as if in thanks as he wrote down the further offense of disrespect.

"Well, at least you didn't get kicked out. You'll still graduate this year."

The Guru smiled. "Don't try to pump sunshine up my ass, Avery. You're no good at it." He looked at his father's *Bugle Notes* and continued: "I heard that my dad got into a lot of trouble as a cadet. He was almost a double-century man. He never got suspended, though. So, I got him there, right?"

"Right."

He nodded.

"How old were you when he died?"

"About two."

He hesitated for a moment and then put the *Bugle Notes* into his backpack.

I wondered if it was the absence of his father that had made Cadet Henry Stillmont into the Guru. The war robbed him of every son's ultimate source of approval. He had to rely on his own judgment, establish his own values, and find his own way almost as soon as he learned to walk. By the time he got to West Point, this self-reliant individualism was too ingrained to be stamped out. He would be his own cadet. Period. It was the academy's task to convince him of its ways.

"So where are you headed for your break? Florida?"

"Hell no, Avery. I am a mountain guy. I'm going home to Colorado, probably to hang out in Telluride."

"Really?" I asked with envy.

"Yeah. It won't suck, but it's only for six weeks. I have to pick a training event for the summer and then serve on a cadre team somewhere. I'm probably going to do Pathfinder School in late June. Then I'll be cadre at Fort Knox for the Armor Week rotations for the new yuks."

"Six weeks away from this place? Not a bad punishment."

"I should be graduating in four weeks, asshole."

"Right. Well . . . when do you head out?"

"I sign out after breakfast formation tomorrow. I think Eifer wants to do it like that so that everyone sees that he won." The Guru stared down at his feet. He looked sad.

"He didn't win, Guru."

"Neither did I."

At a loss for words, I just nodded.

"I really appreciate you stopping by, Sam. You were the first of your class I got to sink my teeth into, and, by God, I think you're turning out well. You're one of my favorites, Avery. I'm not ashamed to say it."

He held his hand out, and I shook it. "Keep your ducks in a row, Avery."

"You too, Guru."

"Too late for that, my friend."

✦ ✦ ✦

The next morning before breakfast, the Guru stood behind the company formation next to Captain Eifer. His suspension was effective, and he was no longer part of the company. The captain looked like a proud hunter standing next to a prized kill. Soon formation would be dismissed and we would march into the mess hall for breakfast; the Guru would sign the final paperwork and leave to serve his suspension. He looked despondent. Resigned to his fate.

Then he saw it.

A smile spread across the Guru's face. The regiment collectively gasped as we saw it, too: swinging prominently from the top of the flagpole in North Area was Captain Eifer's dreaded bicycle.

It squeaked against the metal pole as it swung slowly from side to side, hanging awkwardly by its rear wheel. It had not been treated gently. The frame was bent and the front wheel folded in half. A battle streamer tied to the handlebars flapped in the wind; the writing on it fluttered in and out of sight. "Eifer: Jealous you are not a grad? Fuck off and die!"

Captain Eifer appeared unruffled. Though he must have been boiling on the inside, he betrayed no hint of anger or embarrassment to the assembled Fourth Regiment. Knowing that a thousand pairs of eyes were studying him for the slightest evidence of emotion, he refused us any satisfaction. My respect for him reluctantly increased at that moment. He was saying, "Fuck you, too!" back to us with the only thing he had at the moment: his perfect military bearing. He stood resolutely while the regiment took accountability. When formation was over and the companies were dismissed, cadets gawked at the well-known bicycle and its blasphemous battle streamer as each company waited for its turn to march to breakfast. Then another surprise happened.

After rendering the report to battalion, our company commander did not give the company back to the first sergeant. Instead, as the rest of the regiment looked on, he marched us in a short left-hand square pattern that took us through Delta Company's area. It was obvious that he had coordinated with Delta's company commander, because those cadets were already standing out of our way, applauding.

After two more rapid left-turn commands, we were marching parallel with the barracks and the rear of the formation, where Eifer and the Guru still stood. I realized what we were doing. E4, the worst drilling company in the history of West Point, was passing in review for the Guru.

Realizing what was happening, Captain Eifer swiveled on his heels and walked to his office. The Guru stood. Astounded. The company staff rendered their salute, and then First Platoon executed their eyes right. The Guru returned their salute and lost it. He was crying and laughing at the same time. He raised his arms in a victory gesture as the rest of the company marched by and rendered honors.

"Unbowed, gentlemen!" he shouted. "I am unbowed! I will see you in August! Go naked! Go naked!"

Then, in just a moment, it was over. We continued on to the mess hall. The Guru turned and walked up the steps into Eifer's office and was gone.

The bike was down before lunch formation. No one knew who had hoisted it up there, of course, but I had my own theory. Turtle had taken Eifer's victory over the Guru personally and hard. Turtle considered himself to be the Guru's heir when it came to spirit missions. He was honor-bound to strike back and was also capable of the act. Though Turtle would never admit it to me, I was certain that the Guru had given him the map of the steam tunnels. Handed down to Wilcox by one of our E4 ancestors, it then passed from Wilcox to the Guru and, finally, to Turtle.

Gaining access to Eifer's office via a secret steam-tunnel link would have been easy enough, but Turtle would have needed help. Hoisting the beat-up bicycle frame to the top of the uniform flag was a two-man job, and I was sure Bill had been his second. Bill hated Eifer. He would have jumped at the opportunity. He had also been trained in spirit missions by Wilcox and the Guru, and there was no one in the company that Turtle trusted more.

Finally, this pair understood the unwritten rules of cadet justice. There is no coordination, no high fives or celebrating when done, no winking months later when the story comes up. If the karmic scales need balancing and you are able, you strike. Your buddies couldn't know anything about it because they would surely be asked, and direct questions and orders from commissioned officers cut through all cadet bullshit. No, when you saw the need and had the means to address something, you did it in secrecy. It was the right thing to do.

I never said anything, of course. That was my job. Having figured it out, I was to shut the fuck up. I joined in the regimental conversations about the bike, echoing every other cadet's questioning. No one knew who had done it, but we all knew in whose name it had been done.

NINETEEN

"**C**OLONEL AVERY?"

A voice calling my name from the darkness startled us. I was suddenly aware of footsteps approaching the aircraft.

Because of our illicit intentions, we were all on edge. Pete looked at me with questioning eyes. I stepped forward and prepared for a confrontation.

Sergeant Weber stepped out of the darkness, into the soft glow of the aircraft ramp. He was in full battle dress and carrying an M4 equipped with an M320 grenade launcher under the forward grip. He looked around at our group, smiled, and then addressed me: "Sergeant Weber reporting for duty, sir."

I stood mutely.

Crawford, faster on the uptake than I was, said, "Fucking A, Webs. And I thought you were just a staff weenie. We can always use another gunner. Welcome aboard."

Weber stepped past me onto the ramp and headed into the aircraft. I finally caught up.

"Wait a minute, Weber! What the hell are you doing?" I yelled. Some of the other aircraft had started their engines, and the airfield was getting noisy. My words were swallowed by the loud night.

Pete chuckled and walked toward the front of the aircraft. "Honestly, sir, I don't know how you consistently get this response out of people. Fucking pied piper. I'll be in the cockpit."

"Sergeant Weber, I'm talking to you!" I yelled.

I was now the only person standing at the end of the ramp. Thomas and Wilson, the other two crew chiefs, were walking to their stations outside the aircraft for engine start. Crawford was forward in the cabin with Pete.

"Damnit, Weber!" I yelled into the dark aircraft. "What are you doing?"

"I could ask you the same question, sir," he said, walking toward me.

He stopped at the end of the ramp and looked down at me. I spoke in a low voice: "Seriously, Weber. It's not going to be just the standard mission for us tonight. We have a follow-on mission that is, um . . . it's a volunteers-only thing. It's not exactly sanctioned. I can't let you come with us."

"I'm your driver, sir," he said flatly. "You're my responsibility."

"You don't even know what we're doing."

"I know you're throwing away full bird."

"You made the colonels list, sir?" asked Crawford loudly.

I saw Pete lean into the companionway from his seat and look back at me.

"That's enough, Sergeant Weber," I said as sternly as I could. "Get off the aircraft."

"I'm the pilot in command, sir," taunted Pete from the cockpit. "Weber is welcome on board."

Crawford chuckled. Weber smiled.

"I figure you've got your reasons, sir. It probably has something to do with the friends who came to see you this morning or with the secret meeting you went to without me this afternoon. I'd be better informed about our mission if you had included me."

"I'll brief you up, Webs," said Crawford. "First we get fucking Abdul, then it's a hip shoot to spring the colonel's buddy. There. You're all briefed up."

"Cool. Sounds like a good plan," Weber responded over his shoulder without breaking eye contact with me.

I shook my head. "Weber, get off that aircraft."

"Fuck you, sir. I've got your back," he said as he turned and walked into 458.

"Weber!"

"He said, 'Fuck you, sir,'" said Crawford, walking by me to take up his position for engine start.

"Come on, Colonel!" hollered Pete from the cockpit. "It's time to go!"

I stepped back up onto the ramp and into the aircraft. I glared impotently at Weber as I walked to the cockpit. I tried not to notice Pete laughing at me as I strapped in.

"'Colonel Avery' would have sounded good, sir."

"Shut up."

The first time I watched a Chinook run-up, I was disturbed. The rotor blades bounced and flailed as the large disks start to spin. They intermeshed spasmodically just inches over the fuselage, threatening to sever the synchronizing drive shaft that ran the length of the top of the aircraft like a delicate spinal cord. The landing gear compressed and skidded as the fuselage rocked and wallowed underneath the torque of the engines and the twin rotor hubs.

Inside the aircraft, the run-up felt worse than it looked. Everything was amplified once I was sitting in the nose of the long fuselage. The entire cockpit swayed left and right as the engines labored against the heavy rotor blades. A vertical bounce came and went and came back again as vibrations harmonized and then canceled each other while they worked their way through the airframe. It didn't inspire a lot of confidence.

Now, though, I love the idiosyncratic and bouncy ritual. It's like sitting inside a muscular athlete as she warms up. Stiff at first. Halting. Awkwardly working through hitches in her systems until she gets to speed. It's a short and predictable transition from flail to grace that I find comforting.

In thirty seconds, it was complete. The awkward machine had been replaced by a heaving warbird. Precise. Powerful. Waiting on the crew to catch up so she could start flying. As we worked through the final items on the checklist, I could almost hear her saying, "Come on. Hurry up. Let's go."

We moved quickly through the checklist and then repositioned to join the flight before takeoff. The three Black Hawks, call signs Outlaw 30, Outlaw 31, and Outlaw 32, were in lead, with the two Chinooks in trail. The fat cow's call sign for the mission was Bulldog 70. We were the last aircraft in the formation, call sign Bulldog 71.

At precisely 2040 hours, Outlaw 30 initiated takeoff, and in a blink, our flight of five was moving faster than a hundred miles an hour. The airfield faded away behind us. It felt good to be under way, even though it wasn't yet the mission I wanted to be flying. *Hang on just a little bit longer, Guru,* I thought. *We're coming.*

TWENTY

THE GRADUATION PARADE WAS A HOT ONE. THERE WERE no clouds above the Hudson River valley, and the sun pounded us.

I hung back during the recognition ceremony that followed as the plebes shook hands with the upperclassmen of E4. All I could think about was leaving the post tomorrow and not coming back for two and a half months. I was sick of West Point and wasn't in the mood to shake any plebes' hands. I stood and watched the cadets of the class of '92 hesitantly look around, trying not to appear nervous as they shed the instincts that had been hammered into them for a year. "Cadet Avery?"

I hadn't noticed Morris approaching. "Hey, Morris. Congrats."

"Thank you, sir!" He tried to stop the "sir," but it got out of his mouth before he could swallow it. He shook his head. "Shit."

"Don't worry. By the end of the day, you'll have shaken it off completely. You won't believe you used to call jerks like me sir." I held my hand out. "Seriously. Congrats. And my first name is Sam."

"Thanks. I'm Mike." After a year in the same company, we already knew each other's first names. But it felt right to introduce ourselves.

"What are you doing for leave?" I asked.

"Going to visit my parents for about a week, and then heading out on a road trip with a few of my classmates."

"Very good." I chuckled at the thought of a couple of drunken rising yearlings road-tripping. "Where to?"

"Florida to Austin via New Orleans."

"That's a good one. Always one to excel, aren't you?"

"I try. You trained me well."

"Bullshit. You were ready right out of the box, Mike. Don't pretend you don't know that. It's not becoming of a cadet with your bright future." I wasn't kidding. He was solid.

"Whatever. What are you up to this summer?"

"I start Airborne School on Monday with Dempsey, and then I'm going to Europe for two weeks. Then I've got Drill Cadet back at Fort Benning. I am literally going to walk out of here tomorrow and not come back until the middle of August." I smiled broadly.

"Gotcha. So, will I sound like this when I'm a yearling?"

"Probably."

+ + +

"What a fucking year, huh?" said Turtle, his mouth full and grease dripping from his chin.

The Corps spent that day madly packing up the barracks. Class uniforms, books, bedding, and the rest of our academic-year gear were jammed into trunks and lockers and stashed in the basement of the barracks. Military training gear was stowed in bulging duffel bags, ready for deployment. In less than twenty-four hours, after the graduation ceremony, we would be gone. The end of the semester had been tedious and final exams had been tough, but our imminent departure and the promise of adventure away from West Point had us buoyant. We were excited and impatient to be gone. Emily, Creighton, Turtle, Zack, Bill, Steven, and I sat on our duffel bags in Zack's room in a large circle around five helpless pizzas.

"Oh shit! I almost forgot," Zack said excitedly. "You guys will never guess what I heard today." He put his slice of pizza down and cleared his throat.

"What is it?" asked Bill.

"Captain Eifer is leaving the tactical department and West Point for a special assignment."

We were silent, digesting the news. "Are you sure?" asked Emily.

"Yep. I'm sure. I heard him talking about it. He leaves as soon as the Corps ships out."

"Good fucking riddance," said Bill.

"Amen," said Turtle.

"What special assignment?" I asked.

"White House assignment. I don't remember exactly what."

"White House fellow?" asked Creighton.

"Yeah. That's it."

Creighton groaned. "He is shameless!"

"What's a White House fellow?" asked Turtle.

"It's an extremely prestigious program where supposedly highly capable and accomplished Americans serve as assistants to White House senior staff members, cabinet secretaries, and the like for a year," said Creighton with disgust. "The application process is very selective. It is a very politically advantageous assignment."

"Perfect," said Bill.

"This guy is destined to be a general, isn't he?" asked Zack sadly.

"It would appear so," agreed Creighton. "I must say, he is playing the peacetime army game perfectly. I am impressed."

"Hopefully this will put an end to all those rumors of a scramble," Turtle said happily.

"Yeah. I heard he had been arguing for a scramble for over a year," said Steven.

"Well, good for him, and I say again, good fucking riddance."

"Amen," said Emily.

I didn't care if Eifer was destined to be a general.

"Why are you smiling, Sam?"

"Creighton, if Eifer's departure is an omen of our cow year, I'm feeling pretty good."

+ + +

The next day after the graduation ceremony, I waited under Mac's statue for the colonel to pick me up. Bill approached me.

"Hey, Sam," he said as he came out of the sally port. I turned and looked the other way, out over the Plain.

He walked around in front of me.

"I just wanted to say good-bye. I hope you have a good summer."

"Go to hell, Bill."

"Well. Sincerely, I hope you have a good one. You've earned it."

I looked back at Bill in silence. He fidgeted.

"Sam, I am truly sorry. I know what I did was wrong. But you? Sam, you were looking out for a friend. I know it wasn't totally right, but you've got to allow for yourself that it was not totally wrong, either."

I grabbed my bag and walked away. I had nothing to say. I left Bill standing under Mac's statue. *Sometimes it is too late,* I thought. *Sometimes you can't recover.* I was going to do better from then on. I was going to earn my redemption, but I'd never forgive him or me.

The colonel pulled in a few minutes later and picked me up in front of the commandant's house. He could tell I was in a shitty mood, so we rode in silence to Newark. When I got out, he said simply, "I hope you have a good summer, Sam."

"Thanks, sir. Me, too."

TWENTY-ONE

"**W**ON'T BE LONG NOW," SAID PETE QUIETLY. Chinook 458 throbbed as we sat in the forward aerial refueling point with the engines at ground idle. Five hundred meters away, Bulldog 70 sat on the ground with refueling hoses rolled out from her belly and at the ready. Beyond her, the three Black Hawks idled. They had inserted the ground team into three small fields surrounding the objective house before landing at the FARP. If things unfolded according to plan, the next call we would get from the ground team would be the code word "Athens," signifying that they had Abdul-Ahad in custody and were ready for extraction. It would take the Black Hawks only about fifteen minutes to get back to the objective, after which they would return to the FARP for a final top-off of fuel. We would then cycle through and get topped off as well before falling into last position in formation for the flight back to Kirkuk. Along the way we intended to make a detour, of course. It was going to be a long night.

"Your buddy the Guru is lucky this is not Afghanistan," said Pete.

"Why is that?" I asked.

"We never could have pulled off two missions together like this over there."

I nodded to myself in the dark cockpit. Pete was right. For a helicopter pilot, you could not design two theaters of war that were more different. Afghanistan is a mountainous country with almost 50 percent more land area than Iraq, which is predominantly desert. The towering Hindu Kush Mountains run northeast to southwest across Afghanistan, carving up the country into a flight-planning obstacle course. How much fuel to take because of weight considerations and where to get more when you need it is always an issue there, even for Chinooks. Iraq's predominantly low-elevation desert terrain makes the flying much more straightforward. Had this been Afghanistan, it would have likely been too complex to throw together a hasty follow-on mission to get the Guru. Certainly not on the same night as a high-value-target hit. Fuel, altitude, or aircraft availability would have screwed us. There were at least a hundred variables that could stand up and bite us in the ass tonight, but at least we were still in the hunt.

"This is Badger 51. Toledo."

"Shit," mumbled Pete.

"Toledo" was the code word for a dry hole. Abdul-Ahad was not there. The ground commander's frustration came through on the radio despite the brevity of his transmission. In the background I had heard a woman crying and maybe a kid or two. I could picture it, having been on the ground for a good share of these missions myself. Blown doors, shattered glass, relatives dressed in pajamas seated in flex cuffs, working dogs restrained on leads, families separated for interrogation, sounds of crying, kids huddled together. It's a jarring scene, and that's if you don't add in males who have been killed during the breach lying covered on the floor. The family never took it well. Especially the kids.

It was a huge letdown to go through the intense planning and preparation, fly all the way out, and assault the objective just to come up empty-handed. Abdul-Ahad was one of the slippery ones and had given us a couple of frustrating nights like this. We were itching to get our hands on him. Tonight, though, I was secretly relieved. There had been no firefight and no one had been hurt, so there was no need for us to launch a cas evac. I pulled out the burner phone and sent Zack a text as we had planned. "GTG" meant we were good to go. We would get our shot at rescuing the

Guru. Zack and Turtle would start their movement to the pickup zone, rig the vehicle for a sling load, and prepare for our arrival. They had plenty of time. We were at least an hour and a half away.

Ten minutes later, Badger 51 called for extraction. Once the Black Hawks had returned with the ground team, they cycled through refuel and lined up for departure. We topped 458 off, and soon our flight of five was headed northeast, back to Kirkuk.

We were flying last in the formation, and we hung back a little farther than usual. This phase of a mission is always a letdown. The team, ground and air alike, begins to relax a bit once all of the night's unknowns are behind them. The adrenaline recedes, and the mind is more open to distraction. It's a normal reaction.

It was also a process we were counting on as we made our move. About thirty kilometers out from Kirkuk, we broke away from the formation, making a gentle turn to the north and descending slightly. As we had expected and hoped, Bulldog 70 didn't notice. They were focused on the final leg of the flight into Kirkuk, putting the aircraft to bed, and getting quickly through the debrief. I watched the flight of four helicopters recede rapidly into the distance. The three Black Hawks hung beneath their rotor disks in a slightly nose-low cruising attitude as Bulldog 70 lumbered behind them. They were flying blacked out, with no lights on at all, and I quickly lost them in the dark expanse of the Iraqi night sky.

The operations center would continue to get real-time position information on us from 458's Blue Force Tracker, of course. Pete and I had decided to leave the GPS-enabled system on. If we went down, we wanted them to know where to recover the bodies.

Pete entered the lat/long for the PZ into the navigation computer, and I steered toward it. No one on 458 spoke as we descended and took up our new course, but I could feel the energy shifting. The cavalier joking from earlier, back on the ramp, was gone. The seriousness of our undertaking settled heavily on everyone's mind. Our single-aircraft mission into the belly of ISIS suddenly felt very lonely.

I tuned in the satcom frequency for Creighton and hit Transmit. "Elvis, this is Bulldog 71. We're a go and will be at the PZ in about ten minutes."

"Roger that, Bulldog 71. No changes on the objective." It wasn't Creighton's voice. He had not been on the radio yet. I smiled, picturing him standing behind a couple of co-conspirators in a dark room in Langley monitoring our radio transmissions and a dozen other intel feeds, trying to stay several moves ahead of us.

I exhaled in relief. It was almost midnight now, and I had been worried that we were going to be too late. But they hadn't moved the Guru yet. We had a chance.

TWENTY-TWO

FORT BENNING WAS SET UP LATE IN 1918 TO PROVIDE basic training for units bound for Europe in World War I. The armistice that went into effect on November 11 of that year ended hostilities in the "Great War" but did nothing to alter Fort Benning's trajectory toward becoming one of America's most important military bases. Home to the Infantry School, Airborne School, Ranger School, and numerous other military courses, Benning puts its stamp on just about every combat arms officer in the U.S. Army and on many from the other branches.

After the long drive to Georgia, Zack and I arrived at the base full of anticipation. We were cows now. We were going to learn how to jump out of airplanes, and we were convinced that this skill was going to make it easier to get laid. It was going to be a good summer.

Airborne School, we soon realized, was not the exotic special operations training we'd envisioned. It was an old-fashioned army training slog. Zack and I had been warned that Airborne School was "five days of training crammed into three weeks." We couldn't fully appreciate what that meant until we were covered in sweat and sawdust, standing in the sun, listening to "Sergeant Airborne" tell us for the thousandth time how to execute a parachute landing fall, or PLF. It was a fancy name for a way of landing that can be boiled down to "keep your feet and knees together and roll with it."

Despite the repetitive training, shouting cadre, and sweltering barracks, Zack and I were in heaven. We were away. Free. Liberated from West Point. The training started early, at 0500 hours, but when it ended, at 1700 hours, we were done. We could eat, shower, get in our civvies, and escape. We would take a taxi into Columbus and enjoy the civilian surroundings or just go to the PX and savor the air-conditioning. The training was boring, but after the sprint to the finish during term-end week of the academic year, my brain welcomed the intellectual silence. I also welcomed the absence of words like "duty," "honor," and "country." At Airborne School they spoke in profanities, not platitudes.

The course went by quickly. It was a mindless blur of push-ups and practice landing falls that concluded with Jump Week. They threw us out of a plane five times during the loud, windy, and dangerous conclusion. The first time the aircraft door opened in flight, we were scared. We were suddenly grateful for the insanely repetitive training.

The best thing about Airborne School was Stephanie.

An art history major from UVA, she was living in Atlanta for half of the summer while doing an internship at the High Museum of Art. Zack and I spent the weekend in Atlanta before reporting to Benning, and I met her at an outdoor concert there. She and I randomly bumped into each other during a lull in the music and were immediately and mutually smitten.

She was beautiful. Her wavy brown hair fell easily onto her shoulders and framed a pretty face with large brown eyes and a lower lip that was big and soft and seemed to always invite a kiss. Except when she was sad. Her body was athletic from one angle and curvy from another. Every position she put it in and the way she moved around in it fascinated me.

We spent that entire weekend together while Zack chased ineffectually after one of her friends. I forced Zack to leave Benning as early as possible with me the next weekend so that I could spend it with her. She met me on the stoop of her apartment building and wrapped her arms around me. "I missed you, cadet," she said sweetly. We spent another perfect weekend together before Zack and I went back to Benning for Jump Week. Then, as soon as they pinned our wings on, I raced back to Atlanta again.

"Holy hell, my head hurts," Zack said softly.

"Quiet," I pleaded.

"I thought you guys were tough or something," said Stephanie from the kitchen. It was Sunday morning. We had been celebrating the end of jump school and yearling year for two days.

Stephanie was a good host and so carefree that it was intoxicating to be around her. At West Point, everything was serious. It wasn't just a math test; it was a "critical demonstration of your ability to receive instruction." It wasn't just breakfast; it was an "important opportunity to develop yourself as a junior leader with the plebes." You weren't just deciding what training to sign up for that summer; you were "making critical career decisions that would have ramifications for the rest of your time in uniform." With Stephanie, though, it was just breakfast.

"Eggs Stephanie-style!" she said, bouncing out of the kitchen with two plates in hand, wearing short cutoff sweatpants and a tight tank top. Zack nudged me in the ribs to signal his approval.

"Not so loud," I said in earnest.

"Like I said. I thought you guys were tough."

"We can be when we need to be," I mumbled.

"These are good!"

"Thanks, Zack. You're easy."

"Easier than you know!" He nudged me again with his elbow.

"You do know I notice every time you do that, right?" she said to Zack.

"Um . . ."

"My Lord, that place is really doing a number on you guys."

"Yeah, but look how fit we are," Zack said, flexing his biceps.

"That part I like," she said as she walked back into the kitchen. "Anyone need more coffee?"

"Okay. I'm serious now. Not so loud."

She came back from the kitchen, patted my head gently, and sat down next to me as we ate.

"You're not eating?"

"I'm not much of a breakfast girl," she confessed as she put one arm around my waist and hugged me close while I ate. For a few minutes there was just the sound of silverware clinking and Zack and me chewing. Stephanie leaned her head against my neck.

"What time are you guys heading to the airport?"

"Around noon. Right, Sam?"

"Yeah . . . that's about right." I felt the pang of missing her begin. It was there whenever I took a deep breath. We had talked about it last night. I was headed to Europe for two weeks. In a few days, she'd be driving to Colorado with some friends for the last half of the summer; there they'd wait tables and hike and party. I would have changed my plans if she had asked me to. It felt that good to be with her, to hang out and be normal, but she didn't ask, and I told myself it was because I didn't give her an opening. That I bluffed too well. I was going on a kick-ass trip to Germany and Austria that could not be deterred. Maybe she felt the same. Maybe she would have delayed her trip out west?

"You listening to me, Sam?" Zack asked impatiently.

"No. What did you say?"

"I said, I am going to shower up, get packed, and make a run to the grocery store to stock up for the trip. I'll swing back by at noon to grab you."

"Sure. Sounds good."

Stephanie sat up and took his plate. "I've got this, Zack. You get going."

"Thanks."

She smiled at me as she took my plate also, and I watched as she walked back into the kitchen. I looked at my watch. About ten a.m. My head still hurt as I lay down on the sofa. I let the anxious sadness of an imminent good-bye wash over me while she finished cleaning the kitchen.

When she was done, she walked quietly over to me and knelt by my head. She leaned in and kissed me softly on the cheek.

"I'm going to miss you, Sam."

"I'm going to miss you, too."

She kissed me again, and I turned to meet her lips this time. I put my arms around her, and she giggled as I pulled her up on top of me. She felt perfect in my arms. She could feel me getting worked up again and slowed our kissing down. She pulled back and propped herself up on her hands.

"When do you think I'll see you again?" I asked.

"Well, it sounds like I get back to UVA about the time you wrap up with the drill sergeant stuff, right? You should come visit me."

"I'd like that."

"Me, too."

"So I'll do it."

"Good."

"But what happens then?" I asked awkwardly.

"Whatever happens next."

"Great. A philosopher."

"Ambiguity, Sam. Embrace it." She slowly lowered herself and began kissing my neck.

"I don't know what that means."

She pulled slightly away and glared at me with a look of mock frustration. "Ambiguity about our situation. Not our feelings. Now shut up and kiss me while you still can."

Later, as we drove to the airport, Zack had something on his mind. He shifted his hands nervously on the steering wheel until he couldn't hold it in anymore.

"I gotta ask you a question, Sam."

"Sure."

"What happened that night? Between you and Bill, I mean."

"Not this again."

"You can't ignore me on this, Sam. It's not right! And it's not just me who wonders. You guys are too big a part of the company to get away with a bullshit, unexplained falling out. Everybody wonders. What can happen between two guys who are that tight that leaves 'em basically strangers?"

I looked out the window. The good-bye with Stephanie was bummer enough.

"I was there, Sam. I saw how you looked at Bill. I thought you were going to kill him. Now you don't speak anymore. You didn't even come to blows again later. You were best friends until that one night. It is reasonable for me to ask." He hit the steering wheel in frustration.

"Shame," I said quietly.

"Huh?"

"I think we are both ashamed of what happened, both of us, and we can't get past it."

"You're making no sense. Two best friends are carrying around a bunch of 'shame' about something that happened between them, and they can't get over it, so they stop talking to each other? What are you? A pair of high school girls?"

"Just drop it. Take our example as a cautionary tale."

"How can I take it as a cautionary tale if you won't tell me what you're so ashamed of?"

I had never explained the situation like that before, even to myself. Once I'd said it, though, I realized it was true. Shame. When I looked at Bill, I was ashamed of what I had done. I saw shame in his eyes for putting me in that position. In truth, I was more ashamed of myself than I was mad at him, and I was very mad at him. It felt like a wound that would never heal. Ever. Too much pain. Too much stain.

"For Christ's sake, you guys are West Point classmates! Beast roommates! We're supposed to have a bond! I don't understand how you guys can just abandon each other." At that instant, I got why Zack was so upset. Bill and I were violating his worldview. To Zack, nothing mattered more than friendship, and the innermost, inviolable circle of friendship was your West Point company mates. To Zack, nothing could absolve you of your duty to a friend. Nothing warranted walking away from this. Not even honor.

I continued to stare out the window. I was certain that if I had had the courage to tell him what had happened, he would have told me to kick Bill's ass and get over it.

"Hey, I'm talking to you, asshole!"

"Sorry, Zack. Look, it's complicated—"

"No, it's not fucking complicated. Let me ask you this: if I screw up and do something that you're ashamed of, are you gonna write me off also? Am I gonna get thrown out like Bill?"

"You have no idea what you're talking about. Bill threw *me* out." I was yelling. "*I* was the one who got written off."

"I just don't know what to think." He looked straight ahead past the steering wheel, and a melancholy confusion sheathed his face. I had not realized until then how heartbroken he was about Bill and me.

"Zack, look . . . I'm sure after summer leave, Bill and I will work it out." I didn't believe that.

"You better."

We spent the rest of the half-hour ride to the airport in silence. I pretended to sleep, and Zack pretended to be preoccupied with driving. We pulled up to the Delta terminal, and I hopped out. Zack came around the other side and yanked out my bag.

I smiled wearily at him and put out my hand.

"Get in here, you moody bastard!" He lunged forward and bear-hugged me, his six-foot-two frame enveloping me. "I hope you have an awesome time, drink a lot of German beer, and screw about fifty European chicks, you airborne son of a bitch!"

"Yeah. Yeah . . . drive safe, asshole."

He bounded quickly back to the car. "I will. And don't you worry, Sam. That chick ain't going to be able to get over you. Trust me. She's got it bad!"

Zack dove into his car and revved the engine. He stuck his head out the window, yelled "Airborne!," and peeled sharply out into the flow of traffic, startling everyone around us.

TWENTY-THREE

"**P**Z IN SIGHT," PETE SAID.

"Roger. I've got it. Before-landing check complete."

Zack and the team were waiting for us as planned at the designated spot on a north-south road about fifteen kilometers to the northwest of the airfield. They had rigged their pickup truck for a sling load and were ready to go. I blinked the infrared landing light three times to let them know it was us flying.

Turtle had set up blocking vehicles about one hundred meters to the north and south of the sling-load vehicle. Four armed men were in position at each blocking vehicle. Turtle was taking no chances on us being interrupted.

Pete brought us in smoothly. We touched down with the aft gear first and then rolled slightly forward as he lowered the nose onto the road. As soon as 458 came to a stop, Pete took her to flat pitch. Zack, Turtle, and six commandos hustled on board as Crawford disconnected his helmet from the aircraft's intercom and exited.

Crawford ran forward to the pickup truck and inspected the rigging. External loads are complex and dangerous, even one as light as a single pickup truck. A good crew chief never accepts a load without inspecting it if he can avoid it. Crawford was one of the best. He worked his way around the load.

"Go naked, gentlemen," said Zack after hooking up to the intercom and leaning into the cockpit. Pete looked at me under his goggles and rolled his eyes. He was not familiar with E4's company motto.

"Just got an update from Elvis. No changes to the Guru's location. No indications of movement. We might get lucky on this one. Here's the commo information." Zack handed me a piece of paper with the drone's Common Data Link written on it. I tuned one of the auxiliary data inputs to the drone feed. Now we could see what Creighton saw.

Crawford jogged back to the aircraft, and his voice came over the intercom: "They're good to go, sir. Let's do it."

"Roger that," said Pete. He increased power, and 458 lifted gracefully to a hover and moved slowly forward. In the bed of the pickup truck, two of Turtle's commandos readied themselves. Their job was to hook the top loop of the sling-load rigging onto 458's fore and aft cargo hooks. Pete's job was to fly 458, steadily, to a hovering position inches above their heads so that they could reach the hooks. First the front hook as it passed slowly by, then the aft hook. Putting a large, powerful machine within such close proximity to soft flesh always sets people on edge. A moment's inattention or an unfortunate gust of wind can hurt or kill someone quickly. Doing this dance at night, with night-vision goggles, increased the difficulty and tension even for Pete, who had done this countless times under worse conditions.

The fact that we were on a commandeered section of road was a big advantage. It greatly reduced the amount of dust we kicked up. This made it much easier on Pete and the hookup crew. They didn't get sandblasted, and Pete didn't have to deal with brownout and lack of visual references. We wouldn't be as lucky at the LZ.

"Load passing under the nose," I announced to the aircraft.

"Roger that," returned Crawford. "Load in sight."

I watched the pickup truck and hookup crew pass under the chin bubble. The two men steadied themselves against 458's rotor wash. One of them held on to the static probe, and the other held on to the sling-load reach tube. When we were in position, the static probe man would tap the aircraft with the large metal probe to discharge the static electricity before the hookup man slapped the loop on the cargo hook. It couldn't be done the other way around; the static discharge would have knocked them off the vehicle.

"Bring her forward twenty, sir," said Crawford. "Looking good. Ten more."

Pete started to decelerate 458.

"Looking good. Five more. Four. Three. Two. Hold."

She came to a motionless hover.

"Down two, sir," said Crawford, his voice fighting the wind noise. At this point, he was hanging halfway out of the hellhole, the large square opening in the belly of the Chinook where the center cargo hook hangs. It allows the crew to monitor external loads in flight and gives pilots guidance during sling-load operations. Crawford was performing a critical duty, but it was also another opportunity for a big machine to take a bite out of soft flesh.

Chinook 458 settled two feet lower.

"Good. Right there. Now ease her forward."

The powerful helicopter walked slowly forward, maintaining her current hover height.

"Front loop is on the hook. Keep her easing forward. Aft hook coming into range in three, two, one. Aft loop is on the hook. Crew is clearing the load."

Now we were attached to the load. Even though we weren't lifting it yet, I always felt like the aircraft was already heavier at this point in a mission. It would be a mental stress until we released the load at the other end. It didn't matter that this was not a heavy load, probably only slightly over seven thousand pounds and well below what the cargo hooks could carry.

External loads make everything more complex: hovering, flying, landing, and emergency procedures. All of it is dicey with a large load swinging from the belly of the aircraft.

"Crew is clear. Bring her back to center her up, sir. Good. Five, four, three, two, one. Right there. Checking the rigging."

Crawford scanned the rigging to be sure there were no tangles that could screw up the load as we came to a hover.

"Load and rigging look good. Bring her up slowly, sir."

She rose straight up.

"Slings coming tight."

Chinook 458 stopped rising.

"Rigging looks good. Keep her coming, sir."

Pete pulled power. Her systems hummed faster as her engines produced more torque to drive the rotor blades, which were increasing their pitch to bite more air to create more lift to get us and the pickup truck flying. It's disconcerting to pull power in an aircraft like a Chinook and not gain altitude.

"Load getting light."

Pete pulled in more power.

"Load is off the ground. Bring her up five more. Good. Load at ten feet."

She bounced as she hovered. I read the torque. "We're at ninety percent torque. All indications normal." She wasn't at her limit, but she was burdened now. A low-frequency vertical bounce ran through the aircraft, as if she was feeling out the pickup truck the way a weight lifter adjusts their grip on the bar.

"Load is ready to fly."

"So is 458. Hover check complete."

"Roger that. Let's go."

We began to move forward. She shuddered and vibrated as she accelerated through twenty knots and passed through effective translational lift. ETL is the point where a helicopter outflies its own rotor-tip vortices. The swirling air at the edge of the rotor disk reduces lift. It's a negative factor in hovering flight, but at about twenty knots the aircraft outruns those wingtip vortices and starts to fly through clean air. Once through the transition, 458 started to climb out over the desert without Pete adding any more power.

At a hundred feet of altitude, Pete nosed her over to increase our acceleration.

"How does the load look?" he asked.

"Load's flying well. Steady with no oscillations."

A pickup truck is dense. It wouldn't be a problem in flight. More dangerous are the light, aerodynamic loads. They do some weird things as the aircraft gets going.

"Okay. I'm going to bump up to one hundred and twenty knots."

Our Chinook settled into the flight, and I checked the navigation computer. It was about fifty minutes to the LZ. I looked east. No moon yet, but it would be up soon.

Zack patted me on the shoulder and headed aft. "Just like old times, Sam. Grab your balls and jump."

TWENTY-FOUR

"SO, YOU JUMPED OUT OF AIRPLANES, WENT TO EUROPE for two weeks, and spent six weeks bossing around recruits doing army training. I mean, really, who had a cooler summer than you, cadet?"

Stephanie leaned back in her chair and took another sip of wine, enjoying the warm and breezy night. Her housemates were gone for the weekend, and we were enjoying a last night together before I reported back to West Point. Europe had been great. My second rotation to Fort Benning, as a drill cadet, had been hot and boring. Grudgingly, I'd learned how well-oiled a machine West Point was. Infantry basic covered half the training in twice the time as Beast Barracks. Stephanie had consumed my thoughts through it all.

"It was all right."

"It was all right?" She narrowed her eyes. "What's wrong, Sam?"

"Nothing. Just tired."

She got up from her chair, poured herself more wine, and walked over. "Relax. Your body language is killing me." She leaned over and gently ran her hands through my short hair. She moved them softly down my neck and then rubbed my shoulders. With a tolerant, slight smile on her face, she stroked my arms, and I suddenly realized they were crossed tightly in front of my chest. She grabbed each hand and tugged my arms apart, and I couldn't help but smile as I noticed that my legs were also tightly crossed. She caught me smiling and cooed, "There you go." She nudged my knees apart. "It's like I'm uncoiling a loaded spring." She settled herself into my lap and nuzzled her head into my neck. I put my arms around her and squeezed softly.

"What's wrong, cadet?"

"I missed you, and I know I'm going to miss you more this coming school year. I'll realistically see you, what? A handful of times?"

"I'm here in your lap, Sam. Why are you focusing on the rest of the school year, which hasn't started yet?"

"Don't you think about it?"

"Sure I do, but I don't let it ruin what's happening right now. You've got to relax. I just want us to have a good time together."

"That's what this is? Just a good time?"

She squeezed me harder. "Stop trying to fight with me."

I could feel myself ruining the night. I hesitated.

"Sam, you chose the military. You chose West Point. I didn't. Don't start resenting me just because I made a different choice than you. I really like you. I want to see more of you. I want you in my life. I miss you when you're gone, but, yes, I'm living a different kind of life right now. You've got to stop trying to come up with a map or tactic to deal with this or you're going to ruin it." She kissed my neck gently.

The next day, I returned to West Point.

✦ ✦ ✦

When we reassembled for the start of the academic year, E4 was happy to learn that the barracks renovations had been completed. We moved back into our beloved Lost Fifties.

"Lord, it's good to be home," said Zack, my roommate for the semester. "I hate those long-ass hallways of Mac Long Wing. Absolutely no privacy. Feels like a prison. The Lost Fifties is more, I don't know. Intimate."

"Yeah. Intimate. Exactly how I would describe the barracks at West Point," I mumbled.

Zack and I alternated between hazing the new plebes and sharing our stories from the summer with our classmates. Cow summer had been our first extended time away from West Point out in the "real army." It gave us our first meaningful interactions with ROTC cadets, Officer Candidate School graduates, and all kinds of soldiers. As we digested our experiences together, a common realization percolated through our class: West Point is the longest and most grueling route to get into the U.S. Army. OCS, ROTC, enlisted. These routes are unlike what we were going through. Basic training is only eight weeks long. OCS is only twelve. We were astounded to learn how thoroughly our ROTC contemporaries were enjoying real college experiences during the year, then mimicking what we did for a few weeks during the summers. A joke. One that we envied terribly. But a joke.

No one came close to the four-year, highly regimented, minimum-security-prison insanity that we had ignorantly signed up for and continued to subject ourselves to daily. Combine this with our other major summer learning—that being a West Point cadet pretty much earned one only ridicule out in the real army—and we felt truly stupid.

We realized that the joke was on us. It wasn't that our route was better than ROTC or OCS commissioning tracks; it was that our route sucked so much more. It was ridiculous. Worse than a joke, we were the butt of an inane comic opera. One that had so warped us that the realization actually made us proud. We had chosen the hardest path, one that everyone else thought was ridiculous, and it conferred zero advantage. None. It was actually a handicap in some ways. One that painted West Point commissioned butter-bar lieutenants arriving at their first units with a centuries-old cliché: that they are unique cocktails of arrogance, idiocy, and ambition. And still, we were proud. Probably more proud than we had been up to this point, and more determined than ever to see it through. Together.

Most of us would not have come to West Point had we known what it was really like, but the academy had us now. And in those moments when it got to us, when we weakened and considered leaving, it was because of our friends that we stayed. We had been through too much together. We couldn't leave each other. We would not quit each other. Period. "Fine," we said. "We're going to finish it anyway. And fuck you, too." For the rest of our lives, we would remember how much stupid shit we put up with together. We finished what we started. Outsiders would never understand. We finally were members of the long gray line.

And the long gray line resists change. We respect the old ways. Much of what we regard as ridiculous we maintain because it is rooted in centuries of continuity that has served the country well. The craziness has worked for more than two hundred years. We are scared to fuck with it. So when we arrived back at West Point to find that, for the first time in history, a female had ascended to the highest-ranking position in the Corps of Cadets, a shock ran through the long gray line from end to end. There was a female cadet first captain, and it didn't go over well.

+ + +

Females had entered West Point almost fifteen years earlier, so for my friends and me it was a nonissue. We may not have always liked it, but we could not imagine the place without them. It just seemed logical. As Creighton said to guys who complained, "There are women in the army, gentlemen. You might as well make peace with it here."

The peace was not always easy, though. The implementation of separate physical standards created friction and unfavorable comparisons. During summer training, the differences could be stark. Female cadets usually couldn't march as far as fast with as much weight. It was always noticed.

Then there was the inevitable social status conferred on the female cadets due to their fewer numbers. They made up only about 15 percent of the Corps. No matter how homely, in the cadet area they got a lot of attention from some of their lonely male classmates. This created even more friction, both from spurned suitors and from those who resented the attention and the perceived attitude female cadets acquired as a result of their scarcity.

There were some good ones, though, and, when they were good, they were twice as good as we were. We realized over time that they had it harder than we did, that the females sacrificed more to be cadets than we did. In addition to all the things male cadets sacrifice, women give up more of their identity. However co-ed West Point tries to be, men dominate. Always will. So it took something special to be considered good: an Athena in cadet gray.

An additional burden for Emily and the other women was the constant unwanted high-level attention they received. At least once a semester they were pulled aside to participate in a congressional study of females in the military or an academic panel on women in leadership positions or some other high-visibility talkfest. These august panels usually served only to further isolate the women. Emily hated them. "I wish people would just let me get on with being a cadet," she griped to me.

Sometimes it got worse than congressional committees. I was secretly ashamed and humbled when Emily told me about some of the hazing she'd been subjected to as a plebe. Isolated, spit on, and physically intimated, she'd faced worse than I ever had, and she had never complained or turned in the perpetrators.

But the appointment of a female first captain changed the issue from one that each cadet faced to one that the Corps as a whole faced. My friends and I were bombarded by the protests of old grads and old-fashioned cadets. "The first captain is the Corps' symbol. Our representative," they protested. "The first captain is supposed to be the toughest, strongest, smartest, most squared-away cadet in the whole Corps. Now, for us, that is a damn female! Do you realize that the Citadel and VMI don't even admit women?" They were inconsolable.

On our other flank, we faced the unyielding certainty of our leadership that it was time.

The whole thing was a hassle. "Let's just get on with being cadets," Emily said.

✦ ✦ ✦

Later, at dinner formation, I looked over the new plebes in the company. They were miserable. The blacktop of North Area radiated the heat it had stored all day from the mid-August sun. The plebes had sweat through their shirts and pants. Disgusting.

Mike Morris paced in front of his three plebes as he interrogated them. All three of them popped off with plebe knowledge as Mike nodded.

I picked a plebe in my platoon at random. "Mitchell. Start 'The Days'!" I said sternly.

"Sir. 'The Days.' Today is Sunday, twenty August 1989. There are five and a butt days until Ring Weekend for the class of 1990. There are thirty-four and a butt days until Army defeats Wake Forest at Michie Stadium in football. There are one hundred and eleven and a butt days until Army beats the hell out of Navy at the Meadowlands Sports Complex in East Rutherford, New Jersey. There are one hundred and twenty-one and a butt days until Christmas leave for the United States Corps of Cadets. There are one hundred and eighty-four and a butt days until One Hundredth Night for the class of 1990. There are two hundred and ten and a butt days until spring break for the upper three classes. There are two hundred and eighty-one and a butt days until graduation and graduation leave for the class of 1990, sir!"

"And how about the class of eighty-nine-point-five, beanhead?" said a familiar voice approaching behind me.

"I heard you were back."

"Indeed, Avery. I am back," said the Guru with his customary flourish. His face was tan, and his curls were pressing the limits of regulations again. It made me smile.

"I couldn't believe it when I heard you were allowed to return to E4."

"Yes, well, with Eifer gone the enmity toward me among the tactical department has mellowed. In fact, I believe some of them appreciate my sense of style. Excuse me a moment, my friend." He winked at me as he stepped by and in front of the plebes. He made a show out of bending down to read Mitchell's name tag and then stepped back around to me and said in too loud a voice, "Cadet Avery, do these newly minted plebes belong to you?"

"Yes, they do."

"Do you mind doing me a favor?"

"Of course."

"Would you please tell them that at the first formation of the day, I would like to be greeted with a shortened version of 'The Days.'"

"Sounds reasonable. Preferred format?"

"I think something along the lines of 'Sir, "The Days." Today is whatever the date is, there are however many and a butt days until graduation for Cadet Stillmont, third-generation United States Military Academy cadet, survivor of Captain Eifer, and future armor officer."

"I like it. You guys get that?"

"Yes, sir!" they said in unison.

"Good. Starting tomorrow, the first plebe in the squad to see Cadet Stillmont will pop off with it. Do you understand?"

"Yes, sir."

"Thanks, Avery. It's the little things, you know."

"No problem. It's good to see you."

"Good to be back. Gonna do my time, graduate, and head on down the road to Knox."

"Well, I hope the time didn't mellow you, Guru. Wouldn't be fair to the new plebes or to those of us who have come to depend on you so much."

"I hope you'll find me to be a more circumspect Guru. I can't weather another slug. But don't fret," he said. "I still have work for you."

TWENTY-FIVE

"TEN MINUTES TO THE LZ, ZACK."

"Roger. Ten minutes."

We flew the next minutes in silence. The angry radio call from Brick earlier demanding that we return to base had been an unneeded reminder of what we faced if we made it back. It was good to have actual mission demands push him out of my mind. I could picture the activity in back. Hurried, but not frantic: Zack and Turtle and his six commandos concluding final checks on their equipment and one another, Crawford hanging halfway out of the hellhole monitoring the load, Thomas and Wilson checking their weapons, ensuring that the ammunition belts were properly fed. Miniguns had a frustrating tendency to jam, so you could never check them enough. In just a few minutes, hundreds of essential items would be swiftly and silently checked off by the operators and aircrew.

The operators would be anxious to get off the Chinook. I understood this well, having been attached to several ground units over the past few years as a liaison officer. I loved to fly them, but Chinooks are not a fun way to be delivered to an objective. There is no visibility. The small portal windows in back are worthless, and the ramp is typically shut to keep the ever-present desert sand to a minimum. It feels like wallowing in the back of a submarine. Landing on the objective, you feel like Jonah spit from the whale, rather than a soldier assaulting from the sky. Most operators would rather be sitting on the side of a Little Bird, which is ridiculous because you are totally exposed, but at least you can see what's coming and shoot back.

"LZ in sight," said Pete.

"Roger. I've got it, too. Three minutes," I announced.

"Roger. Three minutes," responded Zack. He would pass the time to everyone on his team.

"Why don't you take this landing, Pete? I haven't done a dusty-goggle landing in a while."

"Come on, sir. It's like riding a bike."

"I've spent too much time drawing lines and circles on maps in the TOC. I'm not even sure I can ride a bike. We need to nail this one. You take it."

"Suit yourself. I have the controls."

"You've got the controls."

"I've got 'em."

Pete took the controls and started a deceleration, lifting our nose up slightly as he lowered the collective. Airspeed began to bleed off. Having a sling load meant we couldn't execute an aggressive assault-landing profile to minimize our time and vulnerability on the approach. We would have come to a hover above the LZ and slowly lower the pickup truck to the ground. Not the optimal tactic when you're trying to get in and out of an area undetected.

Just as important, Pete and I had to be sure we didn't break the team's vehicle when we put it down.

The Chinook shuddered as we continued to decelerate, and the load began to swing slightly.

"Load height twenty-five feet. Oscillating five feet fore and aft," said Crawford from the hellhole.

"Power at seventy percent," I announced. As the Chinook lost the aerodynamic benefits of forward flight, it had to work harder to fly. The imagery on our displays showed 458's speed and height above the ground as a huge rotor-driven dust cloud enveloped us. Like all large beasts of burden, 458 was not happy about being worked this hard. She let us know, bucking and shuddering more obnoxiously as she decelerated below ETL. "Power at ninety-one percent." Shedding the last couple of knots of airspeed, she transitioned to a laborious hover. With a sling load, it was easy to overtorque during this phase of the flight.

The rotor wash under a heavy Chinook exceeds a hundred miles an hour, which means total brownout in these conditions. Were it daytime, the dust cloud would be visible from miles away. At night, under night-vision goggles, it means the pilots are doused in sudden and vertiginous zero visibility. Not comfortable conditions to hover in with an external load.

Most dramatic, though, is the effect of the sand being struck by the leading edge of the rotor blades. The anti-abrasion strips are titanium, which is extremely hard, but the sand is harder. Millions of sand particles smash into the rotor blades as they rotate, knocking off tiny bits of titanium, which ignite in the air. These millions of tiny burning titanium particles turn the churning rotor disks into faintly glowing orange halos that swivel and tilt as the pilot makes control inputs. It's eerily beautiful.

"Load height ten feet," called Crawford. Ground effect had started to work against us, resisting the aircraft's descent.

Pete lowered the collective slightly to take out more power.

"Load height five feet. Four. Three. Two. Contact. Load stable on the ground."

A jolt ran through the floor of the aircraft as, at Crawford's command, pressurized hydraulic fluid snapped open the fore and aft hooks.

"Load is disconnected."

In one fluid motion, Pete slipped the Chinook smoothly forward and down in the maelstrom of dust. Flying completely off the display imagery and using his own feel for the helicopter, he put us down aggressively about twenty meters forward of the vehicle in only seconds.

"Aircraft stable on the ground. Ramp coming down," announced the crew chief. "Team exiting."

"Thanks, Sam. Go naked!"

"Go naked, Zack," I answered, but he was already disconnected, one of eight heavily armed men running in the dust toward the pickup truck.

Exiting a Chinook onto an LZ like this is a strange experience. It is a quick transition from no vision in the back, to tunnel vision running off the ramp, to a moment of expansive vision as you run into the night, followed by the blinding sandstorm of takeoff. It is always at this moment in an operation, running toward the vehicle or rally point, when an operator thinks, *Holy shit, these helicopters are loud. The whole country must know we're here.*

"Ramp coming up."

"Everybody ready?" asked Pete. We had been on the ground for about twenty seconds. It had been only about two minutes since we'd gotten to the LZ.

"Roger that," answered the crew chief.

The engines screamed, and 458 leapt abruptly into the air as Pete pulled an armful of collective. Suddenly freed of the large, awkward pickup truck, 458 felt spry and responsive. He leaned her nose over, and we accelerated away.

As we departed, I swiveled the FLIR pod around to look at the pickup truck. Zack, Turtle, and the team were in a security formation. We had been off the LZ for less than ten seconds and were already more then a quarter of a mile away. Zack would hold the team for about five more minutes, letting their ears adjust from the shriek and pound of a loaded Chinook to the stillness of the northwestern Iraqi desert. There would be no reward for haste now. It was all about stealth.

"Elvis, Bulldog. We're off."

"Roger."

"Elvis, Thayer 6. So are we." Since Zack was really the ground commander of our mission, Turtle had given him the call sign Thayer 06 for the night.

"Roger, Thayer 6. We're monitoring the route to the objective. At this time, it is clear."

"Roger. Thayer 6 out."

We circled wide to the east of the team's route, per the plan. I could feel my body relaxing now that the insertion had been successfully completed. For pilots, the insertion is always an adrenaline spike, followed by a coast down until the next spike: the extraction. For the ground team, the stress was now high and would be ratcheting up continuously until the hit.

We flew toward our next LZ, an isolated location we had picked on the map to conserve fuel and monitor the mission. Elvis would keep us apprised of Zack's progress. We would be airborne again before they hit the house and would be circling an empty spot in the desert only a couple of minutes' flight time from the objective.

After the noise and kinetic energy of the insertion, flying straight and level seemed suddenly peaceful. No one spoke. The terrain zipped by at over 125 miles per hour en route to our next checkpoint. I looked out my window to the east. The horizon was bright with the impending moon-rise.

TWENTY-SIX

BY THE END OF SEPTEMBER, IT WAS CLEAR THAT THE academy was not going to crumble and slide into the Hudson because a female had taken the mantle of first captain. Most of life in the cadet area continued as it ever had, including the feud between E4 and F4.

With the Guru on self-imposed retirement, Turtle led the fight for E4. This was bad for both companies. The Guru's spirit missions, no matter how humiliating to the target, had always been imbued with humor. Like the time he somehow superglued all of F4's sabers to their scabbards before a dinner formation attended by the superintendent and the German ambassador. The Frogs yanked and tugged but were unable to draw their sabers. They had to render hand salutes to the ambassador rather than presenting arms. Everyone laughed, and it was over.

Turtle's spirit missions tended to be more destructive. One of his favorite methods was to screw up the rooms of an offending company at four in the morning before a Saturday inspection, creating havoc with a combination of fire extinguisher spray, shaving cream, and boxes of BBs. He and a small squad of plebes could hit as many as a dozen rooms in under a minute. The results were catastrophic for the targeted cadets, who had to stand for inspection in a room they had no hope of cleaning in time.

The problem with his methods was that they usually resulted in escalation. Particularly when the target was F4. The Frogs knew Turtle's signature well, and they retaliated.

Fortunately for both companies, our cadet commanders intervened and agreed on a truce, but only after a tense standoff. The Frogs stole all of our dress shoes in a bold mission that struck around 1630 hours, when they knew just about every cadet would be out of the barracks and engaged in either intercollegiate or club athletics. Even the Guru was impressed.

We hit back by kidnapping F4's company commander. Turtle and a couple of yearlings intercepted him as he returned from the gym. They tied him up and hid him in our company area. At dinner formation that evening, with all of E4 standing ridiculously in combat boots under our dress gray uniforms, F4 looked around for their company commander. We noted with pleasure that Captain Kendell, the new E4 tac who'd replaced Captain Eifer, didn't know how to react, so he did nothing.

We acted innocent through the formation and dinner and then passed a note to the Frog first sergeant, proposing an exchange: our shoes for their commander. The next day, the truce was agreed to.

The Corps, though, was not at peace. The advent of the first female first captain had added an extra degree of swirl and churn to cadet life. Females at West Point and the role of females in the military and in combat was now a national discussion. Worse, it was also a raging argument within the Corps and among the old grads. The incessant, grinding debate was wearing me out. It was wearing the Corps out. I needed some perspective and looked forward to speaking to the colonel after the weekend's football game.

We were in their living room after dinner when I brought it up.

"So you were there when the first female cadets were admitted?"

"Yes, I was. Why?"

"Just wondering what it was like."

He regarded me for a long moment. "Well, to be honest, it was a crazy and depressing time. We rolled into West Point in June 1975. I taught three academic years, from seventy-five to seventy-eight. The debate about admitting women into the academies had been going on long before that. But by 1975, everyone was arguing about it. I was pissed because my goal at the time was to blend in quietly and study history at Chapel Hill. In 1973, army officers were not very welcome in the halls of academia. Then comes this raging debate about women at the academies and everyone in my grad school wants to talk to me about it and ask me what I thought. Such a pain in the ass!" He shook his head.

"The debate went back and forth, but by the end of that year, President Ford signed it into law. Boom. Done."

"The old grads must have gone nuts."

"Oh, yeah. The hue and cry was deafening, and West Point fought it. The supe at the time, LTG Berry, who'd served in Korea and Vietnam, objected, publicly, from the start of the debate. He had even threatened to resign before admitting women. Think about that."

I did. I couldn't imagine it. It was totally different than the politically correct leaders who seemed to be in charge now.

"The supe ended up regretting his threat. He was a good officer. After the law had been signed, he sent a letter to graduates and friends of the academy saying the order has been given, now we've got to execute."

"Wow."

"That kicked off a bunch of activity. We only had about six months to get ready. It affected everything: barracks, bathrooms, uniforms. You can't imagine."

"I bet the old grads stayed pissed."

"Absolutely. Rings were thrown in the Hudson. All that."

I nodded slowly.

"But it got worse. Add to all that the nasty class of seventy-six cheating scandal that got so much press. Every day for over a year it felt like it was the end of the academy. Seemed like we had gotten lost so badly that we were never going to find our way back. Old grads, the press, and the public all spewed their opinions at us and seemed disgusted with us. The Corps was getting it from every possible angle." He looked at me.

"Okay. I get it. It's not so bad now."

"No. That's not my point. Well, maybe a little bit," he said, smiling at me and leaning back in his chair.

"Sam, you're going to have to make peace with the fact that West Point is of this earth. It's made up of fallible human beings. Sometimes it gets shit wrong. What's worse, it always seems beset by existential crises because it is the kind of place about which people have very strong feelings. It is an institution that some people regard as critical to the nation; other people regard it as useless and expensive, while another group regards it as anachronistic, and still others don't like it just because. So things are never going to just be peaceful here."

"And what do you think?"

"About what?"

"West Point. Is it critical, anachronistic, stupid, or what?"

"Oh. Depends on the day."

"Terrific."

"Sam, you need to relax about this. Remember, you're not here to be a damn cadet. You're here to get ready for what comes after. All you can do while you're here is do your best. Do that, and it's all going to work out. What do you think of your classmates?"

"What do you mean?"

"Your classmates. What do you think of them? Good cadets? Dipshits? What?"

"They're good cadets." I thought of Zack, Creighton, Turtle, Emily, Steven, and the rest. And, yes, Bill. Things had been thawing between us. Being in the same room together had slowly coasted down from me feeling pissed to awkwardness to just coexisting. Billeting two doors down from each other meant we met often in the latrines and locker areas, and we were in a history class together. It was not reconciliation, but the machinery of West Point was wearing our animosity down, proving the value of a common enemy. "They are the best," I said.

"Well. There's your answer. That's the true strength of this place. No matter how stupid, lost, idiotic, or screwed up the academy gets, the regenerative, self-healing, course-correcting process ultimately sets it right."

"What are you talking about, sir?"

"I'm talking about you!" He leaned out of his chair suddenly and jabbed me repeatedly in the chest with his finger. "Cadets like you keep showing up. Every year. Without fail. The next class always shows up. West Point is what it is because of the kids who come here each year. Period. Not because of the old grads or the current TACs and professors or anyone else."

He read the skepticism on my face. "I don't give a shit if you believe me. It's impossible for you to believe me, because you're too young." He smiled. "It's true, though. Every year we get a fresh batch, and every year we do our best to teach you and get you going in the right direction. In a good year, I think we end up getting it about half right. Combine that with a class's youth and goodness in this crazy cauldron for four years, and you usually wind up with a good group of officers. Lather. Rinse. Repeat."

"So you're saying I'm just another number in the system here."

"You can be such a gloomy kid." He chuckled. "And by the way, I know this first captain. She's a good one, best I have seen in a while. She would probably kick your ass, and she is definitely smarter than you. You are well represented, Sam."

TWENTY-SEVEN

"SIR, 'THE DAYS.' TODAY IS, SATURDAY, EIGHTEEN November 1989!" I looked over my shoulder and saw the Guru sauntering up to formation in full dress like the rest of us. He was smiling and came to a halt in front of the platoon, his right hand raised as if acknowledging fans from a balcony. The rest of the plebes in the company had joined immediately in the delivery of "The Days." Even though the Guru had given this special duty just to First Squad, the rest of the platoon had quickly joined the tribute. Within a few weeks, every plebe in the company was participating. Guru loved it. So did the plebes, and so did the rest of the company. It made us all feel like survivors.

"There are twenty-nine and a butt days until graduation for Cadet Stillmont, third-generation United States Military Academy cadet, survivor of Captain Eifer, and future armor officer!" As the chant wrapped up, the Guru saluted the company in general and walked over to First Squad.

"Good morning, Avery."

"Morning, Guru."

"Know what today is?"

"Yep. Last parade of the season."

"Oh no. More than that, young cow. More than that. This is my last damn parade ever."

I shook his hand as the cadet first sergeant gave the command to fall in.

The brigade review was chilly but not unbearable, and it passed quickly. We were glad. It was our last home game and, therefore, the last parade until next spring. The post was crawling with old grads, as this was also the last reunion weekend for the year. Most of the leaves had fallen, but the Hudson River valley had not yet surrendered to the dark ashen gray of winter. The severely clear November day was a fitting way to end the parade season and perfect for fall tailgates.

Emily's parents were visiting from Ohio and laid out a high-quality tailgate spread. After the parade, Zack, Creighton, Bill, and I hiked up past the cadet chapel to the parking lot to join them.

We gorged ourselves at the tailgate. The perfect weather, final game, and reunions had yielded a full-capacity crowd. Pods of proud parents wearing cadet parkas with their cadet's year patch stood next to groups of old grads flying old unit and year group flags. In every cluster there were cadets enjoying positive attention and grilled meat. Like in any good American college tailgate environment, alcohol flowed. It was festive. No alcohol flowed to us, of course. Only firsties could drink on post.

"Lucky bastards," said Bill quietly. He and I were looking enviously at a couple of old grads at the gathering next to us. They were pouring Baileys into their coffee from a well-stocked bar that sat on the back of their pickup truck.

"I bet they'd give you some."

"Right. Good idea. I should go do that. Have a nice Scotch and water with the class of forty-three right out here in public so some duty-dick cadet can turn me in."

"Well, you never know," I said. "Someone might cover for you."

I smiled ruefully. He glanced at me.

"Son of a bitch." He turned his head back toward the festive old grads. "I never thought I'd hear you joke like that."

"Me, either." We stood in silence for a few minutes. I was more surprised than him. My comment had come out spontaneously. Naturally. Without any thought and unobstructed by emotion. I inventoried myself as I stood there and found no anger toward Bill. The shame was still there, as always, but not crippling. *Strange,* I thought to myself. *When did this happen?*

The game against Colgate was a good one. We crushed them 59 to 14, and the stadium was comfortably warm with both the mild weather and the energy of the Corps and old grads. Even better, Thanksgiving leave was the following week. Stephanie and I had worked out our plan. I was going home for the holiday itself and would then meet her in New York City that Friday. I couldn't wait.

✦ ✦ ✦

Late November in New York City is nearly perfect. The weather is not yet frigid, and the city is pivoting out of Thanksgiving, into Christmas. The window displays begin to get festive, and the tree at Rockefeller Center is decorated but not yet lit. The city has the excited sense of looking forward to the holidays, without yet being smothered by them. It was the perfect time and place to spend a weekend with Stephanie.

Cadets execute weekends with their lovers like a Delta Force raid. They obsess over every minute detail and conceivable scenario. They construct and stress-test the timeline against transportation challenges, potential food delays, and unforeseen bathroom stops. They look at the trip from every angle to eliminate all obstacles to achieving their mission: securing long stretches of uninterrupted and athletic bouts of nakedness.

As a result, a weekend escape with a cadet is usually one of two things: a magical whirlwind for their lover in which everything is perfect and flows easily and inevitably toward a passionate and extended finale, or a death march through a mechanical checklist of contrived situations that results in an awkward and frustratingly sexless conclusion. My weekend in New York City with Stephanie was the former.

I had been able to get us a room in the small hotel on Governers Island, a Coast Guard base less than half a mile off the southern tip of Manhattan. A military ID was required to gain access, and a small, dedicated ferry worked its way back and forth between the island and lower Manhattan. There was not a lot of activity on the island, so it felt like our own personal bed and breakfast with access to New York City. Stephanie loved it. After adventures in Manhattan, we snuggled against the chill and alternated our gaze from the Statue of Liberty to the lights of the city as we crossed the water where the Hudson and East River came together.

As perfect as it was, though, our impending separation stalked us all weekend. On Sunday, she cried as we packed to take her back to the airport.

"Am I feeling too much?" she asked.

"Not unless I am also."

"Why is everything so damn strong with you? Why are my feelings so urgent?"

"Is that a bad thing?"

"I think it is." She stopped packing and sat on the edge of the bed staring at the floor.

"Why?"

"It's going to burn us up. It's not sustainable." Tears ran down both of her cheeks.

"I think parting is supposed to hurt, isn't it?" I sat next to her and I wiped her tears with my hand.

"I know that. This just feels so different. It's too much. I mean, I've been in relationships before. I've had to say good-bye and do long-distance. This is different. We always seem to be saying 'good-bye' or 'I miss you.'"

"I feel the same." I leaned in and gently kissed her forehead.

"I'm not saying this to be reassured by you, Sam. I'm just saying what I feel. This doesn't feel good to me. Doesn't feel healthy."

She noticed the alarm on my face, reached out her hand, and gently stroked my cheek. "Don't look so worried. I'm not winding up to anything. I'm just saying . . ."

"Just saying what?"

"I'm worried about us. That's all. I don't know what to do with all these feelings. I don't trust them."

"You can trust me."

"I do. I just don't think we know what we're doing. It scares me." She began to well up again. Her eyes glistened heavily for a moment and seemed to sink beneath the rising tears. She closed her eyes, and a heavy, sad teardrop broke free and ran slowly down each cheek.

I didn't know what to do, so I gave her a hug. She stifled a few sobs and then sat up, her nose running.

"Damnit. Just the way I want you to remember me. Can you grab me a tissue?"

I returned from the bathroom and handed her a box of tissues.

"Could you find us some coffee?"

"You got it."

When I got back, she was done packing and was standing at the window looking out across the water at the city.

"Here you go."

"Thanks." She gave me a kiss on the cheek and walked over to the sofa. Her eyes were red. But she was different. Colder. She had clearly been crying while I was on the coffee run. But she had finished and put on her armor.

We took the ferry back to Manhattan, and I rode with her in the cab to the airport. We held hands and looked out the window in silence as we left the city. On the curb at LaGuardia, I hopped out and grabbed her bag from the trunk. The cab idled at the curb as we hugged and said good-bye.

TWENTY-EIGHT

"ELVIS, THIS IS THAYER 6. WE'RE SET. SITREP, PLEASE."

"Thayer 6, no changes."

"Bulldog, Thayer 6, what is your status?"

"Thayer 6, Bulldog is in position," I answered as we flew a wide left-turn holding pattern five hundred feet above the desert floor ten kilometers to the southeast. At this distance, we could get to the objective to extract Zack and his team in about three minutes. We had the drone video feed called up on our displays and were looking at the objective.

"Roger that. Here we go."

The team broke down the door, threw concussion grenades, and stormed into the house in one fluid movement, like water rushing into a sinking boat. Even from a distant, monochromatic overhead angle it was an impressive display. It was the deadly economy of motion obtained only through tens of thousands of hours of repetition. In that moment, I knew they would get the Guru out.

"That was smooth," Pete said softly in admiration.

We couldn't hear anything, but we watched as window shutters were blown off in successive rooms as the team worked their way quickly through the house.

"How many guys do we think are in there?" asked Pete.

"Elvis says four."

"Shouldn't take long."

I stared at the drone feed in silence. This was the moment in any mission I hated the most: waiting as the ground element executed. Waiting for the next radio transmission. The one that would reveal whether the operation would proceed smoothly or begin to unravel. Whether the fortunes of war had been kind or cruel. Once the call was made, the uncertainty was lifted. For me, it was always easier to know. Was it going to be a hot LZ? Would there be wounded? Was there something we had not planned for? I just wanted to know.

I pictured Turtle and Zack working through the building together. Were it not so deadly a situation, the contrast would be humorous. Since his first day as a cadet, Turtle had been a dense, stout guy. His movements had a deliberate and insistent quality that reflected his stubbornness and the fact that he would never quit, ever.

Zack was lanky and awkward-looking when stationary but graceful in motion. I had been on the ground with him on a few operations since 9/11. He still moved like a lacrosse player: fluid, sweeping, and decisive. I hoped he'd make quick work of things tonight.

No one spoke on the aircraft. Chinook 458 was quiet except for her laboring engines and beating rotors. Out of the corner of my eye, I saw Pete stretch his neck to one side and then the other, limbering up for the coming fight. Crawford was leaning into the companionway, staring over our shoulders at the drone feed on our cockpit displays. The entire aircrew stewed silently, considering all the scenarios that could be dictated by the next few minutes: some good, some bad.

I closed my eyes and took a few deep breaths.

"This is Thayer 6. House clear. No Guru."

"What happened to all that intel you guys were supposed to be getting, sir?" Crawford said from the back of the aircraft.

"Elvis, this is Thayer 6, you copy?"

"Roger, Thayer 6. He should be there. Check again."

"Second fucking dry hole tonight. This is bad," Pete said.

He was right. We didn't have the resources to conduct a search of the next house, let alone the adjacent block or the rest of Tal Afar. We barely had sufficient resources to take down the one target house.

"Thayer 6. Elvis. Any enemy you can question?"

"Negative. Wasn't the profile."

It was a ridiculous question. Zack's frustration came through over the radio. He and the team had gone in to clear and rescue. Not to capture anyone.

"Tell them to check again," said Pete.

"No. They know what to do. Give them a few minutes."

"All the time in the world is not going to matter if your guy is not there." Pete was getting frustrated.

He was right. I was worried. To make matters worse, the assault had been loud. It would already have begun attracting attention. We would be screwed if a ground force found them. It would take too long. They should be back on the pickup truck headed to the PZ now.

"I'm going to feel really stupid flying back empty-handed."

Pete's statement hit my gut like ice water.

TWENTY-NINE

THE MONDAY AFTER A LOSS TO NAVY SUCKS. THE CORPS is back facing exams, gloom period's takeover of the cadet area is close, and the plebes, who have been hoping to "fall out" after a win over Navy, must continue pinging against the walls and eating at attention.

At dinner, I found myself sitting at a table with Bill and the Guru as table com. As the two cows, Bill and I sat across from each other at the head of the table. A month before, it would have been awkward, but we had thawed to the point that I almost welcomed it. I wondered if the Guru had orchestrated it.

The Guru ordered the plebes to execute their duties silently. "I don't ever want to hear announcements during dinner. Just get the drinks and food out and cut the dessert. Always assume eight pieces. Do you understand?"

"Yes, sir!"

"Get on with it."

It was a quiet meal. As soon as the announcements were made, the plebes and yearlings departed. Bill, the Guru, and I sat at the table and drank coffee.

"What a fucking year, huh?" said Bill dejectedly. "Female first captain. Fall of the Berlin Wall. Loss to Navy by a damn field goal with fifteen seconds left."

"Are those all bad things?" asked the Guru.

"I suppose they're all both good and bad," I said. Bill looked at me, puzzled. "Okay. Losing to Navy is all bad, but the other two depend on your point of view."

The Guru shook his head. "Always the philosopher."

"Well, my point of view is pretty simple," said Bill. "It's the Corps' point of view. Having a female first captain is progress but is also a pain in the ass. This place is shitty enough without cause for even more scrutiny and political correctness."

"All progress comes from struggle, Bill," the Guru said.

Bill rolled his eyes and continued: "As far as the Berlin Wall is concerned, same thing. Sure, it's progress for the world, depending on how things shake out, but for the Corps, the beginning of the disintegration of our 'main enemy'? You watch, Sam: by the time you and I graduate next year, all people are going to be talking about is massive military budget cuts. What a wonderful time to be commissioned."

"You'd prefer that Berlin remain a divided city so the Corps can be happy?" the Guru asked.

"Of course not," Bill fumed. "But sometimes I think we're just cursed. Unlucky. This has to be the most overly sensitive, wannabe-professional, watered-down time in history to have ever been a cadet." Bill shook his head. He was dejected. He took a swig of coffee and sighed. "Fuck it."

It was strange to see him like this, if only briefly. To me, Bill had always seemed an indifferent force of nature. He did not get down. Even when walking off more area punishment tours than some entire platoons get in a semester, he had not gotten down. But the cocktail of events and the outside pressures weighing on the Corps this year had affected him in a way that other things had not.

"You guys sound ready," said the Guru.

Used to his cryptic style, we turned our heads toward the head of the table and waited for him to continue.

He warmed up his coffee from the steaming silver pitcher and added a single sugar packet. He stirred the drink slowly and continued:

"For action, my young Percivals."

He held the steaming cup in his left hand as he sat back in his chair. He placed his cadet saber on the table in front of him, then laid his white gloves over his saber. With his props in front and the mural depicting the history of warfare on the wall behind him, he took a leisurely sip of coffee.

"You guys know who Percival was?"

"The knight who found the Holy Grail," I said. "He saved Camelot."

"Correct."

"The Knights of the Round Table were the most glorious band of brothers the world has ever known. After their formation by King Arthur, they rid England of the tyranny and chaos that had plagued it for centuries. Imagine the impressions this group must have made on the young men of the kingdom as they rode grandly about the land, slaying evildoers and dragons, effortlessly seducing every young maiden in their path, and wearing impressive suits of armor when everyone else was dressed in rags.

"One of these starstruck youths was a peasant named Percival. He followed the knights wherever they went, begging for ways to serve them. They scoffed at him. 'Out of the way, peasant!' the mounted knights would shout as they rode off to do their daring deeds. Despite repeated rejection, Percival continued to memorize their histories and grand accomplishments, and to secretly dream that he would someday be one of them."

The Guru took a sip of coffee and looked at us. Sensing that he needed to rope this tangent in quickly, he continued briskly: "Well, as you may know, there was a bad argument and misunderstanding between the king and Guinevere and another knight or two, which resulted in a trial by combat. Lancelot was out of town and therefore unable to stand for the queen's honor. Percival volunteered, and King Arthur knighted him right on the spot.

"As luck would have it, Lancelot rode up just before the combat could take place. So Guinevere's honor was defended and Percival obtained his knighthood."

The Guru leaned forward. "But he was admitted into the brotherhood just as it entered the dark times. Camelot turned out not to be what he'd expected at all. Morale sucked. The brotherhood he thought he had seen from the outside wasn't there; the table was rife with cliques that undermined its spirit of common cause. Arthur seemed unable to cope with the problems within his band of noble soldiers. Percival's dream was destroyed in its realization. He was crushed and disillusioned." The Guru paused for a long moment. He took a sip of coffee and nodded slightly as if confirming something to himself.

"Yet he was the one who risked his life. It was his act of faith that saved the land. Disillusioned, he still found the Grail." He looked at us. "Probably one of the most important spirit missions in history, don't you think?"

The Guru smiled. "Do you guys have it in you to seek the Grail?"

Bill let out a loud sigh and pushed back from the table. "Guru. I love you, man. Anyone who tells Captain Eifer to fuck himself is good in my book. But you're a nut job. I've got to get back and study."

The Guru smiled.

Bill shook his head.

"The goat," I said.

The Guru smiled at me. "Very good, Sam."

The Guru leaned forward and said over his saber, "It hasn't been pulled off in a very long time, fellows. It needs to be done."

"We'd get hammered," I said.

"Don't think of the cost. Think of the reward."

"Seriously, the commandant gets up at the beginning of each year and reiterates the agreement: the truce thing between the two academies. And then, in case you've forgotten, he reissues his command. He says don't fucking do it."

"Even if we did get hammered," mused Bill, almost to himself. "It would be worth it." He was leaning forward now.

As we sat in silence, I realized that the Guru was savoring this moment. Graduation was a week away for him. He was smart enough to realize that he would not exist in his current form after that day. They say there is no rank as high as that of first-class cadet. For the Guru, that would be doubly true. He had mastered this peculiar universe and was totally at home in the cadet area. He would never master anywhere else so well ever again. The moment after he was commissioned he would be just another dipshit butter-bar second lieutenant, unremarkable and unworthy of respect.

"Tell me, Sam, what are the principles of war?"

Only for the Guru would I recite plebe knowledge as a cow. "Objective. Offensive. Mass. Economy of force, maneuver, unity of command. Simplicity. Security and surprise."

"Very good. Bill, tell me which are the most important of those principles if one were to try to steal the navy goat."

"Surprise is definitely one."

"Agreed."

"Security," I said.

"Excellent. Lastly?"

Bill and I thought for a moment. The Guru sipped his coffee.

"Objective," the Guru said gravely. "You must keep the objective in mind."

He set his coffee cup down. "What is your mission, Bill?"

"To get the goat."

"Merely to get the goat?" His voice was heavy with disappointment. "Did Percival seek the Grail merely to find it? The Corps must see it. The Corps must receive it from you. Just to steal it from the navy means nothing."

"The tactical department would disagree with you," I said.

"Yes. They would burn you merely for the theft." Involuntarily, and to my concealed shame, my chest constricted at his words. I had images of walking area tours until the turn of the century, of never seeing Stephanie again.

"That is why security is so important. Once the word gets out that the goat has been stolen, the tactical department is going to go berserk. They will do everything possible to intervene and stop you before the rest of the Corps sees the goat. But that's all right because we can predict what they will do." He leaned back in his chair, the history of war spreading out on the wall behind him.

"The tactical department's tentacles will latch onto every possible lead. So if you leave anything real out there, anything at all that might lead them to you, they will find it. Even worse, the Corps would never believe that the goat had been taken." This possibility hadn't occurred to me: that the tactical department might intervene before the rest of the Corps could see the goat.

"With a little forethought and attention to security, you won't leave anything real out there for them to find." The Guru smiled.

"We'll send 'em down some deep fucking rabbit holes!" said Bill, laughing.

"As you should, but don't overdo it. Use misdirection sparingly—otherwise it won't be convincing. As the end approaches, they will undoubtedly be able to put a lot of heat on you . . . no matter how tight your security is. You must be ready for that.

"Remember, you must avoid getting cornered. Do not give them probable cause to pose a justified direct question. Or, worse, the opportunity to give you a direct order to surrender or return the goat before the Corps has seen it."

Bill and I nodded.

"You must choose your team carefully. No one with a discipline record of any significance should participate." He was pointing at us now. "You must all be able to weather a heavy disciplinary board and still graduate, and you should all be prepared to do so. It may be unavoidable, as your names are sure to become known."

I swallowed hard at the thought of spending my last semester on the area. No time with Stephanie. "Do you think it will come to that?"

"Of course it will."

"So why would you tell me all of this?" asked Bill. "I've had a first-class board, over a hundred hours. I can't take another one."

"Indeed, Cooper. I thought about that. Then I realized you're the kind of cadet that just doesn't give a shit. You will do what you think is right, cost be damned."

"You got that right."

"Avery here is not like that. He is a good strategic thinker but not as devout a risk taker as you are. It would be good for him to have you beside him on this. You'll just have to decide if the risk is worth it to you."

"I think it is."

"Don't answer too hastily. You have time. There will be a lot you can do in support."

"So," I said, "the chain of command will probably come down on us like a load of bricks, huh?"

The Guru regarded my troubled face and leaned forward. "Come now, Sam. This grand institution has been preaching selfless sacrifice to you since the day you arrived . . . none of it sank in?"

"Did I say I wasn't going to do it?"

"Of course not." He leaned back in his chair. "Surprise will be easily achieved if your security is tight enough. This is not to say that it is not essential. It is. The element of surprise must be retained in regards to both the navy and the commandant's office. But since no one has even attempted it in over a quarter of a century, and since the spirit of the Corps is so low . . . no one will be expecting it."

We were all quiet for a moment. "Why didn't you ever do it, Guru?" I asked.

"Who, out of this entire Corps of Cadets"—he gestured outward with his arms—"do you think would immediately be suspected if the goat was stolen?"

"True," I agreed, "but you said that one hundred hours would be a small price to pay."

"Fair point. The truth is, I don't think I could get it to the Corps. They would discover me too soon, and it would be over. Then it would be impossible to attempt for another twenty-five years." When finished, he looked away.

He stood up, strapped on his saber, and began to put on his gloves. "I won't be here, of course. Spare no effort in your planning. Exhaust every possible scenario and have a contingency for all of them."

He took one final swallow of coffee and said, "Never forget that you are doing it for the Corps—otherwise whatever you accomplish will mean nothing."

"How the hell are you so sure we will do it?" I asked.

He just smiled, and then he strode out of the mess hall, master of the myths of West Point.

THIRTY

EXAM WEEK ROLLED OVER THE CORPS LIKE A DAM bursting in slow motion. It struck the different departments in sequence. First the mathematics department was crushed, then foreign languages. The engineering departments, the largest at the academy, took the longest to inundate, but one by one they were all washed over.

The Corps was done, packing and headed for Christmas leave. As we quickly tore down our rooms and stored our personal gear in the basement trunk rooms, the United States invaded Panama. It made a strange backdrop to the ordinarily carefree and joyous departure of the Corps. Cadets and officers alike spent a lot of time in the dayrooms watching CNN. Slowly, we were able to figure out what units had gotten the call, and who of us were in those units. Some of our former company mates from the class of 1987 were getting their first taste of battle.

On Friday morning, I attended the December graduation ceremony at the Guru's invitation. Held in Robinson Auditorium in Thayer Hall, it lacked the scale of the traditional Michie Stadium event each May. There were twenty-one cadets graduating, including the Guru. More than two hundred family members, civilian friends, and cadets were in attendance. The fight under way in Panama gave the ceremony a sense of gravity that hadn't been present at the other graduations I had attended. Even though Noriega was on the ropes already and there was no way any cadet graduating today was going to see battle in Panama, the combat operations hung heavy in the air. The dean struck the right tone of solemn acknowledgment, brevity, and humor as he spoke. Soon the graduates were throwing their hats in the air. A couple of caps bounced off the ceiling as the crowed cheered loudly. I applauded in the back, watching the Guru. He was smiling broadly as his mom and stepfather hugged him.

The auditorium was awash in sounds of loud talking, cheers, and backslapping. I eased toward the front, hoping to catch the Guru's eye. I was halfway down when he saw me, and I gave him a wave and brought my right hand up in a salute. He nodded, and I turned to go.

I was almost to the top of the auditorium when I felt a hand on my shoulder.

"Sam, wait." It was the Guru.

"Congratulations, Guru. You did it."

"Thanks, Sam." He reached out his hand to shake mine, but I saluted instead. He chuckled.

"No. I haven't been commissioned yet. We're doing that in about an hour, so I'm not quite an officer."

I held my salute. "Yeah, but I won't see you then. Let me be the first."

He smiled and saluted me back. As he did so, I noticed his class ring.

"What is that?" I grabbed his hand and looked at the ring. The ugly void had been filled by a shiny, rounded stone. It was gray with colored flecks and had been polished to a smooth, gently domed finish. The dark stone made a striking contrast with the gold of the ring. It seemed to have weight. It looked sharp.

"What do you think?"

"What kind of stone is that?"

"Granite."

I looked back at the ring.

"It's granite from the barracks. I chipped off a big chunk one night and sent it to a jeweler. He tried to tell me it wouldn't work, but I think it turned out pretty well."

"That's cool, Guru."

"Thanks. I got a link of the chain *and* a piece of the mountain." He smiled at me and made a fist of his ring hand.

"It's not going to be the same here without you."

"No. It won't, but that's okay. Another Guru will appear. They always do."

I rolled my eyes at him for the last time.

I realized that he had not set out to be the Guru. As a cadet, he'd simply followed his path as best he could, like the rest of us. But in the rigid ideological landscape of West Point, informal leadership figures loom large, particularly those who offer an alternative worldview. The influence of these figures is outsized because of their scarceness. The Guru had been one of the giants.

"I need to get back to the family. I'm the man of the hour, you know."

"When are you ever not?"

"Indeed. Good luck to you, Sam. Don't let the bastards get you down."

"Thanks. Same to you. Go naked, sir!"

"Go naked, Sam." I watched as he made his way back to his family. He was halfway there when he turned around suddenly. "I nearly forgot—good luck with that thing next year!" he shouted over the crowd. "I'll be rooting for you!" He smiled his Loki grin, turned back into the celebrating crowd, and was gone.

Son of a bitch, I thought. What ever happened to the principle of security?

THIRTY-ONE

"**T**HIS IS THAYER 6—WE GOT HIM."

I smiled to myself in the dark cockpit and tried to picture the scene. *Fuck yeah, Zack!* I thought.

"Bulldog, Thayer 6. Sitrep follows. They had crammed him into a hidden closet. Medic is looking him over now, but he is disoriented and badly dehydrated."

"Thayer 6, Bulldog. Is he ambulatory?"

"Not sure yet. Stand by."

"Now all we need is exfil instructions," said Pete happily. "We may be home in time to be court-martialed tonight, after all."

We flew another two laps in the night, waiting for Zack to give us instructions. He would assess the situation, including the Guru's mobility. All we could do was wait.

"Thayer 6, Elvis. Vehicle convoy headed your way. Five vehicles proceeding south approximately seven kilometers north of your position. Moving fast. Estimated ground speed sixty kilometers an hour."

"Shit," said Pete. That was the problem with our bootleg operation. Even though we were sure our every move was being monitored in real time by Brick and the rest of the command, we didn't have access to what they knew. As a result, we didn't have the theater-wide situational awareness we normally did. We were vulnerable to surprises, and we had taken too long on the objective.

"Roger, Elvis," said Zack quickly.

"Thayer 6, Bulldog. Say exfil intentions."

The radio was silent.

"Fuck it," I said as I banked the helicopter sharply toward the objective.

"Bulldog, recommend you proceed closer to the objective to prepare for exfil and potentially provide suppressive fire."

"Way ahead of you, Elvis," responded Pete.

As big as it is, the Chinook is actually the fastest helicopter in the army. Its counter-rotating rotor disks give it an advantage over single-rotor designs. It will do 170 knots, almost 200 miles per hour. It gets slowed down after we stick a couple of miniguns out the windows and hang flare and chaff dispensers, and numerous antennas on its fuselage, but you can still boogie. I leaned 458 as far over as I could and demanded all the speed her rotor blades could hammer out.

"Thayer 6, Bulldog. We are en route. ETA three minutes."

No reply.

Pete called up the FLIR and swiveled it to look at the objective, now only five kilometers away.

"Thayer 6, Elvis. Vehicles now two kilometers north of your position."

"Maybe they're not going to the objective," Pete said hopefully but without conviction. "Maybe it's not related."

"No," I muttered. "This is bad." Then I spoke to the crew: "This is going to be a hot extraction."

"Roger that, sir," responded Crawford. "Weapons ready."

Not wanting to overfly the objective until we had a better idea of the situation, I altered course to the east. I also hoped the sound of our rotors would spook the enemy enough to slow them down. Funny thing about a Chinook is, it can sound like a flight of four smaller helicopters, particularly at night, when you can't see it.

The vehicles were approaching the objective from the north on the main road. The objective was centered in our FLIR image. The range read one kilometer when a bright streak flashed across the screen.

"Hell," said Pete as the wall surrounding the target house exploded. Dust and debris showered the area, obscuring our line of sight. I banked to the south and decelerated to a better maneuvering speed.

On the FLIR we could see the vehicles as they drove to the breached wall and stopped. Men with weapons hopped out and began to surround the house. It was getting ugly quickly.

"Thayer 6, give us a sitrep," I transmitted.

Nothing.

"Someone tipped them off," muttered Pete. "They knew exactly where they were going."

"Elvis. Little help, please."

"Bulldog, five vehicles and numerous personnel surrounding the objective."

"Do you have eyes on Thayer 6?"

"Negative. We had to take eyes off Thayer to monitor the vehicles. Now the objective is obscured. Searching."

I felt an unwelcome flare of panic in my gut. The FLIR showed foot soldiers sneaking through the breached wall and taking up positions around the house. If we went right now, we might have sufficient surprise and be able to gun enough of them down to pull off a successful extraction. But there was no response from Zack.

"Thayer 6, Bulldog. Sitrep, over?"

Silence.

"Goddamnit!" I yelled into the cockpit, without keying my mike. As if I were screaming underwater, my yell was drowned out by the noise of the cockpit. The same suffocating feeling gripped my chest. It had gone to shit so fast.

"They've got more RPGs," said Pete softly. I looked at the FLIR display and watched as the distinctive silhouette of a man shouldering an RPG pointed at the target house. The flare of launch obscured our view for an instant. The telltale bright streak crossed the display, and the front doorway of the target house vanished in dust and chunks of flying stone.

"Elvis, Bulldog, anything?" transmitted Pete. On the FLIR, the foot soldiers were tentatively moving forward into the smashed house, firing their weapons intermittently.

"Negative, Bulldog. Still searching."

"Thayer 6, this is Bulldog. Give us a sitrep, Zack," I transmitted futilely.

"All right, fuckers," Pete said. "Left side, prepare to fire."

"Been waiting on you, sir," Crawford said.

Pete dumped power and pulled back on the cyclic, and 458 started to decelerate. Then he aggressively pressed on the right pedal. She skidded abruptly out of trim. The left side of the aircraft faced almost thirty degrees into our direction of flight. Chinook 458 wallowed through the air now like a sideways semitrailer.

"Enough?" asked Pete.

"Roger that, sir."

"You're cleared hot."

A loud chain-saw noise erupted from the left minigun. A vibration went through the floor of the aircraft. It felt good.

I watched the IR tracers stream toward the enemy. Crawford was one of the most experienced gunners in the regiment. He quickly dropped two of the enemy closest to the objective house. The others dove for cover and fired futilely in our direction.

Our direction of flight momentarily put the wall between us and the enemy.

"Damnit," said Crawford. "Targets obscured."

"Roger. Bringing us around."

Pete wrestled 458 through the air to try to give Crawford a clear shot. I watched the enemy on the drone feed. They moved into the objective house, crouched and firing their weapons. At fifty knots, one hundred feet above the desert floor, my heart broke. I realized the insanity of what I had done. I had just brought two friends to the enemy so that they could kill three instead of one.

THIRTY-TWO

TURTLE AND I WERE ROOMMATES AGAIN SECOND SEMES-
ter cow year. He had evolved into the quintessential E4 cadet: studi-
ous when he wanted to be, with straight A's in his aerospace major but C's
in everything else; tough and dependable; but always in disciplinary trouble. Despite having chosen the hard-core study of flying machines, Turtle
was determined to branch infantry and was preparing to compete to
attend Ranger School as a cadet that summer, a competitive and difficult
thing to accomplish. He didn't give a shit about the cadet chain of command and was unambitious when it came to his cadet career. But being a
Ranger and, ultimately, Special Forces was something he planned and
prepared for every day. Like Bill, he possessed a clarity of self and purpose that perplexed me.

Turtle tried to tone things down in his third year. He did not completely abstain from spirit missions, but he didn't do anything outrageous,
like the night he clambered up the statue of Washington on his horse and
painted the animal's balls red. He had also stopped launching water balloons out barracks windows with the powerful slingshot device he'd made

from surgical tubing and a duffel bag; he'd been able to put balloons through windows on the other side of North Area. It had truly been impressive. But when he'd started sniping at F4 cadets walking back from nighttime study sessions, he'd gotten hammered. It hadn't been hard to figure out where the projectiles came from.

These days he executed most of his spirit missions in a support role. He either trained plebes and yearlings in the art or acted as security for Disco Bob.

Disco Bob was a cow in Third Regiment who threw secret flash disco parties at the stroke of 0015 on random nights. Turtle was part of his secret communications web. Somehow Bob would get the word out, and in a random place in the cadet area exactly fifteen minutes after taps, at least fifty daring cadets would answer the call and dance like crazy. Disco Bob had lights, equipment, and music. He even had a mirrored disco ball, which he held aloft with an old saber; cadets would shine flashlights on it as they danced around. No one could figure out how he got set up so quickly, how he hid the equipment afterward, or how he put the word out. It was a feat that earned even the Guru's respect. But I did know that Turtle helped Bob pick the nights and the spots. Turtle had a feel for the Corps and had studied all of the officers who served as officer in charge. He knew their routes and habits and how to place the late-night mini disco party on the other side of the cadet area from them every time.

Even better for me, plebes were terrified of Turtle. They feared me as well, simply because I roomed with him. As a result, our newspaper and laundry were always prompt. He even had a small crew that brought us cookies and sheet cakes from the mess hall, after he taught them a way to sneak into the bakery.

As roommates we were a good fit, and the semester ground by.

"Let's go, Avery. You were supposed to be ready at eighteen hundred hours."

"I know, I know. Give me one minute."

Bill and Turtle stood impatiently at the door while I threw on my uniform. We were going to a movie in Thayer Hall.

"I'm going to go grab Zack," said Turtle. "See you guys there."

"Roger that," said Bill. "If this guy ever gets ready."

A few minutes later, Bill and I strode in silence on Diagonal Walk, across the Plain. I looked north past Trophy Point at the Hudson. It was mid-March, and only a few large chunks of ice remained on the banks. The river was still gray, but there were hints of blue and green as it moved past the academy, toward the city.

Our détente had also quietly accelerated over the past few months. We were at ease around each other, and our classmates were at ease around us when we were together. No one asked about what had happened anymore, and I seldom thought about it. When it did come to mind, the world no longer stopped spinning. *I really fucked up*, I would think to myself. *Can't ever do that again.* I realized as we were walking that it had been more than a year since that night. It seemed like a decade had passed.

"So, I was thinking about planning a road trip after spring break," Bill said.

"Where to?"

"Annapolis."

"I see."

"I did some research and found three spots where they might be keeping the goat between games, and I thought we could snoop around a bit. Recon the area."

"Would you want me to come?"

"If you want."

"Sure. I'm game."

"Good." We emerged from the tunnel and cut across Central Area. It had just started to snow.

As we walked, I realized that the potential goat-napping mission had been a salve to our wounded friendship. It had been the catalyst for the thaw by becoming a constructive secret. It didn't wipe out the secret of shame we shared, but it gave us a path forward. I wondered if that had been the Guru's purpose all along, if he hadn't cared whether or not we actually went after the goat. I smiled and shook my head as we neared Thayer Hall. That would have been just like him. And I was grateful.

At that moment, I fought the urge to apologize to Bill. To say that we were cool. That I had grown up a little bit and did not hold what had happened against him anymore. That I did not forgive either of us, but I was done judging and just wanted us to do better. And that our friendship was more important to me than any of it. My pride told me that he should make the apology. And my brain told me that the conversation could wait till after spring leave, which was just a week away.

THIRTY-THREE

HALF OF US WERE OFF THE BUS AND RUNNING BEFORE
it had come to a stop in Central Area. Leaving our bags on the bus,
we sprinted toward our respective company areas. Spring leave would be
over in less than a minute. Anyone who didn't make formation in time
was looking at a no-questions-asked twenty hours on the area. Not the
way I wanted to wrap up my cow year.

I accelerated as I plunged into the tunnel under the mess hall, expecting to hear the command "Fall in!" at any second. We shot onto North
Area to see the regiment shuffling forth to their company formations. It
seemed like most of the cadets in the company were already standing
in their assigned spots, and Captain Kendall was in the rear of E4, survey-
ing the company with pen and paper at the ready. As I sped directly through
the center of North Area with the rest of my classmates, I caught the eye
of the regimental cadet command sergeant major. He smiled at me and
shook his head as we barreled past him. At that point, I knew we had made
it. Tom was from D4 and not a duty dick. He would wait until we made
it to call formation. I skidded into place just as I heard him yell, "Fall in!"

After formation, I started back to the bus to get my bags. As I turned to go, that familiar and awful realization swelled within me. For the past few hours, all of my efforts had been given to making formation. With the crisis now past, my mind got its bearings and figured out just where we were. After a nearly perfect week with Stephanie, I was back in the cadet area. I missed her already.

"Avery!" It was Kendall's voice.

"Yes, sir." I spun on my heels and headed purposefully back to the rear of the formation. Settling into my indifferent cow stride, I organized my defense. The captain's face was sternly set. But I had made formation on time, hadn't I?

As I got closer, he moved away from the post-formation gaggle so that we had some privacy, despite the hundreds of cadets streaming back into the barracks. The guys in the company were watching me as I walked over. I had the awful feeling that the hammer was about to fall, and I wondered which terrible secret about me Kendall had uncovered.

"Sam." Captain Kendall never called us by our first names. "This is not easy . . ." He shuffled his feet a little and looked down. I got nervous. Something was wrong.

Then he put his hand on my shoulder and said, "Bill Cooper was killed in an accident returning from leave. He's dead, Sam. I'm sorry."

I don't remember many things about that night. I don't know how my bags got from the bus to my room. I don't know how I got signed in. I don't even know how I got into uniform, but I do remember leaving the barracks to go to the taps vigil.

Moments of silence for fallen graduates are often held in the mess hall. Prior to "Take seats," an announcement is read naming the officer as well as the time and place of their death. In peacetime, it happens several times a year. During war, more often. But those are graduates. Cadets seldom die as cadets. This was shocking. Even to those who had not known Bill. Not the death part. Death is talked about every day at West Point. Every building, sally port, and windowpane seems to be named after someone who died in battle, or after, or whenever. But cadets walk around this deathscape feeling immortal. Bill's loss was an insult.

The Corps was in dress gray. Mist rose off the Hudson, obscuring the academic buildings and reducing the cadet area to a vague and obscured region of dark shapes and indistinct lights.

Just before midnight, the Corps formed up on the edge of the apron, facing the Plain in a single rank, cadets standing shoulder to shoulder against the darkness. It took a few minutes for all four thousand of us to arrive. Once the icy footfalls ceased, silence fell. The oppressive, tangible quiet thickened the mist and lasted for about five minutes. Just when it seemed that it would crush us, a lone trumpet sounded from the darkness.

The solitary wailing instrument let out a long, slow note. It hesitated for just an instant, as if it were choking back tears of its own, and then began to sound taps. The tragic notes seemed to emanate both from the impenetrable darkness and from us. A dark, wet stain grew on my chest as tears ran down my face and onto my dress gray. The trumpet continued to sound from somewhere on the Plain, and I was unable to keep my vision clear as I peered into the dark.

The trumpet concluded.

Before the silence could smother us, the Corps faced about to return to the barracks. No command was given, but it was done in unison. We left the Plain without speaking a word.

Zack and Creighton sat with Turtle and me in our room after the taps vigil. We were heartbroken and confused. I felt like I had vertigo and held my head in my hands while the others talked.

"I didn't even know he had a motorcycle," said Turtle softly. "Did you guys?" Creighton shook his head, but Zack didn't react.

I hadn't known either, and that hurt. Bill hadn't shared anything with me after our falling out. Certainly nothing like this. We hadn't had that relationship anymore. Now we didn't have any relationship. Never would.

"I did," Zack said. "I was actually with him when he bought it. He loved that thing."

"Why didn't you tell any of us?" asked Turtle sadly.

"It was none of your fucking business, that's why."

"Better you did not know, Turtle. It's against regulations for cadets to operate motorcycles."

"Thanks, Creighton," said Zack in a tired voice.

"I'm not criticizing, Zack. Just giving him context as to why it's reasonable that you didn't tell anyone."

Zack was trying to get angry, but he was working too hard not to cry. His face was red and knotted with effort, and, after a few seconds, he rubbed his eyes with both hands as tears began to run down his cheeks again. Creighton walked over and put his hand on Zack's shoulder. We all looked in the other direction.

"Does anyone know what happened?" I asked.

"I heard he went off the road at the top of Storm King Mountain. I'm not sure where he was coming from," said Turtle.

"The weather here has been so slimy lately. I'm sure the road was slick."

Storm King Mountain rises about thirteen hundred feet above the Hudson River and is a constant overwatching companion to West Point. Its looming, dark granite presence just to the north of post is almost always in view of the Corps and contributes to the isolated surrounded-by-granite-walls feeling of the cadet area. Route 9W runs north along the west side of the Hudson, tracing a route from Fort Lee, New Jersey, to Albany, New York. On its way up Storm King, though, 9W turns back and forth on itself sharply a few times, offering dramatic views of the Hudson River valley and West Point far below. I pictured Bill sailing over the railing at the big switchback, tracing a long, steepening arc as he separated from his bike and fell to his death.

"What did he do for spring leave, anyway?"

"He told me he was going to ride south, turn around, and ride back. Not sure he had a real schedule."

"He was seeing that girl from UNC, right? Did he link up with her? Do we need to get in touch with her?"

"'Seeing' is too strong a word, I think."

"I just can't believe it . . ."

"I guess the academy has told his parents by now?"

"Not sure," Creighton said. "Kendall asked who I thought would be willing to gather his belongings."

"I'll do it," I said. Snot was coming out of my nose, and my breath was ragged. I stood up quickly, walked to the sink, and splashed water on my face. "I'll do it."

"Okay, Sam. Just let Captain Kendall know in the morning."

We stood in silence, unsure what to do next. Zack spoke up first.

"I'm going to turn in."

Turtle closed the door after Zack and Creighton left. "You okay, Sam?"

I didn't answer. I was lying in my bed still in my dress grays. Eyes closed. Tears flowing.

THIRTY-FOUR

E4 MOVED SLOWLY THROUGH ITS MOURNING. THOUGH the Hudson River valley was returning to life and spring injected color back into our landscape, we were stuck in a heavy gray haze. Me, especially. I couldn't accept what had happened. It affected everything. My grades dropped. I found it hard to talk to Stephanie. I withdrew. I felt foolish. Ashamed. Shocked. And over something so stupid as a tire losing its grip. A motorcycle losing its footing. A person flying and then falling.

I helped Captain Kendall pack up Bill's things. It was sad, but he had made it easy on us. He was a good cadet and everything was in its place, even his locker in the trunk room. It was perfectly in order. Everything fell easily into boxes to be shipped home to his parents. The process took a couple of days, and as we worked, I kept hoping to find a journal or note or something that would help me connect to my lost friend. But there was nothing. Bill had not been a journaler. Far from it. I laughed at not finding any letters to him in his room. Most cadets have a precious beat-up shoe box where they keep treasured letters from girlfriends, family members, and friends. Not so Bill. I think he read letters once and threw them away immediately. With the information relayed and received, there was no purpose to the paper anymore. It was tossed.

A couple of us received "compassionate leave" to attend Bill's funeral, outside of Pittsburgh. His parents were destroyed but stoic. His dad, a gruff trucker, shook our hands stiffly and thanked us for coming. His mom was pale and fragile and looked like she hadn't slept at all since the day Bill died. She hugged each of us when we introduced ourselves. Later, when the service was over and we were headed back to West Point, she made a point of finding me and giving me another hug. It was awkward. She held on too long. I could see Zack shuffling his feet out of the corner of my eye. Before she let me go she whispered, "You were very special to him, Sam. Very special. I appreciate you coming."

I pushed myself gently away. "Thank you, ma'am. He was special to me, too. I miss him."

Then we left.

Cow year slid off the calendar as the gray haze of Bill's death slowly burned off. Zack, Creighton, Turtle, and I remained shattered. But we put our heads down and trudged through the rest of the year. Our latent cow anger mixed toxically with Bill's tragedy to render us numb and bitter. "Fuck it" was our mantra.

Our melancholy crust was so thick, an earthquake barely registered as it passed through the Corps. The scramble was announced. The class of 1992 impotently shook their fists in rage when they learned that they would be randomly assigned to new companies when they returned after the summer for their cow year.

I was selfishly happy for my class and myself. We had dodged a bullet. The friendships and bonds that had been formed and tested over the past three years would be allowed to continue to fruition. After Bill, I could not have handled the scramble. But I was sad for E4. Its continuity would decay, diluted by the irresistible annual infusion of a new randomized class of cows from across the Corps. Something would be lost.

I consoled Mike Morris with words I didn't believe: "It's not that big of a deal, Mike. All of the companies are pretty similar."

"You're a terrible liar."

"Look at it this way: you've always been too squared away for E4 anyway. We've held you back, and you know it. This way you'll probably get the recognition you deserve."

Mike just stared at me.

"I actually mean that. And it's a compliment, asshole."

"Whatever. Have a great summer, Sam. I'll see you in August."

"Roger that, Mike."

Zack and I skipped 1990's graduation ceremony, noting as we drove away that we were finally firsties, the highest-ranking members of the cadet area. It actually felt good. Next year promised to be bearable. We would get our rings, cars, find out our branch assignments, and would accelerate toward our own graduation, now only twelve months away.

"Fuck it," Zack said as we cruised out the back gate. We drove up 9W on our way out and stopped at the spot where they thought Bill had gone over the railing.

"It's weird. He's kind of frozen in time now."

"Yeah, Zack. He's dead."

"No. I mean, he'll always be a cow. We will never remember him as a firstie."

"Or a lieutenant."

"Or that, either. That's what I mean. He's stuck in that part of our lives."

"I know what you mean. But now that you mention it, I already think of us as firsties."

"Me, too."

Zack chuckled. "You know he would have been a terror as a firstie."

I whistled. "You are right about that."

We looked down on West Point. The Hudson curved in a great arc behind it.

"Can I ask you something, Sam?"

I cringed. I hated it when he wound up like that.

"It seemed like you guys kind of made up with each other there at the end."

I stared at the river below. Its surface was reflective silver as it wrapped around the cadet area.

"Did you?"

I tried to get mad but couldn't. This was classic Zack. He didn't have discrete relationships. He lived in an ecosystem of friends. Bill and I had been an insult to that ecosystem. He was trying to balance the books.

"I don't know. It wasn't totally behind us. We were still pretty mad, at ourselves and at each other. . . . But we seemed to be moving on. It seemed . . ." My throat tightened, and I started to choke on the words. "I guess . . ." I clenched my teeth as tears escaped my eyes and rolled down my cheeks. "I had forgiven him. And I felt like he knew it . . . and I think he had forgiven me. I just regret not having had the courage to say it to him. I thought we had time." I turned from the river and looked at Zack. He was staring at me, heartbroken. "Hell, Zack, I don't know. I just know I miss him."

"Me, too," he said. "I'm sorry. I won't ask about it again."

I watched Zack as he walked back to his car and got the bottle of Scotch. He was still the same tall, athletic cadet I'd first met three summers ago, but he seemed less stubborn to me now, more steady than knuckleheaded. He still had his moments, but he had become a decisive friend I tended to lean on. I thought about Turtle and Creighton. They also seemed to have grown up a lot. I wondered if I seemed any more mature to them. Whether I did or not, I swore I would never take my friends for granted again.

Zack poured us each a big shot. We raised our glasses in the direction of post.

"To Cadet Bill Cooper," I said.

"To Bill."

We choked down the shot and threw our glasses over the side of the mountain. We didn't hear them strike hundreds of feet below. Zack looked at the bottle of Scotch and then threw it over the side as well. After a long delay, we faintly heard it shatter against the granite.

THIRTY-FIVE

"**B**ULLDOG, THAYER 6. LITTLE BUSY RIGHT NOW. STAND by." If I weren't strapped in, I would have leapt out of my seat. Zack was talking in a whisper, and the transmission was full of static, but his voice was calm.

"Roger that, Thayer 6."

We flew another half a lap in anticipation, watching the FLIR. It looked like there were about fifteen of the enemy now. One of their vehicles had a pedestal-mounted weapon in the truck bed. Looked like twin M240s.

"Bulldog, Thayer 6." Zack came over the radio again, still whispering. "We are at the far west end of the street. I've put an IR chem stick in the yard. We are going to attempt to get to the roof for extraction."

"Son of a bitch," said Pete on the intercom. "Your friend's a crafty fucker, huh?"

I just shook my head in the dark cockpit. He must have bolted the team from the target house the second he'd heard Elvis's report. Standard

Zack decisiveness. His best and worst quality. It had saved their lives tonight. So far.

"Elvis, do you have the chem stick?" Infrared chem sticks were a great tool for identification at night. Invisible to the naked eye, they were easily picked up by infrared imaging, which the enemy over here typically did not have.

"Roger. One block north and approximately two hundred meters west of the objective. Appears to be undetected by the enemy."

I called up the drone imagery and looked at Zack's new location. It wasn't great. A squat two-story building sat between two other multi-story structures. There was a small utility shed on the top floor where I assumed the team would gain access to the roof. It would also obstruct a large portion of the roof from us. The other structures were taller than the extraction point. They would constrain our flight path.

"You're not going to like this," I said as Pete switched one of his displays to the drone feed. "Obstruction on the roof and constraints to the east and west. Approach needs to be either from the north or south."

"Right over the road."

I switched back to the FLIR imagery and looked at the machine guns in the back of the pickup truck. The gunner peered through his sights at the original target house. He could do quick and deadly damage if he got a bead on us.

"Thayer 6, Bulldog. Is it possible for you to continue to evade farther west?"

"Negative, Bulldog. Have two wounded. Can't move them again and need medic ASAP."

"Roger that."

I grimaced. Must be bad if Zack was calling for an exfil like this. He knew the risks.

"All right, guys," I said to the aircraft. "Get ready. Definitely a hot extraction."

"Roger that, sir," said Crawford.

After anxious minutes, Zack made the call: "Bulldog, Thayer 6. We're ready. We are on the rooftop marked with four IR chem sticks."

"Bulldog is on the way."

Pete pointed the Chinook toward the objective and accelerated to about eighty knots. "I'm going to bring her in over the unpopulated area to the west to try to keep us away from the enemy for as long as possible. We'll approach the house from the north."

"Roger that." Pete was thinking exactly like I was. This was not going to be fun. A roof landing is tricky and time-consuming. We were going to be a big, loud, slow-moving target. He was trying to deny the enemy a clean line of sight for as long as possible. Still, the odds were not good. I noted the height of the bright moon illuminating the night and cursed our timing.

"Bulldog, this is Elvis." I was startled to hear Creighton's voice come over the radio. He had not spoken during the mission at all. It had always been someone else on his team. I had not heard his voice in years. It was strange to hear it now.

"Go ahead, Elvis."

"Bulldog, can you delay your extraction three minutes? Working on something here."

"Thayer 6, you copy?" I said to Zack over the radio.

"Roger," whispered Zack. "We can wait. But no longer than that."

"Okay, Elvis," I transmitted. "But you need to expedite."

"Roger that."

"What the hell are you chuckling at?" asked Pete, who had picked up on the mirth in my voice when I was talking to Creighton.

Just hearing Creighton's voice had made me feel better. Despite the fact that we were facing a doomed flight into a hot LZ, I couldn't help but smile at the irony that it was Creighton, a second-generation army armor officer, and not an air force alum, who'd ushered the CIA into preeminence with a robot air force. But, even better, it felt like he was playing Risk in the barracks again, only with us as the set pieces and the Guru as the prize. There was no one I would rather have running the game board. I was hopeful. All I said to Pete, though, was "This ought to be good."

THIRTY-SIX

THE END OF AUGUST 1990 WAS ANOTHER STRANGE return for the Corps. We converged again on West Point for the new cadet march back as the rest of the U.S. military was converging on the Middle East. The nation was preparing for war, and it looked like this was going to be a real one.

After two weeks with Stephanie, I spent most of the summer on a Beast cadre detail training the new cadets. I was surprised to find that I enjoyed it. As a new firstie, I tried to inure myself to nostalgia or anything else that smelled like irrational fondness for West Point. But training the new cadets was meaningful. I felt a connection to the Guru, Wilcox, and beyond to others I did not know.

After marching the new cadets back from Lake Frederick, I prepared my room for inspection. The class of 1991 moved through Reorgy Week like the pros we had become. We were firsties now and could get a room ready for inspection with ease. Zack and I were roommates this semester. We worked well together and alternated between squaring the room away, going to the gym, and sitting in the dayroom watching the run-up to war. Like the rest of our class, we also looked forward to Friday evening, the day we would receive our class rings.

On Wednesday afternoon, we had just gotten back from the gym, and Zack was feeling frisky. He stepped out into the hallway and waited for a plebe to ping by. He didn't have to wait long before Cadet Yun came pinging up the stairs.

"Cadet Yun, post!"

I rolled my eyes to myself as I put on my robe and headed to the shower. Zack wasn't a mean haze, but he did enjoy making sure a plebe knew he was a plebe.

"What did you read in the paper today, Cadet Yun?"

"Sir, today in the *New York Times* it was reported that President Bush told allies that they must bear their share of the cost of the new post–Cold War world. Secretary Baker is being sent to the Persian Gulf to demand contributions to the war effort."

I turned on the shower as Zack ran Yun through his paces. First the *New York Times,* then "The Days," then Schofield's Definition of Discipline, and then a bunch of other random stuff. He was still chewing on Yun when I came out of the latrine.

"Cadet Yun, I'm going to square you away. I'm going to tell you how to have a good first semester here on my floor. Would you like that?"

"Yes, sir."

"First you need to make sure that Cadet Avery and I always have a newspaper."

"Yes, sir!"

"If that means you have to steal a paper from a nasty yearling or mean-ass cow, you do it. I like to read the paper. You understand me?"

"Yes, sir."

"And I don't want a wrinkly, wet, or otherwise fucked-up paper."

"Yes, sir."

I smiled as I went into our room and got dressed. It felt good to listen to Zack laying down the law for the semester. The world was in order.

"The next key to having a good semester is laundry. Don't ever let Cadet Avery or me lose any laundry or have to wait for it to be delivered. Do you understand me?"

"Yes, sir."

"Hello, Sam?" Mike pushed his head into our room.

We shook hands and gave each other a hug. We had not seen each other since the end of the academic year and the Corps' announcement of the scramble.

"So how is First Regiment?"

Mike shook his head. "It's a different world, Sam."

The scramble had landed him in Cadet Company B1. Just as E4 was, to those who knew the Corps, a wayward rebel outpost, B1 was the physical, uniformed manifestation of the Corps' Platonic ideal. Impeccable uniforms. Immaculate barracks rooms. Flawless drill formations. B1 cadets were perfect. But not in the dehumanized way of Captain Eifer. B1 cadets were perfect because they worked their asses off at being cadets. And they did not mind if that effort showed. They were tough and disciplined enough to be perfect, and the rest of the Corps was not.

I had several friends from B1, guys I had gotten to know either at Buckner or in classes. They were great guys. Like the colonel had said, we were more similar than different. They just had a higher standard in the cadet area. And if you were in their sphere of influence, you were going to meet it also. Period. As their friend from E4, I created low expectations from them in terms of military discipline. I met that standard.

B1 hated the scramble as much as E4 did. More, even. Their purity was threatened. Their tradition, the reasons they so reliably created fanatically good cadets, dates back to the beginning of the Corps. Whereas E4 traces its history to the near doubling of the Corps of Cadets from 2,529 to 4,417 in 1964, B1's lineage extends all the way back to the first decades of the academy. It was one of the original cadet units, formed with the other foundational companies, A1, C1, and D1, when the Corps was expanded to 250 cadets. Congress authorized and funded this expansion to meet the need for officers for the looming war against England in 1812.

War and the nation's ever-increasing role in the world have been West Point's growth catalyst ever since. After the academy graduated cadets early to meet the need for officers, first in the Spanish-American War and then in the Philippine-American War, the Corps was increased to 481 cadets in 1900. World War I provided the impetus in 1916 for the Corps' near tripling to 1,332 cadets. This still didn't spare the three upper classes at the time from being accelerated through, graduated early, and shipped to the trenches in Europe to lead doughboys. The Corps was increased again in 1935 and then again to 2,496 in 1942. Again, cadets were graduated early to go to war.

Through each of the Corps' lurching growth spurts, B1 had been a bastion of its true spirit. They hardened each time the Corps, in their eyes, added softness. Their legend became more potent as the Corps diluted.

Their legend also had a dark side. Their resistance to change in the Corps was indiscriminate, but they hated women. There had not been a female graduate from B1. Ever. Females who were assigned there were run out or reassigned. B1's unofficial company name was "Boys One," which they preserved at an even greater risk than E4 did the motto "Go naked." Like E4, their true history was difficult to determine. It was woven through with myth. Some of it ugly.

"It's fine, though," Mike added. "It's a good group of cadets."

"That's good," I said, noting to myself how sad he seemed.

"It's not the same, though," he said, looking at his highly shined shoes.

"Of course it isn't. It's First Regiment."

"That's not what I mean. I feel like I don't belong. Almost like I'm not a cadet anymore."

I realized that Mike was seeking guidance. He needed friendship as he dealt with a monumental change. The sense of fraternity in some cadet companies is so strong, it can be disorienting when it is taken away at graduation. But at that time, the newly commissioned officers have a fresh world of distractions to take their minds off the loss. Mike and his year group had none of those distractions. They trudged through the same institution but now without their tribe. I realized again how fortunate I felt at not being scrambled. I was happy and tried not to let it show.

"Mike, I am not going to tell you this doesn't suck. But I promise you that after a month or so of living in your new company, it's going to be better. It won't be the same. But it will be good. Remember how tight you got with your Buckner company? And that was just eight weeks."

He looked at me and nodded. He didn't smile, but his eyes seemed less sad.

"I'm actually living with the battalion staff. They made me the sergeant major of First Battalion."

"Wow, Mike. Congratulations." I marveled at his ability to move so easily within such disparate cultures. With us, Mike had been squared away without being a duty dick. With B1, he was chilled out without being a slacker.

"Thanks, Sam." He looked genuinely happy as I slapped him on the back. "Remember, you trained me."

"No. Not true and you know it."

Zack yelled in the hallway, interrupting Mike and me, "Are you kidding me, Yun? Did you seriously just say that to me?"

Mike smiled.

"I can't stay long now, Sam, but I wanted to stop by and bring you something." I had not noticed the extra dress white hat in his hand. "I meant to give it to you at the end of last year, but you and Zack were gone before I could find you."

I caught my breath. It was Bill's dress white hat. I thought of him all the time, but not in such a deliberate and tangible way. "Where did you find this? I thought we sent everything back to his parents."

"Yeah. I thought we had, too. But when you guys went to the funeral, I helped Captain Kendall finish the cleanup, and I found it in some of his other stuff."

I looked at the hat brass. It was still perfect. He had been able to do that. I ran my fingers over the brass, picturing him effortlessly shining it.

"Anyway. I didn't find it until we had already sent his things to his parents, and you guys were already gone. So I hung on to it. I wanted to give it to you earlier, but you were . . . well, you weren't good."

"I was a zombie." I looked at him and smiled.

"You seem okay now, though."

"I feel good."

"I think you should have it."

"Thanks, Mike." I turned the hat over in my hands. I felt a stab of pain as I read the name tape: "Bill Cooper '91." And then I nearly choked when I saw the words "The Goat" written in Bill's hand under his name.

The inside of a hat is one of those unexpected places in which cadets find privacy and expression. Most cadets adorn the flat inside of their hats with pictures of girlfriends or family or motivational quotes. Plebes store their cake-cutting templates there and even hide knowledge cheat sheets. Bill, as usual, had never personalized his. For three years, all I'd ever seen in his hat was the standard-issue cadet name tag. But there, under his name, he had written "The Goat."

"I don't know what that means," Mike said. "Were people calling him 'the goat'?"

"Not that I know of. I mean, I guess so. Who knows?" I turned the hat back over and then put it on. It fit.

"I was hoping it would fit."

I took the hat off and looked at him. "Mike. I don't know what to say."

"You should have it." He turned to leave.

"Let's catch up after dinner."

"I'll look forward to it."

Mike stepped out into the hall just as Cadet Yun tried to ping by. Yun came to an abrupt skidding stop but still jostled Mike a bit.

"Holy shit, Yun! Did you just run into Cadet Morris?" screamed Zack. Mike turned and smiled at me and closed the door behind himself.

I could hear Zack rip into the hapless Yun as I stood motionless and looked at the name tape on the inside of Bill's hat. I could picture him that night after our session with the Guru sitting at his desk, pulling out his name tape, and writing "The Goat" under his name. Bill, the cadet who saved no letters and did not keep a journal, had scribbled himself a note. Was it a challenge to himself? An inspiration?

I hadn't thought about the goat since Bill had died. I could see him standing in front of me, jabbing me in the chest with his finger, smiling, and saying, "Do it."

I walked over to the window. The sun was getting low now, sinking below the mountains that ringed West Point to the west. The cadet area was blanketed in shadow, but the far side of the Hudson was still bright.

"Zack, how many hours do you have at this point?" I asked when he stepped back into our room.

"I've only done about fifteen."

"No disciplinary boards?"

"Naw. Been pretty lucky. Just a few inspection dings. Why?"

"I'm going to steal the navy goat this year. I'm going to need help. You in?"

"Hell yes, I am."

THIRTY-SEVEN

DURING THE EARLY PLANNING STAGES, ZACK AND I researched the history of goat-napping. We scoured old issues of *Howitzer*, the West Point yearbook, at tables in obscure corners of the library. Our research also included the memoirs of some of the long gray line's more famous members and newspaper articles from those days. Neglecting our classes, we pored over microfiche, notebooks, and archives.

We knew the rough history of the goat already. For hundreds of years, warships had sailed with livestock. Goats were not only a good source of food but also served well as roving general disposals. The legend at the U.S. Naval Academy is that two ensigns attending a football game there dressed up in the tanned skin of their ship's deceased goat and ran onto and around the field during halftime. This fired up the crowd, and Navy won the game. Years later, in 1893, the USS *New York* gifted a goat, named El Cid, to the naval academy to serve as mascot for that year's Army-Navy game. Navy won. El Cid was a hero. A tradition began.

"I'm convinced this is it. This is the earliest recorded goat-napping." Zack jabbed his finger into the pages of an old *Howitzer* for emphasis.

"Seems late, doesn't it?"

"Maybe. I'm not saying it didn't happen before, but this job in 1953 is the earliest one that made a big enough impression on folks to actually get written about. I even found a reference to it in the *New York Times*." Zack pointed at the image on the microfiche reader. "Hey, Navy! Do you know where your 'Kid' is today?" read the article in the *Times*.

"Nice."

"It says two cadets stole the goat and made off in a convertible driven by an army corporal."

"Shut up."

"Al Rupp, class of fifty-five, and Ben Schemmer, class of fifty-four. I don't know who the driver was. All it says is that he was in the army band. The goat apparently destroyed the vehicle's interior and kicked holes in the roof on the drive back.

"Look, the caption to this photo says they chloroformed the goat to subdue it!"

Zack pushed the *Howitzer* toward me, and I looked at the photo. There in the back of a torn-up old car, a goat with his horns painted blue and yellow slept on the floor, head cocked to his left, leaning on the seat.

I ran my eyes down the faded page until they fell on another black-and-white photo, this one of an army officer. "Who is this?"

"The next day, when the *New York Times* article taunting Navy came out, the shit hit the fan. Eisenhower himself ordered the return of the mascot. He sent that lieutenant colonel along to make sure it happened."

In the black-and-white photo, an officer stood in front of a microphone, speaking, as his right hand gripped one of the goat's horns. Midshipmen stood around him, smiling broadly. He was wearing the World War II–era belted olive-green jacket over khakis.

"I love that uniform."

"It was badass."

"I'll never understand why they changed to the puke-green pseudo-corporate bullshit officers wear today."

"You know why, Sam. Professionalism. Got to look like executives, not like people who are paid to wage war."

I shook my head.

"Anyway," Zack continued, "he had to walk that goat into Bancroft

Hall at Annapolis, surrender the prisoner, and make an apologetic speech. He barely escaped being kidnapped himself."

"Look at this, though."

"That's them walking the goat into the cadet mess hall. How cool would that be?" The goat in the photo seemed terrified. He walked on a leash a few paces ahead of a cadet who smiled broadly as he looked at the cheering Corps. On either side of him, cadets clad in dress gray were cheering and laughing. A bugler walked in front of the cadet leading the goat.

"It's not every day that the president of the United States acknowledges your spirit mission," Zack said.

"Acknowledges? You mean orders you to stop it?"

"Exactly. That's a win in my book."

"Perhaps."

"What are you thinking?"

"I'm thinking it's got to be bigger." I thought of the Guru and the night he gave Bill and me the mission.

"Bigger, like, how?"

"Bigger, like television."

Zack laughed.

+ + +

One night in early September when we got back from a planning session in the library, there was a letter on my desk addressed to "Samuel Avery" in handwriting that looked familiar. There was no stamp.

I opened the letter cautiously. "Dear Sam," it began. "I'm sorry I did not get to say good-bye in person, but my deployment orders came down rather suddenly, and I just couldn't get it all done. I've been called back to my old unit, currently in Kuwait. Please do me a favor and check in on Mrs. Krieger from time to time. She will tell you not to bother, but it will comfort her and mean a lot to me. I'll look forward to your graduation ceremony, which I fully intend to make it back for. Thank you. Sincerely, Col. Stan Krieger."

"What is it?" Zack asked.

"Colonel Krieger got orders," I said. "He's on his way to the desert to join his old unit."

"What is this, his third war?"

"It's weird," I said as I stared at the letter. "If the balloon goes up, he gets pulled into it. Guys who really want to go don't go. And then there are other guys who can't get away from it."

"What's your point?" Zack asked.

"No point. I just think it's weird. It's random."

"Which do you think we'll be?"

"I don't know. But I hope we're like Colonel Krieger."

THIRTY-EIGHT

"THAYER 6, THIS IS ELVIS. KEEP YOUR HEAD DOWN, please."

Pete panned back the FLIR image to give us a wider field of view. "What the hell is he up to?" I muttered. The next instant the armed pickup truck, with two soldiers manning the machine gun, vanished as the screen went completely white. A huge explosion engulfed three of the vehicles, and bodies flew through the air in pieces as a Hellfire missile scored a direct hit. Pete whistled over the intercom. "I didn't know he had ordnance."

The body parts had not even hit the ground yet when Creighton came back over the radio. I could see his Cheshire cat grin all the way from Virginia. "Bulldog, Elvis. I suggest you go now. My Reaper is Winchester. But we will do a few low passes to keep their heads down."

"Roger that. Bulldog on the move." Hearing "Winchester," the code word for "out of ammo," was not good news. But hopefully Creighton's drone had bought us enough time.

"Finally," said Crawford from the rear. "Can we please go shoot some-body now?"

Pete dove 458 toward the ground, picking up airspeed. We leveled off at about fifty feet above the ground and 100 knots. At this altitude and airspeed at night, it would be nearly impossible for anyone to get at us. The rooftop extraction, though, would take some time. A couple minutes, at least. I switched over to the drone feed to assess the damage to the ISIS force.

The scene around the original target house was macabre. Bodies and parts of bodies surrounded three burning vehicle hulks. A couple of fig-ures crawled slowly away from the flames, gravely injured.

"I count about ten bodies, I think," I said to Pete. "Hard to tell. But that leaves about five of them still out there. If one of them has another RPG, it's still going to be messy."

"Always the downside with you, sir," said Pete.

"Bulldog, this is Elvis." It was Creighton again.

"Go ahead, Elvis."

"You guys need to be quick about this."

"No shit, Elvis."

"Six more vehicles headed your way from the north. You've got about five minutes."

"Terrific," I said. "Thayer 6, did you copy that?"

"Roger," whispered Zack. "We're ready. Just waiting on you."

I switched from the drone feed back to the FLIR imagery. I had entered the new extraction location into the nav computer, which put a crosshair on the image of the house. Distance one kilometer and closing.

"Thayer 6, Bulldog. What's the condition of the roof?"

"Bulldog, it's flimsy with multiple obstructions."

"Roger." I turned and looked at Pete. "Probably an aft-gear-only land-ing."

"Ugh," said Pete in a disgusted voice over the intercom. "I am starting to feel picked on." An aft-gear landing meant we had to place just the two rear wheels on the roof while the helicopter hovered over the street. It takes precision. Precision takes time.

"You guys copy?" I said to the crew in back.

"Roger," said Crawford.

I looked again at the moon. It had risen high into the night sky. We were going to be plainly visible to the enemy.

"Be ready on those miniguns. You see anything on the road, light it up." The other unfavorable aspect to an aft-gear-only landing is that the aircraft loses the benefit of any cover from the building. Our gunners would have to suppress any approach from the street as best they could.

Pete banked the aircraft slightly to the right. We were skimming up the riverbed to the southwest of the extraction point. He jerked the nose up and dumped power to start decelerating more rapidly.

The range to the objective read five hundred meters. "Thayer 6, Bulldog. About one minute."

"Roger. We're set."

"Elvis. Bulldog. Status of the enemy vehicles?"

"One kilometer north of the intersection."

We weren't going to make it. When they turned that corner, they would be only a couple hundred meters from our position. We'd be an easy target hovering over the street with aft gear on the roof of the house in the moonlight.

"That's going to be a problem, Elvis. You still Winchester?"

"Roger, Bulldog."

We flew a tight right-hand pattern a block north of the landing site and rolled out pointed due south directly at Zack's rooftop, one hundred meters away. The IR chem sticks were plainly visible. Pete raised the nose further and reduced power to almost zero. The rotor disks went quiet as they freewheeled through the air, momentarily demanding no lift or thrust, and the engines coasted down to a low hum. Chinook 458 was suddenly doused in silence as she shed airspeed. I called up the drone feed to check on the advancing vehicles and saw only static.

"Elvis, we lost your video feed. Can you reestablish?"

It was not a good time to lose our eye in the sky.

"Ready on those door guns!" I called over the intercom.

We were only thirty meters from the building, pointed directly at our landing spot and approaching fast. The objective and the area around it were clear. But they wouldn't be for long.

"Hang on," said Pete softly as he made a sharp input to the left pedal while adjusting the cyclic slightly to the left to level out the aft disk. This turned the aircraft abruptly and perfectly around the aft rotor hub, counterclockwise. Sitting in the cockpit forty feet forward of the aft rotor mast felt like being on the end of a rope swing as we traced a graceful arc above the dirty street. In just a couple of seconds, he had spun the massive aircraft 180 degrees. We were now flying backward. He had also shaved off the last of our airspeed while perfectly maintaining our direction of flight, alignment on the objective, and rooftop altitude.

The maneuver saved us precious time, and for a split second, I allowed myself to marvel once again at the magic an experienced special operations aviator can do with a helicopter. I was going to miss this. Chinook 458 vibrated as she transitioned to a hover.

"All right, sir," called Crawford, who was hanging off the ramp. "Bring her back thirty feet." Out my chin bubble, I could see the street slide quickly by fifty feet below us. "Looking good, sir," Crawford, his eyes on the objective, said calmly. "Twenty more feet."

Sitting in the right seat, I had a perfect view of the intersection at our three o'clock. I looked in that direction and waited for the enemy to appear. The big aircraft crawled rearward. There was no way to hurry this part.

"Looking good, sir. Gimme ten more feet."

The glow of headlights appeared at the intersection.

"We need to hurry," I said.

"Five feet. Four, three, two—hold her there and bring her down two feet."

The aircraft stopped moving forward as if Pete had thrown out an anchor and sank down two feet, resting the rear landing gear on the building.

A Humvee turned the corner and came to a stop. Its headlights washed out my goggles. I leaned my head back and looked under them. The doors opened, and ISIS fighters dismounted. I could barely make out the silhouette of the machine gun turret on top. This was going to hurt.

THIRTY-NINE

"I CAN'T BELIEVE IT," I SAID.

"I never thought I'd see the day."

"It's nothing to be ashamed of, guys," Emily said. "This was bound to happen."

We stood in the company orderly room with half a dozen other cadets, looking in disbelief at the results of last week's graded parades. E4 had placed third in the regiment. We had never seen a result above seventh. Ever.

"What happened?"

"The damn scramble," muttered Zack. He was right.

The infusion of cows from around the Corps was having its intended effect. Cows are a huge influence within a cadet company. They are often more important than the firsties, who tend to be dazzled by their rings, cars, and off-post privileges. While firsties are less focused on cadet life as they daydream about their imminent graduation, cows are still in the trenches of the cadet area. And E4's new cows were improving the company's performance.

"Congratulations, gentlemen," said Creighton, greeting us happily as he walked into the orderly room. Since he was company commander this semester, the results would reflect well on him.

"Shut up, Creighton," said Zack.

"Of course you would be happy that their diabolical plan is working," said Turtle.

I winked at Creighton as we walked out.

That night, Turtle took offense at another diabolical plan: ours.

"You guys are up to something," he said in our room after dinner.

"What are you talking about?"

"I'm not blind and deaf. The weird late-night sessions in the library. The hushed conversations about 'the Grail.' Long periods in your room with the door closed." He glared at us.

Zack and I looked back. Expressionless.

"What's going on?" he demanded.

Cadets live next to, on top of, and with one another twenty-four hours a day. They shit, shave, shower, sleep, study, eat, and exercise together. Cadet company mates come to know one another's every nuance. And Turtle was more than just a company mate to us. He was closer than a brother. We would not be able to bullshit him. Without looking at Zack for consensus, I told him.

"We're planning to steal the navy goat."

Zack gaped at me, alarmed.

Turtle's eyes got big. "I knew it!"

"What the hell, Sam?" said Zack.

"We can't bullshit him."

"I want in."

"No," I said.

"Fuck you. I want in."

"No," said Zack.

"What do you mean, 'no'?"

"Your disciplinary record is too bad. What do you have now? A hundred and fifty hours on the area?" I asked.

"Only one hundred and thirty-five. Why does that matter?"

"Because we're probably going to get slugged hard for this," said Zack. "Maybe a hundred hours. You can't take another major hit like that and graduate."

"Says who?"

"Says us."

"That's bullshit. I'm in."

I thought back to that night in the mess hall with the Guru. He had included Bill and told him that it was up to him.

"Turtle, let me talk to Zack for a minute."

"Sure," he said as he got up and left the room. "But I'm in."

"We should let him on the team," I told Zack.

"His disciplinary record is too bad. He'll never survive the slug."

"True. But he meets the most important criteria. He wants to do it, and we trust him. He won't cave when the heat gets bad."

"I don't know."

"I'm not going to try to convince you of this. If you don't agree, we won't do it."

Zack thought about that for a moment and then smiled. "There is no one else I'd rather have on the team. I'm just scared for him."

"I know. But it's up to him. It's a volunteer mission."

"Okay."

That night we spent a couple of hours briefing Turtle on everything we knew and had planned. We intended to execute the mission the weekend after Thanksgiving leave, one week before the game. We'd thought about doing it the weekend prior to Thanksgiving, but we were concerned about the length of time we would have to survive before the game. I remembered the Guru's caution to avoid a direct query or order from an officer. That would stop us cold.

We felt confident that we could keep the goat hidden and ourselves anonymous for a week, particularly Army-Navy Week, when things would be a little goofy anyway. We felt pretty good, in fact, about the whole mission, except for one small detail.

"What do you mean you're not sure where they keep it?"

"We know it's on a dairy farm, but there are three possibilities for which farm. Specifically speaking." Zack shrugged as he spoke.

"We've got to know for sure. We won't have time that weekend to look around," Turtle said.

"Agreed." I said. "How many weekend passes do you have left this semester?"

"I've got two."

"Then you and I are going to have to take a little road trip," I said. "There's one more home game for Navy this month. It's the weekend after next. There's also another home game in November, but I think that's too late. We need to go this month and have that one home game in November as a contingency."

"The three of us going?"

"No," said Zack. "I'm tied up every weekend this month. It's got to be you and Sam."

"I'll put in for the pass immediately."

+ + +

That Saturday, I dropped in on Mrs. Krieger. I had stopped by a few weeks earlier and planned on doing so regularly while the colonel was away. As he had predicted, she told me not to bother.

The visit followed the same pattern as the first. I didn't stay long. It was initially awkward, until she asked for help with a couple of chores she just happened to have written down on a list. Afterward she asked first about Stephanie, then about classes and the latest happenings in the Corps, while she packed a small care package of cookies she just happened to have made the day prior.

This time, I excused myself to the bathroom while she bagged the cookies. On my way back, I noticed that the door to the colonel's study was open. I couldn't resist.

I took one step into the room and looked around. I was surrounded by the artifacts of a career of military service. They told a warrior's story: a 1967 West Point diploma; a company guidon from B Company, Third Battalion, 187th Infantry Regiment; a painted First Cavalry insignia; a large flag from the 160th SOAR(A); and many other things I didn't recognize. In the center of the wall behind his desk hung the partial beat-up rotor blade. I stared at it, wondering what it meant.

"It's the tail rotor from one of the helicopters he crashed," said Mrs. Krieger from behind me.

"Oh. Ma'am. I'm sorry. The door was open and I, well . . ."

"It's okay, Sam."

She smiled wearily.

"Did he crash more than one?"

"Yes. Two. That was from the second one. He was trying to pull some soldiers out of a bad spot on a hilltop in Vietnam. He had already made three runs carrying out wounded, and they tried to tell him to quit. The enemy was starting to gather, and they'd focus on him when he flew in. The soldiers he was trying to get to thought he was crazy, but he just kept at it. They told me he made three tries and on the third one his helicopter just took too many hits. The engine quit, and he crashed."

"I've never heard that story."

"You never will from him. He never talks about it."

I looked at the artifact on his wall. The fractured tail rotor was fastened in a vertical orientation to a simple wooden plaque, like a raised broadsword. The plaque was carved in the shape of a shield and was made of light-colored wood. Signatures were scribed in thick black ink on either side of the battered blade. There were eleven names.

"Luckily, his leg was broken in the crash, so they sent him home to me early. He got into grad school, and I had him safe and to myself for a few years. But it made such an impression on the guys he rescued that about a month later, at Walter Reed, a few of them visited us and brought that plaque. Every man he pulled off that hilltop signed it."

I tried to picture it. A Huey returning again and again to pull out wounded soldiers. The enemy encircling a tight LZ. Rounds piercing the light-skinned aircraft. The helicopter falling to the ground without power. Bone shattering on impact.

"He loves that thing," she said, gesturing at the tail rotor. "I hate it."

"I didn't mean to snoop, ma'am. I'm sorry."

"It's okay, Sam. You can't help yourself. Gray moths to the flame." She followed me out and shut the door. "Don't forget your cookies."

FORTY

TWO WEEKS BEFORE OUR SCHEDULED RECON, I DEVELoped a scheduling problem. Mission prep had negatively affected my studies, and I struggled on a military history test. My professor, Captain Horatio, told me to stop by his office that Wednesday. Never a good sign.

When I arrived, he was grading quizzes at his desk. He looked up and scowled. "You guys are really something." He gestured grandly as he wrote a big red *F* on the top of the paper and tossed it onto his desk scornfully.

He motioned me forward and pulled my paper out of the stack on the floor. I sat down in front of his desk. He placed my test between us and then leaned back in his chair and regarded me with a skeptical face. I looked at the big red *F* on my paper. It took up half of the page.

"Well?" he said.

"Well, sir?"

"Let's hear it."

"Hear what, sir?"

"Your sob story . . . the reason why you are perfectly justified for submitting this sorry piece of shit."

I didn't take the bait.

"Look me in the eyes and tell me that you studied for this for more than five minutes."

"Sir, I—"

He waved me off. "Don't. Just don't." He sighed heavily. "Look, Avery. I've been where you are." He held up his right hand, brandishing his West Point class ring. "I know what it's like. You're finally a firstie. You've got a car. Can spend more time away from this shit hole. All of that. But listen to me: you're not done yet! The thing that really pisses me off is that I know how smart you are. You've got to try to do this badly. Really try." He paused and regarded me for a long moment.

I felt the urge to tell him what I had been doing. That I had neglected his class for only the most worthy of causes. To prepare for a quest. To steal the goat.

"Here is the deal, Avery. I'm going to give you a choice in this matter. You can take this F and try your luck on the final. You would have to get at least a ninety-six on the exam to pass my course. Or you can attend the Gettysburg staff ride and submit an additional report. Depending on what you get on the additional paper, you will probably only need to score around an eighty on the final exam."

I was stunned. This was not standard West Point professor practice.

"Sir. Thank you. That is very—"

"Don't thank me, Avery. It makes me feel like I'm being soft on you."

"Yes, sir."

"Well?"

"Sir, it sounds like a no-brainer to me. When is the staff ride?"

"It's the weekend after this one."

That was the weekend Turtle and I were going to recon Annapolis. My face must have betrayed my thoughts.

"Not convenient for you, Avery?"

"Oh. No, sir. I mean, yes, sir. It's good. There is no problem. I was just thinking it's actually a really good weekend. I had something planned, but it's nothing important."

"Good. I think you'll get a lot out of the staff ride, Avery. You're making a good decision here."

"I'm sure I will. Thank you, sir."

"What did I say about thanking me?"

"Sorry, sir."

"That will be all, Avery." He gestured at the door and looked back down at his papers.

I walked glumly back to the barracks. *Gettysburg, here I come.*

Zack read me the minute I walked into the room. "So, not your best academic performance?"

"Fuck you."

"But he didn't fail you, did he?"

"No. Not yet."

"Explain."

"He's making me go on the Gettysburg trip section in exchange for a passing grade on the quiz."

"That's actually pretty cool of him."

I sat on my bed and stared out the window at the rump of the mountain.

"Isn't that the trip that Creighton goes on twice a year?"

"Yep. He's the history department's star student. He's almost an assistant professor at this point. In fact, Captain Horatio is one of his main mentors."

"Perfect. You're in for a treat, my friend." Zack chuckled as he pictured it. "I almost wish I was going. Did the captain order you to go on the Gettysburg trip?"

"Nope. But if I don't go, then I'll have to get at least a ninety-six on my TEE to pass."

"You can do that."

"It would be tight, and I would have to study like a fiend."

"That's not something I can picture you doing."

"Me, either. I guess I'm going to Gettysburg." I threw my hat across the room. Zack watched as it smashed into the computer on my desk.

"Sam, other than the fact that the trip is on the same weekend as the goat recon, it's a good deal," he said.

"My own fault. I'll go let Turtle know."

"Let Creighton know, too. He's going to be psyched." Zack laughed as I left.

Turtle took it well. "No problem. I can do it. Probably a waste to have two of us go anyway."

"Maybe. I just hate to back out on you at the last minute like this."

"Seriously, Sam? Look, you've got to do what you need to do to graduate the hell out of this place. Don't give it a second thought."

When I stopped by Creighton's room to tell him, he listened to me with a grin, waiting until I finished to say, "Oh, I'm aware, Sam."

"You are?"

"Indeed. I pleaded your case with Captain Horatio."

"You did?"

"This compromise scenario is actually one I proposed to him."

"You're kidding me. You dick!"

"An unconventional way to say thank you. But I appreciate it nonetheless. You are welcome."

"Why couldn't you propose something that did not involve a weekend's punishment?"

"I did. But he wasn't going for it. Be thankful you have this opportunity at all, Sam. Not everyone in your situation is being given this option. Besides, you might find it to be an enlightening trip section if you're able to participate with an open mind."

"Creighton, I appreciate it. Sincerely. I'm just frustrated with myself right now. Thanks for looking out for me."

"You're welcome."

✦ ✦ ✦

We departed on the four-hour drive to Gettysburg on Friday at noon on a bus full of cadets with Captain Horatio up front. Fortunately, the weather cooperated, because we spent the entire weekend outdoors, walking from one important spot on the battlefield to another. At each stop Captain Horatio would talk for a few minutes, setting the scene, before calling on a cadet to narrate that piece of the fight, after which he would invite group discussion. He called on me often. Fortunately, Creighton had given me a study sheet on the bus. I was ready, and Creighton became more proud each time I performed satisfactorily. Sunday morning we walked day three of the battle, which was mainly Pickett's Charge. After tracing those doomed footsteps to the stone wall, we listened to Captain Horatio's final comments and boarded the bus. We got back to West Point around 2000 hours that night.

Creighton and I were tired and walked through the tunnel to North Area in silence.

"Pretty weird," I said as we emerged onto North Area.

"What's that?"

"After kicking so much ass for years, Lee resorted to 'Hey diddle diddle, straight up the middle' on day three."

Creighton chuckled at the old military adage signifying an overly simple and predictable frontal attack.

"I suppose we all run out of ideas at some point."

FORTY-ONE

"**E**NEMY VEHICLE, NINE O'CLOCK, TWO HUNDRED AND fifty meters!" I yelled. Then several things started to happen at once.

"Ramp is down," Crawford called out as Wilson opened up with the right minigun. "Team moving toward the aircraft." The familiar noise exploded behind me, laying a stream of 7.62mm rounds down the street at a rate of six thousand per minute. The acrid smell of propellant flooded the cockpit.

Two more vehicles, another Humvee and a pickup truck, skidded through the intersection. They rolled toward us. In the back of the pickup, the manned .50-caliber machine gun took aim. They were closing fast.

Wilson doused the second Humvee in a stream of lead. Sparks erupted from its hood and windshield. It veered to the right and struck the building. Two more vehicles rounded the corner at the intersection.

Wilson's minigun stopped firing. "Right minigun jammed!" he cried. At that moment the stationary Humvee started to fire.

"What the hell is taking so long?"

"They're having trouble moving one of the men!" said Crawford from the rear.

Chinook 458 hovered with her aft gear on the roof and the rest of her fuselage over the street. An easy, motionless target.

I looked at the pickup truck with the .50-caliber. It was within 150 meters now and closing. In a few seconds, they would have us.

"Get that fucking minigun going!" I yelled. Wilson screamed something I couldn't make out.

I braced for the impact of .50-caliber rounds.

"Bulldog, this is Elvis. Hold your position, please." It was Creighton.

"What the fuck is he talking about now?" demanded Pete.

I started to answer, but a loud roar cut me off. A huge dark shape zoomed by from left to right. I spun my head to track the object and recognized it at the last moment as an MQ-9 Reaper. It passed a few feet above us in a slight left bank, descending into the street. Its left wing hit the ground about twenty-five meters in front of the oncoming enemy. The drone cartwheeled violently. The airframe shattered as its two thirty-foot wings caught fire and scythed into the lead vehicles. Debris, flames, smoke, and body parts sprayed into the air, obscuring the street.

As the recognition dawned on me that Creighton had just made a kamikaze run with a Reaper, 458's rotor disks choked on disrupted air from the passing drone's wingtip vortices. She lost lift and began to slide forward. She dragged her wheels off the building and sank toward the street.

"Goddamnit!" Pete yelled. He pulled all the power he could. Chinook 458 howled, and the indications all went red. We were cooking the engines to stay aloft. A crash now was a death sentence, even if we survived.

"We're off the building!" yelled Crawford. "Two team members still on the roof!"

Blood sprayed through the cockpit like an aerosol. Pete yelled in pain. "I'm hit. Take the controls!"

The right-side minigun began to fire.

"Enemy dismounts. Three o'clock, fifty meters!" Thomas yelled.

"I've got the controls!" I took hold of the helicopter.

The handoff was rough, and we lost more altitude as 458 swayed left and right.

"Pull up! Pull up! Pull up!" yelled Crawford. "Aft rotor disk is going to hit the building!"

If the rotor blades struck the building, we were dead.

FORTY-TWO

"**W**E'VE GOT A BIG FUCKING PROBLEM," SAID ZACK when I got back to the room.

I dropped my bag and looked at my roommate. Turtle stood next to him nervously.

"Well, Turtle," said Zack sternly. "You tell him."

"Sam, I really don't think it's that big of a deal . . ."

"No. You're right, Turtle. Operational security is not a big fucking deal at all!" Zack waved one hand in the air for emphasis. "I told you this was not just another one of your raids on F4."

"Zack. Please!" I waited until he stopped talking before continuing. "Tell me what's going on, Turtle. You guys are making me nervous."

"I did the recon like we planned. I sat outside the Navy stadium during the game just where you told me to and waited for them to bring the goat out and take him back to the farm. I was going to follow them to the dairy farm and confirm the location." He paused.

"But?"

"But they never came out. I waited all game and for an hour afterward. Nothing."

"Shit."

"Just wait, Sam," Zack said. "It gets worse."

"I was pissed, and not really sure what to do. I had to figure out a way to confirm the location because, like you said, we are running out of planning time. So, I got in touch with a real good friend of mine, Tim Ambizo. He's an exchange cadet there at the naval academy right now."

I started shaking my head.

"He's a fucking cow, Sam," Zack pointed out.

"Listen to me, Sam. Ambizo is a good guy. We're cool."

I was suddenly exhausted. I walked to my bed and sat down. "Turtle. I told you. Team selection is the most critical piece of this operation."

"That's right, you did. That's why I would have never talked to Tim if it weren't mission critical. I didn't know what else to do, and I was on my own since you weren't able to make it. And, besides, we found it. We positively identified the goat's location. We did it." He pulled a map out of the pocket of his short overcoat and held it up. "We know where he sleeps."

I looked at Zack, who glared at Turtle.

"Knowing where the goat sleeps is good, Turtle. But this Ambizo guy . . . this is a big variable now. How well do you know him?"

"I know him very well. I was Buckner cadre this summer, and he was in my platoon. He's tough and squared away. I made him one of my squad leaders."

I imagined the Guru sitting next to me, shaking his head. He would be furious that we had lost control of team selection. Now someone we didn't all know and could vouch for had been read in to the plan. We had been delaying picking the fourth and final team member because we'd wanted to be absolutely sure. Instead, our hand had been forced.

"Look, I know you guys are concerned about Ambizo because you don't know him at all. I get it. But he fits the profile; he's got a spotless discipline record and could take a big hit and still graduate. Even better, he is located at Annapolis and can be our eyes and ears there. And there is something else: his family lives on a small farm near Harrisburg, Pennsylvania. It's an ideal location to stash the goat and hide it for a week, which was a major hole in our plan."

"It wasn't a hole, Turtle. We just hadn't addressed it yet."

"That's what I mean, Zack. This addresses that hole now. If you look at it dispassionately, this solves two major requirements: where does the goat sleep and where do we hide it? If we had thought longer about the team profile, we probably would have tried to get an exchange cadet for our fourth, if possible. You have to trust me on this. He's cool."

"Let me think for a minute," I said, studying Zack. He was still smoldering, with his arms tightly crossed. Anyone else would have thought he was about to explode. He looked pissed. But, knowing him as I did, I could see that he was actually spinning down as he got his head around the idea.

I was feeling less comfortable.

"Sam, you have to trust me," Turtle said urgently.

"I do. But you still might be wrong. You might have slightly misjudged Ambizo. Maybe by only about five percent. But that five percent is now flapping out there in the wind, and when the heat comes, we don't know what's going to happen. The reason we were all supposed to be involved in selections is to reduce risk. Three sets of eyes are better than one."

"You're right. Lately, every time I come back from class or the shower, I look at the door to my room and imagine one of the name tags pulled down." He pointed at himself. "I picture my roommate telling people about his dumbass friend, Cisco Guerrero, who stole Navy's goat with a couple of his buddies and got kicked out.

"All I can say is that I made the best decision I could make at the time. And, yes, I did introduce risk by unilaterally inviting Ambizo onto the team. But remember, I've got the most at risk here. If it goes bad, I am fucked. You guys will probably still graduate. I also confirmed the target's location, acquired a place to hide it, and kept the mission alive." He held up the map in his right hand. I looked at Zack. He wasn't shaking his head anymore, but he wasn't happy.

We were all quiet, staring at the center of the room. I stood up and walked past Zack and Turtle to the windows. I opened the center one and leaned out, putting my hands on the large stone sill and dousing my head in the cold October air. I stared at the massive stone foot of the mountain, less than a hundred feet from our barracks.

"What do you say, Sam?" Zack asked.

I turned around slowly. They were both looking at me. "I'm still in."

Zack nodded and said, "Me, too. Long as there aren't any more fuckups."

"Okay, then. Show us that map, Turtle. And tell us what you saw."

FORTY-THREE

AFTER A FULL YEAR OF THINKING ABOUT IT, A COUPLE of months of serious planning, and lot of driving, mission day was finally upon us.

The U.S. Naval Academy Dairy Farm sat on prime farmland about twenty-five kilometers northwest of Annapolis. It was a straight shot up I-97 from the naval academy, after which you exited onto Annapolis Road. About half a mile up Annapolis Road on the left was the dairy farm's driveway. Called Dairy Lane, the driveway exited to the southwest off Annapolis Road. This picturesque, tree-lined drive ran about one hundred and fifty meters before turning almost ninety degrees to the right to the residential buildings in the northwest corner of the farm. Before it made its turn to the right, an offshoot departed Dairy Lane, heading almost due south and up a slight incline for about fifteen meters before turning ninety degrees to the left to avoid the five main agricultural buildings of the farm. This ninety-degree turn formed a large, north-oriented capital L on the map. The driveway then diverged and curved around and dissolved into a network of muddy dirt roads that interweaved among the grain silos and other utility buildings to the south of the L.

Our target sat on the north side of the notch of that L, where three small fenced fields lay. The fences were designed to contain small farm animals, and in the middle of each field stood small, cinder-block structures that served as sleeping stalls. Turtle and Ambizo's recon had located the goat in the northernmost field. This was good because it meant we could access the northern corner of the field from Dairy Lane and the cover of the trees. We did not want to have to go up the smaller driveway and into the farm itself, either on foot or in the rental van. There was too much light and only one way out. Worse, most nights a roving rent-a-cop in a golf cart patrolled the farm on an irregular schedule. It would be too easy for him to spot and obstruct us.

The plan was for the van to cruise up Annapolis Road around midnight. It would come to a slow roll prior to Dairy Lane, and Turtle and I would jump out of the back. We would ingress under the cover of the dark tree shadows until we reached the point where the northern corner of the field abutted Dairy Lane. We would hop the fence, cross the field to the small building, and confirm that the goat was there. Once that was confirmed, we would assess how to get the goat out.

We brought everything we could think of, trying to cover every contingency: bolt cutters, a power saw, a full ratchet set, and even a blowtorch, which Zack had insisted on. Once Turtle and I had formed a plan, we would radio the van, telling Zack and Tim what we needed for the breach. The van would do another pass, and Zack would hop out at Dairy Lane with the requested tools. He would sneak up to us at the building, and we would do what we needed to do. Then we'd exfil with the goat by cutting a hole in the fence and trotting him out through the shadows to Annapolis Road, where the van would pick us up.

At that point, it would be about a two-hour drive to Ambizo's family's farm outside of Harrisburg, Pennsylvania. We would drop the goat off there and then head back to West Point for the hard part: avoiding discovery until the game.

Everything began according to plan. Turtle and I hopped out of the back of the van as Ambizo brought it to a crawl just short of Dairy Lane. Zack pulled the van doors shut as we ducked into the shadows under the trees, and Ambizo gently accelerated away. After about a minute of jogging, Turtle stopped and knelt next to a tree.

"This is it." He motioned behind himself toward the fence.

"Roger."

We hopped the fence quickly and jogged toward the cinder-block building about thirty meters south of us. There was a three-quarter moon out, and visibility was good. I felt exposed as we jogged across the open field. We got to the building and bounced around the southern corner to peer into the doorless opening. Turtle stuck his head inside.

"Shit."

"What is it?"

"Cows."

I looked around his shoulder and saw two cows lying on the straw, gazing back at us indifferently.

"I thought you guys said the goat was in the northernmost field."

"It was, the night we came out here. He must be in one of these other fields. Come on."

This was not a good start. There were three more fields adjacent to the one we were in. Each one was a little closer to the notch in the L. We hopped the fence and jogged to the next building. It also had an open doorway without a door.

"Nothing," I said. "Not even cows."

We hopped the next fence and ran directly to the building. My heart sank when I looked inside.

"This one's empty, too."

"Damnit," hissed Turtle. There was only one pen left. If the goat wasn't there, we were back to square one after having come all this way. We ran to the fence and stopped. This fence was higher than the others, constructed from a combination of wood and wire. We scrambled over it and ran to the building.

We hustled up to the doorway and nearly smashed our heads into the metal grate of its door.

"I was used to there being no door on these things."

"Me, too."

"What's that?"

I peered into one corner of the cinder-block stall.

"I think it's a goat."

"Is it a goat?"

"It's a goat!"

A wave of relief washed over me.

Turtle put his hands on the door's steel bars and pulled.

"This thing is pretty solid." He heaved on it several times. "Damnit. It's *real* solid." I got out my small flashlight, and we scanned the door. The hinges were on the inside, so we couldn't get at them, and it was secured by a keyed dead bolt. We yanked on the door in unison, and still it didn't budge.

"This is a no-shit door."

"Shhhhhh! What's that?"

The sound of tires crunching on gravel approached.

"It's the guard!" We moved quickly around to the north side of the building. I hoped he hadn't seen my flashlight.

We lay prone behind the building, at opposite ends, each of us peering around a corner. The guard came riding up on the electric golf cart. He drove directly up to the fence in front of us and rolled slowly to a stop. He held up a large flashlight and spotlighted the building we were hiding behind. The light lingered for a few seconds and then shifted to the building in the field to our north. Then the next one. Then the last one. Then the light clicked off and the guard pulled a U-turn and drove off toward the residential area to the northwest.

"He's just doing his patrol. He didn't see anything."

"We need to figure out this fucking door."

"Let's get back to van and make a plan."

"Roger that."

We ran, hunched over, to the north, hopping each of the fences in succession until we were back under the trees on Dairy Lane. We ran all the way out to Annapolis Road and then jogged a few minutes to the south before radioing the van. After picking us up, Ambizo drove a couple miles to the south before pulling into a gas station and parking. The four of us sat in the back of the van while Turtle and I debriefed the others.

"What happened to the goat being in the northernmost field?" asked Zack angrily.

"That's where it was that night," said Turtle. "It's not there tonight. We just have to deal with it."

"Well, I'm glad I brought the blowtorch. Everyone made fun of me, but it doesn't seem so stupid now."

"That's not going to work, Zack," I said.

"Why not?"

"It will be noisy, slow, and highly visible. The guard will be all over us."

"I can handle the guard."

"I know we can handle one guard. But I'm sure he's got a radio, and when he sees us he'll call for backup or whatever his procedure is, and then we're finished."

"I don't know how I feel about damaging navy property anyway," said Ambizo.

Zack almost jumped to his feet at the comment, but I quickly put my hand on his shoulder. The last thing we needed right now was for Zack to beat the shit out of our exchange cadet.

"Look, Tim," I said. "We don't want to do any more damage than we have to. But unless you have a key to that door, there is going to be damage involved in our next step."

Ambizo looked at me earnestly and then looked at Zack. "I understand, Sam. Let's proceed."

"Any ideas that do not involve blowtorches?"

"Take the door off its hinges?"

"Nope. The hinges are on the inside. I checked."

"Sledgehammer to the lock?"

"No. It was a dead-bolt setup. Would be loud and take too long if it worked at all."

"I think we have another problem," Turtle said. "I don't know if you noticed. But we're not going to be able get the goat through that fence to the north like we planned. The wood slats run horizontally and are too close together."

"That's not good." Our plan called for getting the goat to the road on foot, without having to go through the L. "That road is so well lit, the guard will be all over us."

"That would be a long run with a pissed-off goat," said Zack.

We stared glumly at one another for a full minute as we tried to figure out a solution. As we did, a kernel of panic took hold in my gut. I felt it whenever I drew a deep breath. I forced myself to ignore it, but it dug in and began to erode my thought process. I tried to think of options, but I only saw myself telling the Guru we had failed.

Ambizo spoke up: "Look, guys. It just might not be feasible tonight. There's no shame in doing the smart thing. We could always—"

"Shut the fuck up," growled Zack. "We're getting this done tonight." He sounded sure. It snapped me back.

Zack turned his head and talked to me only: "There is only one way to get this done now."

"How's that?"

"Use the van to pull that door off its hinges."

"That's insane," said Ambizo. Turtle put his hand on Ambizo's shoulder and shook his head.

"Go on, Zack," he said.

"That's it, guys. We drive the van up to the door, tie the door to the van with the rope, and then yank the door off its hinges."

We all grimaced. The plan violated three principles we had tried to stick to during our months of planning: do no damage, don't bring our escape vehicle all the way into the constrained farm environment, and don't expose all of us at any one time. It was bold, though. It took the initiative back.

"What about the guard?"

"If we're fast enough, he won't have time to do anything about it," I said. It was starting to seem less crazy.

"That could work. As long as someone went in first and rigged the door prior. We'd also have to get the fence open so that the van could get into position."

"That will be easy," I said. "It's held shut with a chain." I had noted the chain while watching the security guard. My panic was subsiding.

Turtle nodded his head as I laid it out: "This will work. Turtle and I can get back in and rig the door. When we're ready, we'll radio for you guys to bring the van in. We'll cut the fence at the last second and guide you in. Ambizo, you'll have to back the van in. Then we yank the door, grab the goat, and get the hell out of there. The van should be in and out in under a minute." I was nervous as I went through the plan, but it could work.

Zack and Turtle were smiling. I didn't care what Ambizo thought as long as he drove the van. I looked at Zack. "Thanks." I had been stuck. He had saved us.

"Cooperate and graduate."

Five minutes later, the van rolled to a crawl, and Turtle and I hopped out again. I had the rope and a leash and collar for the goat. He carried the bolt cutters for the chain on the fence. I chuckled loudly as we hopped the fence.

"What's so funny?" asked Turtle.

"Hey diddle diddle, straight up the middle, baby!"

FORTY-FOUR

TRIED TO STEADY MYSELF AND, BY EXTENSION, THE aircraft. I shut out everything happening around me and focused on a high-speed cross-check. I flashed back and forth from the hover display imagery to my view out the right window. Lashing her engines, I tried to get 458 to take advantage of the available ground effect. *Help me out here, baby,* I thought to 458. *Give us just a little more.*

Miraculously, she stopped sinking.

"That's it!" called Crawford. "Bring her up five more feet!"

"Get a medic up here!" I yelled.

"Fly the fucking aircraft! I'm fine!" Pete yelled back.

"Up two more!"

"There are a lot of these guys over here. Looks like a whole squad!" yelled Thomas.

"Okay. Good altitude. Now bring her back ten feet!"

I heard a strange thump from the back of the aircraft.

"What was that?"

There was a flash to the right of the aircraft.

"That's Weber and his grenade launcher," yelled Thomas. "Nice shot!"

"Everybody shut the fuck up!" yelled Crawford. He was trying to get flying instructions to me. "Bring her back five more. Three. Two. WHOA!" There was a severe jolt and a loud crunch as the aircraft ramp jammed into the building.

"Stop! Stop! Stop!"

Again I willed myself to steady up. The aircraft rose a few feet and got stable.

"Ramp severely damaged. Losing hydraulic fluid!" shouted Crawford.

Pete lurched toward the overhead panel. With his good hand, he flipped the ramp power switch to Off. This isolated the ramp's hydraulics from the rest of the system. Otherwise our utility hydraulic fluid would bleed out of the damaged ramp and we would lose power to the brakes and other key systems.

"Now back two and down two, sir!"

Chinook 458 seemed to know what I was trying to do. She sank down and back. The two aft wheels planted themselves on the roof.

"Good! Now just hold us there, sir!" Crawford yelled. "Last two approaching the aircraft." I heard another thumping report from Weber's grenade launcher, followed by the flash of an explosion to the right of the aircraft.

"Enemy on the roof!" called Crawford. "They're on the fucking roof!" The sound of machine guns firing erupted from the back. Zack and his team opened up from the ramp. The smell of fresh gunpowder flooded the cockpit.

"RPG on the roof!"

I swallowed hard. If they had gotten onto the roof with an RPG, we were done. "Get those guys on board so we can get out of here!" I yelled.

"One on board now, sir. Other one still shooting!"

"Goddamnit!" screamed Zack. "It's Turtle!"

"He needs to be on this aircraft now!"

"Shit! He's hit! He's down!"

There was a bright flash and a shock wave traveled through the aircraft. Chinook 458 bucked forward, and I felt her tires scrape across the roof as if she were trying to hold us in place.

"Hold her steady! They're grabbing him now."

"Go, Sam," yelled Zack. "Go! Go! Go!"

"What about Turtle?"

"We got him. Go!"

I yanked power, stomped on the left pedal, and leaned her forward. Chinook 458 was as eager as us to get out of the area, and she accelerated quickly toward the dark of the river valley. Both miniguns continued to spit rounds at the enemy. I kept us at rooftop level until we were clear of the buildings and then dove sharply to about twenty feet above the ground. The miniguns stopped firing and soon we were flying at 130 knots. Tal Afar fell behind us.

FORTY-FIVE

WE RAN THE FULL COURSE OF THE L BEND IN THE road to the gate. Turtle quickly cut the chain, and it rattled to the ground as we swung the large gate open.

"I hope the van can get through this," Turtle said. "Does it look too narrow to you?"

I didn't answer. I sprinted through the gate, quickly covering the twenty feet to the stall. I wrapped the end of the rope several times around three of the bars and began to tie my best knot. Turtle made the call on the radio.

"We're set. Come get us."

I heard Ambizo pull the van off Annapolis Road and floor it. It roared up Dairy Lane and squealed as it turned toward our location. I finished my knot and walked the other end of the rope back toward the open gate. The van skidded to a stop and then awkwardly lunged backward as Zack hopped out and helped Turtle guide Ambizo back. I tossed Turtle the end of the rope.

"Tie it to the chassis, not the bumper!" I yelled and then headed back to the building. Zack joined me as I shined my flashlight into the stall.

"There you are, you little fucker," he said gleefully. The goat was nervously crouching in the corner, facing us.

"Ready?" Turtle yelled from the back of the van.

"Do it!"

Ambizo gunned the engine. The steel gate resisted for a few seconds, but before I could get nervous, it gave up loudly. It came off its hinges as the bolt ripped out of the strike plate. The goat, terrified now, rose up and began to shuffle back and forth.

"Get him!" yelled Zack. He blocked the door as I dove toward the animal. He resisted, but I got the leash on him and started dragging him toward the van. At that moment, the security guard's golf cart came speeding down the hill from the residential area.

"Zack!"

"Roger!"

Zack sprinted toward the oncoming golf cart while I wrestled with the goat, who had decided that he preferred not to get into the van with the army cadets. He was strong and heavy enough to make it difficult for me. Turtle saw me struggling and rushed to assist. The goat was in full tantrum mode now, and it took both of us to get him hoisted into the back of the van. His rapid-fire kicks connected with both of us several times, nearly knocking the wind out of me.

"Let's go!" said Ambizo.

Turtle and I jumped in after the goat.

"Wait!" I screamed.

I reached into my right cargo pocket and pulled out a baseball cap. It was printed in a camouflage pattern and had a "D2 Dragons" patch sewn onto it. I tossed it out the back, toward the goat's stall, and yelled at Ambizo: "Okay! Go! Go! Go!" Turtle held the goat's leash as Ambizo gunned the van through the gate. I nearly fell out as we lurched forward.

"What is he doing?"

Zack was about fifty feet in front of us, sprinting toward the security guard and his golf cart, which was headed directly at us. The guard drove with one hand and was gesturing wildly at us with his other.

"Stop and pull over!" he yelled.

Without thinking, Ambizo stepped on the brakes as we watched the confrontation. Zack didn't slow down as he approached the guard and his car. Like us, the guard expected Zack to ease up as he got closer. It wasn't until the last instant that the guard realized he wasn't going to. Zack, an accomplished high school lacrosse player, ran full tilt into the security guard and body-checked him halfway out of the cart. The impact knocked the guard into the empty passenger seat, and he avoided falling completely out of the cart only by a last-second grab at the cart's roll bar.

"Go! Go! Go!" yelled Turtle.

Ambizo, momentarily stunned, snapped out of it and floored the pedal again. The goat and Turtle slid toward me and the open back end of the van. I noticed that the goat was pissing himself just as he slid into my legs, knocking me over and halfway out of the van. Turtle grabbled me by the knees just in time.

A smiling Zack trotted up to the van. The driverless golf cart carried the dazed security guard slowly into the fence. "That felt good," Zack said as he hopped in the back of the van and I closed the door behind him. Ambizo swerved sharply to the right and then straightened out and accelerated onto Dairy Lane. Zack lost his footing on the pee-slicked floor and fell heavily on his ass. Our tires squealed loudly as we hit Annapolis Road and Ambizo took a sharp right. We all shifted again as Zack, Turtle, the goat, and I tumbled over one another. The van rocked back to center after the turn and settled into the straightaway of Annapolis Road.

"What's that noise?" There was a loud clanging just outside the van.

"Shit!" I yelled. "The door! It's still tied to the van."

Ambizo came to a stop, and I got out to untie the rope. I ran back and slid the heavy door off to the side of the road. As I jogged back to the van, Turtle and Zack smiled at each other as they held on to the goat by his big blue-and-yellow painted horns to keep him from jumping out after me. We had done it.

✦ ✦ ✦

The drive to Ambizo's uncle's farm took about two hours and passed uneventfully, without any unpleasantness—other than the stench that filled the van. Turtle and Zack were spared the smell as they followed behind in Zack's car. The farm was perfect and had a nice fenced-in pen with a shelter that Ambizo's uncle had actually used for goats in the past.

Once in the pen, the goat was indifferent to everything that had happened. We took a few hero pictures of ourselves with the goat and then showered. It was after four a.m. when we finally hit the rack in the uncle's guest beds.

The next morning, we spent an hour cleaning the interior of the rental van before returning it and coordinating for the next phase of the mission: getting the goat to the game. Ambizo headed back to Annapolis and the rest of us started the three-and-a-half-hour trip back to West Point. It was a long, droning drive, and despite having gotten some sleep after the mission, we struggled to stay awake.

We made a midmorning gas stop, and I called Stephanie. We had not spoken in a couple of days.

"We did it," I told her. My voice sounded tired but excited. "We got him."

She hesitated. "That's great, sweetie."

"What's wrong?"

"We talked about this, Sam. I wish you hadn't done it. I don't know what I'll do if you get put on months of impediments."

"Restrictions."

"Whatever. I just miss you. I'm going to hate it."

I didn't know what to say, so I made something up: "Don't worry about that now. We may get away with it."

"You're right. I'm happy you're happy, Sam. I've got to go now. Talk soon."

"I love you," I said. But she had already hung up.

FORTY-SIX

"SIR, THERE ARE FOUR AND A BUTT DAYS UNTIL ARMY beats the hell out of Navy at Veterans Stadium in Philadelphia!"

"You're damn right," said Zack as he stepped into the hallway before breakfast formation. It was Monday morning of Army-Navy Week at West Point, and we had a big secret.

I pushed him ahead of me as I stepped out of the room and forced him toward the stairway. "What?" he asked as we landed on the third floor and kept heading down.

"No gloating, knucklehead. Opsec!"

But we exited the barracks into North Area, and I had to smile. Huge spirit posters hung from the top of the barracks, and all the cadets in the regiment, like the rest of the Corps, were wearing their battle dress uniforms. The energy level was building, and it felt good.

I stepped up to my platoon and listened as the plebes recited the daily knowledge.

"Sir, today in the *New York Times* it was reported that Iraq agreed to meet with the U.S. for peace talks with the goal of avoiding a war over Kuwait. The Iraqi statement came a day after President Bush offered to meet in Washington with the Iraqi foreign minister and to send Secretary of State Baker to Baghdad."

"And why do you think the president did that, Cadet Snyder?" said Creighton as he stepped up beside me.

"Sir, I think he is just trying to make sure that the world thinks he has done everything he can to avoid war with Iraq."

"Correct. When does the ultimatum expire, Cadet Snyder?"

"Sir, I do not remember."

"The security council's deadline is the fifteenth of December. So the president has plenty of time to make a good show of playing the peacemaker, don't you think?"

"Yes, sir."

"Cadet Snyder, how many days until the Navy game?" I asked, interrupting Creighton.

"Sir, there are four and a butt days until Army beats the hell out of Navy at Veterans Stadium in Philadelphia!"

"Very good. Do you want to talk about any of this geopolitical bullshit during Navy Week?"

Cadet Snyder smiled. "No, sir!"

Creighton shook his head in mock disgust. "The Corps has." He looked toward the first sergeant and gave the signal to call formation.

"Echo Company, fall in!" commanded the first sergeant.

It was a normal start to Army-Navy Week; there was an expectant buzz in the air. But there was absolutely no indication of our heist.

Zack, Turtle, and I huddled after lunch. "You'd have thought we'd hear something, right?" Zack said.

"I'm glad. The longer we go like this, the better. Remember: no one needs to know anything until that day."

"I agree with Sam," Turtle said.

"I know. I'm just saying."

"Let's count our blessings for now. We've got four more days to go."

"I don't know what scares me more," said Turtle. "Them not giving a shit or them being so pissed off right now that they're making their own plan rather than going off half-cocked."

After dinner, we learned what their plan was.

Plebes streamed passed us to leave the mess hall as we sat at Turtle's table and shared a cup of coffee. He was agitated.

"Not good. Not good." He shook his head and looked around nervously. The stream of plebes had nearly dried up, so he began to speak. "After class, I overheard some of the brigade staff talking about the fact that a major had just arrived on special assignment to deal with an 'unauthorized spirit mission' that has really pissed off the commandant."

"'Unauthorized spirit mission'? Aren't they all unauthorized?" asked Zack earnestly.

"This guy is here to deal with one that is considered way off reservation."

"A major? To deal with a spirit mission? Ridiculous!" Zack said.

He was right. In the army, a major is a big deal. Considered field-grade officers and holding powerful billets, majors command hundreds of troops, are responsible for hundreds of millions of dollars of equipment and budget, or serve on high-level staffs. To task one to find the cadets who'd stolen the Navy goat was ridiculous. We were scared.

"Where did this major come from?"

"Someone said something about the Pentagon."

"Well. Wherever he's from, we need to go to ground. Stay cool. We'll be fine." I was talking primarily to myself.

"Should we get a message to Ambizo?" asked Turtle.

"No. He can't do anything about it, and he might be under scrutiny there anyway."

"This is a good sign," I said.

"How's that?"

"It means we got the right one and they really want it back."

Both Zack and Turtle grinned widely.

As I thought about it, I decided this was a good development. Bringing in an officer from the outside would slow the investigation down. It would take them some time to get up to speed. Without a good understanding of the Corps, its quirks, disparate factions, and baffling heterogeneity, a new player would be lost. The new guy wouldn't have his bearings, much less a theory or any leads to follow before Friday. We would be long gone by then, on our way to Philadelphia with the prize pissing himself in the back of another rental van.

On game day we were going to take advantage of the spirited chaos that occurs at the stadium. It always looks like a NATO circus convention at the utility entrance. Army and Navy personnel mill about in every conceivable kind of uniform as they push, drive, or ride props, mascots, and spirit items into the stadium. Army mules are led in by their handlers, often next to a large, motorized mock-up of a battleship. Small tanks buzz around as howitzers are towed in by cadets in World War II–era uniforms. No one would notice as we pushed a large rolling speaker along in the melee.

The hollowed-out speaker would conceal the goat and our intentions until the prisoner exchange, the moment before kickoff when exchange cadets and midshipmen are marched back to their rightful units to watch the game. The TV cameras would be rolling as we would stride out and add the goat to the ceremony. We were counting on the surprise of the moment to carry us through. Our plan ended, however, at the point where we handed the goat's leash to the Navy first captain. "Just be ready to run," Zack kept saying.

After dinner, I bounded up the steps of the barracks' stoop and headed toward the orderly room. Stepping into the company area, I confronted a nightmare.

Eifer, in all his rigid perfection, stood in our orderly room questioning the midnight cowboy. The CQ was at attention, and Eifer's back was to the door and hallway. Suddenly I was a plebe again, terrified. I kept moving quickly to the steps and down into the basement. He never turned around. But as I'd passed the orderly room, I'd caught the gleam of gold on his shoulder. The gold oak leaf insignia designated the rank of major. He had been promoted while a White House fellow. I walked through the basement to the exit onto the corner of North Area. From the E4 area I glanced over to see Major Eifer walking down the barracks steps and then across North Area toward Washington Hall.

I jumped back into the barracks and ran up to the orderly room.

"Cadet Wells, was that Major Eifer?" I asked in my most nonchalant voice.

"Yes, it was. Do you know him?"

"Unfortunately. He used to be E4's tac. Left for Washington, D.C., right before your plebe year. What did he want?"

"He took our departure book."

"Really?"

"Said they were pulling the departure book from every company."

"Did he say why?"

"No."

"Anything else?"

"He told me to tell Cadet Patterson that all company commanders are required at a mandatory meeting immediately prior to breakfast formation tomorrow."

"Thanks."

I tried to put on a brave face when I gave Zack and Turtle the report back in our room.

"Holy fuck," Zack said quietly. "He's back."

"Major Effin' Eifer," said Turtle in an equally hushed voice.

"Supposedly he has collected all company departure books."

"That should be no problem, right?"

"Shouldn't be. I would think that there are hundreds of cadets who signed out to areas that are within striking distance of Navy. I can't imagine that us signing out to Pennsylvania will lead them to us," Zack said.

"There's one more thing. He called a meeting with all company commanders tomorrow morning."

"That's not good."

"I'm not sure," I said. "The fact is, Creighton doesn't know anything."

"But that straitlaced dork won't play it right. You watch." Zack fidgeted nervously.

"Should we give Creighton a heads-up?" Turtle asked.

"Hell no!" hissed Zack.

I waved my hand in front of Zack to cut him off. "No, Turtle. We can't tell Creighton anything. Even if he figures it out, we can't tell him anything. I actually trust Creighton. He can bifurcate."

"What are you talking about?" Zack asked.

"He will go by what he knows. Not by what he thinks he knows."

They looked at me blankly.

"When it comes to chain of command, Creighton will only deal in what he knows to be fact. What he has absolute knowledge of. He won't act on what he only suspects."

"You think he suspects?"

"I think he will."

"I still can't believe Eifer is back," mumbled Zack.

FORTY-SEVEN

BANKED TO THE SOUTH AS SOON AS WE HIT THE DARK-ness of the river valley. As Tal Afar fell behind us, I noted that 458 felt terrible. There was a roughness in her forward rotor disk that induced an odd horizontal vibration. The blades had probably been damaged by bullets or flying debris. There were numerous holes in the cockpit windows, and wind whistled through them as 458 limped south. Blood was splattered on Pete's instrument panel. He held his left forearm in pain.

"You okay?"

"Hurts."

"Zack, we need the medic up front," I said on the intercom.

"Roger that. He's stabilizing guys back here. Two minutes."

Thomas stepped into the companionway with a first aid kit and began wrapping Pete's forearm.

"Crawford, how does she look back there?"

"Rough, sir. Utility hydraulics are totally gone. No pressure indication at all. Flight hydraulics reservoir reading low, but pressures look normal for now. Temp is a little high. There's hydraulic fluid all over the place. Fucking mess. Lot of holes back here. But she'll get us home."

A red emergency light lit up the cockpit.

"Fire indication in the number one engine!" I yelled.

"Roger that!" yelled Crawford. "Number one is trailing smoke, and we're starting to get smoke in the cabin."

Pete grunted as he shoved Thomas out of the way and reached up to the number one engine lever with his good hand. "Number one engine lever identified!"

I looked up to confirm that his hand was on the correct engine lever. "Confirmed!" You don't want to shut down the wrong engine at a time like this.

Pete yanked the number one engine lever and then grabbed the fire handle. The number two engine screamed as it surged to maintain rotor RPM. "Dumping bottle one!" Pete yelled as he pulled the handle and rotated it.

There isn't much you can do for an engine fire in a Chinook except pull the engine condition lever to stop the engine and activate the fire-extinguishing system. This cuts off the fuel to the engine and dumps a Halon fire-extinguishing agent into the engine compartment. It's a weak system. Ordinarily we would land as soon as possible to get out of the air and off the aircraft. But if we did that now, we'd be hundreds of kilometers deep in enemy territory with several wounded and the entire Islamic State looking for us. We needed 458's systems to work. I opened my window and pressed the left pedal forward to get us out of trim and blow the smoke out of the cabin.

"How does it look, Crawford?"

"Can't tell yet, sir. We're still trailing a little smoke. But it doesn't seem to be entering the cabin anymore."

I let up on the left pedal, and 458 straightened up.

"I'm going to dump the second bottle," Pete said as he reached for the lever. There are two fire-extinguishing bottles in the aft of the aircraft. They are rigged to douse either engine compartment. You can use both on one engine, but once you've used them, that's it.

Pete pulled and twisted the lever. "We're fucked if we land now," he said, leaning back in his seat. "Let's get as far as we can."

"Roger that. How does it look now, Crawford?"

"About the same, sir."

"We'll know soon enough," I said and checked on the number two engine. It was laboring alone now under the full load of both rotor systems. Fortunately, we were flying light with just passengers and not much fuel left.

"Okay. I'm ready for that medic now," muttered Pete. I could tell from his voice that he was in a lot of pain.

The medic leaned into the cockpit to work on Pete's left forearm.

After a few minutes of flying, we were over empty desert and I climbed up to a hundred feet AGL. I flew in silence, trying to get a grip on what had just happened.

As soon as the medic was finished, he stepped back out of the passageway, and Zack appeared. He plugged his headset into the intercom and leaned toward me.

I looked at him, but he didn't speak.

"How's the Guru?"

"He's pretty beat up and weak. But seems okay. He smiled ear to ear when I told him you were up here flying."

"Others?"

"One gunshot wound to the leg. Another has a gunshot wound to the shoulder. The leg was bad. Close to bleeding out. But the medic has it under control. Has an IV in him now."

"What about Turtle? How is he?"

"That lucky bastard. They got him in the prosthetic. He fell forward when his leg shattered. Saved his life, because the rest of the rounds went high. He was able to get a grenade into them. Took out the RPG."

I shook my head as the relief swept over me. Zack put his hand on my shoulder, and we flew without speaking for a few moments.

"He saved us, Sam. We wouldn't have flown far from that rooftop. These things just take too long to get moving."

I nodded. Zack was right. They would have riddled us as we tried to accelerate away. The RPGs alone could have easily destroyed the aircraft.

A few minutes later, two crewmen moved Pete out of his seat and to the rear. His left forearm had started to hurt like hell as the shock wore off. The medic gave him painkillers. SSG Crawford took Pete's seat in the cockpit. Crawford couldn't fly, but he could back me up on radio transmissions and other cockpit tasks. Still, I didn't want to fly any longer than I had to like this.

After Crawford had gotten himself settled, Zack leaned back into the cockpit. He seemed to want to be close by. Like me, he was digesting all that had just happened.

"I've never seen a drone used to clear a street like that," Zack said.

"Neither have I. But it sure as hell worked."

"Creighton is going to have to answer for that, I am sure."

"I think we're all going to have things to answer for tonight."

FORTY-EIGHT

"**S**IR, TODAY IN THE *NEW YORK TIMES* IT WAS REPORTED that Iraqi president Saddam Hussein announced that he has decided to release all of the foreigners held by his forces in both Iraq and Kuwait. This decision would apply to the approximately nine hundred hostages who are Americans. This decision is viewed by most as an attempt by President Hussein to seize a moral high ground to blunt the current momentum toward war in the region."

"No shit, Sherlock," said Zack as we walked by plebes reciting knowledge to their yuks in the hallway. "Guy is a fucking Clausewitz over there."

As we walked out of the barracks, onto the stoop, Major Eifer was already talking to Creighton at the bottom of the stairs, behind the accumulating company formation; he had already held a meeting with all the company commanders that morning.

Zack and I walked quickly to our spot in formation and tried to be invisible.

"Echo Company, fall in!"

The company shuffled to attention as the platoon sergeants took accountability. I imagined Creighton and Eifer behind me at the base of the formation with their eyes on Zack and me. Eifer would let the formation run its course, and when we were dismissed for breakfast Zack and I would be called over and it would be done.

At that point, the executive officer posted the first sergeant and took command of the formation. Telling his XO to take the formation meant Creighton was still talking to Major Eifer. Not good.

Soon the regiment was released for breakfast. The platoon sergeants dismissed their platoons. Most of the company began to shuffle toward the mess hall. I hung motionless. Zack approached me, but I silently gave him a frown that warned him off. He continued on.

Creighton was nodding as Major Eifer spoke. Then he snapped to attention and rendered the major a salute. Creighton walked toward Second Platoon. I caught his eyes as he crossed in front of me. They were intense, but he made no outward sign of having seen me.

He caught up to Emily, who had started toward the mess hall. I stood still as they passed me. I caught Creighton's eye again and, imperceptibly, he shook his head at me. I looked back to the ground and let them go on ahead.

I fell into the midst of the gaggle of cadets about twenty meters behind Eifer, walking toward the mess hall. Eifer strode ahead in a deliberate and slow overwatch of Creighton and Emily, about ten meters behind them.

I studied Eifer's peculiar stalking of Creighton. His gait was a humorous mix of a hunched prowl and his normal, super-erect carriage. *This is how an uptight asshole sneaks up on someone,* I thought.

Creighton and Emily were now only about ten meters from the mess hall. Eifer accelerated.

Eifer reached out and tapped Emily on the shoulder. The two of them stopped, spun on their heels, and snapped to attention.

As I passed Major Eifer, I looked the other way but listened intently. I heard him say, "Cadet Patterson, you are dismissed. You may go to breakfast."

"Thank you, sir."

Creighton fell in behind me as I hopped up the short flight of steps into the mess hall.

I resisted the urge to turn around and demand to know what had been said between him and Eifer. Instead, I went directly to my table, and at

"Take seats" I sat down, spoke to no one, and ate quickly. When we were dismissed, I left immediately. I wanted to beat Zack back to the room so I could grab my books and get to class without having to debrief him. I wasn't ready to deal with that yet. My mind was racing. I was having a hard enough time not panicking myself.

I bounded down the stairs, out the door, onto the stoop, and nearly directly into Creighton, who was waiting for me.

We set off across North Area in silence. Weaving between the hundreds of camouflage-clad cadets now spilling out of the mess hall, we stepped onto the apron, walking quickly. The steps of the mess hall rose above us to our right, and the Plain extended under a thin layer of snow to our left. Past the Plain, the morning sun crested the eastern mountains but left the Hudson still in shadow. I walked at an even pace, waiting for him to speak. He remained silent until we got close to Ike's statue.

"So, you might have noticed that Major Eifer met me at formation this morning. I had to give the formation to the XO."

"I noticed that."

"He actually called a meeting with all company commanders prior to breakfast formation, at which he informed us that an unauthorized spirit mission has taken place. Apparently he has been tasked by the commandant with apprehending the cadets responsible."

I focused on taking casual and even steps as Creighton spoke, so as not to betray my anxiety.

"After the meeting he followed me back to E4's area and interrogated me about the status of my own investigation into the possible participation by E4 cadets in said unauthorized spirit mission."

"What did you tell him?" I stopped walking.

Creighton stopped walking also. Behind him stood Ike's reproving statue. Hands on his hips. Left knee slightly bent forward. Ike was a dark silhouette against the white Plain and sunstruck Storm King Mountain. I thought of Bill. *We tried,* I said to myself.

"I told him I had nothing to report. That there were many rumors involving many cadets of many companies but that I had nothing actionable."

"No shit?"

"No shit."

"Then what happened?"

"He proceeded to ask me the same question in multiple other formats, to which I gave the same answer: Lots of rumors, sir. Nothing actionable."

Creighton stopped talking to allow a couple of cadets to pass nearby. When they were safely distant, he continued.

"During his extensive questioning, I got the feeling he was not convinced. And, since the man is such a predictable officer, I knew that he would be watching me closely. Had I known anything, it would be a natural reaction for me to go immediately to those persons to warn them about Major Eifer."

I started to chuckle. Creighton allowed himself the slightest of smiles.

"So, after formation I picked a random firstie to walk to breakfast with and engaged in a conversation about our upcoming history term-end exam." He stopped and regarded my broad smile.

"I only did this to test my theory, Sam. And for no other reason."

"Right."

"Anyway. As Emily and I were talking, Major Eifer stopped us from behind. He then dismissed me. Emily told me later that Major Eifer interrogated her about an unauthorized spirit mission involving the Navy goat. Emily, of course, did not know anything. She said this seemed to frustrate the major. She said she was gruffly dismissed after only a few minutes."

I nodded slowly.

Creighton gestured toward Mahan Hall, and we started walking again.

"The truth is, Sam, I have not investigated anything. I don't have any actionable information." He sounded troubled. "I hope it stays that way."

I didn't respond. I understood.

FORTY-NINE

WALKED EXCITEDLY BACK TO THE BARRACKS FOR OUR pre-lunch huddle. I hadn't been able to focus at all in class that morning. Creighton had come through for us more than I ever could have expected. I was convinced he had bought us sufficient time to get through the week to the weekend and the game.

"We are so fucked!" said Zack. I smiled. I was sure he had stewed all morning about the portents of Major Eifer's visit to our breakfast formation. I almost felt bad that I had waited until now to tell him.

"Relax, Zack. It's under control."

"What do you mean it's under control? How can you call this under control?" He waved his long arms around.

"Just give me a minute to explain. I actually think we're in better shape than ever now."

"Are you nuts?"

"Sam, I'm not following you," Turtle said dejectedly.

"I spoke with Creighton after breakfast. Believe it or not, he did great." I smiled smugly.

Turtle's head sagged, and he rubbed his temples while Zack went wild-eyed and hissed at me. "What the fuck are you talking about? Does Creighton know Ambizo or something? You're not making any fucking sense!"

"Ambizo? What?"

"Ambizo! Turtle's friend who we let in on our mission. What are you talking about?"

"I haven't told him yet, Zack," said Turtle. "He doesn't know."

"Then why are you trying to tell us it's under control?"

My heart sank.

"Well, Turtle, tell him," growled Zack.

"It's Ambizo. He called me this morning. He said the commandant of the naval academy called all of the exchange cadets into a room this morning and told them that they know one of them was involved. The com said if that cadet turns himself in and the goat is given back, there won't be any punishment. He said failure to do so will result in the naval academy equivalent of a first-class board."

"Their com is bluffing," I said. "How would they know that?"

"I don't know. And it doesn't matter. Ambizo believed him."

"Well, he's going to have to suck down a first-class board then."

"Not this guy, Sam. You got it all wrong!" said Zack loudly.

"Seriously, Turtle. This is exactly what we all talked about. You have to be willing and able to take a first-class slug." I tried to talk around Zack's rage.

"Tell him, Turtle! Tell him what your buddy is all about!"

"Zack, please!" I gestured at him to shut up.

Turtle looked at me with dread and said, "Ambizo says he is on the short list for first captain and doesn't want to jeopardize that."

"Shit," I said quietly.

"That's right," Zack spat. "We didn't know we were on the mission with royalty."

"I'm sorry, Sam."

I tried to think. "When is he going to do it? When is he going to turn himself in?"

"He said the com gave them until tomorrow noon. So he was going to do it tomorrow after breakfast formation."

The three of us stood in a tight circle. Zack's head was shaking with anger. Turtle looked despondent. I glanced at my watch. For some reason, I felt at peace. I wasn't mad or even surprised. I was grateful.

I put my hand on Turtle's shoulder. "It's okay, Turtle. Your buddy did pretty good."

"What the hell are you talking about?" demanded Zack.

"Think about it. In spite of being jacked up by a one-star admiral, he bought us twenty-four hours. He could have turned us in right then."

Zack looked at me as Turtle smiled.

I appreciated what Ambizo had done. Balancing the demands of the institution against those of friendship was a constant task for every cadet. But Ambizo had just faced a greater test than most. Ninety-nine percent of cadets go through their careers with a captain being their highest-ranking menace. Ambizo had had to stare down a one-star and tell the commandant to wait while putting his own potential to reach the highest position in the Corps on the line. The easiest thing to do would have been to give us up on the spot, but he didn't. He found an honorable path he could live with. And, in the process, he bought us precious time.

Zack started to smile as well. "What are you thinking, Sam?"

"We're going to steal that fucking goat again. Tonight."

FIFTY

"SAM, CREIGHTON JUST CALLED ON MY SAT PHONE," said Zack on the intercom. "He wants to talk to you."

"Okay. Bring him up."

Zack came forward and leaned into the cockpit. He handed me the wired earpiece to his sat phone, and I jammed it under my helmet ear pad.

"Creighton?"

"Sam. Good to hear your voice."

"Yours, too. Hell of a thing back there. Thanks."

"Listen, I don't have much time, and I no longer have eyes on you. Can you make it to Baghdad?"

It was a strange question, but I ran through the calculation. We had about two and a half hours of fuel, including our twenty-minute reserve. At 120 knots, we were a little over two hours from Baghdad. Throw in some hover time and it would be tight but manageable.

"We've got enough fuel. Barely. Why?"

"I'm working on something. Stand by."

"Okay. But I also need to check on our medical status. I don't know if they can fly another two hours."

"Find out."

"Zack, what's our medical status?" I asked on the intercom. "Could they fly another two hours if we had to? We might divert to Baghdad."

"I think so. Everyone who needs an IV has one and has been stabilized. I'll check with the medic."

I waited while Zack checked. The sat phone earpiece felt heavy in my ear, and I smiled at how pissed off Brick and the rest of SOCOM must have been at that moment. The CIA's control of the majority of the country's drone operations was a source of major frustration for the Pentagon. Coordination and communication were not the CIA's strongest suit. Several times in the past decade, some in Congress and even the president had tried to transfer control of the CIA's drones to the Defense Department. Each time, they'd been thwarted by the CIA and its bureaucratic allies. The turf wars in Washington had not interested me in the past, but tonight I was damn glad for the dysfunction. Creighton had exploited it to not only make our mission possible but to save our lives.

"Medic says if we have to go to Baghdad, we can do it without endangering the wounded," Zack announced. "But he wants assurance that medical staff will be waiting for us there."

"Creighton, we have the fuel and our medic says we can make it, but can you confirm there will be medical assistance waiting for us?"

"Roger that, Sam. You'll have more waiting for you there than you would have back at Kirkuk. They'll be in the hospital within five minutes of your landing."

"Okay, then. Baghdad it is."

"Very good. I will call you with a lat/long to land at in about half an hour."

"Roger that."

"Wilson, what's 458's status?" I asked over the intercom.

"We've done a thorough check, sir. I stopped counting at two dozen bullet holes. Couple decent leaks but no major damage. The ramp is fucked, though. You really did a number on it when you backed us into the building. Otherwise, 458 is in pretty good shape. She'll keep flying."

"Sorry about the ramp."

"No problem, sir. We know you're rusty."

Crawford shook his head. "It's not okay with me, sir." Damage like this would keep 458 out of the air for a while, and it would take a couple of weeks of work on his part to repair. I didn't have the heart or the energy to tell him they were going to take 458 away from him when we landed.

After a minute of silence, Crawford said, "Your buddies are something else, sir."

"I know."

"How close do you think that drone came to us?"

"I don't even want to think about that."

"Roger that, sir."

Zack leaned into the cockpit. I yanked the earpiece out of my helmet and gave him back his sat phone. "Creighton says go to Baghdad. Says he'll call with a lat/long for landing."

"What do you think?" Zack asked.

"I trust Creighton."

I put the lat/long for the center of Baghdad into the flight computer, and 458 gracefully entered a standard rate turn to the south. I was letting her fly on autopilot so that I could do other things.

Now that we had the Guru and the bullets had stopped coming at us, my thoughts were turning toward the aftermath. I focused on the course change and managing the rest of the flight and tried not to get nervous about the reception we would receive when we landed. Wherever that ended up being.

I looked over my left shoulder at Zack. "I wish I knew what he was up to."

"I bet he's trying to keep us out of jail."

"Just like old times."

FIFTY-ONE

"SAM, THERE'S NOT ENOUGH TIME," SAID TURTLE. "NO way to get there and back before taps and bed check at midnight."

"It's just a little over three hours there. Figure we leave after dinner formation . . ." My voice trailed off as I realized the math didn't work.

We stood silently in a small, sad circle and stared at our feet.

I realized that I had never even debriefed them on how close we had come with Eifer. It seemed like months ago that Creighton had misdirected him at formation. It had only been this morning. It was only Tuesday. This week was going to kill me.

Zack started to speak slowly: "Turtle, it would be great if tonight there was a spontaneous midnight rally of some kind."

Turtle looked at Zack and smiled. "I think you're right."

I started to catch up. I smiled at my amazing friends and said, "Ideally, it would pull the maximum possible number of cadets out of their rooms tonight right at taps, for an hour or so. It needs to really screw up everyone's bed check."

"Understood." Turtle was nodding now.

Zack continued: "It needs to be widespread but not destructive." He wagged his finger at Turtle. "It would not be good if it provoked a crackdown or other aggressive response from the tactical department."

"Maybe somehow suck the officer in charge into the action if I can. Pull him out of the fight."

"Who's the OC today?"

"Captain Gunderson. From phys ed. Nice guy. ROTC commission. Pushover."

I was starting to feel better. Zack had gotten us unstuck.

Zack and I came up with a quick plan. We would attend formation and dinner and then leave promptly when the Corps was dismissed. Go back to our room, change into civvies, and head up the mountain to Zack's car as quickly as possible. We still weren't sure where we were going to stash the goat when we got back. Hopefully a good idea would occur to us on the long drive ahead.

Formation was uneventful. Dinner was loud as Army-Navy Week continued to build momentum and the Corps became more rambunctious. The Goat-Engineer Game would be tonight after dinner. A tradition at West Point since 1905, this full-contact football game, complete with pads, pits the top academic half of the firstie class (the Engineers) against the bottom academic half (the Goats). The players are given equipment and one practice earlier in the week and then go at it in front of the whole Corps, administration, and community. Some old grads swear that "as the Goats go, so goes Army against Navy."

All of this boded well for Turtle's assignment. The more frothy the Corps' spirits, the less of a shove he would have to provide shortly before midnight.

✦ ✦ ✦

US Route 9W hugs the Hudson River's western bank south of West Point. The mountains mellow into rolling hills as the route links up with the New Jersey Turnpike and the Hudson widens in anticipation of the Atlantic Ocean. The river flows under the George Washington Bridge, along the length of Manhattan, and into the sea. Since first classmen have been allowed to own cars, the Palisades has served as the high-speed avenue of escape to New York City or farther south for a weekend. Zack and I did not have the usual happy anticipation on this road trip, however. We drove in determined silence and hoped it would go smoothly.

We got to the farm in Harrisburg just after 2200 hours. We parked about half a mile down the road from the long driveway. Ambizo's uncle was the kind of guy who would keep a loaded shotgun handy, so we wanted to be as stealthy as possible.

It felt good to be walking after the long drive. We trotted quietly into the farm, sticking to the shadows, and went directly to the barn. Creeping inside, we found the goat. I leashed him up while Zack watched the door. I fed the goat a few mess hall carrots, and he decided we were guys he could hang out with. It was an easy trot back to Zack's car. Then things got interesting.

"He doesn't want to get in."

"Are you discussing it with him?"

"No, asshole. Look at him." The goat strained at his leash as I tried to pull him toward the backseat of Zack's car.

"Give me that motherfucker." Zack came around the front end of the car. The goat, sensing Zack's resolve and emotional state, suddenly went limp. Zack picked him up and tossed him roughly into the backseat, where he lay still, stunned by his sudden change of fortune.

"See?"

"You're a regular Doctor fucking Dolittle."

"Just get in. Let's get this drive over with."

Zack started the car and pulled out onto the road. Our second theft of the Navy goat in a week was complete.

The drive back was equally uneventful, other than the goat eating most of the upholstery in the backseat of Zack's car. He was a slow but deliberate eater, and all we could do was hope that the material wasn't toxic. We needed him to live at least another three days. Zack moaned with every rip and tearing sound that emanated from the rear, but we kept driving. We didn't have time to figure out anything else.

"Those guys back in the fifties were smarter than us, huh?" said Zack.

"What do you mean?"

"Remember that picture of the goat knocked out by ether? We should have done that."

"Where the hell do you get ether these days?"

Zack grunted and faced the road again.

We did figure out where to hide the goat ahead of its Army-Navy game debut.

"Pelly's," Zack said out of nowhere.

"Huh?"

"We should keep him at Pelly's."

"She loves cadets, hates tacs, and would dig it."

"That's perfect. But we're not going to get there until about one in the morning."

"So, we'll wake her up."

With a large, rambling piece of land several miles off the post, Pelly was a legend among cadets. For a small monthly fee, she let underclass cadets hide their vehicles at her place. This was a violation of cadet regulations, of course. Only firsties could have cars. The tacs tried to keep the illicit car storage from happening. She looked after her cadets, though, calling the police anytime a tac came snooping. Even though there were usually more than a dozen cars hidden in the trees at Pelly's, no one ever got busted. Pelly was proud of that.

Two hours later, we pulled into Pelly's. Rather than continuing on to the wooded back where underclass cadets kept their secret vehicles, we stopped in the front. We sat in the dark car for a moment and looked at her front door.

"This is where Bill kept his motorcycle, isn't it?" I asked.

"Yes."

We got out of the car and slowly walked up to her door.

"Well, here we go." Zack rang the doorbell.

We stood for a full minute in silence, then rang the bell again. We waited there for another minute. As Zack raised his hand to press the bell a third time, the door unlocked suddenly and swung open. Pelly didn't crack it to peer out to determine who was on her front step. She opened the door wide and took a step forward, almost knocking us off the stoop in one catlike motion.

"Who the hell are you?"

"Good evening, ma'am. My name is Zack, and this is Sam. Sorry to disturb you, but we have a huge favor to ask."

Pelly narrowed her eyes at Zack as he spoke.

"Um. You see. The thing is, we have just returned from stealing . . . I mean, borrowing the naval academy's mascot. A goat. And we need a place to hide him for about a day or so. Really about two and a half days."

"Wait a minute. Shut up. You did what?"

"We stole Navy's goat, ma'am," I said. Now her eyes were narrowed at me. "And we really need a place to hide him until Friday about noon."

She looked past me at Zack's car. It was rocking slightly from side to side as the goat jumped around in the backseat, finishing his destruction of Zack's interior. His painted horns flashed blue and yellow behind the car window.

A smile slowly spread across Pelly's face until her smoke-stained teeth were showing.

"It's always something with you cadets. I just love you guys."

"Is that a yes, ma'am?" asked Zack softly.

"That's a hell yes, son. Pull around back to the garage." She stepped back inside and shut the door. Zack and I gave each other a high five. It was 0118 hours. I wondered how Turtle's impromptu mischief was going.

FIFTY-TWO

"ATTENTION ALL CADETS, THERE ARE FIFTEEN MIN-utes until assembly for breakfast formation. The uniform is battle dress uniform. Fifteen minutes, sir!"

Zack and I got out of bed as the minute caller popped off. We dressed and then walked slowly to formation, arriving just as the first sergeant gave the command to fall in.

At breakfast, we began to get a sense of what Turtle had wrought.

"Was that the craziest BP cart race you have ever seen, or what?" asked Zimmer, a cow at my table.

"It was crazy," I said, sipping my coffee. I smiled. BP carts were large rolling carts used by the barracks police, or janitors, as they went about their custodial chores. They were five feet long, three feet wide, and a little over three feet tall and served well as general-purpose carryalls. Put a cadet inside one, however, and have four other cadets push it at a sprint, and it became a careening, barely controllable chariot of ridiculousness.

"I've never seen a race that big! Have you, Sam? Was there anything like that when you were plebes?" asked Montman, the other cow at my table.

"No. No, that was definitely the biggest. How many carts do you think were involved?"

"At least three dozen! What do you think?"

"Three dozen at least. Maybe more."

By lunch formation, Zack and I had pieced together an outline of what had happened. The diversion had kicked off with a spontaneous dance rally just before taps in front of the supe's house, with about two dozen cadets cheering and inviting the supe to come out and do a "Rocket" with them. There were several uniformed cheerleaders involved, which is probably why the supe felt like he had to oblige. He stepped out and gave the Rocket cheer, which dates back to the first days of Army football and seems ridiculous now but is beloved by cadets and old grads. After completing the Rocket, Turtle's troops politely grabbed the supe and placed him into a BP cart that had been painted black and gold. He was either having a good time or had been shocked into silence, because he never ordered the cadets to let him go. Cheering, they pushed him all the way to Central Area, where they demanded that the OC join in. Then cadets started pouring out of the barracks. They'd heard the noise, looked out their windows, seen the superintendent in a BP cart surrounded by screaming cadets and cheerleaders, and had been sucked into the melee.

By the time the OC came out and was put in a BP cart, there must have been a thousand cadets in the area. Soon, BP carts began to show up from all directions, being pushed by cadets in silly outfits and carrying passengers holding aloft their company guidons. It didn't take long before the chant "Race, race, race" was sounded. At that point it was unstoppable, and the BP carts surged onto the apron, where they were greeted by Disco Bob's disco party equipment, set up and blaring on the mess hall steps, where at least fifty cadets danced beneath a lit mirrored ball.

At that point I'm sure the supe and the OC realized that the only way to get the Corps back under control was to let it get its gun off. So they went with it. Beat Navy.

Taps room checks across the Corps were blown off.

It was a masterpiece. Both vintage and new Turtle. The vintage was the "Fuck it, let's start at the supe's house" audacity. The whole fragile, critical undertaking could have been squelched before it even began had the supe come out and barked angrily at the nascent uprising. But he didn't. It worked. The new Turtle was evident in that he wasn't the wedge breaker. He didn't run up onto the supe's porch and pound on the door yelling, "Beat Navy, motherfucker!" Rather, he had proved to be a planner. A strategist.

Turtle came to our room before dinner with news.

"I talked to Ambizo today."

"What happened?"

"He turned himself in to their commandant this morning and told them where the goat was being held. The military police went directly there to reclaim it, but it wasn't there, of course. They interrogated his uncle, but he hadn't even noticed the thing was gone."

"That's right, you nasty squids!" laughed Zack.

"Then they hauled Ambizo back to the com's office and braced him pretty good. Demanded to be told what he knew. "

Zack got quiet.

"Did he give up our names?" I asked.

"No. He didn't. All he said was 'Sir, I wish I could be of more assistance, but I do not know where the goat is now.' Said he was in the admiral's office for over half an hour. Same question over and over. Says he never cracked."

"Wonder why he did that? I thought he wanted to be first captain."

"Doesn't matter. He found his path."

"That's great. I also heard that Major Eifer tore into Second Regiment today," Zack said. "Word is that he hit D2 really hard."

I smiled. "He's chasing rumors."

FIFTY-THREE

THE CORPS' ENERGY LEVEL AT DINNER WAS HIGH, AND the mess hall was loud. Only a day and a half stood between the cadets and the big weekend. Across the mess hall, last-minute link-up plans were being made, girls' phone numbers shared, and transportation details confirmed. When the command was sounded for the brigade to come to attention for orders, it took longer than normal for quiet to descend.

The cadet adjutant made the typical mundane announcements as I refilled my coffee cup. Then there was a shuffling noise as he turned the microphone over to someone else. When the officer spoke, I froze.

"Attention all cadets. My name is Major Eifer, special projects officer for the commandant of cadets. Some of you may have heard the rumors about the Navy goat being stolen last weekend." A ripple of whispers propagated through the Corps. I resisted the urge to look at Zack and Turtle. "As you all should also know, this is an expressly forbidden activity. We are in the process of trying to locate the Navy's stolen property. In support of this effort, any cadet who signs out on pass to attend the Army-Navy game this weekend will be affirming that they did not participate in the theft and have no knowledge of the whereabouts of the Navy goat. A cadet who so affirms and signs out to the game for the weekend and is found to have been involved in the forbidden activity will face an honor board as well as disciplinary action. That is all."

The Corps was silent for a moment as it digested what it had just been told. I looked down at my coffee. My heart sank. I couldn't believe it. Eifer was erecting a barrier between us and Philly.

As I rubbed my eyes, I noticed a sound. A murmur growing to a buzz, then to a rush, then to a roar. I looked up. Cadets were pounding the tables and climbing onto their chairs. They began to cheer. They swung their napkins over their heads. I was confused.

"We got the goat!" The plebes at the end of my table were jumping up and down. I smiled. In an effort to cast a wide and inescapable net, Eifer had confirmed the rumor. The goat had been stolen. The Corps believed it now. True, Zack, Turtle, and I were screwed. I didn't see a way through this. But the Corps was happy.

The noise died down as cadets began to head back to their barracks.

"Pretty cool, huh?" said Zack, smiling broadly. "They fucking love it!" He gestured around at the mess hall.

"I don't know what you're so happy about, Zack," I said. "In case you haven't figured it out yet, we're done."

"Oh, what? That guy?" He pointed in the general direction of the man in the sky, Major Eifer. "Fuck him. We're not doing that."

"What do you mean?" asked Turtle.

"I mean, fuck him. It's an improper question. We sign out. We don't mean it. We go. What's the problem?"

"I suppose you're right."

"Cheer up, Sam!" said Turtle, slapping me on the back. "You coming to the Firstie Club with us?"

"No. I'm beat, guys. I'm going to hit the rack."

"Okay, I'll see you after," said Zack. He and Turtle bounced out of the mess hall.

I fell asleep feeling despondent. I was trapped. I wasn't going to sign a false report again. Period. I didn't see a way out of this one.

I didn't hear Zack get back to the room that night. I slept fitfully until morning, when he jostled me awake.

+ + +

"Sam! Wake up! You've got to see this."

Zack dragged me to his desk. He sat down in front of his computer and pointed at the screen.

"Look at this, Sam. It's a fucking uprising."

I read the entries on the class bulletin board. The Corps was raging.

"'This type of mass-issued improper question is totally inconsistent with both the spirit of the honor code and the letter of regulations,'" Zack read out loud. "'I, for one, agree with those who say we should sign out in a way that indicates clearly that we are only signing out for the weekend and nothing else!'"

Zack glanced at me over his shoulder in glee. "See, buddy? No moral crises for you here after all!" He stood up and started getting ready for formation. I looked quickly at all of the bulletin board headers, then threw on my uniform and grabbed my hat as the minute caller popped off for breakfast formation.

Walking into the mess hall, I realized how widely this position in the Corps had spread since dinner the night before. On every table there were several printed flyers. Zimmer read from one as we sat down: "'Major Eifer's sign-out directive for the Army-Navy game is not in keeping with the highest traditions of the Corps' honor code nor the letter of regulations. As the chairman of the Cadet Honor Committee, I do not support his actions and I encourage all cadets to sign out with the explicit caveat that they are making no statement regarding the Navy goat. Cadet Stanley, Honor Committee Chairman. Beat Navy!'"

I looked around and saw every table going through the same sequence we were: one cadet reading the flyer aloud, then everyone agreeing and exhorting one another to resist.

The movement spread so quickly because there were not many occasions in cadet life when the Corps was right and the system was wrong. Usually, we begged for forgiveness when we screwed up. We did our time when we got caught. We groveled daily as we fell short of the ideal. But every once in a while, we were in the right. The system would briefly reveal itself as fallible, and the Corps would seize on it. Seldom receiving mercy ourselves, we never extended any when it was ours to give.

On the way to class, I smiled and shook my head. Thursday morning. One more day. It looked like we were actually going to make it to Philly. Sometimes it's better to be lucky than good, as the Guru would say.

But when I got back to my room after class and found Creighton waiting for me, I didn't feel like I was either.

FIFTY-FOUR

BAGHDAD AT NIGHT UNDER GOGGLES IS A BLINDING constellation of lights in the desert cut in half by the snaking Tigris River. I had 458 pointed at the city's center and was ready to put her down. She was ready to be done as well. The whole way from Tal Afar, her vibrations and roughness had gradually worsened. Her one good engine ran hot most of the flight. She was tired. "Almost done," I told her.

Creighton had given us a lat/long. Zack laughed when I showed it to him on the map display. He looked at the imagery of the parking lot about half a mile to the west of the American embassy. "In the Green Zone? Well, that's convenient for our arrest, I suppose."

"Let's get ready to land, Crawford."

"Roger that, sir."

Crawford started working through the landing checklist as I drove 458 down to rooftop level and kept her speed at 120 knots. We weren't making any radio calls, and I wanted to minimize any chance of us getting hit, at the end of our journey, by a pissed-off air defense site or a just a lucky bastard.

"What is that, sir?" said Crawford. "About nine o'clock. Same altitude. Closing rapidly."

I leaned forward and craned my neck to see around Crawford. The glare of two landing lights flying in close formation approached quickly from our left. They separated gracefully as they got closer, and one passed behind us. The glare of the other shifted as the aircraft banked and its light swept ahead of us.

"Where were those guys when we needed them?" I grumbled as the two Apache gunships assumed a tight escort formation on either side of us.

"That's a little fucking dramatic, isn't it?" said Zack from the rear.

"Oh joy," said Crawford. "Regular army aviation saves the day."

I scanned my navigation display. We were five minutes out.

"Looks like he wants to talk to you, sir," said Crawford.

I glanced out my window at the Apache on our right. The pilot was waving furiously and pointing at his ear. He wanted me to get on the radio.

"Fuck him. They're not going to shoot us down."

Our reluctant formation of three flew over the heart of the city. Lining up on the assigned landing spot, I could see the Crossed Swords and Unknown Soldier Monument off to our left.

"Lot of activity at our landing site," said Crawford. A dozen vehicles ringed the landing area. Numerous armed soldiers stood at the ready around them.

My pulse quickened, and I tried to focus on putting the aircraft down safely. I raised the nose and dumped more power. Chinook 458 decelerated and sank toward the earth. The Apaches slowed but maintained their altitude. They started doing easy clockwise laps above us.

The Qadisaya Expressway was empty as we passed over it, flying slow and descending. "We are clear of obstacles," called Wilson. The vehicles' headlights combined with the streetlights in the area to wash out my night-vision goggles. I brought 458 down to the asphalt for a landing.

She hit too hard, and a bouncy jolt went through the aircraft.

"Damnit, sir!"

"Sorry."

I set the brakes and started to run through an abbreviated shutdown checklist with Crawford.

"Soldiers approaching the rear of the aircraft," said Thomas. "Looks like a medical team."

"Let them on."

"Roger. There are also armed soldiers surrounding us."

I looked out to see ten armed men encircling the front of the aircraft, just outside the spinning rotor disk.

"What do we do, sir?" asked Crawford.

"We shut her down and face the music."

We quickly shut the number two engine down, and I jammed the rotor brake forward. As the forward disk came to rest, I noted several ragged bullet holes in each blade.

After switching off the APU, I removed my helmet and unstrapped. I motioned to Crawford. He nodded and headed aft. I ignored the commotion in the rear of the aircraft and looked at the tail number badge on 458's center dashboard. "Thanks, old girl," I said softly and switched her battery off. All of her systems went dark, and I left the cockpit.

The rear of the aircraft was jammed with people in motion. Each wounded man had two medics working on him. Chinook 458's floor was slick with a mixture of hydraulic fluid and blood. At least a dozen spent IV bags were strewn on the deck and seats.

Pete was the farthest forward toward the cockpit, sitting just behind the right minigun. He had an unlit Backwoods cigar in the corner of his mouth. He smiled crookedly and gave me the middle finger with his good hand. I saluted him slowly. He nodded.

Next I caught the Guru's eye. He waved me over.

Seated midship on the left side of the aircraft, he was filthy. Dust and grime covered his clothes and skin. An IV bag hung just above his head, feeding fluids into his left arm, while his right hung in a sling. His face looked weary. Gone were the crazy curls he had maintained even as an officer, replaced now with stubble. His ragged, closely cropped beard was matted with dirt.

He stood up as I approached. He was wobbly and almost inadvertently yanked the IV out of his vein. I steadied him by the shoulder, and he reached out to grab my arm.

"Go naked, Sam."

"Go naked, Guru. Now sit back down."

"No. I'm fine. Just as I told this young man, who pestered me the whole flight, trying to get me into a stretcher."

I looked at the medic. He shook his head disapprovingly at Stillmont.

"You outdid yourself tonight, Sam."

I smiled. "Does it rank with moving the reveille cannon?"

"It sure as hell does for me." He smiled. It was his Loki grin, only much older. The muck on his face crinkled at the corners of his eyes, making him look a hundred years old. But he was still as charismatic as ever, and it still made me chuckle.

"I doubt you'll get off with just a few hours on the area for this one, though," he said.

I nodded. I didn't know what was going to happen next. Truthfully, I was starting to get nervous about it. True to form, he read me immediately.

"I'm honored you came for me, Sam. Thank you. I'm sorry for what it's going to cost you."

I shook the apology off. "Bullshit. I can't think of a better final flight. It's not every day you get to save a guru."

The grin vanished, and he shook his head. "There are no gurus over here. You saved Henry Stillmont tonight, my friend. And I am very glad you did."

Then I heard Admiral Brick's voice. He must have caught a quick flight to Baghdad when our destination became obvious.

"Roger that, sir," he said. "I am on board the aircraft now. I think they got him. Confirming. Stand by."

He approached while holding a secure sat phone to his ear. Two armed guards followed behind him. He alternated between barking commands to the team on the helicopter and speaking into his phone. Henry and I dropped our arms to our sides.

"You Henry Stillmont?" Brick asked.

"Yes, sir. I am."

"What is his status?" he asked.

The medic gave Brick a thumbs-up.

"I've got eyes on him," Brick said into his phone. "He's good, sir."

Brick began to work his way aft, checking on each of the wounded. I watched him and then waggled my eyebrows at Stillmont and followed Brick.

Turtle's guys were stable and doing well. One had taken a bad hit to leg and had nearly bled out. He was moving now, though. Across from him, the man with the shoulder wound was bound and leaning back in his seat, enjoying his pain meds.

I eased past the admiral as he spoke into his sat phone.

The commotion outside to the rear of the aircraft began to come into focus as I moved aft. There were several spotlights, and I could barely make out what looked like dozens of people. Zack and Turtle stood under the aft transmission, gazing off the ramp, out into the lights.

Turtle had a hand on Zack's shoulder to balance himself. His prosthesis had been severed a couple of inches below the knee. They had cut back his pants leg. Fragmented carbon fiber dangled beneath the opening.

"That hurt?" I asked, stepping next to them.

"Not like in 2003."

"Good."

"Sucks, though. It was my best one. Going to take months to get a new one made."

"Any regrets?"

"None. You?"

"Nope."

"Good."

Admiral Brick stepped up behind us, still speaking into his phone: "Roger that, sir. We are all accounted for here, and the wounded are being moved to the medical facility now. . . . Yes, sir. . . . Brick out."

He put his phone into his cargo pocket. Even in the glare and shadows, I could see the transformation take place. Brick was a good officer. His first concern was the welfare of the wounded. But now that they were secure and receiving treatment, anger overtook him. By the time he took the last step in front of us, he was steaming. The two armed men followed closely behind him.

Brick didn't slow down until he was inches from me. One of the armed men actually reached out and grabbed his shoulder to stop him. Brick shoved the guard's hand away and jabbed his finger into my chest. He started to speak a few times, but he was too mad. He couldn't get anything out. Giving up, he gestured at the guards. The medics and wounded men pretended not to notice as Zack, Turtle, and I were handcuffed and shoved down onto the bench seats.

FIFTY-FIVE

CREIGHTON SAT AT MY DESK, HOLDING HIS SABER AND still wearing his gray hat.

"Hi, Creighton. What's up?"

He stared down at his saber.

"You okay?"

"Why did you guys leave me out?" he asked without looking up.

"Leave you out of what?"

He shook his head and took off his hat, still without making eye contact. He put his hat in his lap and rubbed his eyes. He kept his hair closely cropped, and I could see the muscles on the side of his dark head ripple with tension. Then he looked at me. "Don't insult me, Sam."

I pulled Zack's chair out and sat down facing Creighton.

"I'm not the oblivious idiot you and Zack think I am. Turtle is involved too, right?"

"Involved in what, Creighton?"

"Don't insult me, Sam! I can't believe you would do this!" He closed his eyes and took a deep breath. I started to get nervous.

"If you're going to do something like steal the Navy goat," I said, "you have to keep it secret. You can't let anyone figure it out. Even those who don't want you to get caught."

I looked back at him, unsure of what to do. I didn't want to admit to what we had done yet. I wanted to find a path through this.

"I thought we were friends," Creighton said.

"Of course we're friends. Why would you say that?"

"Why didn't you guys ask me to go on the spirit mission with you?"

The question surprised me.

"First of all, I'm not admitting to anything here. But you would never do something like steal the Navy goat, Creighton."

"You don't know that."

"Would you ever disobey a lawful, direct order from a general officer?"

"Of course not."

"You ever willfully broken a regulation?"

"Never."

"You don't see how that might make someone overlook you when they recruit for an 'unauthorized spirit mission'?" I wanted to yell, but I spoke as deliberately and kindly as I could. "For fucksake, Creighton. We're all going to work for you someday anyway . . . that's not enough?"

"No."

His anger started to anger me.

"This is a ridiculous conversation."

"I agree."

"Here's a tip: if you want someone to pull you into a spirit mission, try not to be the perfect robo-cadet."

He glared at me. Angry and hurt. I suddenly felt sad. This was an unanticipated consequence. Now we were in a difficult spot.

Creighton was an army brat hoping to become a second-generation armor officer legend. He loved the military and thought of nothing else. He excelled because he'd gotten here already living by a code. Violating regulations was something he simply could not do. So when his good friends did it for a cause he viewed as worthy, he was stuck. And now he was in a double bind. Not only did he feel hurt because of being left out; he also had to decide whether or not to turn us in. I was confident I could talk him through this.

"Creighton, I thought that after Eifer questioned you at formation, E4 was in the clear."

"Unfortunately not, Sam. His attempt to bind the entire Corps to a sign-out statement backfired. The Corps' refusal only temporarily saved you. He has regrouped."

"I expected nothing less."

"And it has been another forty-eight hours. A lot more has happened. You guys have been sloppy. He is calling company commanders in one at a time now. He is interrogating them and making them sign an official report that they do not have any knowledge of the stolen goat."

He stared at me. He was searching for a sign. I didn't even blink. I regarded him passively as my mind raced.

"He is starting with First and Second Regiment tonight after dinner. Third and Fourth Regiment commanders will go first thing in the morning after breakfast."

We looked at each other for a moment. I was frozen. I didn't know what to do or say. It was a good move by Major Eifer. His Corps-wide honor-focused approach had been heavy-handed and was a sign of how much pressure he was under. But now he had dialed into the cadet chain of command. Though Zack, Turtle, and I were dismissive of the posts, we understood that they carried a real burden. The hardest people in the world to lead are your peers. The cadet chain of command was leaned on constantly by the tactical department. They often had to mete out punishments to and take privileges away from fellow cadets. Their roles were hard. Particularly in a company like E4, where the ethic often put the company at odds with its cadet commander. Creighton had navigated the role well because he understood the company and we understood him. Neither side took any of it personally. Until now.

Eifer's pivot now put the concept of command behind his effort. In the army, a commander is responsible for every aspect of his unit: military proficiency, physical fitness, mental soundness, family health, morale, everything. West Point makes the same demands of its cadet company commanders. The fact that the goat had been stolen meant that it was fair game to ask every company commander if they knew anything. And not just in the investigative, conversational way in which Eifer had engaged Creighton after Tuesday's breakfast formation—also in the focused, "on your honor" way that Eifer was shifting to now. Eifer could also leverage the fact that the Corps is so tightly woven that in a cadet company it is hard to miss the slightest change in your company mates. The fact is, a good company commander should have figured it out by now. And Creighton was one of the best.

By making all the commanders sign and swear to a report, Eifer was exploiting the dynamic that Creighton and I were dealing with now. Creighton knew. Period.

Creighton looked away from me and back down at his saber. "I just really wish you guys had asked me to be on the spirit mission."

He stood up and left the room as the realization hit me.

"Creighton, wait," I called after him, but he didn't stop.

I sat and continued to stare at the spot where he had been. I was para-lyzed by shame. Had I learned nothing? I was doing to Creighton what Bill had done to me.

FIFTY-SIX

WE STOOD IN A TIGHT CIRCLE UNDER MAC'S STATUE after lunch. I didn't want to have this discussion in the barracks. Zack and Turtle were nervous. They could tell this was going to be bad news.

"We have a problem," I said hesitantly. "Major Eifer is interrogating the company commanders one by one. He is making them submit an official written report regarding their knowledge about the goat. Creighton goes in front of Eifer first thing tomorrow morning."

"Fucker," said Zack quietly.

"What is Creighton going to do?" Turtle asked.

"It doesn't matter," interrupted Zack. "Creighton is a big boy. He can take care of himself. Do the math. Even if Creighton does give us up tomorrow, it will be Friday morning. Too late for Eifer to get to us."

"That's right," Turtle joined in. "If we skip out immediately after breakfast and get on the road, he won't be able to get us. He'll never find us in Philly before the game. We'll have the initiative. At that point, we just execute the plan. Sneak into the stadium. Get on the field. Heroes."

"Exactly," agreed Zack. "We'd be adding a missed formation to our offenses, but at this point that's just a rounding error. It's a good plan. We can still do this. I'll call Pelly and let her know we'll be grabbing the goat earlier than planned tomorrow."

"What do you think, Sam?" asked Turtle.

"No."

They looked at me, startled.

I understood what they were going through. The overwhelming desire to succeed. Fuck Eifer. We are so close. We can do this.

"Are we going to put Creighton in that position?"

"He did fine at formation the other day, didn't he?"

"This is different."

"How so?"

"It's more than forty-eight hours later. We didn't hold things close enough. With all of the running around we had to do—sneaking off the post again, re-stealing the goat, Turtle's late-night diversion—there was just too much going on. Too many opsec violations. Creighton knows. And not because he was trying to figure it out. We allowed it to happen. And now he knows."

"You sure?"

"Yes."

I let it sink in for a moment.

"We've said from the beginning that we had to be ready to take a big slug to do this. The Guru taught us that a spirit mission like this is going to demand a price of everyone who participates. But we never said that our plan would be to have friends cover for us. Or that we would put them in a position of having to choose."

"What do you mean, 'choose'?"

"Between their friends and honor."

Zack winced when I said the word "honor." Turtle's face twisted with anguish.

MacArthur's statue looked over Turtle and Zack's shoulders as they stared at the ground and worked through the problem. The old general's right hand was in a fist on his right hip, and he held his trademark leather bomber jacket over his left arm. Mac's determined gaze swept out over the Plain toward Trophy Point and the Hudson. He had seen it all and was ready for a fight. Ready for anything. Quotes from the general were inscribed on large marble slabs circling us at the edge of the statue's memorial area. One of them finished with "Duty. Honor. Country."

"I'm sorry, guys, but we can't put Creighton in a position to have to make that choice. As much as I want to get the goat to Philly and beat Eifer, it's not worth doing at the cost of Creighton's honor. Nothing is. He's a cadet. And he's our friend."

Zack held up his hand, cutting me off. "You're right, Sam."

I looked at Turtle. He nodded sadly. "Absolutely."

"I am so disappointed," Zack said. "I really wanted to be on television."

"I am too, Zack. But remember, all that matters is getting it to the Corps."

"You got something in mind?"

"Yes. But we don't have much time."

FIFTY-SEVEN

HOURS LATER, WE WERE BACK AT MAC'S STATUE. THIS time, instead of the BDUs being worn by the rest of the Corps, we had donned our full dress uniforms with sabers.

We skipped dinner formation and fidgeted nervously as the rest of the Corps filed into the mess hall.

"There she is."

Pelly's old pickup truck turned onto Scott Place. I glanced quickly at the mess hall steps. Most of the cadets were inside now. Soon they would be taking seats for the evening meal. A couple of officers milled around just outside of the massive mess hall doors. But no Eifer so far. That was good.

Pelly stopped alongside Mac's statue, and we jogged over. Her truck was fitted with a beat-up camper shell. Zack lowered the tailgate and raised the rear door. The Navy goat looked at us, lying on a bed of old, dirty blankets.

"That is one ornery animal," said Pelly, who had gotten out and come to stand beside Zack.

Zack yanked on the goat's leash, trying to pull him out.

"He won't agree to anything unless you offer him food." Pelly waved a carrot, and the goat moved slowly toward the tailgate.

"Come here, you bastard," said Zack. "We're tired of this, too. You might get to sleep in your own bed tonight."

Zack and Turtle lowered the goat to the ground. Turtle snapped another leash onto his collar. He and Zack could now stand on either side of his head and hold him on course.

"Thanks, Pelly." I said. "Really appreciate your help."

"It was my pleasure, cadets. You guys have fun." She hopped back in her truck and drove off.

I looked at the mess hall steps, then at my watch.

"Anything?" asked Turtle.

"Nope. Nothing yet."

It would have been entirely like Eifer to suddenly appear from around the corner, just as he had when he'd busted Bill for vomiting. We would be done. Even though we had the Navy goat only a few hundred meters from over four thousand cadets, the Corps would never know. Eifer would make sure of that.

I stared at the mess hall steps. I felt exposed.

Finally William, the rugby team's captain, stepped out of the mess hall and stood in the middle of the steps.

"There he is. Let's go."

We jogged quickly to the mess hall. Fortunately, the goat went along with our plan and picked up an easy gait with Zack and Turtle by his side. It helped that I was in front holding one of Pelly's carrots.

As we climbed the mess hall steps, William was laughing. "Holy shit! I can't believe you guys actually did this." His eyes were wide.

"Focus, William," I said. "You know what to do?"

"Don't let anyone get to you. Not complex stuff." He spun on his heels and leapt up to the center door. He yanked it open as we got to the top, and we stepped into the small foyer and were soon in the midst of the Army rugby team.

"Form up!" yelled William as his guys started to fixate on the goat. "No one gets through us. No one!"

As the team formed a cordon around us, I noticed that there were two captains in the foyer with us. I did not recognize them as tacs. They smiled and shook their heads, but they didn't do anything to stop us.

The cadets at the tables nearest to the foyer were looking our way now to see what the commotion was. Some of them stood up to get a clear line of sight through the large windows in the swinging doors between the foyer and the mess hall. One by one, as they spotted the goat, they grabbed a buddy, their eyes widening in disbelief. Within seconds, everyone at the first twenty tables was standing up, looking our way. We were so close.

Then I spotted Major Eifer at the far end of the mess hall. He saw the commotion and started walking toward us.

"We need to move!"

As we made ready, the doors suddenly swung open and a full-bird colonel glared at us. It was Colonel Lenz, the head of the civil engineering department. He had graduated from West Point in 1969 and been shipped to Vietnam. There, he'd served as a 155mm battery commander at Firebase Bastogne in 1972, when it was overrun. He was a tall, gruff hard-ass who enjoyed hazing firsties most of all. My heart sank. We couldn't have had worse luck.

Over Lenz's shoulder, I could see Major Eifer. He was now striding purposefully our way. We had seconds before he would arrive and shut us down.

If we did not get the goat into the mess hall, the best we could hope for was a persistent rumor that we had gotten it. We were one verbal order away from total failure.

William glanced back at me in terror. I felt Zack and Turtle, just behind me, waiting for my word. Colonel Lenz's bearlike body filled the doorway in front of me.

I stared at Colonel Lenz. His normally intense face looked like it was about to burst into flames. He was clearly enraged. He inhaled deeply and started yelling.

"Beat Navy!" The old man smiled from ear to ear and started pumping his fists in the air, hollering all the while. He stepped to the side and held the door open for us. He never stopped yelling.

I nodded at William, and the rugby team stepped off in a wedge formation. I drew my saber and held it high in the air as we burst through the doors. I joined the colonel in his chant, bellowing, "Beat Navy!"

Eifer was ten meters away from the door as it swung open and we stepped into the mess hall, but he was too late. Cadets leapt from their tables and exploded in cheers. He was jostled to the side and out of the way as thousands of cadets rushed forward to see our prisoner, the Navy goat. I didn't see Eifer again in the mess hall.

William and his team were able to keep the path clear for us, and we kept moving forward toward the brigade staff's table. The Corps went nuts. Since it was the Thursday of Army-Navy Week, there was a mixture of elements in the crowd: cadets, officers, cheerleaders, military police, and civilian VIPs. All with gaping mouths and pie-pan-sized eyes. All going crazy. It was louder than when President Reagan gave the Corps amnesty. My ears were ringing, and my heart was full.

The goat, though, had a different reaction. From his perspective, it must have seemed like hell itself had risen to devour him. Certain of his doom, he collapsed in a pool of his own piss. Turtle and Zack had to drag him the last twenty meters to the first captain. Fortunately, because of the piss, he slid easily across the large stone tiles.

With thousands of cadets watching, I stepped up to the first captain, Cadet Stephens, and presented arms with my saber. He shook his head in disbelief.

"Cadet Stephens, please accept this prisoner."

Zack and Turtle handed him the leashes. Stephens smiled as he looked at the goat and returned my salute.

"Beat Navy, Sam," he said with a nod as he took hold of both leashes.

Zack, Turtle, and I turned, and several of William's guys led us out. We passed through the E4 area as we jogged out of the mess hall and through the Fourth Regiment wing. As we got to the door, I saw Creighton in the crowd.

Creighton, the cadet whose military bearing never cracked, was going bonkers. He was swinging his cadet scarf like a bullwhip, and veins were poking out of his neck and forehead. He and I made eye contact, and he raised a salute. I returned it at a jog.

We ducked out of the mess hall and walked slowly back to the barracks. Before we entered the Lost Fifties, we stood on the stoop and savored the roar from the mess hall. Despite the stone walls and our distance, it still sounded loud.

"I wish Bill had been able to make it," Zack said.

"Me, too."

FIFTY-EIGHT

"**Y**OU ARE GOING AWAY FOR A LONG TIME, AVERY. A very long fucking time!" The admiral had found his voice and was leaning down over me, screaming into my face in the back of 458. Spit flew from his mouth as he yelled. I wanted to wipe my face, but my hands were bound behind me and one of the guards had his hand firmly on my shoulder, to make sure I didn't so much as stand up.

"Do you realize we had to cancel real missions tonight because of your fucked-up joy ride?"

"I'm sure you can reschedule the bombing runs on the camels and wagons to tomorrow night, sir," said Zack, sitting to my right.

The admiral almost came to a three-foot hover in rage. He howled at Zack: "And you, asshole! Do you even know who I am?" The admiral did not wait for a response. "I'm Rear Admiral Brick, task force commander, goddamnit. I'm responsible for JSOC's resources and responsiveness in-theater. This is my fucking helicopter! I've been on the line with MacDill and D.C. all night, trying to explain how and why it was stolen. Do you know how embarrassing this is? And from the looks of it, this bird won't be able to fly again for months."

He stopped to take a breath and surveyed the inside of 458. "I don't know how the hell this thing kept flying," he said, almost to himself.

The admiral swiveled back to me. "This is a hell of a way to go out, Avery. Steal a United States Army helicopter in a war zone . . ." He shook his head. Now that the wounded were secure and he had us back under control, he was having a hard time believing what had happened. Truthfully, so was I.

The admiral was interrupted by the medics as they started to move the wounded off the aircraft. One of them looked at Admiral Brick for permission. He nodded and gestured aft, off the ramp. First Turtle's two commandos. Then the Guru, and then Pete. Once the wounded had been removed, there were eleven of us still on the aircraft, other than Brick and his armed guards: Zack and me, Turtle and his four remaining commandos, Crawford, Wilson, Thomas, and Weber. We all sat, handcuffed, and awaited our fate. Someone came running up the ramp.

"Admiral Brick!" It was Major Obrien.

"Yes. What is it?"

"Sir, you better come see."

"Okay. Let's go then," Brick said over his shoulder to our guards. We started to get up to follow him.

"Sir . . . um . . . I recommend you leave them on board for the time being." Obrien gestured at us, looking terrified.

"What is the problem, Obrien?"

"Sir, it's better I show you."

"Fine." Brick pointed at the guards and me. "Hold them here until I get back."

"Yes, sir."

Brick strode out after Obrien. They disappeared off the ramp into the glare of spotlights. As they did, a wave of fatigue swept over me.

"You okay?" Zack asked.

"Yeah. Just tired."

I hung my head. I looked at the blood smears and hydraulic fluid on the deck of 458. It had been a long night. It had been a long career.

If I could have, I would have put my head in my hands. I could feel my mind and body reacting to the realization that the mission was over. That we had survived. I closed my eyes. My mind raced. I saw the rockets go into the house again. The vehicle with the .50-cal. rounded the corner. It had us. I started to shake slightly and was glad my hands were behind my back so that the guard could not see them twitching. I saw the drone cartwheel into the enemy. Aft rotor disk inches from the building. The impact of 458's ramp.

I focused on my breathing. My meditation was interrupted by the curses of Rear Admiral Brick.

"Goddamnit!" He stomped back onto the aircraft, followed by Major Obrien. They did not walk all the way in. They stopped under the aft transmission. Obrien was talking to someone on the sat phone.

"Yes, sir. Yes, sir. I will, sir. Here he is, sir." Obrien handed the sat phone to Brick.

"This is Brick." His voice sounded agitated. He had seen something that he really hadn't liked outside.

"Yes, sir. They are. I'd say at least a dozen. Maybe more." He shrugged his shoulders. "I have no idea, but it is clear that they were tipped off. They know a hell of a lot already. It's a fucking disaster."

I looked at Obrien. He was fidgeting, his head swiveling back and forth between Brick and whatever was outside of the aircraft.

"Sir, I really don't think—" Rear Admiral Brick straightened suddenly. Whoever was on the other side of the conversation had cut him off. "Yes, sir. I understand, sir." His body language was tense, screaming the opposite of what he was saying. "Yes, sir. I will. No . . . it's not a problem, sir. I know what to do."

Brick put his other hand up to his face and kneaded his forehead. "I will, sir. Yes, sir. I will call you afterward." He handed the phone back to Major Obrien and took a deep breath. Then he walked toward me.

"Stand up, Avery."

I stood slowly, still sinking into the adrenaline letdown.

"Uncuff them."

"Sir?"

"I said, uncuff them, goddamnit."

As the guards worked their way through our group, removing handcuffs, Brick stepped in front of me.

"Now, you listen to me, Avery. You're going to walk off this aircraft next to me and follow my lead. If you stray one fucking micron, I'll shoot you myself and bury you out here in the desert. You got that?"

"Not really, sir."

"That makes fucking two of us."

"The rest of you are going to stay on this aircraft until we can find a way to get you off. Do not fucking leave this aircraft."

"Yes, sir."

Brick pointed to one of the guards. "You stay with them. If they try to get off the aircraft before I come back, shoot them."

"Yes, sir."

"Let's go." He turned and walked toward the ramp, with Obrien on his heels. I looked around the helicopter at the guys. Weber and I locked eyes for a moment. The expression on his face told me he wanted to go with me to watch my back. I just smiled. He nodded.

I followed Brick and Obrien. Breathing deeply, I walked off 458's bent ramp and stepped onto the ground, a couple of paces behind the admiral and the major.

The glare of the spotlights was intense, and I slowed involuntarily as my eyes adjusted. Noticing this, Brick reached back to grab me by the arm. He pulled me up even with him as he pushed through a line of armed soldiers, into a throng of civilians.

Then I saw the cameras and microphones. Finally, I put it together.

"Admiral Brick!" said a young woman holding a microphone. "May we speak with you, sir?" She didn't wait for an answer, decisively moving next to Brick and then fluidly swiveling back to face her cameraman. She was a pro and recognized an easy target.

"This is Linda Cogner, CNN, live from Baghdad. I am here with Rear Admiral Brick whose special operations troops have just completed a daring midnight raid that successfully rescued an American hostage from ISIS. Under the cover of darkness, their team achieved total surprise over an enemy that had no idea they were even in the country. It's a proud night for America, isn't it, Admiral Brick?"

FIFTY-NINE

"THE COMMANDANT WILL SEE YOU NOW, GENTLEMEN."
Zack, Turtle, and I looked at one another and breathed deeply.
Zack went in first. We stepped in front of the com's massive desk, and Zack
rendered our report: "Sir, Cadets Dempsey, Avery, and Guerrero reporting
as ordered."

The com eyeballed us gravely, then slowly returned Zack's salute.
Behind the com, to his right, stood a glowering Major Eifer. Cadet Stephens, the first captain, stood behind the com to his left. Several other
officers stood off to the side, but I didn't dare gaze around to see who
they were.

General Franklin looked at us for a moment, then glanced over his
shoulder slightly, toward Major Eifer. The major handed him a folder.
The general placed the folder on the desk in front of him and opened it
slowly.

"Gentlemen, you are here to answer for the following behavior." He
read from the 2-1 form: "Error in judgment with major effect: participating in an activity which had been explicitly prohibited by the chain of

command—misappropriating the Navy goat. Compounded by repeated failure to rectify the situation as directed by senor officials and return the aforementioned property by the designated deadline." He exhaled forcefully and leaned back in his chair.

"Gentlemen, not only did you exercise poor judgment when you decided not to adhere to or support command directives . . ." He raised his hand and stabbed a finger into the air.

"You failed to support your chain of command, the United States Corps of Cadets, and the United States Military Academy by willfully disobeying a direct order." The second finger extended.

"And, worst of all, none of you displayed the moral courage necessary to halt what each of you knew was prohibited activity." The third finger extended, and Major Eifer nodded in disgusted agreement.

"That is three strikes, gentlemen." The general slowly lowered his hand.

Major Eifer shook his head in disapproval. Stephens looked at us with pity.

"Do you know the main reason why we forbid the stealing of mascots, Cadet Dempsey?"

"No, sir."

"It's not because we don't have any spirit. It's so you dumbasses don't do something stupid and get yourself hurt, hurt the animal, or damage property through your buffoonery."

"Yes, sir."

He looked back at his folder. "Are you aware that you gentlemen did several thousand dollars' worth of damage on that farm, Cadet Guerrero?"

"No, sir."

"Well, you did. And the academy had to cover it."

The general glared at us.

"But the minor damage you did and the reasons why we forbid stealing mascots don't matter that much to me. What matters to me is that three cadets can get this far in my academy and think it's okay to disobey direct lawful orders. What am I to make of that?"

You learn on day one as plebes not to answer rhetorical questions. Doing so never ends well. We looked straight ahead.

"That was not a rhetorical question, gentlemen."

General Franklin had graduated from West Point in the early sixties and had seen combat in multiple conflicts. He knew the deal. And he was getting more pissed as time went on.

"Cadet Dempsey, what am I to think about this situation?"

"Sir. No excuse, sir."

The general shook his head in disgust.

"I want an answer, goddamnit. Why, Guerrero? Why did you think it was okay to disobey a direct and lawful order? Where at this academy were you taught that?"

Turtle's voice trembled as he spoke: "Sir. I do not know. No excuse, sir."

"Fine. How about you, Avery?"

"Sir, I didn't think it was a serious order."

In my peripheral vision, I could see Stephens's eyes get big.

"You didn't think it was a 'serious order'? You thought I was joking?"

"No, sir. Not joking. But . . . it was an order you had to give, sir. It's given every year." I stalled. I was walking the plank. I should have dummied up.

"So I just give this order every year for no damn reason?"

"Not for no reason, sir. But . . . I didn't think you really expected it to be followed . . . strictly speaking."

"Look at me, Avery. Do I look to you like the kind of general who gives orders he does not expect to be followed?" He was incredulous. I suddenly realized how stupid I sounded.

"Sir, may I ask a question?"

"Go ahead, Dempsey."

"Sir, we are about to fight a war in the Middle East. Do you really want a Corps of Cadets that does not try to steal the Navy goat? Seems like we—"

The general quickly held his hand up, palm toward us, in a "shut the fuck up" gesture. He leaned his head forward and rubbed his eyes with his other hand.

"Don't talk to me about war, Dempsey. Please." He raised his head. "That's all I think about, unfortunately. My cadets going to war." He kneaded one of his fists in the other hand. He looked old and tired.

"And what I want is a Corps of Cadets that knows how to follow orders. That knows how to evaluate between right and wrong. I want you men to lead, to fight, and to live well. Not to play games with your honor. It's too precious. And once lost, it is really, really hard to get back."

His voice sounded earnest, and though I believed we had done nothing wrong, I felt vaguely ashamed. West Point did that to you occasionally. You would go into meetings expecting to get your balls crushed by
an officer, and at some point in the meeting it would pivot and they'd be
teaching you a lesson. It was hard because the lesson was being taught as
a result of some way you had fallen short. But you always left those meetings feeling good, maybe because you realized that the officer gave a shit
about you and the army and the future of both. Rather than simply writing you up, they took the time to try to teach you something. You left
those meetings feeling strangely obligated to apply the lesson. To live up
to what they were telling you to do. To make their time worthwhile. To
get strong and be ready for the next meeting at which, invariably, your
balls would be crushed again. And here was the commandant of cadets,
a one-star general, who had every reason to bash our heads in, seeming
more troubled than anything else, weighed down by a burden we couldn't
yet see or feel.

"What should I do with you three?" Another rhetorical question. No
one answered.

"You cadets think I'm just asking rhetorical questions, for my health?"

"No, sir."

"What should I do with the three of you? What would you do if you
were me?"

I spoke to fill the void: "Sir, I recommend that no disciplinary action
be taken."

"On what basis?"

"The victory over Navy, sir. And the positive effect our mission had
on the Corps' morale."

He shook his head. "Good try. Not going to happen." He gestured at
someone behind us, and an officer stepped forward with a large folder.

The general flipped it open.

"What rank did your father retire at, Cadet Guerrero?"

"Command sergeant major, sir."

"Did he know General Schwarzkopf?"

"Yes, sir. They served together in Vietnam and then later at Fort
Lewis."

"That would explain the phone call I got from the general after the
game, then. Called me from the damn desert. He has a strong opinion

regarding your spirit mission. As do other members of the class of fifty-six. Every living member of which has tried to contact me over the last seventy-two hours."

He shifted his eyes to me. "Colonel Krieger is your sponsor, Cadet Avery?"

"Yes, sir."

"Got a call from him, as well. In addition to pleading your case, he let me know that the SEALs he is working with were pissed off about the goat."

I nodded, not wanting to speak.

"And who the hell is Second Lieutenant Stillmont?"

"He graduated from E4, sir," said Zack.

"Well, that son of a bitch gave my e-mail address to everyone with a computer in the sandbox in southwest Asia. You know how many e-mails my office has gotten regarding the goat and the disposition of your discipline board?"

I started to speak.

"That one is rhetorical, son."

"Yes, sir."

"The real pain in my ass, though, is *Good Morning America,* ESPN, and the others. They want to talk to the daring group of cadets that stole the Navy goat on the eve of war in the Middle East."

He looked at us evenly. "Who the hell reached out to the networks?"

"Sir . . . I wouldn't say we reached out as much as answered their inquiries," I said shakily.

The general rubbed his eyes again and leaned back in his chair.

"Here is what is going to happen. I'm giving each of you a hundred hours on the area."

My breath constricted, and my heart sank. I wouldn't be able to get away to see Stephanie at all next semester. She would crumble. We were done. And there was no way we could walk that many hours off by graduation. We would graduate late. I didn't know if I could get through it.

The general stared at us and let it soak in. Then he looked down and slowly filled out the paperwork. We stood at attention, waiting to be marched out.

He put down his pen and regarded each of us in turn. "However, gentlemen, I must consider the fact that your spirit mission did succeed in raising the morale of the Corps, the academy as a whole, and even some of our troops getting ready to fight downrange. That means something to me.

"So, at great hazard to you cadets in the form of the lessons you will draw from this, and in light of the mitigating circumstances and in exchange for the performance of duties I intend to assign to you . . . I am going to suspend the punishment contingent on the following—"

Major Eifer leaned forward and took a small step toward the general. "Sir, I don't think—"

"At ease, Major!" The general's voice took on the hardest edge we'd heard yet. His head had swiveled sharply as he spoke, his right hand rising instantly to a knife-edged ready position. He hesitated until Major Eifer had fully returned to his former spot. The general lowered his hand.

"I am suspending your punishment contingent on your communicating to the media that you are busy with exams and not available for any interviews. You will tell *Army Times* as well. No more articles about the Navy goat. You will contact this Lieutenant Stillmont and get his e-mail campaign stopped. Guerrero, your father will get Schwarzkopf to call off the dogs in the class of fifty-six. And each of you will get the word out to the Corps. Mascots are off-limits. Period. Do you understand?"

"Yes, sir," we answered in unison.

"You'd better. If a single goat, dog, falcon, or any of God's creatures is stolen from any of our opponents while you are still cadets, these one hundred hours will go immediately into effect. Do you understand?"

"Yes, sir."

"Furthermore, I am holding the three of you responsible in this area for the rest of your lives. I'm serious. I don't care how many years from now it happens or where you are in the army. If any cadets steal any mascots, I will track your asses down. Is that clear?"

"Yes, sir."

Cadet Stephens was smiling. Eifer shifted angrily on his feet. He was roiling inside.

"You are dismissed."

✦ ✦ ✦

We rejoiced, got through exams, and took off for Christmas leave. We complied with all of the commandant's commands, of course. Fortunately, the media cooperated as well. Soon they were on to other stories.

Surprisingly, Creighton was the only one of us to do any time on the area. Major Eifer wrote Creighton up for his "failure to properly command his company," and the quill stuck. He got twenty hours on the area for failing to uncover our unauthorized spirit mission. An even greater surprise, though, was Creighton's reaction to having his spotless discipline record stained by such a sizable slug. He could hardly contain his pride.

He swaggered to area formation each Friday like a peacock telling anyone within earshot how he had earned his quill.

"I was involved in the goat-napping. I can't really talk about it. But, yeah . . . those were my friends." In Creighton's mind, each of the twenty hours on the area cemented his relationship with us. It was a small price to pay for proof of his place and role within our tight circle of friends.

We were quiet firsties, and when we got back for second semester, we kept our noses clean. Creighton and I were roommates again. The war in the Gulf kicked off shortly after we returned to classes and was over in just a few weeks. Many of us cursed our luck at missing it, but Creighton laughed. "It isn't over. Trust me. Nothing has changed over there. We'll be fighting this one for a long, long time."

Colonel Krieger returned to West Point in late March, and by April the national conversation had turned back to "the peace dividend" and plans for the drawdown accelerated. I got posted to aviation, Zack and Turtle got infantry, and Creighton was assigned to his beloved tanks.

Stephanie was accepted into an internship at a museum in Europe and was headed to Paris at the end of the academic year. I was headed to Fort Rucker, Alabama, for flight school. She broke up with me during our last weekend together before graduation. "I'm sorry, Sam," she told me. "I just can't keep saying good-bye."

Graduation took place on the first of June, under a clear sky. The view looking north, up the Hudson, went on forever as the river flowed beneath Storm King Mountain. Dressed in our India White uniforms, we filed excitedly into Michie Stadium and sat as a class in front of the speakers' platform. I wore Bill's dress white hat. We listened to President Bush's commencement address in disbelief. Had this day really arrived?

When the ceremony finally ended and our class was dismissed, I threw Bill's hat into the air with the rest of my classmates. It rose high with a thousand others against the severe blue sky, and then disappeared as it fell to the ground.

SIXTY

"COLONEL ANDERSON WILL SEE YOU NOW."

"Thank you, ma'am."

I walked past the secretary's desk, into the history department head's office. Colonel Anderson crossed the room to shake my hand.

"Lieutenant Colonel Avery. Thanks for stopping by. I promise this won't take long, and then we can both get out there to watch the march back." He glanced at his watch and gestured toward two leather chairs by a large window that overlooked the Hudson River.

"Yes, sir. I'm looking forward to that. Haven't seen it since I was a cadet. Actually, the daughter of a classmate of mine is marching back with them as a plebe."

"Who's your classmate?"

"Colonel Zack Dempsey."

"I've heard of him. Good officer."

"We were in E4 together."

"That's great. Now I know who to go to for blackmail material on you."

"Trust me, sir. You don't have to go far for that."

"I get the feeling that's true." He smiled. "Are you settling in okay?"

"Yes, sir. I appreciate you helping out with the quarters situation." Colonel Anderson had stepped in when they'd tried to billet me in the bachelor officers' quarters, a crappy condo-like building full of newly minted lieutenants who had stayed back a year to help with athletics and unmarried mid-grade captains fresh out of grad school back to teach their first courses. He'd thrown his rank around and had gotten me situated on the end of Lee Road, just two houses down from where Colonel Krieger used to live.

"No problem. They can be so uptight at this place. It's bullshit."

I smiled.

"What's so funny?"

"Sir, if I had known when I was a cadet that full-bird colonels and department heads still referred to 'they' and 'fucking West Point' when they talked about this place, I would have been very confused."

"It's a hell of a thing to become the 'they' one used to rail against as a cadet."

"Do 'they' really exist?"

"All I know is this: I've heard the superintendent, a three-star general, complain about 'they' and 'fucking West Point.'"

"I don't know if I should cry or laugh."

"You should laugh. You'll feel better."

"Well, your getting me into those quarters meant a lot to me. Thank you."

He nodded, and we both looked out the window at the river.

His office in Thayer Hall faced the Hudson. The trees and rolling hills on the other side were a lush green.

He spoke without turning away from the window: "As nontraditional as your assignment process has been, Sam, it's still really good to have you here. It's good for the cadets to have instructors with your experience."

"Thank you, sir." Colonel Anderson had been on the faculty at West Point for almost a decade and looked more professorial now than soldierly. He'd done a few hard years after 9/11 as an MP in Afghanistan and then Iraq, though. The academic paunch covered scar tissue, physical and psychic.

"You ever going to tell me how all of that happened? First I see you on CNN after that mission, and then a couple days later the supe calls me in his office and tells me to make room for a lieutenant colonel coming to the history department. The next day you show up. Was it a reward for something?"

"Not exactly, sir."

"Come on. Guys line up for years to get assigned here. Particularly to this department."

"Sir. I'm sorry. Part of the deal was not to talk about it. Ever. I'm going to follow through on my end." I looked back at the river. It was narrower in this spot than most, and it seemed a little faster. "To be honest with you, I don't want to talk about it at all."

The only thing that had saved us from being charged after our bootleg mission in Iraq was the press. Creighton tipped off a few of his contacts in leadership positions at key networks and made sure they got to us in Baghdad before Brick and his crew were able to take us away. Thanks to Creighton, the coverage was immediate, widespread, and positive. Minutes after we landed, CNN and the others were broadcasting live breaking news reports about a "daring and successful rescue operation." After Benghazi and the inability to rescue any of the Americans in Iraq prior to their beheadings, the administration and the Pentagon were not about to correct the public record. They accepted the praise and talked convincingly about our mission exemplifying a new period of ass kicking against terror in general and ISIS in particular.

In private, they were incandescent with rage, not only at what we had done but also at the fact that they couldn't punish us. Thanks to Creighton, we were on the right side of the public relations wire, and the army displayed its customary institutional reluctance to cross that wire.

Admiral Brick had kept the rest of the crew sequestered on 458 until the impromptu press conference was over. Mine would be the only face associated with the mission. It became clear that none of us were going to jail, but for those of us in uniform there was a price.

Zack was taken out of consideration for squadron commander. He was assigned to another dark corner of JSOC where he could continue to serve. These days there is always a new black ops unit being spun up for duty somewhere. It's the only growth sector left in today's army, and no one is better at it than Zack.

Pete was given a medal and medically discharged with full benefits. Weber and the rest of the aircrew were quickly and honorably discharged and were then quietly scooped up by Thayer Tactical. They were now making three times the money I was.

Turtle and his guys were also kept on the aircraft until it was clear. The government did not want to acknowledge the help of private military contractors. They snuck away when it was all over. Turtle flew back to the States the next day and went to his friends in San Francisco to get fitted for a new leg.

Later that night, after Rear Admiral Brick finally calmed down, he shook my hand and told me how ballsy we were. He said he was glad we had gotten Stillmont back. Then he calmly told me that if it had been up to him, he would have sent us to directly to Leavenworth as soon as we landed and thrown away the key. He assigned an armed escort and put me on an immediate flight out of Baghdad, back to MacDill.

After a long debriefing, I was told I was done forever with Special Operations Command. My clearance was revoked, and I was removed from flight status. They also canceled my promotion. They thought it would be best, however, not to make me retire right away. It would look funny.

There was no way they would want me to stay at MacDill, though, so I spent a few days there organizing my stuff while I waited to hear. I got a call from Creighton.

"Sam. How are you?"

"Good. I'm just packing up. I'm expecting to be put in charge of latrines at Fort Polk, Louisiana, any day now. How about you?"

"Not bad. Still tied up in an investigation of a recent drone mishap."

"I bet."

"Had one suffer an engine malfunction while on a mission. Crashed and burned. Wasn't pretty."

"It sure as hell was pretty to me," I laughed.

"I bet that's true."

"How do you think you're going to make out after all this?"

"I'll be fine."

Knowing him, I believed it.

"Thanks again for that, by the way. It was the most epic save I can never talk about."

"You're welcome, Sam."

"I hope we get the chance to get together soon."

"I will make sure of it. Let me know where you land. Go naked, Sam."

"Go naked."

Luckily, someone decided that Fort Polk would look funny, too. I was floored the next day when they asked me where I wanted to go.

"Are you serious?"

"Within reason, Avery," said the major general they had sent from the Pentagon to lay out the deal. "You're not going to fucking Schofield. And no one wants you within a hundred miles of D.C."

I smiled. Playing out the clock in Hawaii would have been nice. But it was clear they were determined that this not be too good a deal for me.

I spoke without thinking:

"I'll take West Point, sir."

The general blinked a few times. "Are you sure?"

"History department."

"Avery, I'm going to ask you one more time. I've got better things to do than work on your dead-end career. Are you sure about this?"

"Go naked, sir."

"Huh?"

"Nothing."

"Very well. I'll give you a week to get your shit together. Then report to West Point."

"Roger that, sir."

"And remember: we better not see you on TV, or online, or in a magazine, or anywhere else. Casper the fucking ghost, Avery. That's you. Got it?"

"Yes, sir."

"That goes for the next week. The next year. The next decade. For the rest of your life. You don't say shit about your ridiculous mission in the desert. That's the deal. You break it, your next post is Leavenworth."

When I told Creighton, he was jealous.

That had been a week ago. Now I sat across from Colonel Anderson. My boss for the next three years, he was wondering what to do with his new officer who was totally unqualified to teach history.

"How about the goat mission, then?" he said, smiling.

"Sir?"

"I heard you were one of the guys who got the goat back in nineteen ninety. That right?"

"Yes, sir."

"Well, then you can tell me about that spirit mission sometime instead."

I looked out the window at the Hudson. "But it's all a spirit mission, isn't it?"

"What do you mean?"

"Going to West Point. Being a cadet. Serving as an army officer. Looking back now, it all seems like one big spirit mission. Risky. Thankless. A compulsion more than a choice. But for the greater good."

"Would you do it again?"

"Which part?"

"Any of it."

"The sick thing is, I probably would."

The colonel chuckled.

"You're not going to make me do plebe year again, are you, sir?"

"No. I'm glad you're here, Sam. Though I'm not sure how to put you to work." He picked up a folder from the small table between us and leafed through the papers inside. "It's been a long time since you were in an academic classroom environment, and you don't have a postgraduate history degree."

He didn't look up from the file he was reading. I could see that it was thick.

"Getting you ready for the classroom is going to be a little bit of a project, Sam. They made it clear to me that there was no budget to send you to grad school with, and the fact is, I'm going to need to get you up to speed quickly. I am shorthanded."

"I get it, sir. I'm ready to work."

"Good. Well. If I let you point yourself at an era, what would it be? World War II? Vietnam?"

"Actually, sir, I'd rather not study anything from our enlightened modern times."

"The classics?" His eyes twinkled.

"Yes, sir."

"Good man." He abruptly stood up and walked to a large bookshelf on the rear wall. He looked at his watch, grabbed two volumes, and gestured for me to stand up. "We better get going. They'll be marching by soon." He handed me the books.

"Thucydides and Marcus Aurelius."

"It's a good place for you to start."

We shook hands, and I left his office. Exiting Thayer Hall, I strode quickly by the library and passed behind Patton's statue, taking Diagonal Walk across the Plain. As I walked, I was greeted by upper-class cadets back from summer training. They were everywhere, and my right hand whipped up and down, rapidly returning salutes. They looked so young.

The Hudson yawned to the north, and Storm King Mountain loomed immediately to its west. All these years later, I still looked at the shadowed base of the mountain and tried to calculate where Bill had landed.

The crowd thickened as I neared the superintendent's reviewing stand. The August sun was bright, and the crowd was festive. It was a happy mix of parents, other family members, officers, and cadets.

I was almost to Mac's statue when the first company of new cadets rounded the corner on Washington Road and turned onto the final stretch in front of the supe's quarters. The day was hot and their stride fatigued. I quickly gave up trying to spot Zack's daughter. The new cadets all looked the same as they sweated through their BDUs. They were anxious, their eyes nervously drilling straight ahead to avoid drawing any attention. Upperclassmen looked on skeptically, arms crossed.

The first company's guidon snapped down as they presented arms. The next company followed closely behind. And another behind it. And another curving around the corner of Washington Road, like the Hudson flowing around the rocky west point of the mountain.

ACKNOWLEDGMENTS

I started *Spirit Mission* in 1992 as a second lieutenant in flight school while still digesting my West Point experience. Twenty years later, David Weinstein was the first to read it. He became my first editor, meeting often at a coffee shop to discuss the manuscript.

I could not have written this book without the help of numerous West Pointers, military veterans, friends, and family: Jeff Weber, Jim Isenhower, Brad Paulsen, Jen Ruiz, Jeff Jack, Doug McCormick, Tom Barnett, Pete Gaudet, Andy Ulrich, Kevin Virgil, Mike Coachys, Dan Ruiz, Matt Smith, John Daniel, Terry Cope, Tim Pierson, Charles Darnell, Kirby Andrews, Jack Kinsler, Jon Henry, Don Thurman, Shawn Botteril, Jason Gettig, Yvette Daniel, Tommy Arnold, Zack Harmon, Greg Horn, Elizabeth Hardaway, Robert Hardaway, Richie Sheridan, Billy Satterwhite, Blake Ray, Mike Russ, and Jean Russ.

Several others helped me think through some of the tactical aspects of the story. I'm not going to name them. They're still in Special Operations, where discretion matters.

Spirit Mission found its way to publication because of Susu and George

Johnson. They believed in the manuscript and got it into the hands of Ed Victor, the one man Delta Force of literary agents. I'll always be grateful.

Michael Signorelli, my editor at Henry Holt, helped to polish *Spirit Mission* into a finished and professional novel. I can't imagine a better partner for an author.

Finally, and mostly, I am grateful for my wife, Anna, who not only served as a terrific beta reader, but also provided a supportive environment for creativity while dealing with the mood swings of a fledgling author. You're the best, baby. I love you.

ABOUT THE AUTHOR

TED RUSS is a graduate of the United States Military Academy at West Point. He served as an officer and helicopter pilot, ultimately with the 160th Special Operations Aviation Regiment. After leaving the army in 2000, he received an MBA from Emory University and now lives in Georgia with his wife, Anna, and their dog, Henry. *Spirit Mission* is his first novel